Children
of the
Dragon™

RICHARD E. DANSKY

EXALTED FICTION FROM WHITE WOLF

TRILOGY OF THE SECOND AGE

Chosen of the Sun by Richard E. Dansky
Beloved of the Dead by Richard E. Dansky
Children of the Dragon by Richard E. Dansky

AND FROM THE SAME AUTHOR

Clan Novel: Lasombra

For all these titles and more,
visit **www.white-wolf.com/fiction**

Children of the Dragon

Author: Richard E. Dansky
Cover Artist: Ghislain Barbe
Series Editors: Philippe Boulle & Stewart Wieck
Copyeditor: Jasmine Milberger
Graphic Designer: Matt Milberger
Art Director: Richard Thomas

ISBN: 1-58846- 802-X
First Edition: September 2002
Printed in Canada

White Wolf Publishing
1554 Litton Drive
Stone Mountain, GA 30083
www.white-wolf.com/fiction

Dedicated to Saul and Irene Dansky, for years of support and love, their endless encouragement, and most of all their admonition not to be so hard on Ratcatcher this time around.

Chapter One

They cut Ratcatcher down on the thirteenth day after he'd been left behind, thirteen days of torment authored by Holok and Unforgiven Blossom. For close to a fortnight, he'd hung in the branches of the tree, his arms twisted and broken. Insects and birds had fed on his flesh, and spiders nested in the unruly thatch of his hair. The only water that had passed his parched lips had come from two brief rainstorms, and he'd tasted no food in all that time.

He'd not slept at all, and for thirteen days and nights he'd hung, awake, on the tree. At first the pain had kept him from drifting off, the stabbing agonies in his arms anchoring him to consciousness. Then, when pain had ceased to matter, he found himself strangely immune to slumber, and instead had stared out from unseeing eyes both night and day.

Finally, the visions had come. In one, he had seen the great carrion bird, Raiton, who had taunted him and promised to send his servants to feed upon Ratcatcher's rotting corpse. In another, the Prince of Shadows had turned away from him sadly, cloaked in fire and bleeding from both palms. Ratcatcher had tried to call out to him, but his throat was so dry he could make no sounds other than a weak, dry squeaking. He'd heard his hounds baying off in the distance, and once he'd thought he'd seen them, but they remained maddeningly elusive.

And on the last day before succor came, he'd seen her. She'd stood before him, demure as always, in the robes she'd been wearing on the day she had taken his life. Her protector was nowhere to be seen, and Ratcatcher had strained mightily against his bonds in an attempt to free himself and choke the life from her hateful, delicate throat. His efforts failed, though, and he sagged against his restraints, spent, and she began to speak.

"You and I will meet again," she had said.

"This wheel is still spinning." Then she had leaned forward and kissed him on the brow. Then, she vanished, and all he could taste was dust.

•   •   •

The men came to cut him down the next day. There were a half dozen of them, and they rode strong black horses that bore signs of hard riding. "There he is," one said, and they spurred their horses over the ridge and down the slope to where he hung.

They were not gentle when they cut him down. Wide-bladed knives slashed at his bonds; rough hands pulled his twisted limbs free of their confinement. He would have screamed in agony, but no sound emerged from the parched flesh of his throat. And so they took him down off the tree, roughly, and bore him to the ground nearby. One brought water and bathed his face, then moistened a piece of silk and bade Ratcatcher suck the precious fluid, drop by drop, between his cracked lips. His broken limbs were straightened, crudely but effectively, and a folded blanket placed beneath his head.

"Who are you?" he finally managed to croak, after sufficient water had passed his lips. "Why have you come for me?"

"We serve the Prince of Shadows," one of the men said. "He bade us find you. We did so, for it is not wise to fail the prince."

Ratcatcher laughed, raggedly. "No, it's not."

The man nodded.""So we have been told. The prince rides forth, even now, and Pelesh rides with him. We were told to tell you of that as well."

"Pelesh?" Ratcatcher coughed. "Things must be up-side down for that old spider to leave his web. What is the world coming to?"

"I do not know. I simply know I was told, along with my fellows, to find you, to cut you down, to tend to you, and to pass along these tidings. I was also given one more charge, which I may not speak of to you."

"Oh?" He struggled to rise, then fell back against the ground. "What might that be? And when will we be leaving? I'll be strong enough to travel soon, I think. Water is what I need, water and a little time."

"We'll be leaving soon," the man replied softly. All around him was the hustle and bustle of the other men preparing to depart.

"We will?" Ratcatcher looked around. "I don't see a stretcher, or a travois. Will I be riding behind you?"

"No," the man answered, and cut Ratcatcher's throat.

There was surprisingly little blood, a mere trickle. The man who killed Ratcatcher covered him with the blanket which had served as a pillow, and let the thin flow of his blood water the earth.

"Forgive me," he said, and left the knife on the corpse's breast. "It is better that you be judged and reborn. I envy you your journey." Then he, too mounted his horse, and the entire pack of horsemen rode away to the south and west.

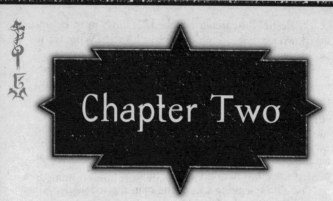

Chapter Two

In the days after the town's entire population had been slaughtered, Qut Toloc acquired a reputation as a haunted place. Travelers who'd stopped in seeking shelter or a meal found instead piles of scorched bones, livestock dead in the streets, and a desecrated temple. Walls stained with blood and offal provided no clues to the fate of the inhabitants, save that it was violent and sudden. The temple's fate was just as mysterious, as the idea of the Immaculate Order abandoning a holy site was almost unknown. Yet here the temple stood, its doors hanging off their hinges and birds nesting in the sanctuary. No industrious monks repaired the damage; no devout ones prayed in the corridors. A few brave souls dared as far as the heart of the temple, where they found shattered doors lying on the floor of a roughhewn chamber, and a gaping doorway whose maw exhaled foul vapors.

A few were brave enough to steal temple artifacts. None were foolish enough to venture into the darkness. All spread the story of the horror at Qut Toloc wherever they went, and those whom they told spread it even wider. Prudent women and sensible men heard the tales, and chose to hurry past the ruins on their journeys. Sage mapmakers modified their wares accordingly. Those whose products had been so detailed as to show Qut Toloc now removed it; those who'd ignored the hamlet before now marked it as a dangerous, ghost-ridden place. Itinerant priests began using tales of the destruction of Qut Toloc as abject lessons in their sermons, and the Thousand Gods turned their faces away and would not speak of it when asked.

And so, in a mere handful of months, Qut Toloc went from a deserted outpost, a secret few had heard of and fewer still cared to remember, to a name bandied about far and wide by the tale-tellers and wags of Creation. It became a place to be shunned and feared, a town whose name was heavy with the stink of death.

Which, of course, is why the treasure hunters immediately found the place irresistible. They expected to find beasts to slay, relics of the First Age for the taking, and treasure and glory scattered on the streets of the village like shells on a sandy beach.

What they didn't expect to find was Eliezer Wren, coming up out of the long dark.

• • •

The instant he reached the top of the spiral stairs, Wren knew he wasn't going to get the bath he was hoping for. Dim light and stale smells flooded the air as he approached, and he could see that the doors sealing the catacombs off from the temple proper had been torn from their hinges by some angry force. Brown stains on the floor and walls could only be blood, and he could see deep gashes in the stone that had clearly been made with malicious intent.

Absently, Wren scratched his forehead and stepped into the room. The air here was a bit cleaner than in the catacombs, but it was scented with old rot and animal smells. Bird droppings marked the floor where the blood didn't, and cobwebs filled every corner.

If Kejak ever saw this, Wren decided, a lot of monkish heads would roll immediately. If the heart of the temple was such a disaster, the Unconquered Sun alone knew how bad the rest of it was.

He stooped to examine the pattern of bloodstains on the floor, and frowned. These were old, older than he would have expected, somehow. From footprints left in the dried gore, he traced the steps of the battles that had been fought in the room, and didn't like what he saw. Gashes in the stone belied the ferocity of the combat. A bloody handprint against one wall made him shudder; the deep cut into the stone behind it spoke volumes.

"This is wrong," he muttered, and stood.""Someone should have been here to consecrate the temple anew. To see to the dead, at the very least. To shut the doors on the catacombs." He looked over his shoulder and down into the dark. Nothing stirred there, which was exactly what he wanted to see.""The fact that no one from the Order has been here tells me that something is very wrong."

That the temple was apparently bereft of monks wasn't necessarily a bad thing, Wren decided as he followed the smeared trail of blood through the temple corridors. While most guests, particularly fellow Immaculates, were guaranteed some form of hospitality within the temple walls, Wren was fairly certain that his Exaltation would preclude any friendly reception. At best, there'd be awkward questions about the daiklave and what he'd been doing down among the dead men. At worst, there would have been an impromptu Wyld Hunt staged in the temple's chambers.

Even so, caution seemed wise, so Wren passed slowly through the temple's halls, stopping often to examine the evidence of carnage. Looters had been here, he saw. Sconces for torches had been ripped out of the walls, and braziers and tapestries had been either savaged or stolen. Everywhere, the tale of the temple's destruction was written in dried blood, smeared on the walls or spattered on the floor.

One man had done this, Wren decided. One set of footprints led from slaughter to slaughter, and the hacks and scores marring the walls were all of a consistent size, shape and depth.

"One man," Wren said softly, and whistled. He recalled the endless mornings in the courtyard for training, the incomparable speed and grace of his peers and instructors. To think that one man could have simply strolled through the temple and dispatched so many monks with such ease was unthinkable.

"Ratcatcher," he whispered. No one else could have done this. The odds against it were too great. The man who'd dragged him, a prisoner, to the Prince of Shadows' dungeon had carved himself a bloody place in the war against the heavens here.

A war, he realized, in which he, too, was a soldier.

More than just a soldier, he suddenly knew. All at once, it struck home. This was no game, not even one of Kejak's intrigues. The powers among whom he moved were mighty and terrible, capable of miracles or slaughters with either hand. When heh'd rejected the dead god's offer, he his mind had simply refused to comprehend what he had done. The power was too vast, the scale on which it worked beyond his comprehension. Even Idli, treacherous, vicious Idli was simply too alien to be comprehended, save when the blows flew and the demands of combat put all philosophizing out of his head.

But this, this brought it home. Ratcatcher was perhaps the lowliest of the creatures he'd striven against thus far, a vain, arrogant, sadistic toady. He danced at the end of the prince's strings, intrigued with the prince's other servants, and upon occasion wiped out entire temples full of trained, dedicated Immaculates.

With a chill, Wren realized what sort of enemy he'd made in Ratcatcher. His survival of the duel in Unforgiven Blossom's chambers now seemed like a fluke, a joke played by the Unconquered Sun.

And if the Unconquered Sun had not chosen to Exalt him, he too, would have died, would have fallen to the rage and power of the Anathema....

Of course, he was now Anathema, too. Gently, gingerly, he tickled awake the power inside him. While it seemed likely that Ratcatcher was long gone, there was still the chance he might have returned, and the depth of the scores in the walls told Wren that now was not the time to take chances.

He continued on, working his way inevitably toward the central sanctuary. There was no reason to go there, he knew, save a morbid curiosity and a lingering faith. Perhaps

Ratcatcher had at least left the sanctuary alone. Perhaps, Wren told himself, it still mattered.

He came around the last bend and nearly doubled over in shock. The sanctuary, or what remained of it, lay before him. Time had not been kind to it. Birds nested on the altar and in the eaves, and their droppings bespattered the room. Old stains on the walls and floors were precisely the wrong shade of brown, and a lingering stench told Wren the extent of the desecration. All of the temple ornaments were gone, either stolen or destroyed. By the smeared trails on the floor he could see that bodies had been dragged out of here, many bodies. It was clear that the sanctuary had become an abattoir, with priests and their servants the beasts to be slaughtered.

Feeling sick to his stomach, he turned away. Those who used the word "abomination" should first come here ere ever uttering it again. This, he saw, was a true abomination, not what he had become. This was the real horror. For the first time, he felt he truly understood why, on a day in the dim and distant past, Kejak and his advisors had felt it necessary to call the first Wyld Hunt.

The fact that the Hunt would now ride him down just as gladly as it would the author of this desecration was not lost on him, however, and he was quite certain that if anyone found him here they'd lay the blame for the slaughter at his feet. Never mind the sheer impossibility of it all; people tended to be less than logical where mass death and the Exalted were concerned.

He had even, Wren admitted to himself, been guilty of it a few times himself.

Now, however, was not the time for self-recrimination, or a reflection on the ironic nature of things. A quick glance around had told him that there were no bodies needing to be buried and no souls needing their way hastened. That, at least, was a blessing. He would leave the temple, scour whatever lay outside for supplies, and depart. The weight of the sword at his back was a reminder of the debt he owed the ghosts from the catacombs below; his sudden thirst was a reminder of a more immediate need.

With haste he worked his way through the temple corridors and out away from the sanctuary, hoping against hope that there might be a village nearby.

He felt a sudden heat on his brow, and amended his wish: a village of the blind, or foolish.

• • •

There were still traces of blood on the temple steps when Wren emerged, not that he had expected anything different. The elements had done their work here and softened the memory. Given enough time, they'd tear down the temple's ceiling and do their work inside as well.

There had been a village here once, Wren saw. Most of the buildings still stood, though some showed signs of having burned. There were perhaps a couple of dozen homes, a stable, a blacksmith's shop and a few other buildings at whose purpose he couldn't guess, all in greater or lesser states of disrepair. Some bore scorch marks, others were little more than outlines of burned timbers on the ground.

In the center of the gathering of huts was a rough town square, and at its center was a pile of well-burned bones. Animal skeletons lay in the street, leading Wren to believe that the bones in the square were human remains. No doubt those of the town's inhabitants, he thought, and loped down from the temple.

There was no smell of death in the streets, and for that Wren was thankful. There was only dust and soot, which rose up in choking clouds with each step he took. Looking behind him, he saw the breeze whip the dust away. Anyone in the area would know someone was here, and if they were clever, they'd know he was alone. The thought did not fill Wren with confidence. He slowed his pace and lightened his tread, and was gratified to see that the puffs of dust rising behind him were correspondingly smaller.

The town square, when he reached it, proved to be roughly paved with massive cobblestones. Thus, it was mercifully free of dust, save for that which the winds had blessed it with. The mound of bones lay in the square's center, and at a glance Wren could see it for what it was: a pyre. This was not part of the slaughter. This was part of the aftermath. Someone had been here after all, had seen the destruction and done what they could for the victims. It hadn't been much, but there had been some effort made to give the corpses of the dead protection from scavengers, and to give their souls a reason to rest.

But who had made the effort? The question nagged at Wren. If it had been Immaculates, why had they not cleansed the temple as well? And who else would have done such a thing? Surely looters wouldn't have bothered. Perhaps the townsfolk had been friendly with local spirits? None of the explanations seemed satisfactory. He took a step closer to the pile of charred bones and frowned. *Did it even matter?* he wondered. *After all, they were long dead in any case.*

The sound of hooves interrupted his woolgathering. With a half dozen quick steps, Wren left the square and faded into the shadows between a pair of relatively sturdy huts, ones whose exterior walls seemed unlikely to collapse in a strong breeze.

Two riders came into view, riding slowly. The leader was bearded, burly, and heavily armed. He wore riding leathers that had seen better days, and a necklace of tyrant lizard teeth. There were throwing knives prominently visible on his vambraces, not to mention other bits of metal. A hat that was red with road dust slouched on his head, and there was a wicked-looking short blade strapped to his thigh. He looked around with mild interest, methodically scanning the square.

The second rider was a woman, tall and wiry. A wicked scar ran down her right cheek, pushing her across the border from plain to ugly. Her black hair was tied back with a silver clasp, and she wore leathers much like her partner's. Not for her, though, were the numerous blades her companion favored. Instead, a short bow hung from her saddlebow, and a full quiver was strapped to her back.

Watching them pass by, Wren frowned. By all rights, he should have seen them long before he'd heard them. The dust alone should have seen to that.

Unless, he realized, they had already been in the village when he'd walked out of the temple.

"Halloo!" The cry came from the square. It was deep and loud and not at all good humored, and Wren felt himself disinclined to respond to it.

"Halloo!" The call came again, this time from the woman. "We know you're here. Just come out and show yourself, and you won't be hurt."

Wren had to stifle some laughter at that. They wouldn't hurt him? Oh, they might try, but as for actually hurting him, regardless of the effort they made, he was quite certain they wouldn't be able to hurt him. Still, he remained in the shadows, curious to hear what they had to say next.

It was the man who spoke again, riding in slow circles around the blackened remains of the pyre. He seemed impatient, while the woman behind him remained phlegmatic and professional. She, Wren decided, was the dangerous one of the two.

"Look, there's enough treasure in that temple for the three of us. Come out and we'll cut you in for a share. Keep hiding and you'll get nothing."

Ah, Wren thought, *That explains it. They were treasure hunters, and they'd somehow heard tales of the fabulous treasures of this lost temple. Well, unless they've got a buyer for a two-foot mound of pigeon shit, they're going to find themselves sadly disappointed.* For a moment, he thought about warning them of what lay within, but decided against it. He had nothing against treasure hunters, grave robbers or other looters of the dead, having been one himself numerous times. What he did object to, however, was the profession's notoriously homicidal attitude toward interlopers, competitors, claim jumpers and witnesses. Wren suspected that the two regarded him as falling under one of these categories. It would certainly be a more believable explanation than the truth, namely that he was a newly Exalted fugitive who had just emerged from the Underworld after defying one of its rulers and escaping from the Prince of Shadows' dungeons by hurling himself into oblivion. Mentally, he sighed and held himself still. With luck, the two would soon grow bored and either wander off or head into the temple, and then he could raid their camp for supplies and vanish. He didn't intend to take much, but in the wake of the duel he'd fought in the catacombs he had no wish to indulge in any particularly strenuous exercise. Besides, he wasn't quite sure he was up to dodging arrows, at least not yet.

Out in the square, the sounds of horses' footfalls on the rough flagstones abruptly ceased, and Wren could hear the two sliding off their horses. "If you're not going to come out," the man said, "we're going to have to find you. You won't like that." Then came the rasp of a blade being pulled from a sheath, and the soft moan of a bow being strung.

Mentally, Wren cursed. They were being stubborn. Moving silently, he faded back away from the square. Finding a window, he flipped himself backwards through it and landed on dirt floor covered with tattered and rotten mats of woven straw. They rustled when he landed, and Wren hoped devoutly that the sound wasn't as loud as it seemed ot his own ears. He scuttled away from the window, then crouched on the floor. Barely breathing, he listened.

In the alley outside, there were stealthy footsteps. "There's footprints in the dust," he heard the woman say.

"Those are yours, or maybe mine," the man retorted. Silently, Wren cheered him on.

There was a pause, and then, "Since when are either of us barefoot?"

The man cursed, loudly, and then came crashing in through the wall with his long knife drawn. Before the debris had settled, Wren was on him. One hand slapped the flat of the man's blade, knocking it away. The other came in under his chin in an open-fisted punch to the base of the throat. The man gurgled, half spun, and collapsed.

Some instinct told Wren to collapse along with him, and he was thankful for it when an arrow whistled just overhead. Twisting out of his fall, he rolled into the alley and sprang to his feet just in time to avoid another arrow.

The woman stood there, fluid as water as she nocked, drew, fired, and reached for another arrow. Wren admired her form for a long instant, then leapt into the air as a cloak of light shimmered into existence around him. Straight up he went, and then over onto the rooftop opposite. Another arrow whizzed past, and he threw himself to the roof, willing the flare of power around him to melt into him.

"Bright Crow," the woman called, her eyes never leaving the spot where Wren had disappeared over the roof's horizon. "Are you all right?" The only response she received was a gurgled moan. "Damnation," she muttered, and loosed another arrow.""He's up on the roof."

There was a pause in the rain of arrows, and Wren took advantage of it by wriggling over to the other side of the roof to see if the next building was within jumping range. It was, or would have been if it still had a roof. But fire had destroyed half of it, and the elements had taken care of the rest. Wren realized that unless he wanted to make a target of himself, he was trapped.

There was a soft plopping sound, followed by the crackling of burning straw. Wren looked up, and saw an arrow with a burning rag tied to it sticking out of the rooftop. The flames were already beginning to spread.

"Oh, hell," Wren muttered, and jumped as the flames swept towards him.

He landed on his feet in the alley on the other side of the house from his bow-wielding assailant. A cloud of dust rose up as he landed, but the sound of his heels hitting dirt was masked by the rising roar of the fire.

He could, Wren realized, simply run at this point. There was nothing to be gained by prolonging the conflict, and much to be said for moving on as rapidly as possible. But the woman's casual attempts to exterminate him rankled, and her partner's clumsy bravado was irritating. They had begun this, not him. There was nothing wrong with finishing it.

He stooped and closed his hand around a shard of pottery. It was heavy and thick, and one side was painted with what looked to be a pattern of dancing cranes. Wren looked at it for a second, decided it was hideous, and tossed it in his hand. The weight was suitable for his purpose. Silently, Wren glided to the right. To the left was the town center, a space much too open for his liking.

The fire was growing now, the heat forcing him back away from the hut's smoldering walls. Dimly, he could hear the woman on the other side still calling out for her partner. Wren smiled, and crept around the side of the building. He took a moment to gauge distances, then tossed the pot-sherd into the mouth of the alley between huts.

It was an old trick, of course—toss the distraction to the right and then go left. Wren had no intention, however, of going left. No doubt the woman had seen this before and would react by looking left, bow drawn, ready to perforate him as he came around the corner. Instead, he'd go right, following the path of his crude missile, and surprise her.

That, at least, was the theory, one which Wren found to be gratifyingly accurate as he slipped around the corner of the burning building.

She stood there, her back to him and an arrow sighted on the other end of the alley. Wren smiled and leapt. His intent was to land a single kick at the base of her neck. At the worst, she'd stumble forward and drop the bow; at best, it would kill her.

With a shout, he struck. She half-turned at his cry, her mouth open in surprise and her hands coming up instinctively to block his attack. His heel struck the side of her neck with both his weight and the force of his leap behind it.

By all rights, it should have shattered her neck, sent her spinning into the dust as her arms and legs flailed wildly. By all rights, it should have killed her.

Instead, there was a flash of pale light, and an unpleasant shock that ran up Wren's leg. He gasped, recovered, and landed to the woman's right, between her and the flames. His right leg felt numb.

She finished her turn and smiled grimly. Her hands still held the short bow; the string still held the arrow. On her breast he could see a small white stone hanging from a golden chain. It was glowing, softly, and he cursed himself for missing it before.

"First Age charm against the strike of the hand," she said, smirking.""You find a lot of these in our line of work."

"Really?" Wren said, and threw himself to the left as the arrow came whistling at him. He rolled, the hilt of the sword he bore digging painfully into his back as more arrows exploded into the dust where he'd been. The woman drew and fired swiftly and easily, and for a brief instant Wren wondered if she'd had Immaculate training. The range was too short for her to keep missing forever.

His shoulder brushed the wall of the hut he'd hidden in, and he sprang to his feet. Another arrow whizzed under his chin, and he flipped himself backwards, out of the way.

"Mind you, I don't think we'll find any of those here." She paused for a second in her rhythm as her fingers slipped off an arrow, and in that instant Wren counterattacked. A flare of light trailing from his fist, he threw himself forward.

He struck, not at the woman, but at her bow. The wood was lacquered and strong, the bow itself a remarkable bit of craftsmanship. But at his touch, it shattered. The string whipped back and cut her face, and she cried out in pain. Half-stumbling backwards, she struck blindly with the arrow she held, but Wren caught it and spun it out of her hand. She turned to run, but he caught the falling shaft with his left hand and thrust it forward, low. It caught her ankles, and she tumbled forward into the dust. In an instant, he was on her, the arrow held at the base of her neck and her face pressed into the dirt.

"You know," he said pleasantly,""none of this was necessary. I didn't want anything except a look at a map and some water, you know, and the temple's empty anyway. Oh, you can try the catacombs underneath, but I don't recommend it. I've been down there, you see. Now, where's your camp?"

She spat, and made an attempt to wriggle free. Dispassionately, Wren reversed the arrow and struck her on the spine with the butt.

"That was stupid. Not as stupid as your friend, whom I don't expect will ever speak again, but fairly stupid nonetheless. You don't have to answer me. This isn't a large village. I expect that once I kill you, I'll find it on my own soon enough. It's up to you, of course."

The woman coughed. "You did this, didn't you?" she said thickly around a mouthful of dirt. Wren found himself wondering if he'd knocked any of her teeth loose.

"What, the slaughter? Hardly. Near as I could tell, I was half a world away. I know the man who did it, though, and he wants to kill me, if that makes you feel any better."

"Liar!"

"No, just thirsty. You do have water at your camp, don't you?"

She refused to answer, and, with a shrug, Wren struck her in the nerve cluster in the side of the neck with the shaft of the arrow. She stopped squirming, blessedly unconscious, and he dragged her into the next hut with her still-moaning companion. The charm around her neck he took for himself, though a rumble in his gut warned him against donning it.

"Watch her," he said, once he had her inside.

"I don't think you're going to be good for much else." The man she'd called Bright Crow cowered back in a corner, and Wren shot him a look of disgust. A disgrace to the trade, this one was, and possibly better off dead.

He turned to go. "You may want to move her, if those flames spread," he added as he walked through the impromptu entrance the man had made. "You may want to do that quickly."

Scrabbling sounds behind him told Wren his warning was being heeded.

•   •   •

The horses were in the square, and a quick check of their saddlebags showed Wren that they in fact carried everything he needed. Water, food, maps—it was all here for the taking. For a moment, he pondered the moral implications of leaving Bright Crow and his friend here without their steeds or equipment, but he brushed it aside. It was part of the trade. No doubt they'd done this to others; no doubt they'd shown less mercy than he had.

He mounted up and tethered the second horse, the man's horse, to his own. Both were surprisingly docile, which he took as a good sign. He clucked and dug his heels into the horse's flank, and headed toward what the maps had assured him was a road.

Behind him, the fire grew. Wren ignored it.

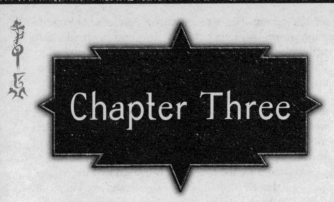

Chapter Three

The problem, Chejop Kejak thought, was not that good help was hard to find. Good help was everywhere, assuming you didn't ask too much of it. After all, he had no shortage of perfectly competent underlings, servants, allies, bound spirits and pawns all quite capable of doing whatever he requested of them. Then again, what he asked of most of his agents was usually quite simple: smiting unbelievers, securing the interests of the Immaculate Order and its sponsors, and occasionally riding out with the Wyld Hunt to eliminate threats to the stability of the Realm.

No, Kejak decided, the problem was that *smart* help was difficult to find. A man in Kejak's position inevitably was beset with difficult, delicate circumstances, ranging from covering up sexual scandals at outlying temples to tracking down First Age artifacts that had passed illicitly through a dozen hands, and those tasks called for at least a modicum of intelligence. Unfortunately, finding willing (or at least pliable) agents with the right combination of wit, skills and temperament was heavens-bedamned difficult, and of late it had been impossible.

And that was why he had spent so much time recently looking for Eliezer Wren.

He'd tried to find Wren, of course, numerous times. Messages had gone out to his agents across the Threshold and

beyond: "report in if you see Eliezer Wren." A dozen false alarm.
were reported, checked out, and dismissed and their authors
suitably chastised. But of Wren himself, there was no sign.

This, in and of itself, was not *too* alarming. Creation was
large, after all, and Wren was just one man with a knack for
concealing himself. On the other hand, Wren was privy to
enough of Kejak's secrets to make him a valuable prize, and
if he'd decided to leave the Sidereal's service he'd no doubt
have plenty of other suitors. If Wren were dead, as seemed
likely—there'd been no word from him at all since he'd left
the temple in Stonebreak half a year ago—that would be one
thing, one that Kejak could deal with. He was just a man, as
Holok had been so fond of pointing out, and ultimately
replaceable. If he was alive, however, he would have to be
found and either brought back into the fold or eliminated.

Kejak stood and scowled. The room he currently occupied was a bare monk's cell, an attempt to get himself as far from
the ambience of the crumbling orrery as possible. There was
now a brace of monks in the chamber around the clock,
constantly shoring up moldering bits of the ceiling or replacing
celestial spheres that had fallen. Soon, he decided, it would be
time to brick the damn thing up and start over. Having the
stars over his head as he made plans had been useful for
centuries, but now it was crippling him. All of his astrological
predictions were off, and he felt blind. It would be difficult to
find another site so perfectly suited for the purpose, but it
couldn't be helped. This, undoubtedly, was enemy work, and
if something was striking at him in this manner then he needed
every weapon in his arsenal at his disposal.

In the meantime, however, he was cut off from one
source of intelligence, and it irked him. He'd tried to
substitute other resources, but time and again, he'd failed.
It was irritating.

More importantly, it was time to do something about
it. If magical and human intelligence were both denied to
him, he was crippled. He had to have at least one of the two,
and then he could work on regaining the other.

And that, he decided, meant that it was time to find Eliezer Wren. He struck the small gong that sat on a shelf near the door of the cell. Almost immediately, a monk appeared in the doorway, his face serene but inquiring. "May I assist you, Revered One?"

Kejak scowled. "Obviously, or I wouldn't have called for you. Have the Chamber of the Unbroken Circle cleansed and purified. I'll need seventeen braziers in there, all bronze, and herbs for meditation. Also, bring me salt and a leather thong knotted around nine stones."

"Revered One?"

"You have three days. At the end of that time, I will need a few other things, but that will do for now. And while you are about, inform the kitchens that I'll be taking no sustenance for a while. That is all."

"Yes, Revered One." The monk bowed and vanished. Kejak smiled. Good help, at least, he still had.

• • •

Kejak sat, cross-legged and naked, on the bare stone floor. Small bronze charcoal burners sat in significant locations around the perfectly circular chamber, fragrant smoke rising from them. An acolyte named Roben Salashi, carefully chosen, wandered the chamber as she constantly placed small bundles of herbs over the flames.

Kejak, as was appropriate, ignored her. Hands placed palm to palm in the air in front of him, posture ramrod straight, he closed his eyes and chanted an incantation that was as familiar to him as breathing. It had been three centuries and more since he'd recited it, but there was no hesitation in his voice, no lapse in his memory.

The price he had paid in order to learn it ensured that.

There was no protective circle on the floor, not that there was any need for one. The creature he was summoning was too powerful to be held in check by a mere circle of chalk, and might be insulted by the attempt. Kejak had more powerful protective measures at his disposal, but he judged their use to be not worth the effort. He wished to approach what was coming as an equal, not a cringing postulant. Doing so might make the negotiations easier.

And so, he had ordered the chamber prepared, its walls and floor scrubbed with fragrant oils. Seventeen braziers had been placed in the chamber, and the sweet scent of dried herbs that flowed from them was unending. Kejak himself had fasted for three days and three nights before beginning the rite, and had purified his flesh with salt and ritual flagellation as well.

Most of this, he suspected, was deeply unnecessary, but it made the rather irritable deity he was summoning happy, and so he submitted to it. It usually paid, he had learned, to make the spirits comfortable in dealings of this sort. It let them forget, at least for the moment, the true nature of the position they were in.

A gong sounded somewhere in the distance. It was followed by another, and then a third. The sound of birds exploding into flight filled the chamber, and a breeze rushed down from the vaulted ceiling. Clouds of scented smoke swirled through the air, and the acolyte shrieked as the wind tore the carefully knotted bundles of herbs from her grasp. These flew up into the air, dancing, as the din continued, while she ran vainly back and forth across the chamber trying to catch them.

"Who calls me?"

Kejak ceased chanting and opened his eyes. The din of wings was deafening now, and the shadows of birds swooped and dove along the chamber walls. The acolyte, her hands full of loose strands, was on her knees against the chamber wall, staring up in horror. Kejak almost felt sorry for her.

The center of the chamber was filled by a titanic figure, roughly man-shaped but twice as tall as any man could be. Its unsexed body was formed by a shifting, screeching mob of birds of all shades and hues. Above it, the room's ceiling had vanished, replaced by a swirling vortex of cloud and shadow.

A constant stream of feathered shapes flew into and out of the room, mingling with the monstrous form of the bird god before splitting off and fleeing once again.

Kejak stood. "I call you. I call you by the wind that lifts you and the earth that holds safe the nest. I call you by the fire that is in your blood and the iron of your talons. I call you by the water of your eye, which is clear and sees all. And I call you because great is my need of your gifts, and I ask that you grant me your succor."

The man-thing's shape shifted, giving the appearance of peering down at where Kejak stood."'Ah. You. I should have known. You have no bond on me. I am here because I will it."

"You are here because you have been summoned, and I have made the chamber of your summoning fragrant for you. I have purified this place and myself, and I have brought for you an unsullied gift." He pointed to the acolyte, who on cue dropped her scattered bundles and shrieked.

The bird-god laughed. "She's not unsullied. Ask her about her evenings in study with Most Dignified Wielder of the Pen Peleps Danini."

"That's not true!" the young woman called out, but Kejak ignored her. "She's not?" His voice was full of surprise.""But she assured me, as did my servants! Father of Wings, how can I assuage this insult I have accidentally given you!" He bowed his head, his posture utterly submissive.

Again, the bird-god laughed.""It is no insult. You are only human, after all, even though you bear the mark of the skies. You can be fooled. I cannot. My children's eyes are everywhere. I see what they see. I know what they know. They bring whispers to me, and tell me no lies. Can you say as much for your flock?"

Kejak shook his head. "No. Great is your wisdom and strength, and loyal are your children. I envy you that. Would that mine were so faithful."

The bird-god's shape shifted, mimicking Kejak's posture. "They are not, I see. Shall I tell you how many nights this girl has spent in her tutor's arms? How loud her cries where? The holy places she has defiled with her lust? You, Chejop Kejak, need to discipline your charges."

"You see all, Father of Birds. Great is your knowledge, greater still your wisdom."

"Indeed." The man-shape broke apart for an instant, filling the air with chattering birds before it reformed. This time, the shape was shorter and broader, with longer arms and shorter legs. "What boon would you ask of me, and what price would you pay for it?"

"She is not sufficient, then?"

"That depends." The bird-god's voice was fluting and sweet, the sound of songbirds at dawn. "If you were to ask me the location of a trinket you'd misplaced in your ablutions, perhaps. If you were to ask me the name of seven in this palace who plot against you, certainly not, not for her and a dozen like her. What do you wish to know? Then I shall name my bargain."

"Oh, it is but a trifling thing for one who sees so far. I do not need the names of those who plot against me; those I already know. But I do wish to know where I might find a man who is loyal."

"Interesting." Again the bird-god's shape fell into chaos, and when it reconstituted itself it did so in what Kejak recognized as an desexed effigy of his own form. "It seems a trifling favor. Why call upon me?"

"Why, because it is a trifle for *you*. If I cannot accurately judge the purity of a member of my own household, surely my eye is not keen enough to spot a wandering servant. For you, however, it would be just a matter of a moment."

"You go to a great deal of trouble for a trifling matter, Kejak. I like this not at all."

Kejak bowed. "Then go. I have no bonds on you. No circle holds you. I would not insult you thus."

The bird-god's shape melted and flowed, now little more than a dark, hovering cloud. "You speak of insults. Be careful, lest you speak of them too often. Now, what is this boon you would ask, this trifle for which you have moved mountains? Tell me quickly. I am curious."

"I wish to find a bird who has flown from my nest. A man named Eliezer Wren, a priest who was in my service."

A great screeching arose, and the rough shape in the air collapsed completely. The wind from above rose to gale strength, overturning burners and scattering hot coals on the stone floor. Feathered shapes beat against the walls of the chamber, the din of their shrieking rising above the sound of the rushing air.

Kejak stood and watched the spectacle. The birds swirled around him, never touching him, even as they descended on the hapless acolyte. She beat at them with her fists and cried out as they tore at her hair, her clothes, her soft skin.

Then, abruptly, the din ended. The wind ceased, and figure of the bird-god once again overstrode the chamber. "Is that all?" the creature asked.""You wish to know where the man Eliezer Wren is?" The god's voice was harsher now, the croak of a carrion bird mixing with the nightingales' tones.

There was an odd emphasis on the word "man" that Kejak disliked, but he merely nodded.

"This, then, I give to you. It is a gift from the Father of Birds, Chejop Kejak, one that I give freely. The man Eliezer Wren is dead. He died in the dungeons of the Prince of Shadows, and thus has passed from your service. My children have few eyes in the Underworld, but they say he has been seen there, traveling with strange and fell companions. Your servant is lost to you."

"Ah," was all Kejak said, a wealth of bitter disappointment in a single syllable.""I had feared as much. I thank you, and I will honor your children in the gardens of this temple. Twenty-five pans of bronze and silver will be filled with grain and left in the temple's courtyard for them to feed upon. This shall be repeated every day for a month, to honor the Father of Birds."

"Do it every day for a year, and I may consider it an honor. For a month, it is simply prudence."

Kejak nodded. "As you wish."

"I do," said the Father of Birds. "And do not call on me again for such tiny things. There are other gods in the world who are weak enough to be bent to your will. I am not one of them." It exploded upwards in a shower of winged shapes, which passed into the swirling storm overhead and vanished. A single red feather drifted down from above and then, as if it had never been, the vortex of cloud vanished.

Kejak reached out, and, with two fingers, caught the feather as it fell. He smiled.

"Is it gone?" The acolyte sat huddled in a terrified ball, peeking out from between her fingers. Her hair and clothes were torn, and her bare arms were scored with scratches.

"It's gone," Kejak said, looking upwards. "And it won't be back."

Little by little she unfolded, and stood on shaky feet. "Were you… were you really going to offer me to it?"

Kejak laughed unpleasantly, and kicked away some of the coals that had spilled near his feet. "I knew you were unsuitable to its tastes. That's why I chose you to attend me tonight."

"You knew?"

"Girl, everyone in the temple knows. The Father of Birds isn't the only one with eyes. Or ears." He paused for a moment.""Or a nose, for that matter. Peleps Danini doesn't bother to wash you off her fingers half the time before her next student arrives." Salashi sputtered, but Kejak swept on, ignoring her. "If I'd offered up someone useful, he'd have known that the matter really was important. If I'd admitted to knowing about your dalliances, I couldn't have flattered him into giving it away. And if you so much as breathe a word of this to anyone, even your esteemed calligraphy tutor, I will have your head on a pike and your hands cut off and tossed in the sea faster than you can even think about lying to me again. Am I understood, oh Acolyte whose silence buys her a continued place in the Temple?"

The girl nodded, unable to speak.

Kejak dusted his hands. "Good. I am glad we understand each other. Here, take this." In two strides, he walked over to her and handed her the feather. "Wear this. Consider it part of your penance. And tell your lover it came from me. She'll know what that means."

"Yes, Revered One." Salashi dropped to her knees, her head bowed. "I serve, in this as in all things."

"Yes, you do," Kejak agreed, and turned to go.

"Revered One?"

He turned. She looked up at him, confusion on her face." "Yes?" he said, impatient and unused to waiting on his lessers.

"If I may ask, who was Eliezer Wren? I've never heard of him."

"A dead man," Kejak said, and left her there.

Chapter Four

"You should stand," the voice said.""The dead gods are waiting."

Ratcatcher opened his eyes. Before him was a vast and empty chamber, carved from black stone shot through with strands of turquoise and gray. The light was dim, but he could see perfectly as he glanced from side to side, taking in the massive pillars and titanic statues that held up the arched ceiling.

He could see perfectly...

"My eyes," he said, and sat up. "My eyes!" His hands—perfect, smooth-skinned hands—flew to his face in wonder. His skin was unmarred, his features his own as he remembered them. He looked down and saw his own form, naked and unscarred. The stone beneath him was pleasantly cool, and it was the pleasant sensation of temperature he felt, not pain.

For the first time in gods alone knew how long, there was no pain.

"Where am I?" he asked, knowing it was a foolish question but unable to help himself.

"You know where you are," the voice said, and its owner bounded into view. "But you can ask if it makes you feel better."

The creature was man-shaped, in much the same way that a scarecrow or a child's first doll might be. Ragged strips of cloth hid its nakedness, and mingled with the ragged strips of flesh that hung from its rotting bones. One eye socket bulged with squirming maggots, which dripped and wriggled and fell onto the floor. The other eye was perfect and beautiful, bright blue in the gloom. Its chin was sharp, its features elongated, and its hair thin and long. It was male; the scraps of cloth failed to hide that much, though its voice was higher and thinner than one might expect. The figure moved with easy grace, though, and Ratcatcher could feel the sheer power the thing possessed. It was, he decided, consciously reining itself in, and for that he was thankful.

"I know better," he said cautiously, "than to ask who you are."

The thing nodded, smiling. "You've learned something, I see. Satisfy yourself with the knowledge that I am a messenger, and trouble yourself no more with questions. Now, get up, get up. You've rested long enough. Stand, Ratcatcher. You've business elsewhere."

Ratcatcher stood, slowly and awkwardly. He was expecting pain, he realized, expecting agony in the limbs that the Immaculate priest had shattered, or in his oft-abused eyes. But there was no pain, only strength and power that he'd been missing since a long-ago night in the rain when he'd first incurred his master's displeasure.

He laughed, then, and the sound chased its own echoes off the chamber walls. Experimentally, he tried a few mock thrusts and parries, his imaginary blade sharp and bright in his mind. Each move was smooth and effortless, the muscles of this body knowing every trick of the old. "Yes!" he exulted, and moved with more confidence. The guide watched him, bemused, and even applauded politely after one particularly convoluted mock passage.

Embarrassed, Ratcatcher stopped, turning his head and bringing his hands to his sides. "I apologize," he said. "You said we should be leaving…"

The creature nodded. "And so we should. But there was time for this, I think. It will help you choose, later."

"Later?" Ratcatcher echoed him.

"Later," it said, and led him from the chamber.

•　　•　　•

They walked for a long time, though Ratcatcher felt neither hunger nor thirst. The air, such as it was, was pleasantly cool on his bare skin, and he reveled in the sensation of each footfall on stone, or on soft earth, or on rusty and heated metal. They passed through corridors that had been built by industrious hands, and those that looked as if grubs had gnawed them out of the earth. Each was lit to a pleasant dimness, and each led gently but inevitably downwards.

Ratcatcher accepted this, even as he accepted that he was unlikely to tread the path upwards. Very little went up in this place. Very little at all.

Eventually, they came to a spit of weathered, gray stone that projected out over a vast, unlit abyss. Barely the width of a man, it arched impossibly over the blackness, and winds from the depths howled up and over it. Involuntarily, Ratcatcher shivered, and his guide smiled.

It walked to the base of the precipice, looked out over the edge, and then peered back at Ratcatcher where he stood, several paces away. "You're cold," he said.

"Yes."

"As well you should be. It's them you feel. If it were merely cold, you'd feel nothing. Not in this place, with you as you are. But they give you a different sort of chill, don't they?" The creature grinned, rotting gums bright red against its perfect teeth. "They're waiting for you down there, you know. Impatiently, but they are waiting."

"For me?" Ratcatcher found himself unable to look away from the pit. Was there light in the depths? Faintly, he thought he saw something glow, a faint white light like a band of stars cutting across the night sky. Fascinated, he looked on. The light had a shape, he was sure, one that he could almost discern. Just another moment, and he'd be able to see...

With a cry, he threw himself back from the precipice, his hands and feet scrabbling on the stone. The wind from the pit grew stronger, grew colder as he did so, and he found himself looking for handholds in the rock that he might cling to if the gusts might try to carry him away.

There were none. For a second, he felt unbridled panic, and then his guide's laughter brought him back to himself.

"Oh, you're a blessed one, Ratcatcher. You saw them, didn't you? That's not a boon they give to all their little ones." The thing's chuckles subsided into a rough cough, but amusement still glinted in its one good eye. "And you took it so *well*. They chose well with you."

Ratcatcher opened his mouth to reply, but the beast held up a hand to forestall him. "I know all of your questions, better than you do yourself. Permit me to speak for a bit, and to ask you. Then, perhaps, you'll know what you wish to know. Or need to. Perhaps even both. Is this agreeable?"

Slowly pulling himself to a squatting position, Ratcatcher nodded grimly. "It seems unlikely I have any other choice."

"Oh, there's always another choice," it replied, and gestured toward the pit. "But that, I suspect, is not what you meant. Am I correct? Excellent. Then let the interrogation commence. You, unless I have been misinformed, wish to know what is expected of you, and why you are here." A quick glance over its shoulder and a head cocked as if to listen gave ample evidence as to the source of its information.

"Yes." Ratcatcher bit his lip. "I should not be here. I should be…" He trailed off in a moment of wonder and pain.

"Dead? Yes. Well, you are dead." The creature's laugh was a dry wheeze. "But this is the wrong *kind* of death for you, is it not? That is what puzzles you."

"Yes," he said again. Gingerly, Ratcatcher knelt. He did not know why he did so. It simply seemed appropriate, and it gratified him out of all proportion to see the being opposite him smile benignly at the sight. "I should be elsewhere. I've failed. Failed many times. I don't deserve—" he held up his hands and gazed at them "—this."

"And what is 'this?' Do you know all that is to befall you in this place? Do not be in too much of a hurry for pain, Ratcatcher." Its long tongue snaked out from between its lips nervously.""You think you should be punished, then? Punished for your failures? Whipped with scorpion stings and flayed with serpent's fangs? You poor, poor fool."

Ratcatcher lifted his head, uncomprehending. "I don't understand," he said. "When I failed the Prince of Shadows, I was punished. Surely I've failed those who dwell in darkness as well, and thus I shall be punished by them?"

Unexpectedly, Ratcatcher's guide grimaced. "Is that all you've learned? No wonder you're a poor tool," it said, and spat maggots onto the floor. "Do not presume to know the will of the dead gods, or to decide whether or not they are pleased with you. The servant who is lashed too often becomes timid, not obedient. The difference is important."

"I see."

"Perhaps you do. I do not think so. It does not matter, and will not, until you have servants of your own. If," it added hastily, "you ever do. That is not today's matter. What remains is the matter of your service. That is why you were cut down from the place of your torment and your soul brought here. You are here to be judged on your failures, and on your successes. Perhaps you will be required to make a sacrifice. Perhaps you will be rewarded. Perhaps you will be utterly destroyed. It is all the same to me. I am merely your guide and your tutor. The final decision lies with those in the pit."

"I am their servant."

"Yes, and they are well aware of this." It took his hand in its rotten one and pulled him to his feet. "Come with me."

It strode out to the base of the jutting stone tendril that leaned out over the dark. "You go," it whispered. "The place of judgment is at the very end. Go on."

Numbly, Ratcatcher went. *Hold your eyes high*, he told himself. *Don't look down. Not again, anyway. Not yet.* He gingerly shuffled along the beam, his feet seeking purchase on the cold, slick stone.

"A little further," his guide called. There was no amusement in its voice anymore. Briefly, Ratcatcher considered the notion that if the guide had meant to do him harm, then surely he would have taken an opportunity before this one to do so. But the memory of games of sadism and pain played at the Prince of Shadows' knee reasserted themselves, and he found himself very nervous indeed. He took a slow step, and then another, and then suddenly his toes dangled over emptiness as he stood naked against the wind.

Below, the light grew stronger, its color shifting from white to bruised, angry violet. He could feel the pressure of it on his skin, and for an instant he thought it would lift him and carry him away. Then the light grew brighter, so bright he had to shut his eyes against it, and the force against his skin grew irresistible. He felt his feet slipping and screamed, then flung himself to the stone itself so that he might clutch it with both arms. A shuddering crack met his ears as he did so, and he knew that the stone promontory which he clung to so tightly was breaking. The light assaulted him, his closed eyes burning with the brightness of it, and then he was falling with an armful of cold stone and no expectation of ever reaching bottom.

Forgive me, my prince, he found himself thinking, and then he thought no more.

•   •   •

He awoke, once again, to the ruined and smiling face of his guide. "Welcome back," it said. "You kept them long in debate. Hours. Days, perhaps. Possibly years. Time here is not as it is elsewhere."

Ratcatcher groaned. "I fell," he said. "I remember falling…."

The guide nodded. "That you did. Though you did not fall in the same way a leaf falls from the tree. Rather, they reached for you and brought you to them. They were curious, you see. Very curious."

He sat up, his head throbbing. "And?"

"And what?"

"Have I been judged?"

The thing looked at him quizzically. "Do you still exist?"

Ratcatcher looked down at his body. It remained as it had been before, still unmarred and pale, corded with muscle.""I would assume so, yes."

"Well then, you have been judged, and found at least partially worthy."

"I have?" He found it impossible to keep the relief out of his voice. It must have been on his face as well, for the guide smiled gruesomely back at him.

"You have. Hear the judgment of the dead gods. They say unto you,'"You have served us poorly, and by doing so you have served us well.'"

Ratcatcher blinked, and bit his tongue to prevent himself from saying anything foolish. "How?" was all he could trust himself to ask. The messenger's face was twisted with pain, the voice issuing from its lips not its own.

"You have failed at every task you were set, and yet in your failures you have revealed our enemies' designs. You have laid your hand on the child who bears the hope of light, though you loosened your grasp upon him. You brought a blade to your master, but it was stolen by his most trusted servant—and yet this, too, is according to our wishes. You have fought with the chosen of the sun and you have lost, and yet by losing you have discovered the measure of your enemies. And you have shown us that we should hunt Raiton, whose sponsorship of the boy can no longer be denied. You have paid for all of these services, paid with your limbs, your flesh, your eyes. These we renew unto you. Go now, if you seek vengeance. Go with our blessing and make sacrifice of blood unto us. Make the rivers forget that water once flowed in their banks, and the sea paint the shores fresh crimson at every tide.

"Or, if you desire it, you may seek oblivion or torment, should either please you. We will grant this unto you, for your failures are our glory. Choose."

Ratcatcher wet his lips nervously. To be reborn in his own body, to be given the mandate to slaughter—this was a reward! He could hear the screams now, smell the smoke and hot blood. No more fool's errands for him, no more fetch and carry—he could render service and praise unto the dead gods without fear of being sent off to bring back a wandering priest or a whiny boy.

Oblivion would be sweet, he thought. Nothingness, an end to pain—perhaps when his labors were done. But now it was the hour of vengeance. He'd been made a fool of, humiliated, and beaten. Priests and boys and old women; they'd learn whom they'd trifled with. They'd learn before he killed them.

"I choose resurrection," he said, in a voice shot through with excitement. "I choose blood and plunder to your greater glory, and I will make great sacrifices unto you when I am reborn."

"So be it." The guide splayed its hand against the ground and muttered a word which Ratcatcher could not hear, then stood back. Stairs sprouted from the ground, each hewed from black iron and blacker stone. A cruel, spiked railing grew out of the stairs, and the tines of the spikes were stained with rust.

"That way lies your path," the messenger said, in its own voice once again. It sounded empty and hollow and sad, and for an instant Ratcatcher pitied it. "You will find a door at the stairway's end, a door to a familiar place. It will be open for you. Your sword and armor will be waiting on the threshold, and there will be servants there to gird you for battle. Take up your former service, for this too is the will of the dead gods, and go to your prince. He is in need of you."

Ratcatcher bowed, humbly. "I will do so, and with joy." He set one foot on the stair and tested his weight upon it. It seemed solid enough, and he took another stride.

Something cold and clammy caught at his elbow. He turned, and the guide's hand had him. "And, Ratcatcher," it hissed, "Find Wren. Find Wren and kill him, and you will be richly rewarded."

He smiled. "Is this also a command from the dead gods?"

"No," the guide said. "This is my wish, and in this, they humor me."

"And who are you that the dead gods show you such favor?"

The guide bowed, mockingly. "I am called Idli. Give Wren my regards before you kill him. I'll do so afterwards."

"I understand," Ratcatcher said. "Count the hours until I send you his soul." And with that, he strode up into the darkness.

Idli watched him go with mild interest. The judgment had surprised him, as had the revelation of the dead gods' uses for the man. But now he seemed renewed. Transformed. Possibly even effectual.

He decided, after a moment's reflection, that he would have felt sorry for Eliezer Wren, if it were in his nature to feel sorry for anyone or anything at all. "I'll see you again, priest," he whispered to the air. "I'll see you very soon."

Chapter Five

Yushuv left an hour before dawn. Dace was sleeping soundly under a pile of furs and blankets on the floor of the tent they shared, and Yushuv spared him a last, fond look before gently pushing the tent flap aside and stepping out into the cold night.

Winter had not yet arrived, but a cold wind through the trees served as a harbinger. Tattered brown leaves rattled on the branches that vainly clung to them, and more swirled along the ground with every gust and eddy. The stars were still bright in the heavens, peeking down through the lattice of bare boughs, and the full moon sat, sullen and yellow, just above the horizon. The camp's firepit sat a few feet from the tent mouth, its contents nothing but cold ashes. Animal hides hung, stretched, on a drying rack, and their faint but pungent aroma hung over the clearing. Trophies of war—plundered charms, pieces of armor, broken weapons—dangled from other branches, and a neat pile of bones marked the detritus of the last night's dinner.

Yushuv's bow and quiver lay resting on a flat stone next to the tent, alongside his knife and pack. Gingerly, he reached out for them, not daring to make a sound. The knife was cold and heavy in his hands, and he shoved it into his belt hurriedly. The pack, which he'd carefully stuffed with jerky, a blanket, and other traveling essentials, rested lightly on his back, the tightness of the straps reminding him of how much he'd grown in even the short time he'd been here. His bow, now marked with thin strips of hide from all the types of prey he'd hunted down, he took last, the quiver fitting neatly against his pack.

A sudden urge took him, and he knelt down by the firepit. With two fingers, he dug deep into the ashes, then traced a series of lines down his arm and across his face. Then, confident that Dace was still sleeping, he turned his back on the encampment and headed east at an easy lope.

Dace would be able to catch him, he knew, but only if Dace knew which direction he'd gone in. That's why he'd spent the day laboriously preparing a false trail which led almost due west, under the guise of hunting. In truth he'd been able to bring down a stag almost immediately, and had stashed the carcass in a tree while he'd laid down the false trail. Dace, he hoped, would never suspect a thing.

Confident in his deception, he put his head down and ran.

• • •

"Going somewhere, Yushuv?"

Yushuv stopped and looked up. She was waiting for him, as he'd known she would be, and he was simply thankful she'd waiting until he'd gotten this far before stopping him. Two full hours had passed since he'd left the encampment, and he'd covered a fair bit of distance.

Enough distance, at least, that Dace probably wasn't within earshot.

A female figure swung down from the branch she'd been perched on and landed lightly on the path in front of him. She was tall and lithe, with intricate tattoos down her arms and legs. Her face was sharp and angular, and had more than a hint of the beast in it. Her feet were bare, as was much of her legs and arms, and a brace of javelins were strapped to her back.

It was his other teacher, Lilith. She was dressed, Yushuv realized, for hunting.

"Nothing to say?" Lilith took a step forward and, involuntarily, Yushuv took a step back. Almost involuntarily, his hand went for his knife, and he had to forcibly restrain himself. A knife in hand wasn't going to help him, not against her.

"Tell me, why are you in such a hurry to leave? And such bold markings." Faster than he could react, she reached out and traced a line along his arm. A streak of gray marked her fingertip, which she held up wonderingly to the light.""Ashes. Whom are you going to kill? Those are hunter's marks you have on, you know."

"You know why I'm leaving," he said.

She nodded. "I do. But I didn't know if you did. I was wondering if you'd tell me what you think your reasons are. If they're good enough, I won't sling you over my shoulder and carry you back to Dace."

Yushuv adjusted his posture, easing ever-so-slightly into a defensive stance that she herself had taught him. A smile quirked at the corner of her mouth when she saw this, the expression of a teacher proud of her pupil.""I don't think I'm as easy to carry off as I once was."

Lilith threw back her head and laughed, a sound that to Yushuv's ears was eerily close to a howl. "Really! Good, that means you learned something from me after all. Well, you almost sound as if you were challenging me to try." Suddenly she stopped laughing, and her face was a mask of serious intent once again. "But I asked you a question. Why are you leaving?"

Yushuv tensed for a second, then relaxed and sat down in the middle of the path. Carefully, he reached into his pack and pulled out a strip of jerky. "It's simple, really. Will you share breakfast with me while I explain?"

The woman grinned. "I brought my own," she said, and pointed to a brace of skinned rabbits hanging from a nearby tree.""But you go ahead and eat yours. I'll listen." So saying, she walked over to where the rabbits hung and cut one free. A few drops of blood fell from the corpse as she shifted it to her other hand, then she turned and sat on the path cross-legged, facing Yushuv. "Go ahead," she said, and took a bite of the rabbit. There was an audible crunch, and she smiled bloodily.

Yushuv blinked, once, then tore a strip of his jerky off with his teeth and began to chew. "The problem is," he said between bites, "that Dace is honorable. He said he'd been sent to find me and to teach me, and he did that. But I don't think he's ready to let me go."

Lilith nodded. "He went looking for you because I told him to. I'd gotten a number of signs—an emissary from a coalition of spirits, for one thing, very insistent—that I should send him to you. Well, not to you precisely, since I had no idea who you were, but," she waved aimlessly, "out there, to look for the one who'd been spoken of. Which turned out to be you. And you're right." She paused to lick her fingers, where were stained red.""He's got another twenty years' worth of things to teach you before he considers you possibly ready to go off on your own. And even then he'd tag along, just to make sure you didn't waste any of his teaching on street brawls or something else suitably unworthy."

Despite himself, Yushuv chuckled. "That's Dace, yes. He'd never let me go. All for the best reasons, of course, and he'd certainly be right about some of them. But not about me staying. It's time to go."

"So you've said. But all you've told me is that it was time to go because Dace wouldn't let you go. That's hardly a good reason to sneak off in the middle of the night."

Yushuv swallowed a mouthful of dried venison. "I know. It's hard to explain. I just know that it's time. It's not that Dace hasn't been a good teacher, or that you haven't, either. It's just that, well, it's time."

"You're not telling me something," Lilith announced, and delicately spat a bone onto the ground. "Dace didn't tell you how to lie."

"He's not very good at it himself."

"No, he's not. But that's beside the point."

"You're right. But he also didn't teach me how to explain this sort of thing."

She grinned determinedly. "Try. As a favor to your other teacher, try."

Yushuv licked his lips, nervously. "All right. But I don't think it will make you happy. Three weeks ago, I started having dreams."

"Dreams?" Lilith quirked an eyebrow inquisitively. "What sort of dreams?"

"Death dreams," he said simply. "Qut Toloc. The temple there. Bodies in the streets. I can still remember the flies, you know. They were so loud. That was the first week of dreams."

He leaned forward, voice low. "Then the dreams started changing. It wasn't just places I'd been, or people I knew. There were cities I'd never seen, and everyone in them was dead or dying. There was fire everywhere. Buildings falling down. Like what Dace and I saw in that city in the crater, but worse, because these cities had been alive."

"And you have the sense that somehow it's all your fault? That if you don't go, this will somehow happen?" Lilith leaned back. "We've all had those dreams, Yushuv. It comes with the Exaltation. It's a great deal of power, and not every one of us—particularly not every one of the sun-chosen—has used it wisely."

"You don't understand," Yushuv said quietly. "It wasn't that I failed to prevent all that by not going. It was that I caused it all by staying. The one thing alive in all those dreams was me."

"Ah."

He nodded. "I was much older, but it was me. There was a sense that you had been with me, and Dace, but that you were gone. And everything I was doing was because of that. I had a sword, too, though I don't remember much about it. I suppose it must have been important, though."

"And you feel that if you stayed, you'd learn enough to make all this come to pass?" Lilith's voice was quiet now, nearly drowned out by the myriad forest sounds.

"Something like that. So I'm leaving. I figure I'll find the man who killed my family and either kill him or die trying. Maybe I'll find that priest. Or I'll go hunting Fair Folk. There's a lot out there."

Lilith frowned. She tapped the ground twice with visible impatience, and shook her head. "That's not it. It's a good story, Yushuv, but that's not it. You're too smart to run off just to get yourself killed. And if you wanted to die, you would have done it already. What's really going on?"

Yushuv finished the last of his breakfast and stood. "All of that is true, actually. I promise. But there was one more dream I haven't told you about. It was a message."

"A message?"

He nodded. "From the Unconquered Sun. He told me that I have to go meet a man, the man who's carrying the sword from my dream. I don't know who he is or where he is now, but I know what he looks like, and I know pretty much where I have to go." He shrugged. "The rest is up to me. Or fate. Or the man carrying the sword."

Lilith stood, and stepped off the path.""I think you're mistaken, but I'm not going to stop you. You want to go, and I'm not going to spend the energy that it would take to keep you. Besides, I don't think you'd learn a damn thing anymore anyway." She gestured in the direction Yushuv had been running. "There's your path. Go."

"Goodbye," he said, and stopped. He turned, and looked intently into the seemingly empty forest to his right. "Goodbye," he said again, then started to walk off.

"Wait," Lilith said. "Before you go." She spat into her palm, and Yushuv stopped.""Something for you," she explained, and dipped a finger still red with the rabbit's blood into her hand. Then, she drew a single line across Yushuv's brow, and two more underneath each of his eyes. The red of the blood made a sharp contrast to the gray of the ash.

"For the hunter," she said. "Now go."

"Thank you," he replied.""For everything." Then, with a lighter heart, he ran.

•   •   •

Lilith watched him go, until he crested a sharp ridge that rose up out of the forest floor and vanished from sight. "You can come out now," she called without turning.""He's gone."

A section of the forest floor exploded upwards, leaves flying everywhere. A second later, Dace stood there, shaking bits of leaf matter and forest mold out of his greaves." "Took you long enough," he grumbled. "I had more grubs crawling on me than a dead man."

"Think of it as practice," Lilith said sweetly. "You heard it all?"

Dace shook his head. "I did. But I don't like it."

"Neither do I. But you can't keep him."

"He's not ready!" Dace stamped his foot for emphasis, and a flock of birds rose up out of the treetops in alarm. "The boy barely knows anything. If the Unconquered Sun is sending him out into the world, it's for no reason I can see. Damn it, I feel helpless."

"You are helpless," Lilith reminded him. "But you know he has to go. Otherwise, you would have tried to stop him yourself."

Dace looked down, refusing to meet her eyes. "I know. And you know. But I still smell disaster in all of this."

"Possibly. But I smell something else, too."

"What?" He looked up, startled.

"Breakfast. Do you want your rabbit cooked, or will you eat it sensibly, raw?"

•   •   •

Some distance away, Yushuv heard a faint sound that might have been laughter. He turned and looked back, but all he saw was trees preparing themselves for winter's onslaught. He frowned, then inspiration struck him. He strung his bow, the nocked an arrow.

"Burn," he whispered to the shaft, one that Dace had made for him shortly after they'd first arrived at Lilith's camp. "Burn." He drew, aimed at a point in the gray sky near where the sun should be, and released.

Halfway up, the arrow cascaded into a flare of golden light, arcing across the heavens. It rose upward, going ever higher, until it looked like the clouds swallowed it. There was a muffled blast, and then the light from behind the clouds faded.

Yushuv smiled, and unstrung his bow. *That*, he decided, *was a much more fitting goodbye, and proof to Dace that he might have learned something after all*. Still smiling, he turned and once again ran east, but his footsteps were lighter than they had been.

Chapter Six

There were four hundred steps that led to an open door, and a single dim torch beyond it.

Ratcatcher found himself counting as he ascended into the dark, his left hand on the thorny rail beside him. Occasionally a barbed hook would catch in his flesh, but it would not tear, nor did he bleed. At first he wondered at this, then curiosity took over and he deliberately began to seek out the most jagged, vicious edges he could find. None would so much as scratch him, and he laughed. Even the pain this inflicted was slight, just a vague reminder that in a sane world, such wounds should render him gasping with agony.

"I wonder if this will hold true in the lands above," he asked himself, and looked at his hand again. Probably not, he decided, but he'd do well to test it before risking injury. Before presenting himself to the prince, he'd find some quiet chamber and a knife, and test its edge on his flesh. If it cut him, then he'd be cautious in his dealings. If it didn't, well, then perhaps the prince would learn a few lessons himself the next time he tried to exact some discipline.

He recognized the doorway, of course. It was the entrance to the Prince of Shadows' dungeons, a route he'd taken many times before. He did not recall there being quite so many stairs, but he shrugged this inconsistency off after a moment. Things down here *changed*. That was the only constant; that and shadow.

The doorway itself was open, the door still on its hinges. The lintel was surmounted with sigils and runes, all glowing a soft, poisonous green. Ratcatcher read them with mild interest. They were warnings and guardians, an announcement of the prince's curse on any who'd dare trespass on his domain. There were threats of torment as well, detailed scripts of vengeance to be enacted, and a few other less interesting notations.

"Unusual," Ratcatcher said, and reached up with a bare hand to caress the runes. They snapped and crackled at his touch, and small gouts of energy splashed over his fingers. He felt an unpleasant warmth, but nothing else, and abruptly the glow faded. The signs were still there, but dull and dark. He sensed that they still had power, but instead of warning they would now ambush. Sooner or later something would come crawling up out of the dark, see the open doorway, and attempt to shamble through. Then the runes would strike, and the twisted remains of whatever made the attempt would serve as a better warning than any message the prince had left behind.

The thought made him smile, and he stepped through the door.

As he did so, a tremendous roar rose up behind him. He turned, hands instinctively curling into fists, but nothing was pursuing him. Instead, the stairs behind him were dropping away, growing jagged cracks and crumbling to dust even as he watched. Within seconds, nothing lay beyond the doorway save gloom, and the faint whisper of a cold wind somewhere off in the distance.

The meaning of this was clear, he thought. There was no turning back. With one hand he reached out for the heavy door, and swung it silently on its hinges. It slammed shut with a sound like a hammer on armor and stayed shut. After a moment's search in the dim light, Ratcatcher found the scarred and heavy bar that should lay across the door, and hefted it. It was lighter than he remembered, or perhaps he was stronger. In either case, it slipped easily into the brackets made for it, and he slid it across the post. The stairs were gone and the sigils still waited, but something still might climb up out of the Labyrinth to pound on the prince's door, and where magic might fail honest timber and iron might still prevail on occasion.

Besides, he mused, it's always better to have a locked door at one's back. It tended to remove the temptation to retreat.

And with temptation thus excised, he strode forward in search of his armor and sword, and if the dead gods were kind, some boots as well.

• • •

The armor was waiting for him in the next chamber, a small room graced with a low stone table and nothing more. Two torches burned in brackets, filling the room with more smoke than light, and the doorways were so low that Ratcatcher had to stoop to enter.

The armor itself was laid out on the table, along with some leggings, a soft white shirt of some unknown fabric, and thick wool socks. There were also, he noted with relief, black leather boots adorned with traceries of silver. His adder-bladed sword lay to the armor's left, and a small round shield with a single gleaming spike in its boss sat at the foot of the table.

"This is new," Ratcatcher mumbled, and lifted the shield. It was made from heavy wood banded with steel, and the entire thing was lacquered over in black. The spike in the center looked to be pure silver, its point sharp enough to punch through most armor. He slipped his hand inside the leather straps, and was unsurprised to find that the grip fit him perfectly. Clearly, it had been made for him, and left for him to find. But by whom? The prince? The dead gods? The mysterious Idli?

There was a scraping sound on the stone behind him, and he turned to face it, shield first. His right hand reached back and closed around the grip of his sword, and as it flashed into his hand he knew that it was indeed *his* sword. Something like joy flooded through him, and he brought the blade up over his head into a striking position, the asp's head pointed directly at whatever lurked beyond the torchlight. "Show yourself," he commanded, and took a step forward.

Two shapes came tumbling through the doorway, short and squat and dressed in shapeless gray robes. They were men, Ratcatcher realized after a moment, though men with pale skin and bulging eyes from years spent underground. They made no move to attack. Rather, they prostrated themselves before him, softly cooing his name in thick, wet voices. Momentarily confused, he took a step back. "Who are you?" he asked, his swordpoint never wavering.

The one on the left looked up, even as his companion continued his obeisance. "We are nothing," he said. "We are servants." Without waiting for a response, he pressed his face to the stone again.

Mildly revolted, Ratcatcher prodded the other with the flat of his sword. The servant looked up, horrified, and scuttled backwards in a whirlwind of pudgy feet and hands. Ratcatcher poked him again. "You. Slave. What is your name?"

Bulging, bloodshot eyes met Ratcatcher's. Fat, blubbery lips quivered. A thin line of drool spilled from one corner of the soft mouth. "I… we have no names, Lord Ratcatcher. We were told to forget them. We are merely here to serve." The last was a pleading whimper, a whine that rose in pitch until Ratcatcher found himself gritting his teeth.

"We have something in common, then," he said, more to cut off the whining than to admit any commonality with these pathetic specimens.

"You are here to serve me? Then tell me who sent you."

"Pelesh the Exchequer," said the first of the two, who by now had ceased his devotions.""He told us to wait here against your return, and to guard your armor against any who might seek to seize it. We have been waiting for you."

"We repaired your armor as well," the second chimed in. "Oh yes, made it better. Healed the gashes and cuts, rewove the straps, polished the buckles. Made the shield, too, down here in the dark. We have been," and there was a certain satisfaction in his voice, "*devoted*."

"Ah," Ratcatcher said, his mind racing. Pelesh was the last man he expected to succor him or cherish his memory. The last time the two had shared time under the prince's roof, Pelesh had tried to have him poisoned, and Ratcatcher tended to look dimly on that sort of thing. This, then, was more than a little bit of a surprise. "Take me to Pelesh, then. He and I have some matters to discuss."

The two servants shrieked in horror, their pudgy hands waving in desperate gestures of denial. "No, no, no, we cannot do that," the first said. "You are not properly dressed," the second added, and the first nodded in almost comical agreement. "We cannot let you go into the citadel unclothed. It would be a most grievous insult to the prince, yes, and to Pelesh as well."

"And surely you would not slight our service by refusing to wear what we have tended for you so carefully, for so long." The two nodded back and forth and babbled, so much so that Ratcatcher could not tell which was speaking.

"Enough!" he said, and cast the shield aside so he could grip his sword with two hands. He lowered the blade so that it chucked the servant on the left under the chin. The fat man shuddered, but did not move.

Ratcatcher chuckled. "Excellent. You can serve after all, it seems. Very well, then. Garb me, then lead me to Pelesh. Rest assured, your labors will be rewarded."

The one on the right bobbed his head vigorously, then looked over at the blade against his partner's throat and swallowed. "We will dress you, yes Lord Ratcatcher. We will make you look so fine, so noble…" The blade flicked from his friend's throat to his own, and suddenly the bobbing and gushing ceased.

"And then Pelesh?" Ratcatcher asked.

"Dressing first. Pelesh later," the first servant said, and Ratcatcher could have sworn he heard the man suppress a chuckle.

•　　　•　　　•

The flabby little creatures had done a marvelous job, Ratcatcher had to admit. The armor fit him better than it ever had before, the boots were supple and comfortable, and the shield (once one of the servants had cooingly dusted it off) rested lightly on his arm, almost weightless. They fussed and fidgeted over him, tightening an armor strap here and flicking away an imaginary dust fleck there. Ratcatcher benignly allowed them to do this, basking in their attention even if the touch of their soft, cool fingers was disquieting.

At last, all that remained was the helmet. It sat on the table, gleaming in the reddish torchlight. Ratcatcher had considered carrying it tucked under one arm, but the shield made that impractical. Instead, with a shake of his head, he reached for it.

"Lord Ratcatcher, no!" It was the first of the servants again. Ratcatcher had begun to think of him as""Mold," and his partner as "Mushroom," and their nervous antics made him think of court eunuchs he'd known in years past. "You mustn't put on your own helm. Besides, you are not ready for it." The last was stated firmly, so firmly that Ratcatcher felt his eyebrow raise involuntarily.

"I'm not?" he said pleasantly?""And why do you say that?"

"You're *missing* something," said Mushroom, who without another word scuttled off through the doorway.

Ratcatcher watched him go. Mold cowered before him, hands twitching in nervousness.

"Where did he go?" Ratcatcher demanded.

"To fetch, Lord Ratcatcher," was the reply. "To fetch what is yours."

Further discussion was cut off by Mushroom's return, a cloth-wrapped bundle gripped tightly in his soft hands. He was smiling broadly, which gave him an uncanny resemblance to a toad, and waddled forward as fast as he could. "This is yours, Lord Ratcatcher," he said, thrusting the package forward.""This we made for you."

Hesitantly, Ratcatcher set down his sword and took the bundle. "Why was it not here with the rest of my gear, then?" His fingers worked at the clever knots that held the cloth in place, and they parted.

"We were afraid," whined Mold piteously. "Afraid others would see it and covet it."

Ratcatcher looked up for an instant. "More so than the sword and armor?"

Mushroom and Mold nodded in unison.""Oh, yes, yes." Ratcatcher opened his mouth to retort, but then the last of the shabby cloth fell away, and a weight of cold metal sat in his gauntleted hands.

"It's marvelous," Ratcatcher said softly, and meant what he said. What he held was a silvery half-mask, polished smooth and inlaid with tears of ruby and jet. The features of the mask were his, but subtly altered. They were fiercer, less human, and seeing them, Ratcatcher felt his lips curve back into a smile. "You made this?"

Mold nodded emphatically. "Oh yes. For you, Lord Ratcatcher, all for you. Pelesh gave us the metal, gave us the old mask, but we made it better. We made it for you."

Ratcatcher nodded, then dropped the mask and grasped the squirming little man by the throat. "This is deathmetal, you little worm. Pelesh wouldn't part with tin for the likes of me, let alone this. Who gave you this? Where did it come from?"

The fat creature gasped and choked, his soft fists beating ineffectually at Ratcatcher's gauntlet as he was hoisted off the ground. Mushroom began wailing, and Ratcatcher backhand him across the chamber.""Answers! I want answers, now!"

"We tell! We tell! Only stop the hurting, Lord Ratcatcher! Please!" Mold's face was red, shading to purple, and his efforts to free himself were growing more and more feeble. "Please," he repeated, softly.

"Damnation," Ratcatcher said, and dropped him to the floor. "Tell me. Quickly. Or next time I see if you have a neck to snap under all that fat."

The fat man prostrated himself once again. "Great Lord Ratcatcher, you are merciful. You will understand. You will understand that Pelesh is not our only master, but that all we do is for you, yes, for you!"

Ratcatcher prodded him with a boot.""Who?"

By way of a reply, Mold lifted his head and pointed fearfully in the direction from which Ratcatcher had come. "Down there," he said. "Pelesh doesn't know *that*, but you do. Now please, Lord Ratcatcher, show mercy?"

Nodding, Ratcatcher stooped to pick up the mask. "I see," he said. "Mercy." Mushroom crawled back into the room, one foot twisted at an odd angle, and Ratcatcher spared him a half second's glance. "Arm me, then." He placed the mask on his face and reached for his helm.

"Oh, yes, lord. You are merciful, so merciful!" The two hefted the helmet and bade him kneel, which he did. With infinite care they placed the casque on his head, cooing and chirping at the nightmare visage he now presented. Then one brought his sword to him, the other his shield. He took both, sheathing the blade and strapping the shield to his left arm. He was, he decided, ready.

"Take me to Pelesh now," he said, and the sound issued forth from his helmet like a big cat's growl.

The two glanced at each other fearfully. Hesitantly, slowly, Mushroom spoke. "Great lord, we cannot do that now. Pelesh is gone, gone with the prince. They rode out many days ago, leaving us and other servants behind. Do not hurt us! We can lead you to them, we promise!"

A red haze crept over Ratcatcher's vision, and he bit his lip in order to stave off the frenzy he felt coming. Salty blood filled his mouth, and a distant part of his brain noted that he was not, in fact, invulnerable any longer. Good to know, he thought, not that either of these two could hurt him. Blinking, shuddering, he forced the rage back. "They've gone?" he said. "Where?"

"We can show you the path, if you let us. We have a horse for you, yes, something very much like a horse. You will like it. Let us journey with you, and we will bring you to the prince."

Ratcatcher considered. If the prince was indeed gone, then any help in finding him would be welcome. On the other hand, a pair of guides he felt compelled to strangle within five minutes of setting out would do him little good. He thought for a moment, then stared down at the two little men.

"You may guide me," he said. "But you will guide me in silence, unless I give you leave to speak." An image flashed through his mind, that of the prince forbidding him to voice utterance, and he smiled grimly at the reminiscence. He'd been unable to restrain himself, and he'd been punished. He suspected these two would do no better than he.

"Oh, thank you! Thank you!" They bowed and scraped, one going so far as to kiss the toe of his boot. With a short kick, Ratcatcher flung him off.

"Go. Pack our provisions. Prepare for the journey, and meet me in the courtyard…" His voice trailed off, as he realized he had no idea what time, or indeed what season or year it was.

"Come fetch me when all is ready. We'll spend the day here, and then leave at sunset."

"Yes, Lord Ratcatcher," said Mold. "Where shall we find you when all is prepared?"

"The chamber of the orrery," Ratcatcher heard himself say, and strode off toward the stairs that led into the citadel proper. Behind him, the two plump little figures clucked and worried, and then scampered off after him.

Chapter Seven

The camp was set in a dry valley between two low hills, and offered as much luxury as the country north and east of Reddust could provide. Pelesh had fretted long and loudly over the possibility that they had set up camp in a flood gully, and pointed hysterically to the heavens on no fewer than six occasions to point out clouds scudding low overhead.

The Prince of Shadows had found this amusing for a little while, and let Pelesh ramble on for a good hour before finally silencing the Exchequer with a single gesture.

Now, Pelesh sat at the top of one of those hills, ostensibly keeping watch against the return of the men the prince had sent out, and nervously glancing behind him as if silently expecting a wall of water any minute. This, too, the prince found irritating, but it simply wasnAu't worth the effort to do anything about it. Instead, he sat in the center of his camp, watching the hustle and bustle around him, and waited for results.

The camp itself was large enough to be mistaken for a small caravan. The prince had brought forty servants with him, equally divided between the living and the dead, and with them they had pack animals, a few small wagons, riding beasts and spare mounts. The wagons and pack horses were loaded with tents, foodstuffs, wine, and weapons, along with some of the prince's monies, and trade goods that Pelesh had insisted on bringing along.

The prince had not wanted to bring the wagons. He'd wanted to ride out with a few companions, set a few towns to the sword, and ride whither the spirit moved him. That seemed, he though, the best way to reenergize himself, and that was what he'd thought Pelesh intended.

Pelesh, however, had argued strenuously for the wagons, and noted that without them, the prince would not be able to travel in the luxury which he preferred.

Pelesh was doing this more often, the prince realized with a start. Arguing with the prince, telling him what he really wanted, and worst of all, making *suggestions*. The prince hated suggestions. As far as he was concerned, they were a sign of cowardice, of a spirit that would not stand by its own convictions. He resolved to have a little talk with Pelesh when the man came down from the hill.

Around him, the camp lay sprawled across the valley. Guards trudged to and from positions on the heights, though they'd not been so much as threatened during the entire long journey. A makeshift blacksmith's station had been set up, and a burly slave wearing a leather apron and nothing more ran a nicked blade along a whetstone. The singing of metal on stone filled the air, while the sword's owner stood nearby and watched with visible impatience. A younger slave tended to the horses and horse-like things that the prince and his servants rode, feeding and watering them while warriors shouted encouragement, or laughed when one of the steeds nipped at her fingers. A cookfire blazed at the north end of the encampment, near the mouth of the would be valley, and the prince's personal chef had set up rough tables on which to work beside it. The wagons sat, their wheels blocked, at the camp's south end, and from where he sat, the prince could see sentries' legs dangling from the wagons' mouths as they watched for movement on the horizon.

It was, the prince decided, supremely boring. He roused himself and stood, then shooed away the slave who came to assist him.

The thought struck him that he didn't used to need slaves like that when he rode out. Perhaps he didn't need them still.

With easy steps, he climbed the hill on which Pelesh sat. He noted with some satisfaction that the man had seen him coming, and did not seem pleased at the prospect. Good, the prince decided. It was time Pelesh felt fear again.

The hill itself was nothing much, a low dome of red dirt and redder stone that jutted from the countryside. Some scrub plants clung to it determinedly, grasses and shrubs with the occasional optimistic sapling, but nothing more. There were burrows of small crawling things here, and the prince had heard big predators roaring in the distance at night, but now the only animal life he heard was a hawk, crying out as it circled overhead.

"My prince." Pelesh bowed deeply as the prince reached the crest of the hill. "You honor me with your presence."

"No," the prince corrected. "I terrify you, and you sincerely wish I were back in the camp. But the lie is of no concern, at least not at this moment." He looked the Exchequer up and down. The man seemed to have aged another decade since the journey had begun, no small feat for a man who'd been old when he'd first entered the prince's service. He wore nondescript clothes of brown and tan and a sad, small hat. His hands constantly brushed the reddish dust from his sleeves and trews, but ineffectually, and once the cook had caught him trying to steal water in which to wash his garments.

Pelesh flushed, and shuffled his feet. "As you say, my prince. How can I assist you?"

"In many ways, my trusted exchequer, in many ways." The prince yawned expansively, and Pelesh took an involuntary step back. "For one thing, when we finish here you can go down into the camp and decide what we really need from those damned wagons of yours. Keep that and burn the rest. I don't care how much it costs. Then, decide if any of the slaves are expendable, or likely to be unable to keep up. If so, kill them as well."

"My prince?"

"You heard me. This has turned into an old woman's holiday, not a hunting expedition. That ends now."

Pelesh shuddered, and cast his eyes at the ground.""As you say, my prince."

"That," said the prince, "is how it should be." He shaded his eyes against the late afternoon sun and gazed out over the endless rolling hills.""Any word from the men I sent out this morning to find your missing friend?"

"None, my liege." He pointed to the north. "That is the direction they rode off in, an hour before sunrise. It seemed, according to the signs and entrails, the most likely route to take. You could see their trail for several hours afterward, but there's been no word from them since." He shrugged slightly. "I am unsurprised, I confess. This is unkind and trackless territory, and we're looking for one man. We don't even know which face he wears any longer."

"Oh, they'll know him when they find him," the prince replied confidently.""All they have to do is follow the carrion birds."

●　　　●　　　●

The pillar of flame from the first wagon reached higher than the surrounding hills, which gave the prince no small amount of satisfaction. He stood on the hillside, watching the destruction at a small remove, and a small smile creased his lips.

His men, the ones he wanted with him, were attacking the excess baggage with a will. There was a tremendous crash, and then a cheer as the second wagon was tipped over. Men swarmed over it with axes, hacking at it and reducing it to firewood. A cask of wine sat near the fire, its top bashed and half its contents on the ground. Nearby, the prince's cleaver-wielding chef was being forcibly restrained by two men as three others chopped his work tables to kindling.

One of the men glanced up at the prince, who met his eyes and nodded. His knife came out, and then the chef fell to the ground with a gout of hot blood jetting from his throat. Someone threw his body on the fire, and the smells of scorched meat and bubbling fat filled the air.

Pelesh ran here and there through the carnage, directing the men here and restraining them there. Not *all* of the foodstuffs should be immolated, he could hear the little man trying to explain, and there wasn't a need to burn *all* of the wood just yet. Oddly enough, the men seemed to listen.

The prince watched, amused. Pelesh was scared again, and that was a good thing. It made him more efficient, and the prince valued efficiency in his servants.

Idly, he wondered if the pillar of flame rising from the camp would attract any unwanted attention. *Let it come*, he decided. There was nothing in this wasteland that frightened him.

The sound of riders to the north suddenly caught his attention. He strode up to the top of the hill to get a better look, and even as he did so he noted with satisfaction that his men had left off plundering their own supplies to seal off both ends of the valley.

There were three riders, not the six the prince had set out, and they clung to their exhausted horses in obvious terror. Even as the prince watched, the hindmost steed stumbled and fell, throwing its rider to the ground. It tried to rise, whinnying piteously, but it was obvious that one of its forelegs was broken, and it sank back down to the ground. The rider, for his part, staggered to his feet and ran for all he was worth. He was, the prince noted, shrieking, and neither of the other two riders slowed or made any effort to return for him.

They reined up just in front of the camp's defensive perimeter, and now the prince could see that they were in fact his men, albeit shaken, pale and terrified. The ranks parted to let them through, and they dismounted with obvious relief. Pelesh sprinted over to them, demanding to know what had happened.

Out in the dark, there was another scream. The prince drifted forward along the line of the hilltop, his eyes searching the darkness until he once again located the fallen horse.

Something was standing over it, something huge and hungry. It was a black shape against the blackness, easily the size of the horse it was feeding upon. The prince saw it tear great hunks of flesh out of the downed stallion's belly, and then it lifted its muzzle to the skies and howled.

In the camp, the reaction was immediate. The two riders bolted for the safety for the fireside, their lathered horses following them. The men in the line shifted uneasily, making signs against the darkness or looking to the prince for guidance. Pelesh, for his part, considered the situation, and then climbed into the one remaining wagon.

The shape was moving now, the prince saw, running easily and swiftly across the landscape. The downed horse's rider was perhaps a hundred yards outside the firelight now, the warriors holding the line shouting encouragement to him as he stumbled forward.

The prince put the doomed man's chances for survival at a hundred to one.

The black shape swept forward through the darkness, howling again. The man heard it and redoubled his speed. He was bleeding, the prince could see now. A makeshift bandage was tied crudely on his left arm, and even from his vantage point the prince could see the seeping red stains that had soaked it through.

He'd heard the howling, that much was obvious, and his response was to drop his sword in an effort to make more speed. The prince tsked. It still wouldn't be enough, he decided, and the sword might have lent the man's death some dignity.

Fifty yards outside the firelight now, barely forty from the line. Hope streaked across the man's features as he put on a final burst of speed. The shouting from the men in the line rose to a crescendo as he streaked forward.

Inevitably, the creature came out of the dark. It was wolf-like, in much the same way a lioness is akin to a small and pampered housecat. Fresh blood stained its muzzle and fur, and its eyes gleamed bright, angry red. One eye, the prince could see, was ringed around with scars, and he silently commended the bravery of anyone who got close enough to inflict that sort of wound.

The shouts of encouragement stopped. The beast leapt forward, and in three bounds it was on its prey. There was a shriek, a short one, and then the man's upper torso flew one way while his lower was going another, and a spray of blood and offal filled the air.

There was a second's shocked silence, then the men edged forward. The wolf, if wolf it was, looked back at them.

"Come between me and my prey and you'll all be next," it said, thickly but unmistakably. A shudder ran through the prince's troops. Sensing the indecisiveness, the wolf-thing bared its fangs in a grin and trotted closer. The front of the line bowed back away from him.

This, the prince decided, was quite enough. Summoning the power to him, he leapt into the air. His cloak of Essence flared out behind him, leaving a trail like an ill-omened comet behind him as he descended.

He landed before the line, between his men and the beast. Violet lightning slithered around him, and marked his footfalls as he strode forward.

"These men are mine," he said softly.""Do not presume to claim them in my presence."

The wolf-thing laughed.""Ah, a child of the Abyss. I would not dream of discomfiting so noble an ally. This creature, then" it said, and pointed with one gory paw to the torn cadaver,""was yours?"

"Was, yes, and will be again. They serve me in death as they served me in life. Some of them, in any case."

The wolf nodded. "I see. You should take better care of your things, child of shadow. I found six playing at being Sijanese in the hills north of here, and the stink of new death was on them. They shouldn't have wandered so far."

"They were about my business, dog," the prince replied, and was rewarded with a bristling of the thing's fur. "Do not presume to tell me what that business is."

"I'm no man's dog, and no Abyssal's either," the thing growled, its hackles raised. "Don't tempt fate too often, small one. I've still room in my belly."

"You'd do better to find a meal you could stomach better. What is your name, spirit, and what is your business here?"

"My business is hunting, and my name is mine to give." With a snarl, it hurled itself at the prince, who nimbly sidestepped and swatted the beast on its haunches. It gave a howl to freeze the blood and skidded to a halt, and the prince's men rushed forward to engage it. "Fools!" it roared, "Come to your destruction!" One jabbed at it with a spear. Its great jaws closed on the shaft, and then tossed both spear and wielder aside. Other men were laid low by savage swipes from the beast's massive paws. They hacked and hewed at it, but their blades caught in its thick fur or were turned aside by its claws. Meanwhile, the vicious jaws snapped and tore, and hot blood sprayed in the air.

The prince watched for a moment, then strode forward. His men had the spirit fenced in with sharp steel, but more men fell every minute, and the ring of blades grew thinner as each warrior went down.

A half dozen paces brought him to where the beast stood at bay. He concentrated for a moment, and his hands glowed with sullen light. "A good dog knows when to heel," he said, and struck. There was a sharp, sizzling sound, and the smell of burnt hair and meat. Flashes of light erupted where his fists struck the wolf's hide, and it gave a sound that was half howl, half whimper.

"You dare?" it said, and turned. Its jaws opened wide as it sought to snap the prince in half with a single bite. A soldier, braver or more foolish than his companions, leapt to stand before his prince but was knocked away effortlessly.

"I'll send you back to hell!"

The prince said nothing, waiting until the last second before acting. Then, as the spirit's lunge carried it forward, he dropped to the ground, turned and thrust straight up. His hands caught the beast's fur over its heart, and a second's thought was all it took to send searing pain through his fingertips.

The beast skidded to a stop and bent its head down between its legs in an effort to root out the figure that crouched there. In response, the prince swatted it on the nose. Again, there was a crackle of energy and the horrid scent of burnt dog.

With a yelp, it rolled onto its side and lay there, panting. "I yield," it said, weakly.

His face utterly without expression, the prince rose to his feet. "You don't have much choice," he said, and placed his foot on the beast's throat. It shuddered once, but did not move. "Now, tell me your name before I decide to dispose of you."

"Bonecrack," it whimpered. "I am called Bonecrack."

"I've heard of you, I think," said the prince. "The dead gods alone know where. But it's of no matter. Why are you out here, Bonecrack? This land hosts lions, not wolves."

"I was hunting," it snarled bitterly. "I have prey bound to me by oath."

"Oh do you? That's fascinating. My men swore no oath to you, did they?"

The beast grinned, an ugly sight. "Your men were merely convenient." It chuckled, a sound that was abruptly cut off when the prince dug in his heel. "Them I claimed from hunger. The other, I claim by right."

The prince spat, deliberately, onto its muzzle. "You claim nothing that I do not grant you, dog. Do you understand me, Bonecrack? I can destroy you whenever I please." Abruptly, he turned and walked off. "Give me a reason to keep you alive, and I may permit you to serve me. Don't, and your carcass will feed the worms."

"Mighty one," it said, and its voice was wheedling, "there's no need for us to work at cross-purposes, I think. You have the look of the hunter about you as well. Perhaps we can hunt together."

The prince rubbed his chin with one long, pale finger. "An interesting proposition. What are you hunting?"

With a snarl, the wolf said, "A boy."

"A boy?"

"A boy with the mark of the sun on him. I owe him pain, and he owes me his soul."

"Ah." The prince licked his lips. This was unexpected, though considering the way omens had run amok of late, perhaps not entirely so. Too many threads were converging now. It could not be coincidence.""Your suggestion has a certain merit to it."

The beast chuckled.""I thought you might agree. Now, shall we seal the bargain?"

"My word is not good enough for you?"

"I've had problems with that sort of thing of late," the wolf rumbled. "Here is what I propose: For the duration of the hunt, I shall be as a servant to you. I shall tell you what I know of the boy and his companion, of his adventures, nightmares and doom. I shall travel with you until such time as he is hunted down. His possessions and companions are yours, as is his corpse, and I shall swear an oath not to lift claw or fang against you unless you strike me first. In return, I get his soul, and perhaps a small offering of goodwill now to seal our bargain."

"A small offering?"

"The two who fled from me. I want their flesh." He adopted a wounded tone. "You hurt me sore, and I need sustenance if I am to heal."

The prince considered the matter. Behind him, his surviving men shuffled uneasily. The beast would be an ally of uncommon power, and surely it had been brought here for a purpose. The prince did not trust chance meetings, did not believe they existed. Someone or something had called the wolf to this place.

"Swear now," he said.

"Very well," the beast said tiredly.""I, Bonecrack, seal a bargain with you to lift neither claw nor fang against you unless you strike at me. I will travel with you, aid you in your hunt and take no more than my share of the kill. So do I swear, and if I break my bargain you may bind me into servitude for a hundred years and a day." It yawned. "Is that sufficient?"

"Seal it with blood."

"Of course." It lifted one massive paw to its mouth and bit down. Reddish-black blood flowed, spattering and hissing on the dry soil as the spirit repeated its oath. "Do you wish to drink from the wound?"

"That is not necessary, I think," the prince replied, and turned to his men. "Make a sleeping place for Bonecrack in the camp. And send forth the two who rode before him. Our guest is hungry."

Chapter Eight

The prince's citadel was mostly empty, and Ratcatcher found that surprising. While ghosts and other unliving functionaries still scurried along the halls, not speaking to any save their unliving brethren, most of the living servants—and all of the prince's most trusted ones—were gone. Their chambers were empty, though their possessions still remained. Even Pelesh had gone—the fat little men had told the truth on that score—and dust coated stacks of ancient coins on the wizened little man's unoccupied desk.

There was something new in the air, too, a sense of undirected, panicky fear. Ratcatcher felt it as never before. Always, when he had walked these halls previously, the only terror within these walls had been terror of the prince's wrath. Now, there was something else. He couldn't decide where it came from, nor would any of the swarming servants tell him, but it was as palpable and clammy as midnight fog.

Eventually, he gave up in disgust and walked to the prince's throne room. The great doors were barred and shuttered, but he unlocked them carefully. They protested, groaning, but swung wide open. A small eddy of dust followed them, dancing out into the corridor, and Ratcatcher finally entered the throne room sans summons.

It was not a wreck, as he had been half-expecting. All of the tapestries were there, though dim now with dust. The throne still sat on a dais in the center of the room, its single red cushion looking oddly forlorn. There was no devastation, no damage. No enemy had sacked this place and hauled off the prince's treasure. Instead, it had the air of an abandoned bird's nest in autumn branches, a place that had served its purpose and been left empty through deliberate action.

He strode up the dais steps and examined the throne. The prince's mace was not in its accustomed place at the throne's side, nor was the prince's helm. He considered the absences to be a good sign. With a single finger, he reached out and traced a line through the dust on the throne's obsidian arms. It was thick, though not the thickness of years. Briefly, he considered seating himself on the throne, but decided against it. The prince had a way of knowing such things, he was quite certain, and even a symbolic usurpation of the prince's station probably would not make his renewed service an easier burden to bear. He did, however, lift the cushion and dust it, motivated by an urge to maintain some sort of propriety in the midst of abandonment.

He turned then, his heel squeaking on stone, and took two steps down away from the throne before he saw the marionette. It lay, legs smashed and half its strings cut, on the floor to the left of the great doors. It wore jester's clothes, crimson and yellow and green, and its face was a painted mask that reminded Ratcatcher uncomfortably of his own. In another few strides he was upon it, scooping it up off the floor so that he might examine it more closely.

This was no crude toy, he realized when he held it. The face and hands were carved from ivory, the cloth of its pantaloons and blouse woven from silk. The cut strings were silk as well, and the wood of the crosspiece was polished mahogany. The stuffing beneath the silk was soft, the body shaped delicately and in proportion. Whoever had made this had not wanted to abandon it, Ratcatcher realized. Here was another, smaller mystery within the larger one.

The puppet moved.

Ratcatcher dropped it in shock. The thing's head had turned toward him, he was certain, and it had winked. But now it lay, unmoving, on the floor, and surely a mere puppet couldn't have moved on its own? Not here, in any case, where things only moved at the Prince of Shadows' whim.

It twitched again, and stared up at him. One tiny hand reached out, clutching at his heel, and Ratcatcher took a step back. It crawled forward, its useless legs dangling behind and crosspiece scraping across the floor. It moved impossibly quickly, faster than it had any right to, and for a long moment Ratcatcher found himself dancing across the throne room floor to get away. Unreasoning fear clutched him, far out of proportion to any threat the marionette might represent. Even in the prince's throne room, *especially* in the prince's throne room, this thing simply should not be.

With an effort, Ratcatcher mastered himself. This was a puppet, he told himself, a toy that he could crush beneath his heel if necessary. He stared at it. Relentlessly, it advanced.

And crush it he did. His boot came down on the center of its back with a sickening crunch, and it cried out, the first sound he had heard it make. Again he brought his boot down, and again came the sound of splintering wood.

"You," said Ratcatcher in between savage blows, "don't… belong… here." It twitched and squealed, but to no avail. In seconds, it was a ruin, a shape of torn cloth and distended stuffing. Ratcatcher stared at it for a long moment after that, but whatever spirit had motivated it was gone now. Broken-backed and splintered, it lay still.

"I ought to find a fire to chuck you into," Ratcatcher growled, and stalked off. The puppet lay still behind him until the doors slammed shut and the light faded.

Then, slowly and deliberately, it began moving once again. Even in the dark, it knew where it was going.

Inch by inch, it pulled itself toward the prince's throne. On its face, the painted smile grew wider.

• • •

In the stables, two servants labored to load something that, to the untrained eye, looked like a gray gelding with gear and supplies. A closer observation would have revealed certain inconsistencies, such as the bright red of its eyes and ears, or perhaps the fact that it had cloven hooves, but to the casual observer it seemed to be a horse and nothing more, and that was good enough.

The older of the two, whom Ratcatcher called Mold and who had long since forgotten his own name, sighed. "He will not like what he finds, no."

The younger shook his head sadly. "No. And he will blame us." He squatted and rummaged in the darkness for a spare sword, which he strapped to the saddle with resignation.

"He will. But it is our lot. Are our mounts ready?"

Mushroom nodded.

"Yes, and the pack animals, too. We will be ready to leave when Lord Ratcatcher wishes. That should make him happier, at least."

Mold shrugged. "Perhaps. Very little makes dead men happy, except more death. He will kill us, you know."

"I know." Mushroom tightened a girth on the gray's saddle. "And then we will return to our other master, and we shall be rewarded."

"With pain?" Mold's voice was hopeful.

Mushroom nodded. "Yes. With pain." And with that, they returned to their tasks wordlessly.

•   •   •

By contrast with the throne room, the orrery chamber was a disaster.

Ratcatcher entered it slowly and cautiously, perhaps expecting some agent of Unforgiven Blossom's vengeance to have remained here. But there was nothing, only wreckage and sparse signs of the woman's presence.

All of her personal belongings were gone. Any furniture that remained was splintered and broken, mute evidence of the duel Ratcatcher had fought on the orrery that long-ago day. Broken porcelain crunched underfoot as he walked, and here and there scorched and rusted bits of the prophetic device itself sat broken on the floor. The center of the orrery still stood, its wheels and gears now exposed for all to see. A few, he noted with astonishment, still whirred and clicked of their own accord. For a second they reminded him uncomfortably of the puppet in the throne room, but he shrugged the notion off and strode deeper into the room.

Mushroom and Mold had made no mention of Unforgiven Blossom during their squealing recitation, and her apartments were an empty ruin. That, Ratcatcher guessed, meant that she'd left of her own accord, and not due to the prince's wishes. That he found very interesting.

At the back of the chamber he found Unforgiven Blossom's workbenches. Some attempt to rebuild the orrery had been made here, he now saw. New globes sat half-fashioned on the bench, cast from precious metals and encrusted with gems. But the work seemed sloppy and disinterested, the craftsmanship shoddy. Springs and other, less identifiable elements of the device's construction lay scattered, mixed in with tools that had not seen use in many months.

At the end of the table was a series of scrolls, which Ratcatcher took from their cases and unrolled. The first was a blueprint for the orrery, much commented-on and worn. He put that down and took up the next, which proved to be a list of tea blends, along with a detailed catalog of spices and their potentially magical effects. The fourth scroll was more of the same, and the fifth was a personal diary that Ratcatcher read with alternating amusement and disgust.

The sixth, however, was nothing more than a portrait. Ratcatcher stared at it. The face it portrayed was fine-boned and dark, beardless and delicate. It was a man's face, one with lines around the eyes and evidence of too many frowns around the mouth. Ultimately, it was a mediocre portrait of an average face, a depiction of a man one might pass by and ignore a hundred times in the marketplace.

Except, Ratcatcher realized, that it was a portrait of the face he'd worn in Sijan.

With a curse, he tore it in two, then tore it again. Everywhere he went, the damned woman was one step ahead of him. Even in death, she'd found a way to fox him. No doubt she'd flummoxed the lumbering fool of a Sidereal to protect her knowing that he was on the way; no doubt she had other surprises waiting for him even now.

"I have a surprise for you, too, my unloved and unlovely blossom," he muttered, and swept the table clean. Metal clattered onto the floor; glass shattered. Delicate tools broke and heavier ones smashed the items they'd once been used to create.

Ratcatcher drew his sword. A black flame whipped around it now, and another cloak of blackness flared out behind him. This was somehow wrong, he knew, but he didn't care. The power flowed through him, and it felt sweeter than his first new breath of air.

"Everything of yours," he howled, and brought the sword down on the table. It broke with a crack, and the two halves collapsed thunderously onto the floor. Whirling, he hacked at the half-finished globes on the floor and left only twisted scraps of metal behind. The core of the orrery he butchered mercilessly, and the few other evidences of Unforgiven Blossom's presence were destroyed as well. With each stroke, he howled, and each howl echoed through the chamber to mix with the sounds of destruction.

When there was nothing left to destroy, he tried his blade on the walls, and it cut deeply. He tore great gashes out of the floor, then flung the rubble into the air and swung wildly at it. It shattered at the touch of his blade, the serpent head hissing and coiling even as he swung. "I'm going to kill your memory, you hag," he cried out, "and then I'm going to kill you. Can you see that, Unforgiven Blossom? Can you see me coming?"

In a final paroxysm of fury, he brought the sword down on the jagged stump of the orrery's base. A cloud of sparks burst up, and then suddenly, there was silence.

Ratcatcher's anima faded away, and suddenly he was very tired. He leaned on the sword and surveyed the damage around him. It was near-total. Wearily, he smiled. Soon, he promised himself. Soon it would be the woman herself. And her protector. And Wren, and the boy, and—

There was a timid knock at the door.

"Yes?" Ratcatcher said, alert again.

The door opened perhaps a hand's width. Mold, or perhaps Mushroom, peered in. "Lord Ratcatcher?" he said querulously.

"Yes?"

"All is in readiness, my lord."

"Good." He permitted himself a small smile.

"The sun will sink in four hours. You should sleep, Lord Ratcacher. You should—"

"Enough." The servant fell silent. "I will retire to my chambers. You and your companion will meet me there, so that I may remove my armor and rest. When the sun sets, you will find me again, and we shall depart. Do not speak to me unless spoken to. Do you understand?"

Miserably and dumbly, the servant nodded.

"Good. You may go."

The door slammed, and Ratcatcher could dimly hear the receding sound of fat feet slapping against a stone floor. He looked down. There was an unbroken hemisphere of beaten brass by his foot. Mercury, he supposed, or something like it. Somehow, it had survived his rage.

"You're very lucky," he said to it, and picked it up. "Very lucky indeed. I'll use you to catch your mistress' blood when the time comes, and then we shall see what she prophesies. Not much, I suspect. Not much at all."

Chapter Nine

When he stopped for the night, Eliezer Wren bought himself a hat. It was wide-brimmed and floppy, made from brown felt and banded with old, tough leather. Mendicant priests often wore hats like this one, Wren remembered, and the thought made him chuckle.

The man who sold it to him, a heavyset, clean-shaven shopkeeper with a barrel chest and barrel-shaped arms and legs to match, didn't see the humor in it. He charged Wren twice what the hat was worth, and called it a bargain without blinking.

Wren didn't argue. It was clear from the expression on the shopkeeper's face that he recognized the horses Wren rode in on, and just as clear that the extra cost of the hat was the price of his silence about it.

So, humbly and gratefully, Wren paid the cost of the hat, then paid more for stabling his horses, and took a room at the local inn. There was talk in the common room that night about the haunted town of Qut Toloc, with townsfolk and rare travelers trying to top each other with tall tales of the place's mysteries and treasures. Wren chose not to join in. Instead, he sat in the corner, slowly scooping dollops of stew onto hunks of rough bread and listening with amusement.

Some of the stories, he noted as he ate, were actually good, if highly improbable. There was one woman, an enormously fat farmer with a shaved head and earrings that dangled to her shoulders, who swore that on the day the village had been destroyed, she'd seen a bird the size of a horse circling over the temple and singing prayers of mourning. When pressed, she admitted that she hadn't actually seen it, but had heard about it from a friend who had, and then the rest of her protestations were drowned in laughter.

Another woman, whom the rest of the locals addressed as "Grandmother," told in hushed tones of the ghosts who'd walked the streets of the town, rending the flesh from any living man who dared stay there overnight. Only the intervention of a priest, she said, had saved this town from the same fate. He'd gone riding in, she said, with a host of companions behind him, and fought the ghosts for a day and a night. When he'd finished, he burned every body in the place and put his sign on it, so that no one with half an ounce of sense would ever set foot in that place again.

Wren listened to that one with half an ear. It sounded vaguely as if a Wyld Hunt or some such had made a fast sweep of the place, burning the dead and proclaiming victory without doing any work. He snorted over his stew. It was typical, really, and the fact that the local peasants had made it into an epic worthy of the Five Dragons was typical, too.

It was hours later, when the stew was all gone and the majority of the tale-tellers were snoring under benches, when the hosteler finally lumbered out from behind the table at which he sat and pulled up a bench near the central fire. The others hushed, looking up at him expectantly, and despite himself, Wren felt his curiosity piqued.

The hosteler was not a large man, nor was he an attractive one. A spade beard hid what Wren suspected was a weak chin, but his shoulders were broad and his walk was that of a man used to long marches. His left arm ended in a stump just below the elbow, to which some enterprising smith had attached a long and wickedly sharp hook. A wad of clay sat on the hook's end at the moment, a preventative measure against accidents, but Wren had no illusions as to how useful it would be if the man decided his hook needed to come into play.

Scars ran up and down both of the man's arms, white against his heavily tanned skin. He'd clearly been a soldier at one point, and when he spoke his words had an Isle accent to them.

This, Wren decided, was very interesting indeed. He leaned forward and listened.

"I remember the night Qut Toloc died," the man said, and his voice was so low it could barely be heard over the flames. "I could see the carrion birds flying overhead. None of them were praying, though," he added, and shot a glance at the farmer's recumbent form. There was a ripple of laughter which quickly died, and the man continued.

"You don't get much traffic on the road from Qut Toloc. Never did, really. Every traveler who comes up from that way," and he turned his gaze on Wren, who met it, "stands out a bit. The one who came through the next day stood out more than most.

"He was a tall man, and thin. Black armor on him, and long sword. He looked like he should be guarding caravans down on the south side of the Inland Sea, maybe, on prancing around the Imperial Manse pretending to be a noble. Arrogant, he was, and almost handsome enough to make it stick."

There was a murmur from the crowd, and those who were still awake leaned in closer. Wren sensed that most of the stories told here tonight were old ones, well worn and comfortable, but this had the air of something new, and dangerous. He pulled his stool closer to the fire.

"He had a horse, a big black one. Mean. Didn't like being stabled with other horses, and they didn't like being stabled with it. Only the goats liked it, Dragons know why. Not much baggage on him, though, like he expected he'd be able to buy whatever he wanted, or maybe to take it. Pale skin, too, but he moved like a fighting man.

"In any case, he rode out from Qut Toloc way the next day, and showed up just after dawn. Now, the road between here and the town isn't much for danger, but still, it's not one you'd ride all night if you had a choice. Wise men stopped in Qut Toloc back in those days, and started up again with the sunrise. Not him, though. I asked him why he hadn't stopped there, and he said "I generally stop at the first town I come to.' I didn't ask any more questions after that.

"He asked a few questions himself, though, mostly about the roads to the east. I answered him, fed him, and set him up with a room. There were more birds in the sky that day, all headed in the direction from which he'd come. I got the feeling there wouldn't be much Qut Toloc traffic any more."

"And then what?" Wren surprised himself by asking. All heads turned to him, the hosteler's last of all.

"Since you came up that same road, maybe you know. He stayed till supper, then rode off into the dark. The next night, two things happened. All the dogs set to howling a couple of hours after moonrise, then cut off all at once, and a man came riding in with news of what he'd seen down the road. Had to pour wine down his throat till he was sensible. Took an awful lot of wine." There was an appreciative chuckle at that, a small one.

"Ah." Wren felt his cheeks burn with something akin to embarrassment.""And you didn't go after the man who stayed here?"

The hosteler shrugged. "Didn't see the reason in it. If he wasn't the cause, no sense chasing him. If he was, no sense in having him do to us what he did to them." He paused, took a swig from a heavy leather tankard, and wiped his mouth on the back of his arm. "I did charge him extra, though. He had enough jade for ten."

"I've got some jade," Wren said diffidently, and hefted the purse he'd lifted from Bright Crow's saddlebags.

"That's why I'm charging you the same I charged him," said the hosteler, to general laughter.

Wren waited for it to die down.""I have jade, and I have questions about this man."

"Why? He a friend of yours?"

The former priest snorted. "Hardly. He's tried to kill me once, if the man you saw is the one I'm thinking of."

A low murmur ran around the room, and Wren realized he'd made a mistake. He'd admitted to surviving an encounter with the fiend who'd wiped out an entire village. It was clear that the good folk sitting around the fire didn't quite know what that made him, but they did know it made him unusual. And unusual, in these parts, tended not to fare very well.

"It was in a brawl. In Stonebreak," he added quickly, knowing that few if any of these folk had traveled that far. "He was using loaded dice, and someone called him on it. Things got ugly, and he started laying about. It took a pair of priests to roust him, and there were a half dozen dead men on the floor by the time he was done. I got out with a cracked skull and a new appreciation for the evils of gambling." An approving murmur went around the room, and someone stuck a mug in Wren's hand. He looked into it, regretted doing so instantly, and forced a smile onto his face. Apparently, here as in every tavern on the Threshold, dice was a killing matter.

For his part, the hosteler took another swig of wine. The others sat silent, waiting for his reaction. "Well," he said, and Wren breathed a small sigh of relief. "A man who'd kill like he did at Qut Toloc would kill over dice. He was no friend to me, I tell you. Cut down my traffic, he did. Ask your questions."

Quickly, Wren described Ratcatcher. At each detail, the hosteler nodded. When Wren sought to test him and described a shield device Ratcatcher didn't carry, the man shook his head. Clearly, he'd seen the genuine article.

"What are you going to do to him?" the man asked, when Wren's questions finally wound down and jade had exchanged hands. "The trail's long cold, and a dice brawl's not a good reason to hunt a man."

"A dead village is," Wren said, surprising himself with his answer. "I've got promises to keep to a lot of people, and that's one of them. Some of the priests at that temple did me a good turn once." And that, he thought to himself, was close enough to be true that he could believe it when he said it.

The man nodded. Most of the others had departed, or drifted off to sleep. "Seems about as sensible as anything else I've heard tonight. He'll kill you, you know."

"Maybe. He couldn't before." Wren shrugged, and raised the mug of water he was drinking in an impromptu toast. The hosteler responded.

"I didn't catch your name," the man said.

"I didn't give it."

"Didn't think you had. Good luck hunting him."

"Thanks." Wren rose to go and set the mug down on his stool. He took a step, and felt a tugging at the sleeve of his robe. Turning, he saw the hosteler with a thoughtful expression on his face.

"I just remembered one more thing."

"Yes?"

"A couple—maybe three—nights after this friend of yours passed through, we got the first stories about the ghosts of Qut Toloc walking. All the women were fretting because something had come along and stolen bread from their ovens and clothes from their lines. Me, I didn't see any ghosts. I figured it for a survivor, heading the same direction as the killer. Struck me as a bit curious."

The ghosts had mentioned a boy, Wren realized. He imagined the child running, traveling by night, stealing what he needed to survive...

Shaking his head to clear the images, he pursed his lips. "Seems likely. Even the worst butcher might miss someone."

The hosteler nodded. "He might indeed." He stood, and lifted the heavy iron pot off the fire with his hook. "Can't let this cook all night. The bottom will scorch. Good night, friend. I expect you'll be off in the morning."

"Yes," Wren replied. "Good night."

He retired to his rented room, then, and stretched himself out on the rough straw mattress sitting on what passed for a bedframe. But sleep would not come, and all night he saw images of a small boy running, half-blinded by tears of grief and rage.

Chapter Ten

He was awakened by the sound of wings.

Yushuv had been dreaming of his old village, of the days spent running the catacombs with his siblings and friends. Around each bend he found treasures, more than he could carry back with him. But the font of riches was never-ending, and all of the children laughed as they carried gold and jade and orichalcum back up into the light.

It had been a good dream, and he was sorry to lose it. But the flapping of wings was too loud and too insistent to ignore, and the dream flew away even as the sound got closer.

He opened his eyes and looked up. Above him, the branches of a tree cast a net to catch the bright stars in the dark sky. It was still late, perhaps an hour past midnight, and the waning moon gave enough light to tell him that he was alone on the ground.

Rubbing his eyes, he stood and stretched the stiffness from his limbs. Overhead, something large circled patiently.

He thought he knew what it was, and decided that it was best to go up to meet it.

The tree proved a relatively simple climb, with thick branches at regular intervals. Yushuv scampered up until the branches groaned under his weight, and then perched on the thickest one he could find. One hand rested against the trunk for balance. The other, he put to his lips as he whistled.

A heavy thump at the end of the branch he sat on told him that he'd been heard.

"Hello," he said, not bothering to turn. "I didn't think I'd see you again."

"You won't," said the huge black bird that scuttled down the branch until it sat next to Yushuv. "We will not speak again after this."

"You've said that before," Yushuv replied, not bothering to hide the pleasure he felt at seeing Raiton again. "When you told me who you were, and about my father. It seems like a very long time ago. I suppose it is." His tone grew wistful, before brightening again. "But here you are."

"I was not supposed to be here, Yushuv. For you, I have worked wonders. For you, I have paid a price." He lifted his wings, and in the moonlight Yushuv saw the dark blood that flowed, unceasing, from a wound on each.

"Who could do that to you?" Yushuv asked. "And why?"

"Why? Why? The boy-child wants to know why!" Raiton laughed, and there was a bitterness in his laughter that Yushuv had not heard before. "Oh, you know why!"

Yushuv bit his lip and thought. "Me?" he said suddenly. "This is because of me?"

"Of course it's because of you. I've done you favors, hidden you from the heavens, blinded your enemies' servants and guarded you while you slept. Did you not think your enemies had patrons as well, gods who were displeased with me for favoring you so? Oh, I have suffered for you, Yushuv, and I will be suffering long years after you're gone. They made sure of that. And I'm not allowed to speak to you any more. They're watching me, you know." He laughed again, and there was no joy in it. "Gods and spirits don't do well with pain, boy. We're not used to it."

"I'm sorry," Yushuv said. "I wish there were something I could do."

Raiton's head jerked up, his wickedly sharp beak narrowly missing Yushuv's face. "Do? Of course there's something you can do. It's to keep on, boy, or this is all for nothing."

Yushuv nodded."I understand. This was all planned, wasn't it? My father's gifts to you—someone told him to do that, so you'd have a reason to be kind to me. Am I right?"

"Very clever, Yushuv." Raiton hopped from foot to foot, and spatters of his blood landed wetly on Yushuv's hand. "You've started to think about causes. It's a habit that will serve you well. Just don't look so hard after yesterday you forget today. It's all for naught if you make a mistake now."

"I'll take that for an admission," Yushuv said, and leaned back against the tree. "Dace said much the same thing, you know."

"That is why Dace was selected to be your teacher. One of many reasons." Less agitated now, the bird settled down against the branch. "Your path will be entirely your own sooner than you know. Follow it. That will make all the pain worth it. I trust in your teachers, and I trust in you."

"Thank you."

"And well you should thank me." The bird looked from side to side, then cocked its head. "They are looking for me. If I stay here much longer, they will find you as well. That is not something either of us wishes for." He leaned close to Yushuv, and whispered urgently. "There is a tomb in your future boy, an empty tomb. Something waits for you there, something from dreams. I cannot tell you more."

With a shocking suddenness, Raiton leapt into the air, his wings folded against his body. He plummeted as Yushuv watched, horrified, then at the last second gave a mighty flap against the air and soared upward.

"Goodbye, boy," was the last thing Yushuv heard him say, and then the great black bird was just another shape against the stars.

• • •

For a long while after Raiton's departure, Yushuv simply sat with his back against the trunk of the tree and his eyes on the forest floor below. Perhaps a quarter of an hour after the spirit's departure, a series of large shapes came snuffling out of the deeper forest and sniffed around the base of the tree, paying extra attention to the hollow he'd been curled up in. Had it not been for Raiton's summons to the treetops, Yushuv knew, he could have had himself a much more rudes awakening.

Clearly, despite his words, Raiton wasn't quite finished doing favors for him yet.

He looked at his left hand, where the bird-spirit's blood had splashed him. It was an iridescent, oily black in the moonlight, and when he moved his hand he was surprised to discover it was still liquid. Real blood—mortals' blood—would have long since dried.

Gingerly, he reached for the small waterskin he'd taken from Dace's encampment as a backup. Using only his right hand, he unstoppered it and drank half its contents, then poured the rest onto the ground far below. Then, with the utmost care, he scraped the precious drops of blood into the skin.

Like quicksilver, they all slid in. None spilled, and nothing remained to stain his hand. With a sigh of relief, he sealed the skin again, and settled in for a few more hours' sleep.

With luck, he'd even dream, and that was something he hadn't wished for in a very long time.

Chapter Eleven

The window was a good fifteen feet off the ground, but that bothered the thief not at all. She crouched on the ground in the dim moonlight, watching the shadows of tree branches dance across the inn's walls. Nothing stirred in the window, which lay open to the world. There was no light and, apart from the sound of some titanic snoring, no sound. It would be, she decided, an easy evening's work.

She called herself Vicious Whisper, and she was dressed in black. Such was her wont when she was working, swathed in it from head to toe. Black boots muffled with black cloth were on her feet, and black leather gloves covered the constantly twitching fingers of her hands. She crouched in a patch of shadow and waited, patiently.

Minutes passed. A stableboy hurried past, rushing to an assignation with a lover, and never noticed her. A snake wound its way lazily by where she squatted, flicked its tongue at her twice, and then moved on. Still she waited, until the sound of snoring became regular and drifted down gently through the open window.

It was time. She gathered herself, took a deep breath, and leapt.

The leap took her up into the air, her toes landing on the windowsill with barely a whisper. She balanced there for a second, then tumbled forward into the room. The soft black cloth muffled the sound of her hands and back striking the floor, and she rolled to her feet in front of a low, rough table next to the room's single door. A glance behind her revealed that the inhabitants of the room were both still asleep, the woman in bed, the man wrapped in blankets and sawing away on the floor.

Satisfied, she turned back to the work at hand. The table was covered in purple fabric, a drape that extended down to the floor. On it rested a dagger, a blade of exquisite craftsmanship that gleamed gold even in the weak light from outside.

She smiled to herself. It was indeed orichalcum. The information her contact at the inn had sold her was correct. Here was a treasure truly worth stealing, rather than the petty caches of jewels and jade she normally had to filch. Here was a challenge, and a prize worth having. What it was doing in a place like this was beyond comprehension, but that was the problem of the sleeping couple behind her. She, on the other hand, had business to attend to.

Dropping to a crouch, she inspected the table for traps. A few minutes' thorough observation convinced her that there were none. Once, the massive, bald man on the floor snorted in his sleep, and she froze in place until he resumed the rhythmic cacophony of his snoring. The woman in the bed, for her part, rested peacefully, a picture of fragility with her lined face surrounded by a halo of white hair.

Slowly, steadily, the thief extended her hand. It hovered over the dagger like a spider descending on a thread of silk. With each heartbeat it descended, until the blade was caged between her fingers. She waited a moment, then under the cover of a snore she grasped the dagger by the handle.

"I would not do that if I were you," said a woman's voice. It was full of pity.

The thief whirled around, her hand still clutching the dagger. The old woman, she saw, was sitting up in bed, her knees drawn up to her chest and her hands clasped in front of her. Her eyes were wide and open, and she had a look of sadness on her face. Impossibly, the man on the floor was still snoring.

The thief didn't waste time with words. Instead, she sprang for the window, clutching her prize to her chest.

She never made it. Halfway there, a sudden cloak of darkness descended on her and a heavy blow caught her on the side of the head. She spun to the ground, even as she realized that the thing covering her was nothing more than a blanket and that the hideous din of the snoring had stopped.

Hitting the floor hard, she rolled to the left and spun out of the blanket, a mere second ahead of a thunderous blow that hammered the floor behind her.

It had been a trap, she realized. Neither of them had been sleeping. What a fool she'd been, thinking she was the patient one while they waited for her, grinning in the darkness.

Rage flooded her limbs. It was almost a shame that they'd been so clever, she thought. The trap would have caught any normal thief. It would not, however, catch her.

She reversed her grip on the dagger and swung it on a wide arc as the bald man charged at her. A crackling trail of fire hung in the air behind it, and he barely managed to leap over the curve of her swing, and the blade's edge caught the trailing hem of his robe. He was barefoot and bearded, she saw in that instant, and in his eyes was an unmistakable glint of recognition.

"Dragons' asses, Blossom, we've got an Anathema in here!" The man was clearly startled, but not so startled as to refrain from launching a kick at her head. She snapped her head back out of the way, even as she caught his ankle with her left hand. Giving a shove, she toppled him backwards. He went over with a crash, and she surged forward.

A whisper of instinct told her to duck, and an instant later something sharp and metallic whistled overhead. A flash of light told her that there was a single sliver of metal quivering in the wall next to the window. A look over her shoulder showed her that the old woman was on her feet now, a wicked array of silver gleaming in her hands.

"You should have stayed in bed, grandmother," the thief sneered, and started a spinning kick.

"And you should talk less," came a male voice from behind her, even as her other leg was swept out from underneath her. She broke her fall with her free hand, bounced, and spun in the air to see the man bearing down on her. With a curse, she flung the orichalcum dagger at him. It trailed fire as it flew, a purplish, bruised ribbon of flame leading back to her hand. Straight and true it went. She was too close to miss; he was too close to dodge, and she fully expected she'd be plucking the blade out of his chest in a minute before he hit the ground.

Instead, he caught it. His hands clapped together on either side of the blade, stopping it a hair's breadth from his chest. A soft halo of light shimmered into existence behind him while the dagger sat, dwarfed, in his grip. "My," he said. "That would have hurt."

"You're not a priest," she hissed, eyes wide in shock.

"That's open to debate," he replied, and flipped the dagger around. "I am, however, very experienced at dealing with the likes of you." The weapon waggled threateningly. "You really should pick your informants more carefully."

"That is enough chatter, Holok," the old woman said from behind the thief. "Do you intend to bore her to death?"

"I merely thought, oh radiant Unforgiven Blossom, to inquire whether she was here of her own accord, or she served another. Knowing that might make for fewer nights spent pretending to snore."

"You do snore," she retorted, while the thief looked from one to the other in increasing disbelief.

"You're both insane," Whisper announced, and threw herself at Holok. A haze of purplish light streamed out behind her, mixing with his glow and bathing the room in eerie radiance. She threw a punch and then another, and then lost herself in a flurry of blows. Holok caught each one on the flat of the dagger, deflecting every punch and sidestepping each kick. Sobs of fury rose in her throat as she threw everything she had at him, swinging and kicking faster than the eye could see. Her hands and feet were a blur, leaving strange shadows to flicker on the walls. But Holok met every blow and turned it aside, a look of beatific bliss on his face.

"Fall, damn you, fall!" she screeched, and redoubled her efforts.

Wordlessly, Holok countered her.""You can surrender, you know," he said, the steady light from his anima as calm as his expression.

Instead, she flipped backwards. With a backhanded blow, she spun Unforgiven Blossom aside. The woman's head caught the side of the table with an audible crack, and she slumped toward the floor. Without looking back, Vicious Whisper reached for the door. If she could make it downstairs without Holok catching her, she'd be able to dodge him through the kitchens and then make her escape. He was good, but wasn't fast; not as fast as she was.

"Blossom!" he bellowed, and there was real rage in his voice. "Damn you, when I get my hands on you—"

Whisper didn't hear the rest of the sentence. She leapt through the doorway and slammed the door behind her, then vaulted over the railing of the walkway. Her feet hit the thick wood of a tabletop even as she heard the door splinter behind her, and Holok appeared in the doorway.

She bounded off the table and ran for the kitchens. Behind her, a heavy thud told her that her pursuer had followed her course. A crash an instant later told her of the fate of the table.

This is fine, she thought as she leapt over a drunk sleeping on the floor. *He can chase me but he can't catch me. He's too slow.*

She burst into the kitchen and leapt onto the slab that served as a preparation counter. Ducking to avoid the hanging cheeses, she sprinted down its length leaving wisps of purple light behind her. Sleeping figures on the floor stirred at her passage but she paid them no mind. Hopefully, they'd slow Holok.

Grinning at the thought, she reached the end of the table, then realized that one of the kitchen scuts hadn't quite done his job. Her foot found a patch of fat that had not been scrubbed away, and she tumbled forward. Her head hit the wall and she lay there, crumpled, for a long instant. Behind her, Holok burst in the kitchen, his shout of "Where is she?" echoing off the walls. Terrified sleepers awakened, screaming, as he thundered through.

Whisper uncoiled and picked herself up off the floor. A shrieking woman grabbed her sleeve, and instinctively she landed an open-handed punch to the woman's face. She crumpled, blood jetting from what had been her nose, and Vicious Whisper ran.

The back door, she now saw, was only a few feet away, held shut by a simple wooden bar. Behind her, Holok pushed his way through the confusion of bodies, incoherent with rage.

With a single blow, she smashed the bar. A kick shoved the door open, and she burst into the night. She'd done it. She was free. She might have failed at her self-appointed task, but she'd escaped. She drew her anima into herself and sprinted forward into the darkness. There was no way Holok could catch her now.

The sudden, sharp pain at the back of her neck told Vicious Whisper just how wrong she was. She took another stride, then suddenly her legs ceased to obey her will, and she tumbled into the dirt and cornstalks of a field that had long since given up her harvest. So great was her speed that she flipped twice, spinning through the air like a rag doll hurled in anger.

Finally, she came to a stop, face down in the cracked soil of a furrow. She could feel the hot wet blood seeping from the back of her neck, but nothing more. Her arms and legs refused to obey her commands. She was very warm, though, she realized. She'd expected dying to hurt more.

Suddenly, Holok's face was beside her own. "You'd better pray she's all right, girl, or death's not going to be enough to keep you from me. Who sent you?"

Vicious Whisper laughed weakly.""No one sent me. I'm a thief, or I was. I worked for myself. I heard about the dagger from one of the stable boys. He used to tell me about good targets. Used to." She found herself laughing again, but tears gathered at the corner of her eye.

Holok grunted. Up close, his face showed a few faint lines of age, a few strands of gray in the fiercely bushy beard. His eyes were so dark as to be nearly black. "If you'd said that earlier, you would have earned more mercy. What's your name?"

"Whisper. Vicious Whisper."

He nodded. "You're going to sleep now, Vicious Whisper. Tell the Unconquered Sun not to be in any hurry to send your soul back to earth again, and pray that Unforgiven Blossom's not waiting on the other side for you. I'm the gentle one." He said this and reached out with one of his massive, gnarled hands. His fingers found her throat, slick with her blood, and closed.

For an instant she felt one last spasm of pain, and then even the warmth went away. Her last thought was that her killer's hands were too gentle for the job, and then she knew nothing.

Holok rose, and slung the dead thief's corpse over his shoulder. A crowd had gathered at the back door to the inn, kitchen staff and scullery maids and freshly awakened guests rubbing their eyes and demanding explanations.

He stalked toward them, pausing only to pluck the silver pin of Blossom's that he'd borrowed out of the back of Vicious Whisper's neck. Carefully he wiped it clean against the thief's sleeve, and then trudged back across the field.

The questioning throng evaporated as he got close enough for them to see the look on his face. Soon there was only one figure by the door, that of a pale, slender old woman wrapped in a woolen cloak.

"You're well?" Holok said, dropping the body at Unforgiven Blossom's feet.

"I am," she said, sparing the corpse a single glance.

"She did me no real harm, and I thought that the possibility of an injury to myself might inspire you to stop playing."

"You… you allowed yourself to be struck?" he sputtered, his face reddening. She nodded.

"Of course. Otherwise, I would not have positioned myself between her and the door, and then waited." She paused, as if considering the wisdom of her actions. "I suppose I could have interfered in your sparring session, but that struck me as being potentially more dangerous. She is dead now, yes?"

Holok gaped. "Yes, she's dead. She claimed to be a simple thief, and she was stupid enough in her approach that I'm inclined to believe her. She heard about the dagger from one of the workers here. He's been selling travelers out for some time, so we shouldn't feel especially blessed by her attentions." He nudged the corpse gently with one toe. "I haven't searched the body. I doubt we'll find anything interesting."

Unforgiven Blossom nodded. "Then dispose of it. The orichalcum is safe. You dropped it when you leapt after her." She bowed her head, ever so slightly. "I must confess I had not expected your response to be quite so… vehement."

"I live to surprise, my lady," he growled, and pressed the pin into her hand lengthwise. "This, incidentally, is yours. I borrowed it on my way out, and it did me great service. I see why you carry so many."

"You begin to see," she replied. "Should you do something with the body?"

"Only if you do something about getting us another room. I don't think ours has a door any longer."

• • •

Ultimately, they settled for hanging Unforgiven Blossom's cloak across the doorway, as the innkeeper barricaded himself in his room and would not come out despite Unforgiven Blossom's most persuasive entreaties.

Rather than return to bed, Holok sat himself on the floor cross-legged. The dagger rested on the wooden floorboards in front of him, and he noticed a dried drop of blood along the edge. "I must be getting sloppy," he told himself. He checked his hands for nicks and cuts, and, finding none, decided that the blood must have been the thief's. The thought cheered him a little, but not much.

Unforgiven Blossom, too, was awake, swathed in blankets like a corpse prepared for burial. Her eyes gleamed in the dim light of the room as she looked down on him.

"It is beautiful, is it not?" she said.

Holok nodded. "Beautiful and dangerous. We need to do something with this, you know."

"So you have been saying since first I joined you," she replied, her tone gently mocking. "Yet we have done nothing for months but wander from hostel to inn and inn to hostel. You've managed to convince a quarter of the Threshold that you're a deviant priest with a taste for old women, and I've developed feet like a washerwoman's, but other than that, what have we done? And where would you take it, that it would not attract even more attention?"

He sighed. "The Isle," he said, knowing her response. "It needs to go to the Isle. If one of the sun's chosen—or worse yet, a servant of the Abyss—gets his hands on this, you'll see a small river of blood flow to the Inner Sea. Let me take it to the Isle and lock it away, so that it'll never be used. I'll see you get anything you want in exchange for it. A new orrery, a laboratory, jade, a country estate—anything you wish."

She pursed her lips delicately. "All I wish is not to go to the Isle. They'd kill me there. In your heart, you know this. The stain of my previous service is not so easily washed away."

"Then give me the dagger and wait for me! You know I'd come back."

She smiled sadly. "I know you would try. But I cannot allow that." She paused, and considered. "Let us sleep on it. Tomorrow, I will cast divinations as to what our best course should be. If the auguries say the Isle, then the Isle it is. I will abide by their omens if you will. Will you?"

"Of course," he grumbled, and took the weapon in his left hand. He rose to his feet and walked over to the table. With a single blow, he rammed it down, point-first. It sank half its length into the hard wood and sat there, quivering.

A low hum filled the room, and by the time the sound ceased, Holok had once again wrapped himself in his blankets on the floor.

"Tomorrow," he said, and closed his eyes.

"Tomorrow," she agreed, and watched him until sleep came, and years fell away from his face.

•　•　•

She owed him a debt of her life, Unforgiven Blossom decided later that morning, when she was many miles from the inn and the sun rose at her back. That was why she had sprinkled a potion to ensure deathlike sleep on his lips, and then drawn the orichalcum dagger across the back of both of his ankles. The blood had flowed, but she was reasonably sure he would not bleed to death. He would not, however, be following her.

Indeed, it was highly unlikely he would ever walk again.

She withdrew the dagger from the jury-rigged sheath she'd made for it and gazed at it in the morning light. Somehow, it was still wet with his blood. She frowned, and wiped it on the ground. Some of the blood scraped off, while pale dust clung to the rest. With a grimace, she resheathed it and continued walking. Sometime soon, the friend she had crippled would be awakening, and she wanted to be far away when he did.

Chapter Twelve

Six days after he bought the hat, Wren sold the horses.

It was a sensible decision. He had little use for most of the gear they carried, and felt vaguely uneasy about making such an obvious target of himself on the roads. In the eyes of roadside bandits, a lone man on foot was one thing; a lone man leading a pair of heavily laden horses was entirely another. While Wren had no doubt that he'd be able to deal with any bandit troop smaller than an Imperial Legion, he didn't necessarily want to have to do so. Besides, he'd have to hide the bodies after any attempt was made, and that would take time he didn't particularly want to spend.

Of course, he could leave the hypothetical bodies behind. Doing so would serve as an effective warning to the next generation of highwaymen, but it might raise questions. Travelers would come along and wonder, asking themselves things like "Who killed all of these bandits?" and ""Why are there no marks of weapons on the corpses?" or possibly even "How did that one end up hanging from a tree branch twenty feet off the ground?" Those questions, Wren felt, would beget more questions, none of which had good answers. They would attract attention.

The last thing in the world Eliezer Wren wanted right now was more attention, from anyone.

Such were the thoughts he amused himself with in the days leading up to the sale of the horses, days of uneventful travel and slow progress. The horses were gentle enough—Wren suspected they were quite happy to get away from Bright Crow and his murderous companion—but they were not a mode of transportation he was comfortable with any longer.

Furthermore, he had a sneaking suspicion he'd make better time walking.

So better than a week from the corpse of Qut Toloc, he sold the horses and nine tenths of what they carried to a redheaded, tattooed horse merchant who was all teeth and no chin, and who spent more of the transaction talking to the horses than to their owner. She paid him jade almost desultorily, threw in a walking stick and a pack as part of the bargain, and vanished to her overcrowded stables to show off her new prizes. One of the horses cast a reproachful glance at Wren as it was led away, while the other made its opinion known in a more traditional manner.

Then they were gone, and Wren was alone in the horse trader's office. He hefted his pack so that it sat easily on the daiklave, and wriggled his shoulders until both sat comfortably. That done, he tested the weight of the staff, adjusted the brim of his hat, and lacking any further reason to delay his departure, set off.

An hour later, he finally admitted that he was surprised the horses hadn't run off after him.

Chapter Thirteen

It wasn't the constant growth of brambles across the trail that disturbed Yushuv. It was the sense that something had hurriedly planted them there. Several times, he stopped and checked the offending stalks for signs of Fair Folk-induced modification, but none of the vines dripped blood, sprouted tumors or sang off key hymns to elemental chaos. They were annoying and omnipresent, but strictly mundane.

The latest incarnation of the annoyance sprouted directly in front of him, a six-foot tall wall of bramble that sat directly across the path. It at least had the decency, Yushuv noted, to look appropriately withered for the season, but the growth was impressively thick. He looked to the left and right, only to see that going around the obstacle was not an option. The path—more accurately a game trail—ran along a valley floor. The spot where the brambles sprouted was a natural bottleneck, formed by a place where the jutting rock faces on either side of the valley pressed toward teach other. There was scarcely room on either side of the thorns for a squirrel to get through, much less a boy who'd put on twenty pounds of hard muscle under Dace and Lilith's tutelage.

Sighing, Yushuv drew his knife and started hacking away. The brush was surprisingly resistant and springy, and it took a good half hour before he'd cleared enough of an aperture to be able to squeeze through. Even so, he still lost some skin doing so, and a series of scratches along the flesh of his left forearm bore evidence to the fact that he hadn't cleared out quite enough.

Yushuv examined the tears in his shirt and arm and looked up. The sun had already vanished behind one of the hills flanking his route, and he estimated that he had perhaps an hour left before it grew dark. It was time to find a campsite.

From where he stood, the path plunged precipitously down as the valley deepened. He could see ahead to where a small but energetic waterfall burst from the cliff face to his right, to tumble into a small pool on the valley floor. That, he decided, was a good enough spot, and he picked his way downhill with something approaching great care.

The pool, it turned out, was where the game trail ended. It opened to a grassy shelf overlooking the clear water, and a plethora of animal tracks were in evidence. Yushuv chose for himself a spot near the edge of the clearing, so as to avoid being trampled in the night, and set about gathering fuel for a fire. That task accomplished, he laid snares by the water's edge in hopes of catching a hare or two, then settled in to start the fire.

It took several tries to get the wood to catch. The spray from the falls made everything just damp enough to smolder, but not to burn, and he was finally forced to indulge in the use of a touch of power to kindle a flame. Once lit, it blazed merrily, and he sat by the fire listening to the rhythm of the falling water. Supper was a strip of jerky from his pack, augmented by some dried fruit, and then he let the sound of the falls lull him to sleep.

Yushuv awoke three hours later. The valley was dark, and his fire had burned down to embers. He looked frantically left and then right, searching for the disturbance that had roused him. There was none. No creatures blundered through the brush, no warriors held aloft shining blades, no eyes glowed redly in the darkness. Nothing seemed out of place.

His fingers found a pine cone from his kindling pile, which he jammed onto a stick and rolled in the embers until it caught. It burned fiercely, and he squinted in its glare as he searched for the cause of his unease. The light cast long shadows among the trees and reflected off the still waters of the pool, and then Yushuv realized why he had awakened.

For where there had been a steady torrent of water when he had made his camp there was now only dark gray stone, shot through with seams of white and gleaming in the torchlight. The waterfall itself was gone.

It had been the silence, Yushuv realized. That is what had disturbed his sleep. He walked down to the water's edge, the torch before him, and looked up to see if he could discover what had stopped the flow. Cautiously, he peered up to the edge of the firelight.

Suddenly, the waters rushed forth from the cliff face, redoubled. The roar cut through the night, and underneath it all, Yushuv thought he heard a voice, bellowing his name. He stared out at the water, but saw nothing.

After a moment, the water flowed normally once again, and the tormented voice—if voice there had been—faded to nothing. The night noises resumed, and Yushuv was left with the feeling that he had somehow missed something important.

He knelt to extinguish the torch in the water, then shambled off to bed.

• • •

It was nearly noon when Yushuv awoke again, this time to a far more pleasant sound. A rabbit had stumbled onto one of his snares, and was energetically thrashing about by the waterside. Yushuv roused himself, splashed some water on his face, and then took a moment to wring the creature's neck. With practiced skill he skinned it and impaled the carcass on a pointed twig, then set about rebuilding the fire. This accomplished, he roasted the rabbit and ate it with obvious delight. Lilith, he thought, would be scandalized at the wasted effort, but the sizzling meat was exactly what he needed to restore himself. The strange events of the night before told him it was time to move on. He gnawed the last bit of meat off the rabbit's corpse, tossed the bones aside, and went to wash the grease from his fingers. He leaned over the water's edge and reached down toward the pool's smooth surface.

A watery hand reached up before he could do so, clasping his right wrist in a powerful, but gentle embrace. Yushuv had a moment of panic, and then a hulking figure rose up from the depths. A jagged split in its rough head passed for a mouth, and two dull orbs were its eyes.

"Shooth!" Yushuv said, and stopped struggling. "What are you doing here?"

"Looking for you," the spirit said, and released its grip." "Found you, too."

Yushuv felt himself grinning. The last time he'd seen Shooth, the water spirit had saved his life from the wolf spirit Bonecrack, and while that had been months ago, Yushuv had retained a certain fondness for it. "Yes," he said, "you found me. Good thing, too. I was just about to use you to wash my hands."

"Shooth will wash you," it said, and before Yushuv could protest he was doused by the spirit's attentions. A wave descended upon him, soaking both Yushuv himself and his bedroll, and putting out the last struggling bits of campfire. He staggered back, shaking his head and spraying water everywhere.

"That's not quite what I meant, Shooth," he said wryly, and shook both his arms in a vain effort to dry them. The spirit started to stammer an apology, but Yushuv waved him off. "No, no, it's no matter. It'll all dry soon. So why were you looking for me?"

"Dace asked," the spirit replied, and shuffled uncomfortably." "Dace said to find you."

"He doesn't want you to bring me back, does he?" Yushuv leapt back, his hands instinctively curling into fists. "I won't go, Shooth. Not even with you."

"No," the spirit said, shaking its head slowly. "With message."

"A message?" Yushuv asked, relaxing a little. "For me?"

The spirit's head nodded slowly. "Yes. From Dace."

Yushuv blinked. "Well, what is it?"

"Oh. Shooth tell now."

He chewed on the inside of his cheek in an effort to hide his annoyance. "Yes. Please tell me."

"You need to go."

"Go?"

"Out of the woods. Hurry."

"Hurry?" Yushuv's brow furrowed. "Why?"

"Danger." The spirit scratched its head ponderously. "Dace says you need to stop wandering though the woods. You'll be safer if you go west, where they don't have so much power." It shrugged, or at least gave the impression of doing so. "That is all Dace told me."

"Did Dace say what I was in danger from?" Yushuv was already packing up his meager campsite. He glanced up at the spirit, who had not moved from the center of the pool. "Why didn't he come himself?"

"He said he was busy fighting, Shooth thinks. Shooth does not know. Lilith said you would know."

"Fair Folk." Yushuv finished tying his pack shut and sprang to his feet. "I should go back and help them."

"No!" Shooth was surprisingly vehement. "Shooth was told to tell you to go. Shooth will not let you go back." It raised one arm and pointed, away to the south and west. "Go. Shooth will tell them you listened. They will be pleased."

Yushuv stared at the spirit. It looked back, implacable.

"Fine," he said. "I can't keep running away forever, you know."

"Shooth doesn't know much," was the reply, and then the water spirit sank back down into the pool.

Yushuv carefully buried the bones and the evidence of his camp. Satisfied, he refilled his waterskin, hoping he didn't catch any of Shooth's substance in it. His preparations complete, he took one last look around the site. Overhead, the sun had already started the second half of its daily trek. It was time to move. With a last look backward, Yushuv put his head down and walked off. This time, there were no thorns to bar his way.

Chapter Fourteen

None of the prince's remaining servants paused to watch Ratcatcher go. He rode off in the gloom of a misty evening, his two companions and a pair of pack animals trailing behind him like rags tied to a tattered kite. No one emerged from the heavy wooden doors to shut the citadel gate behind them, so Mushroom and Mold dismounted and did so themselves while Ratcatcher watched. The gate clanged shut with the sound of a hammer on a cracked anvil, and then the two figures hurried to remount. Ratcatcher gazed back at the citadel one last time, and then rode off. The others, their eyes respectfully averted, followed.

Three days out from the prince's citadel, Ratcatcher finally admitted to himself that he had no idea where the expedition was going. Camped in a small but dry cave under a limestone overhang, he watched Mushroom (or was it Mold?) industriously turn a spit on which two unlucky rabbits had been impaled, while his companion hauled water to the cave from the nearby stream. The mounts were tethered to a bare-branched shrub by the water's edge, and from time to time one dipped its head to the stream and drank. A thin pillar of smoke spiraled up from the fire and crept along the cave ceiling, mercifully blowing out and away.

Ratcatcher squinted at it. "We should do something about that fire. Someone will see the smoke."

Mushroom looked up from his labors, a look of horror on his soft, pudgy face. "Oh, no, we couldn't do that. There's no one here to see, and even if there were, surely no one would dare attack your campsite."

"You haven't been paying attention to my personal history, have you?" Ratcatcher said sourly, but he restricted himself to poking restlessly at the flames with broken-tipped stick. A tiny geyser of sparks burst from one of the embers as it split under the relentless prodding, and Mushroom gave a frightened shriek.

"Please, Lord Ratcatcher, do not interfere with the fire. You'll scorch the dinner."

"Scorch the dinner?" Ratcatcher raised an eyebrow, slowly. "After all I've been through, you honestly think I give a damn about burning dinner?"

He pulled the stick from the fire, and the end glowed cherry red. Unsmiling, he leaned forward until the smoldering wood was directly under Mushroom's nose. "I don't care if I burn the dinner. Do you understand?" Mushroom opened his mouth, and Ratcatcher added quickly, "Don't speak. Just nod."

Slowly, carefully, Mushroom nodded. Ratcatcher smiled. "Good. Now that we understand my priorities, let's see if you have answers to a couple of other questions that have been troubling me. You will try to answer them, won't you?" Again, Mushroom nodded, his eyes wide with terror. "Good," Ratcatcher said softly. "This doesn't have to hurt if you don't want it to."

"I will answer anything you want, Lord Ratcatcher, anything." Mushroom's voice was a squeal so high pitched as to be nearly unintelligible.

"You say that," Ratcatcher replied, "but I wonder if you mean it. I suppose there's only one way to find out. Where are we going?"

Mushroom gulped, his Adam's apple bulging out obscenely as he did so. His protruding, bloodshot eyes blinked once, and he stammered an answer. "To find the Prince of Shadows, of course. Like we told you."

"That's not good enough, I'm afraid." The stick, now glowing faintly, inched closer to the fat little man's throat. "Where is the prince that you're taking me to meet him?"

"Ah." Mushroom swallowed again. "You may be angry with us when I tell you."

Ratcatcher's smile grew wider. "Oh, I'm angry now. Why don't you just tell me the truth before I get any angrier?"

"Very well. Hear me out, I beg you. We are not taking you to where the prince is, Lord Ratcatcher."

"Ah." Ratcatcher sat back and considered the confession for a moment, not coincidentally taking the opportunity to refresh the heat at the end of his makeshift prod. "I had suspected as much, actually. Now, until recently I would have taken that confession as a perfect excuse to spit you like one of your precious rabbits. I might even have roasted you as well. But I'm a different man these days, and I've learned not to act hastily. That's why I'm going to give you a minute to explain why you lied to me, and where you're actually taking me. If your explanation is good enough, I might even let you live." He yawned elaborately. e "I doubt it, of course, but where there's life, there's hope, yes?"

Mushroom released his grip on the spit and prostrated himself. "If it pleases you, Lord Ratcatcher, we are not taking you to the place where the prince is, for it is a long journey and by the time you reached it, he would be long gone. Rather, we are taking you to where he will be." He peered out from between knotted fingers, looking up at Ratcatcher in supplication.

"And where might that be?" The makeshift tent of sticks in the middle of the fire collapsed, and Mushroom winced at the sound.

"A place you know," he said, his face pressed to the cave floor. "Do not ask for more. I cannot tell you."

"Are you sure about that?" Ratcatcher gently prodded his forearm with the butt end of the stick, and Mushroom whimpered as the smell of burned flesh filled the air. "Quite sure?"

"He cannot tell you, gracious one." The dead man looked up lazily to see Mold standing at the mouth of the cave, his arms filled with firewood.""We are not permitted to do so, no matter how much we might wish to."

"And do you wish to?"

"Of course. But our wishes matter little." He stepped into the cave and over his companion, then carefully began setting the wood down by the fire.

"It seems"*my* wishes matter little as well." Abruptly disgusted, Ratcatcher stood. The stick dropped from his hand and rolled toward the fire, only to be grabbed by the industrious Mold and stacked with the rest. He stalked off, muttering, and a minute later Mold heard the sound of splashing down by the water.

Mushroom slowly unknotted his fingers and looked up.

"It's safe now," his companion said.""He is gone for the moment, and while he is not satisfied, he is willing to trust us for a while longer. He will follow until we reach the Howe."

"I wish I could kill him," Mushroom replied, his voice quavering. "I will watch him when he sleeps, and dream of killing him."

"We are not permitted. You know that. We must serve instead." Mold's voice was as even as if he had just commented on the weather.

"I know. And he will kill us." Slowly Mushroom sat up, his eyes glancing fearfully toward the cave mouth. No ominous shadow filled it.

Mold looked at him reproachfully. "He is supposed to, remember?"

Mushroom cast his gaze at the floor. "I remember."

"Then that is enough. See to the dinner. It is burning."

"I shall," Mushroom said, and bent to his task.

Chapter Fifteen

The problem with the lands west of the forest and south of the ice, Unforgiven Blossom had long since decided, was that they were too damnably large.

She'd left Holok behind in a pool of his own blood six days prior, stealing a horse from the stables and taking with her nothing but a small pack, some food and water, and the dagger. It was by far the heaviest thing she carried, and not just because of its unnatural weight.

She'd begun to suspect the dagger months before. It seemed to find trouble, and to enjoy bloodshed. Where it went, ill luck had followed. Wren, Ratcatcher, the prince—all of them had suffered reversals after taking it into their possession. The Guild merchant who'd shown it to Wren? Dead as well, and sources told her that the factor who'd bought it from the boy (Wren had been most garrulous about its history in the moments before Ratcatcher interrupted their tea, long ago and far away) had met some misfortune, too.

Now, it seemed, it was her turn, though if there were a curse of some sort laid on it, it was too subtle for her meager arts to detect. And Holok, poor trusting Holok, had paid what seemed to be the heavier price this time around. Her regret was something she could at least carry away.

Six days of travel had yielded little in the way of excitement, however. The land over which she walked was, if not dead, then at least in mourning. Low, rolling hills skirted flat plains, each covered with a variety of dry, gray grass that supported precious little life. Rare herds of deer bounded across her path, sometimes pursued by wolves, but she apparently had too little meat on her bones for any predators to bother her. She did not stop to hunt, nor were there any roots or berries worth pausing to gather. The food she'd brought with her had proved sufficient thus far, and she required little sustenance these days. At times, she imagined herself living on nothing more than air and darkness, then the fancy passed and she would tear off a small piece of jerky or dried fruit from her meager supplies. The horse, at least, seemed able to feed off the land.

She'd followed the road that curved past the tavern where she'd abandoned Holok for two days, until it became clear that it eventually curved west, to the sea. Frustrated, she took the next fork that led north, then struck out on her own a bit to the east when it showed promise of too much traffic. The thing she was looking for, she was quite certain, would not be found on a crowded thoroughfare.

• • •

Toward the end of the sixth day, Unforgiven Blossom made for herself a more permanent camp than the one she had constructed in the recent past. Set in the lee of a limestone hill that rose up out of the plain like a breaching whale, it was little more than a rough tent, as she took her lone blanket and fastened it to both the stone wall and the ground before it. The horse she tethered some distance away, giving it some potent herbs to keep it quiet. She'd need all her concentration for what lay ahead, and being distracted by a nervous horse's hallucinations would not help matters in the slightest. It looked at her with woozy eyes, then sank onto its haunches in order to best contemplate the dried grass before it.

Satisfied, Unforgiven Blossom retreated to her tent. A small fire smoldered just outside it, and into this she sprinkled a fistful of dried leaves. The fire's scent immediately grew pungent, though the thick, heavy smoke crept along the ground rather than rising into the skies. One tendril of it poked at the horse, which whinnied blearily, and then lazily snaked past it and onto the plain.

She exhaled, realizing she'd been holding her breath. The first part of the augury was done. Now, it was time for the second. She'd have to accomplish it while the fire still burned, and without adding fuel to buy herself more time. That left her, by her experienced estimate, somewhere just over an hour. Damning the paucity of firewood available, she patted the sheath inside her robes to make sure the dagger was still there, then set off at a lope in search of prey.

• • •

It took Unforgiven Blossom nearly the full hour before her hunt was successful. She hurried back into camp, a brace of throat-slashed partridges tied together by their feet and slung over her shoulder. The tendrils of smoke were everywhere now, prying into her tent and crawling up over the hill. She stepped over them carefully, then lay the birds down by the fire. Squatting next to them, she gutted both and pulled out their vitals with a practiced hand.

The first one's liver was normal, and she cut it out before throwing it on the fire. The scudding tentacles of smoke reacted immediately, recoiling on themselves and shrinking back into the fire. Now only one remained, casting this way and that like a broken-backed snake. Rearing up, it struck dangerously close to where Unforgiven Blossom crouched, but she ignored it. It struck the ground again, and she made an impatient gesture. The smoke shrank away, and she glared after it. Cowed, it slunk off to the other side of the fire.

"Damnation," she muttered, and dug her hands into the belly of the other bird. A second later, they emerged, smeared with blood and offal. The bird's liver was clasped between her fingers, a diseased, mottled thing.

She studied for a moment, turning it over several times and making note of the markings. Then, satisfied that she had learned what she needed to know, she tossed it on the fire.

The pillar of smoke shot straight up toward the heavens. Tongues of flame licked through it, illuminating it from within and bathing Unforgiven Blossom in an eerie glow. Higher and higher it stretched until it was five times the height of a man.

Then, abruptly, there was a sharp crack, as if something precious had just been broken, and in a heartbeat the flames were snuffed out. The smoke collapsed to the ground. It lay, twitching helplessly and pointing to the east. Even as she watched, it shifted slightly to the south, then shifted again. Then, its work done, the smoke simply sank into the ground. A black trace on the dead grass remained behind, mute evidence of the augury's direction.

Disappointed, Unforgiven Blossom stood and stretched. The augury had spoken. There was no doubt about that. But daylight was fading, and the direction offered by the birds' livers had been vague in the extreme. It would be best, she decided, to camp until morning, and then to follow the smoke column's direction to her destination. In the meantime, she needed to gather more fuel for the fire. The night promised to be cold, and the thought of roast partridge for supper cheered her. Slipping off into the gathering gloom, she restored the dagger to its hiding place and went hunting a slightly different sort of prey.

•　　•　　•

The horse, she had noted before allowing herself to sleep, was still quiet. This was a pleasant surprise. She'd not named the animal under the assumption that she would soon have to either sell or kill it, and the constant noise it had made over the first week of travel had inclined her toward the latter. The herbs had worked magnificently, she told herself as she drifted off to sleep. Perhaps a lighter dose would be effective for when she traveled.

In the morning, the horse was gone. A series of footprints in the broken grass near where she'd tethered it told the story: a man, or men, had visited her campsite in the middle of the night and made off with her horse. They'd gone off to the west, and there was no way she could catch them. She cursed her cleverness in having sedated the animal to excess. No doubt it would have given some warning of the theft had it not been too drugged to do so

A shiver ran through her as she realized that only luck had kept the horse thieves from creeping into her makeshift tent and dispatching her as well. Perhaps the thieves had thought an old woman alone on the grasslands would perish on her own soon enough, or perhaps they lacked the fortitude to do the deed. It did not matter. She was alone and on foot, with no way of turning back and only an omen-haunted marker before her.

"It was a good horse," she said to no one in particular, and began the process of breaking down her tent. It was likely to be a very long day.

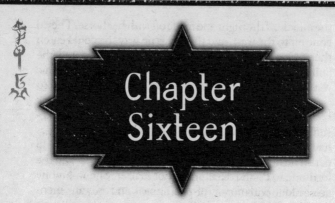

Chapter Sixteen

It was a grand Wyld Hunt that mustered on the quays of the Imperial City, one the likes of which had not been seen in years. Banners of all of the Great Houses snapped and cracked in the breeze, while the smaller, more humble pennons of less reputable bloodlines whipped madly alongside them. Dragon-Blooded warriors stood resplendent in their armor, surrounded by servants, family members and slaves. Baggage was hauled onto a full dozen ships with alacrity, teamsters and house servants working together with a will. Here and there someone's anima flared into life and then sank away to nothingness, while around them other Dragon-Blooded sniggered at the breach of protocol. Swords and axes were taken from scabbards and tested against one another—in friendly fashion, of course. Steeds snorted and whinnied and stamped their feet against the flagstones of the harbor, as grooms led them one by one onto the waiting ships.

Kejak watched the assemblage through a lace-shaded window and sighed, then let the curtain drop into place as he turned away. This was the flower of the Isle's youth, the ones he could pry away from boozing and whoring and their petty little plots long enough to make war on behalf of all Creation. The crowd outside on the quay wasn't a collection of second sons and rebellious daughters; it was bastards and by-blows, hell-raisers and failures sent off on the Wyld Hunt by parents who frankly wished to be rid of them. A daughter who'd been ejected from the House of Bells for cowardice was a liability; that same daughter dead to an Anathema was a hero, and her memory could be used as another tiny piece on the board of the great game.

They didn't know what they were really after or whose ends they were truly serving, of course. Officially, this was a Wyld Hunt called to scour certain lands of the Threshold whose princes and satraps had been afflicted with Anathema of late. The host's presence had been requested by those noble potentates, the plea for assistance forwarded to the Mouth of Peace herself. She had issued the call, not Kejak, and the gathering outside was here at her command. The fact that those satrapies that had called for help were all blessed with advisors who owed their allegiance—and positions—to Kejak was surely a coincidence. To any observer, his hands were clean.

He paced the small chamber, unaccountably nervous. It was Spartan, as befitted a monk—nothing but a reed mat on the floor and a small writing desk of lacquered wood. A stool sat by the window, and a half-empty bowl of oil with a scorched wick in it rested near the doorway. The floors were wood and the walls plaster, and only the lace of the curtains bespoke any touch of luxury.

Kejak kept this apartment for times when his other dwellings grew intolerable. This was such a time. The decay of his divining chamber had not spread further, but it gave the sense of waiting for the right time to do so. Several acolytes in the temple had reported seeing either large rats or serpents in the corridors, and while the claims were patently ridiculous, they had set tempers among the postulates on edge. Terrified shrieks, Kejak noted wryly, were not conducive to meditative exercises.

And so he had come here, and from this place he had given the orders that led to the muster outside his window. From the window he had watched the young ones arrive, the nervous first-timers jostling for pride of place, the arrogant ones arriving in their own time with their worthless entourages, and the stragglers desperate not to miss the great adventure. He'd heard the arguments over which ship would carry which riders—this Peleps refused to share a vessel with that Iselsi, and so on and so forth until he swore the very stones creaked in protest. But now they were all here, and the time to loose them, all unsuspecting, upon the world had come.

There was a tentative knock on the doorframe. Kejak turned. Standing there was a priest, garbed in the robes and insignia that indicated that she was a Most Revered Pursuer of the Ancient Enemy, a monk of the Fifth and highest coil. Her skin was tinged blue, and she carried with her the smell of fresh water running through farmland. It cut through the salt tang of the sea like a surgeon's knife, and shocked Kejak out of his reverie.

"All is in readiness, Revered Teacher," said the monk, and she bowed ever so slightly as she clasped her hands before her.

"Excellent." Kejak gestured her into the room. She bowed her head again and entered, leaving wet footprints behind as she did so. "I trust there were no problems?"

None whatsoever, Excellency. The ships are provisioned, the berthing assignments resolved, and the Mouth of Peace's blessing on the enterprise secured." She sat, cross-legged, on the floor, and nodded. "All that remains is the final address before departure, so that they might know what they hunt."

Kejak smiled.

"Ah. And you are to give that address, are you not?"

She nodded.""I am Nellens T'fillit, Most Revered Pursuer of the Ancient Enemy. I have led the Wyld Hunt three dozen times, and I have taken the kill on fifteen occasions. While I care not for such things, my family has extensive holdings in several of the disturbed provinces, and it is my duty to both my ancestors and Creation to end their depredations."

"Ah. And that is what you will tell them?" Kejak sat across from her, his smile grown thinner.

"It is the truth." A faint frown crossed her face, and her flawless brow grew ever so slightly wrinkled. "And in enterprises like this, the truth is important."

Kejak threw back his head and laughed. "By the dragons, woman, you're perfect. The heavens knew what they were doing when they sent you to me."

The woman who called herself T'fillit permitted herself a small chuckle. "I am glad you think so, and that I play this part so well for you. I've spent fifty years in the Palace Sublime, and still no one suspects that I'm more than a simple priestess." She shook her head in mock disapproval.""Really, Kejak, is it necessary? You created the Order; it dances to your whims. Must you spy on it as well? Five decades of playing masquerade grows tiresome."

"Why should they suspect you are other than what they think you are? You look remarkable, the very soul of water. And yes, your labors are important. Sometimes a subtler guidance is necessary. They must think they are self-led, and we cannot allow them the luxury of straying from the path we have set. That way lies schism, and then tolerance of the foulest evils imaginable. We know what lies beyond that; the auguries have shown us as much. Destruction. Chaos. Oblivion. Be content in your service, and know that it is appreciated. I heed your counsel, which is not something many can say. And the Immaculates—they heed you, do they not?"

"They do. They heed me, they obey my teachings, and they listen to my counsel, for I am wise in the ways of the Elemental Dragons—and in the ways of killing Anathema." She coughed delicately into one bluish hand. "They appreciate the practical experience."

"I'll wager they do," said Kejak, and rose. He walked to the window. After a minute, his visitor joined him.

"You do know what this is all about," he asked, and waved vaguely at the gathering below.

"Besides the hunt?"

"It's a question of whom you're going to be hunting. There's Anathema out there, a little sun-boy who whipped

Holok and butchered the Hunt he led." He paused, and gauged her reaction.""Does that surprise you?"

"Frankly, yes." She stepped away from the window, shaking her head.""Holok's not an easy man to whip. There's some power behind this boy."

"There is," Kejak agreed. "Some of the others know of him, and there's been much debate over what to do. I sent Holok out to find him once, and Holok came back with the boy's knife in his gut. I sent Holok out again, and he vanished."

"Do you think he's dead?"

A slight ripple of his shoulders passed for a shrug. "I doubt it, but it's a possibility. Wren's dead, though, or so my sources tell me. The boy's still at large, the heavens are hidden from me, and there's been a rash of disturbances across the northeast corner of the Threshold."

"And that's where we're going," the woman said grimly.

Kejak nodded, twice.""That's where you're going. Officially, you're there to hunt the Anathema. You don't need to tell the children that they're hunting something that's already got a half dozen notches in his dagger. They're going to be enough trouble as is, each trying to outdo the next. Let them know that the boy's a prize, and they'll be tripping over one another to be first to be decapitated by him. No, just let them know there are monsters out there, and that they're to make a grand progress from province to province, satrapy to satrapy flushing them out."

He turned, his expression brooding.""The ones you trust—and I expect they'll be few and far between—you can tell that you're meeting up with an advance scout, namely, Holok. They may not believe you, but they'll at least be on the lookout for him, and won't do something foolish like play"ride down the Itinerant.' Some of them have a less than respectful attitude toward the Immaculate order, you know."

She rolled her eyes. "That, with any luck, will be the least of my worries."

"I know. But I'd hate for any of them to pick a fight with Holok, thinking he was another district priest they could bat around at will. You'll need to instill some respect in that lot."

"I think I can do that," she said softly.

Kejak grunted something that might have been an agreement. "Are you thirsty?" he said suddenly, and when she nodded in the affirmative, he clapped twice. The sound of scurrying footsteps rose up from the first floor, servants rushing to heed their master's call. A face appeared in the doorway, round and plump and poorly shaved. The body attached to it was equally plump, and garbed in the robes of a postulant.

"How can I assist, Revered One?" he said, not daring to peer more than halfway across the threshold into the room.

"Tea," Kejak replied. "Bring tea."

"Yes, Revered One," the acolyte said with pathetic eagerness, and scurried off.

"You'll enjoy this," Kejak said when the acolyte was gone. "It's the finest tea on the entire Isle. Grown in the shadows of the towers of the Lap, if you please. The mountain air does it good."

"I look forward to trying it," the woman said.""I seem to recall, though, that Holok never liked the stuff. It was part of his adoption of the Immaculate creed, never mind his hand in its origins"

"You recall correctly." Kejak replied, an edge of impatience in his voice. "He preferred boiled acorns. Something about his rustic roots, and my having become soft after too many years of comfort in the Imperial City."

"Mmm. Perhaps that's what he's doing out there, you know—living in some hut somewhere boiling oak leaves and calling it finer than wine." She paused, reflective for a moment. "It's a pity I may have to drag him back to civilization."

"He doesn't have the luxury of his preferences, T'fillit," Kejak said brusquely. "None of us do, not the way the portents are looking these days. Find him. Bring him home.

Kill the boy if you can. Kill anything else suspicious you find. And don't philosophize over whether Holok's earned the right to squat in a hovel on the shore of the River of Tears eating tubers and brewing nettles. Am I understood?"

Her face was a frozen mask of duty.""Yes," she said softly. "I know. I understand."

"Good," Kejak said, his voice quiet but his eyes full of menace. A footfall thudded out from the stair. He smiled, then, but the smile did not reach his eyes. "The tea is coming. I insist you share a cup with me before you set sail. I'm sure you'll enjoy it."

•   •   •

The ships ended up not sailing until the following morning. A handful of servants wearing the colors of House Mnemon had gotten into a brawl with an equal number of sailors, and the scrap had escalated until a half dozen Dragon-Bloods were slugging it out in full battle regalia by the harborside. The rest of the huntsmen were no help, encircling the combatants, making wagers and hooting encouragement. The situation had only been resolved by the intervention of a handful of monks under T'fillit's leadership, who'd efficiently thrown all of the offenders off the quay and into the water. One nearly drowned, and the excitement dimmed after that, but by the time all the ruffled feathers were soothed, it was late in the day. The Dragon-Bloods and their servants repaired to family apartments or expensive hostels for the night, the sailors sighed and stowed gear, and Kejak watched impatiently out his window.

Come dawn, the renewed muster was surprisingly swift, though many of the would-be huntsmen seemed somewhat the worse for wear. Under the baleful eyes of Immaculate monks, they trooped on board, listened to T'fillit's exhortatory address, and prepared themselves for the voyage. Birds wheeled overhead as lines were cast off and winds bellied out the sails. Below decks, the beat of the oarmaster's drum could be heard, its sound echoing from one ship to the next.

By the third hour after dawn, they were gone, their sails vanishing into the haze of distance out on the water. Kejak stood by his window and stared out after them, even after mist and distance hid them from his view. A cold cup of tea, untouched since yesterday, sat on the windowsill. He glanced at it now, and lifted it to his lips.

"Pfah," he said, after a single swallow. "Bitter." He put the cup back down and gazed into it. A few leaves floated in the dark green liquid, and he addressed them. "You've been steeped in your own squeezings for far too long. But then again, perhaps so have I."

He put the cup to his lips once again, and drank it to the dregs, then clapped his hands and called for more. Downstairs, the servants scurried to obey.

Satisfied with the sounds of their response, Kejak returned to the window. The empty teacup he let fall to the ground below, and it shattered on the stone of the quay. A few drops of bitter tea were no doubt scattered among the shards, and silently he commanded them to seek the sea, to make it as harsh to his enemies as the tea had been on his lips.

A messenger wearing the badge of the Deliberative hurried by the house, and her sandals crunched the pieces of broken porcelain. Without slowing, she continued on, leaving behind shards crushed to powder.

Kejak barked laughter at the sight. The spell was broken, and he turned to await the new day's offering from his servants.

This day, he promised himself even as he ordered the postulants to bring him honey with his tea, would not be bitter. T'fillit's hunters would succeed in at least one of their tasks, and this morning's labors would ultimately be sweet indeed.

Chapter Seventeen

It was the sound of fighting that finally lured Yushuv out of the trees.

He'd been planning on coming down out of the woods for several days now, but ever-present fear had told him that as long as he could keep moving roughly southward, he was better off staying in the cover of the trees. Beyond them, where the last low hills surrendered to flatlands, was a broad, grassy plain that offered no cover whatsoever. In warmer seasons the grass would have likely stood tall enough to hide him from prying eyes, but now the desiccated stalks had been trampled down by wind and weather. Once he left the shelter of the forest, he'd be visible for miles in any direction, and the thought of distant Fair Folk archers sighting down their slender arrows at him made the skin between his shoulder blades itch. Dace and Shooth had told him to get out of the trees, but Dace and Shooth weren't here.

He'd seen no evidence of the pursuit Shooth had warned him about, but that didn't mean it wasn't there. He also saw nothing of Shooth, or indeed, of anything else larger than some oversized squirrels which he routinely caught for his supper. A nagging feeling of uneasiness, however, drove him on, and he made better time through the thinning woods than he thought possible.

It was not so much that he was being pursued, Yushuv realized after a few days. It was that he felt like he was being led.

For more than a week, he traveled like this, waking every morning with the anticipation that today would be the day when his destination would be revealed—or when the Fair Folk would come charging out of the brush and render all such hopes irrelevant.

And then, a little after noon on the ninth day, he heard the unmistakable sound of combatants trying to do grave injury unto one another. The noise traveled clearly through the thin scrim of trees separating him from bush-spangled plains, grunts and screams and once, the instantly recognizable snap of a thick bone breaking. There was no sound of weapons striking one another, but a second's listening provided him with the sound of something heavy and metallic hitting the ground.

The urge to run out and throw himself into the fray surged up, but Yushuv throttled it. '*No sense getting involved if I don't know what I'm getting into—or who I should be fighting for,* he told himself. Instead, he contented himself with shimmying up one of the slender pines that marked the edge of the forest, and peering out into the plain for a look.

It took him a moment to locate the source of the disturbance, as it was further out from the trees than he'd anticipated. Sound, it seemed, traveled well here. But after an instant of searching, his eyes caught what he was looking for, and silently, he watched.

Perhaps thirty yards from where he perched, an unarmed old woman in a plain gray robe was beset by bandits. There were five of them, and they were circling her at a wary distance. One held his left wrist as if it were in great pain, and the others held wicked-looking knives. Even as he watched, a heavyset fellow with his greasy hair tied back, launched himself at his victim. His blade, poised on high for a killing blow, caught the afternoon sunlight.

The old woman turned and, without a single wasted motion, stepped inside the bandit's downward stroke. The knife cut the air behind her, and even as it did so she ducked and struck a blow to the man's ample belly. The air went out of him in a whoosh, but before he had time to double over she threw another punch. This one took him in the groin, and he made a sound that spanned the distance between a scream and a whistle in no time at all. The knife dropped from his nerveless fingers, and he folded into himself like a piece of poorly made origami. Before he hit the ground, she had already turned to face her next opponent.

Yushuv had seen enough. He leapt from the tree and hit the ground running, his fingers already closing on the hilt of his knife. For a moment he'd considered using the bow to pick off the highwaymen from his perch, but dismissed it as unworthy. Besides, he admitted to himself as he ran, getting his hands dirty again might be fun.

Another bandit was down by the time he reached the rough circle. The man was on his hands and knees, puking his guts out onto the dead grass. His own knife stuck out of the back of his right hand.

The man with the bad wrist turned as Yushuv approached. He was dressed like a farmer's idea of a robber, a scarf tied around his head and dirty rags knotted around his fists. He was thin, but not skeletally so, and his hair was close-cropped to his skull. A ragged beard covered his chin, and his eyes were wild. "It's just a boy," he said, and set himself in position to receive Yushuv's charge. He'd found his knife somewhere, and it gleamed in his good fist. "I don't know where you came from, little one, but you'll be sorry you found this place."

Yushuv, for his part, said nothing. He feinted high, drawing the man's knife away from his belly, then thrust low. Amused derision turned to stunned surprise on the man's face, as he looked down to see the haft of Yushuv's knife sticking out of his belly.

"You should be more careful of your targets," Yushuv said, and then pulled the blade free. The man collapsed, clutching his leaking gut in an attempt to halt the bleeding even as he fell. Yushuv pivoted, scooped up the man's knife, and turned back to the fray.

The fray, he soon saw, was nearly over. While he'd been dealing with the bandit with the bad wrist, the old woman had taken down another opponent. There was only one man still standing, and he held his knife out in front of himself like a talisman against evil spirits.

"Don't come any closer," he said, his gaze flicking back and forth between the two nervously. "If you take another step, you'll be sorry."

"If you say so," replied Yushuv, and threw the knife he'd taken from his opponent. It flew straight and true, catching the startled robber in the eye. His hands flew up to defend himself, but too late; the knife had already struck home. Staggering backwards a step, he said, "Not fair," weakly, and clutched at the knife's handle futilely. The blood made the grip slick, and his fingers slid off even as he collapsed. His one good eye stared blankly up at the sky; the other was a ruin of dark blood.

Yushuv turned to address the woman he'd rescued, but she'd already taken swift steps over to where the surviving bandits were huddled on the ground. She stood over them, her face dispassionate, and for the first time Yushuv could see she had a heavy dagger at her belt. Reaching for it with one slender hand, she drew it forth.

Where the other blades had caught the light, this amplified it. The gleam of sunlight on the blade made the dead grass seem vibrant and alive, made the rough clothes of the bandits seem to be lined in gold. The blade itself was marked with subtle animal patterns, and Yushuv could see that the hilt was carved into the shape of a roaring lion's head.

"This is yours," the old woman said, her eyes still on the crawling figures on the ground. "I expect you recognize it?"

"Yes," Yushuv breathed. "But how?"

"I stole it, just as you did. Now is not the time for foolish questions. Phrase for yourself some wise ones instead." She caught one of the moaning bandits behind the ear with a kick, and he thudded to the earth.

"We should do something about them," Yushuv said, ignoring her challenge.

The woman nodded, and rendered another one of the survivors unconscious. "Yes, we should. What do you suggest?"

Yushuv chewed on his lower lip. "They don't seem to be any danger now. Do you think it's necessary to kill them?"

"I do not know. Is it?" The last of the surviving bandits saw her coming and tried to crawl off, but she easily outpaced him. He gave a whimper of terror, an instant before she brought the pommel of the dagger down on the back of his neck. Like his friends, he collapsed instantly. "There. Now we can talk freely."

"We can?" Yushuv sidestepped warily, his own knife still out. "I don't even know your name, or why those men were attacking you."

Instead of responding immediately, the woman lowered herself to the ground and sat, cross-legged. She placed the dagger, hilt-first, on the ground in front of her, then folded her hands primly in her lap. "They were attacking me for this. I suppose I should not have been displaying it quite so prominently, but after several days it seemed the best way to lure you from your concealment."

"To lure me?" Yushuv made no move to claim the dagger. "You've been following me?"

"Say, rather, that I have been anticipating you. The bandits, on the other hand, have been following me, and I was finally kind enough to slow down and permit them to catch me." The woman paused, and cocked her head at a curious angle. "They may now wish they had not done so."

"You could say that." Yushuv scanned the horizon and frowned. "We should be getting away from here. All that blood's going to bring predators."

The old woman laughed, a delicate sound. "I do not think you or I have much to worry about from animals. You have been marked by the wolf and the carrion bird; it is your time. Any beasts who feast on the dead here should bow down to you."

He took several steps back.""How do you know all of this about me?"

"I know what I have been told," she replied calmly.""No more, no less, and I do not understand all that I know. There are times when I wish I knew less, or that the auguries were less clear. Believe me, child, it brought me no pleasure to bring this trinket to you. Knowing what you may do with it brings me less."

"Then why?" Yushuv stopped backpedaling, but held his ground. In the distance, he could see some clouds scudding low along the horizon. They promised rain, if not worse.

"Explaining this would take longer than we have, unless you wish me to render my assailants unconscious at regular intervals throughout our conversation." She frowned, and smoothed a stray hair back into place.""Take the dagger. The rest is unimportant."

"If you tell me your name, I'll take the dagger," Yushuv blurted out.""If you don't, I won't."

"There is no time for games," she said angrily. "My name will mean nothing to you."

Yushuv folded his arms across his chest. "Nevertheless, I insist."

The old woman sighed. "I am called Unforgiven Blossom, for reasons that make themselves more apparent to me every day. Are you satisfied?"

Nodding, Yushuv darted in and grabbed the dagger. The weight was oddly familiar in his hand, the serpent-shaped grip oddly warm. He doubted the heat from her tiny fingers was responsible for the effect.

He thrust it through his belt, then paused and extended his hand to the old woman. Her eyes widened, and she clasped it with both of hers. "Come on," he said. "It's going to rain."

"What about them?" she asked, the sweep of her head indicating the men who lay unconscious on the ground. "Or are you not worried that wild animals will find *them*?"

"They've got a better chance than they might have had with just you," he said. "I think there are a lot of things you need to tell me."

"I think, rather, there are a lot of things you think you would like to hear." Unforgiven Blossom allowed herself to be pulled to her feet. "Under the trees, then, until the storm passes."

Yushuv looked south. The clouds were drawing closer. Up ahead, the forest beckoned invitingly. "Until the rain ends," he said, nodding. "Let's go."

Chapter Eighteen

Eliezer Wren woke up surrounded and forty feet in the air.

Below him, he could hear an unfamiliar voice shouting, "Hoy! Hoy up there!" and for a moment he wondered why the mice living under the flagstones of his chamber were so loud. Then he opened his eyes, and his unpleasant circumstances revealed themselves to him in full.

Wren lay wedged between two enormous branches of a massive, ancient oak tree. A woven mat of smaller branches and leaves was tucked neatly in beneath him, to provide support and a softer resting place, and further along the branch an enormous golden sword had been lashed to the bough with thongs of leather.

All of this Wren remembered. After all, he'd climbed the tree the night before in order to find a safe place to sleep, and he'd tied the daiklave to the branch with his own hands. One couldn't be too careful, he told himself, even in the relatively civilized lands near the Inner Sea. Even if one were a combat-trained Immaculate monk (*Former monk*, his conscience told him, and he shushed it) who'd been Exalted by the Unconquered Sun and filled with unholy power by one of the dead gods, one still had to nap occasionally. And as such, to prevent himself from being perforated as Anathema while he slumbered, he'd taken to sleeping in trees or other suitably inaccessible locations.

He'd also taken to letting his hair grow out beneath his hat and stealing clothes from isolated farmhouses, but that was a whole other matter. A common thief would not be remembered. An Immaculate might be. An Anathema most certainly would be, and Wren had long since deemed any notice at all to be extremely hazardous

Now, however, he looked down from his perch and saw that someone rather unpleasant had in fact noticed him. A quartet of armored riders was clustered around the base of the tree, looking up at him. The apparent leader wore heavy armor, lacquered in a pattern of green and blue swirls, and he was pointing with apparent unfriendly intent. His right hand held the reins of his steed, which looked vaguely horse-like underneath its barding, and a thunderously heavy mace was slung across his back. His helmet was off, and from where he lay Wren could see what looked to be pleasant enough features, slightly flushed with exertion.

Dragon-Bloods, he thought. *What the hell are they doing out here?* Instantly, his mind supplied the answer: *They're hunting me.*

"Hoy again! You, in the tree! Who are you?" Wren noticed that none of the other three had their helmets off, and indeed two of them had made not-so-subtle movements in the direction of their weapons. None, he saw, had bows, however, and that was a good thing.

They did, however, stand between him and the ground.

Grumbling at the ache in his back, he rose to a crouch. The branch he had slept on was wide enough for him to stand on, but he didn't feel like exposing himself quite that much. Running his hands over the stolen tunic and leggings he wore to smooth them, he shouted down "A simple traveler who was trying to get some sleep, thank you very much."

The leader of the quartet laughed, without much humor. "There's a hostel a half-hour's ride from here. Why didn't the weary traveler stay there instead?"

"The weary traveler is too poor for hostels, I must confess. Is that all?"

"I'm afraid not." The man in the enameled armor smiled affably, while his companions dismounted and moved to positions around the perimeter of the tree's foliage. "A man who climbs halfway to heaven to sleep is a man of rare talent. That sort of talent makes me curious. Who are you?"

Wren sighed. While he didn't know the Dragon-Blooded loudmouth below by name, he certainly knew him by type—young, officious and eager to let the world know how powerful and important he was. No doubt this idiot had been poking his nose into the business of everyone and everything around him since disembarking in the Threshold, with his three friends assisting. It was just Wren's bad luck to have caught the man's eye on a morning when he hadn't already been distracted by a fox or a peasant wench in a low-cut blouse, or a shiny trinket laying in the dust.

Best to attempt something near the truth, then, Wren decided, and hope for the young idiot to grow bored and go away.

"I'm an Immaculate monk on an itinerant mission of five years' duration," he shouted down, "and if you have any other questions, you're going to have to go ask my abbot. Satisfied?"

"I hate to doubt you, revered one, but you don't, ahhh, you don't *look* like a priest." The young Dragon-Blood scratched his head with due affectation.""Care to explain the hair, for one thing?"

"I lost my razor, and felt it would be presumptuous to buy another one, as I'd clearly proven unworthy to care for the last. Are you always this impertinent?"

By means of a response, the man reached to his belt for a leaf-bladed knife, then flung it underhand and straight up. It smacked into the bottom of the branch Wren stood on with a solid *thwock*, striking hard enough to make the entire bough shudder perceptibly. "Yes," he said. "And surely you could have gone to another temple to tend to your ablutions. And, for that matter, your robes." One of the other riders called out something, too low for Wren to hear, but from the look on his inquisitor's face he knew it wasn't good.

"Priest!" the man said, "my friend here just found some chicken bones in the ashes of your fire. I thought itinerants weren't allowed to eat meat. Do you have an explanation, or have we just treed a common thief?"

Wren cursed. Not only was the idiot persistent, he was observant as well. "Look," he said wearily, "whether you believe it or not, I am a monk. I could tell you my rank and temple assignment, but most likely it would mean absolutely nothing to you, and the only people who can verify it are a fortnight away. There are very good reasons for my looking like I do, dressing like I do, and acting like I do, but they're between me and the man who gave me this assignment, and he'd be extremely cross if I shared them with you. It would emphatically defeat the purpose of the entire exercise, if you take my meaning. If you don't believe me, that's fine, but I'm up here and you're down there, and that's not going to change at any point in the near future. Get comfortable, if you can afford to wait. I'm not coming down any time soon."

"Is that so?" The man gestured to his companions, and one drew a massive double-bladed axe from a holster slung across her back. "You're not a wagering man, are you, priest? Because if you were, I'd say now would be a perfect time for us to make a bet."

The figure with the axe, a broad-hipped and broad-boned woman in black enameled armor that only emphasized her girth, stepped up to the tree. The axe head was black as well, its handle dyed a sullen blood red. She hefted the weapon for a moment, then swung. There was a deep groaning sound, and the ax-head bit deeply into the wood. The entire tree shuddered, and Wren found himself involuntarily grabbing the branch he stood on to steady himself. "It's a big tree," he called out. "This might take a while."

"We've got time," the Dragon-Blood called back, then gestured to the woman with the axe. "Again, Shelesh. Harder."

She obliged, swinging with a will. Again and again the tree shook under the blows. It wouldn't be too long, Wren realized, before either he was shaken out of the tree or the tree itself went over. He found himself hoping fervently for a second or two that it just might land on the young idiot's head, but dismissed the thought as unworthy. If something was going to happen to the loudmouthed fool, Wren was the one who was going to have to make it happen.

Stepping lightly, he ran to where he3'd secured the daiklave the night before. Ignoring the constant stream of catcalls from below, he worked the leather thongs that held it to the branch loose, then quickly strapped it to his back. The improvised scabbard was good enough for travel, he'd found, but acrobatics and combat might be an entirely different matter. Frowning, he looked down, and estimated the distance to the ground.

"What's that you've got there? Something else you've got that you can't tell me about, priest?"

Wren looked down. There were more than enough branches between where he stood and the ground to make a leisurely, safe descent possible. At the end of that slow route, however, was likely to be an extremely unsafe reception. The tree quivered again, and Wren considered his options. Down was the only way to go, and now was the only time to do it.

But, he reasoned, there was no reason not to do it in style. He tested the slight breeze with a finger, then hitched his leggings and relieved himself. An outraged shout from below told him that he'd once again been precisely on target (*a skill they didn't teach you in the Order*, he thought with a smirk) and then flung himself into space.

His anima flared out behind him like ragged streamers as he fell, shouts of alarm from below letting him know that his display was all too visible. He'd have to kill them all now, he realized, or the survivors would send the Wyld Hunt on his track. His hands reached for another branch, catching it and sending him spinning earthward, even as the strands of light around him began to coalesce into something greater and more terrible.

He landed just behind the woman with the axe, his hands already a blur of motion even as his feet sank into moss that surrounded the wounded tree's roots. She turned and swung at him, a bellow of rage ringing out from her featureless helm. Wren ducked and wove out from under the flurry of blows she threw, then landed a solid kick to her armored midsection. A hollow clang rang out, and the force of the impact drove her back a half step. The wicked curve the axe cut in the air dipped, and in that instant Wren stepped inside the arc of her swing.

"I don't think you're putting that axe to very good use," he said, and rammed two hooked fingers into the eyeslits of her helm. There was the sound of something wet popping, and she made a half gasp, half shriek before collapsing amidst a thunderous clatter.

"Anathema!" Wren heard the voice behind him, but didn't turn. Unbidden, the lessons he'd learned in the Labyrinth, the torturous uses of power that the dead god had burned into his brain, surged up from the dark recesses in which they'd been waiting. He understood, now, exactly what he was capable of, and why it was proper for the humble Dragon-Bloods to fear him.

He felt the impact across his shoulders, and turned. The leader of the Dragon-Blooded band was there, mace in hand and an expression of disbelief on his face. Wisps of greenish flame trailed off behind him, but their light was pale and wan compared to the glow that emanated from Wren's anima. "You... I struck... how?"

Wren reached out and tore the mace from his nerve-less fingers. "You're young, aren't you? All you know about the chosen of the sun comes from tales to frighten the children. Well, little Dragon-Blood, you're a child. Be frightened." He brought the mace up on the backhand and connected with the man's chin. There was a sickening crack and he flew backwards, landing on the ground a dozen feet away. His two remaining companions held to a safe distance, weapons out, circling warily.

"Stop," said Wren. His voice was quiet, his tone commanding. The mark on his brow glowed with something just short of hunger. His shadow stretched on the ground as his anima flared into new prominence, towering over the former priest.

Slowly, agonizingly, the two Dragon-Bloods obeyed. Wren could see the strain in every muscle. Their hands trembled, their legs quivered. Like leashed hounds, they yearned to be free so that they could leap to the attack, and his will was the only leash that held them.

"Kneel," he said. Slowly, cautiously, the two knelt. They still held their swords before them, but their hands were trembling. One's anima flickered behind him, a ragged series of red flares, while the other's had guttered out. Their eyes were on Wren, reverent and terrified, and both were sobbing softly.

Wren walked over to them. "Drop those," he said, almost conversationally, though he could see the men flinch at each word. First one, then the other did so. "Excellent. You had poor choice in friends, you know. Try to explain that in the afterlife." Without meeting either man's eyes, he struck. Seconds later, two bodies toppled to the ground.

Suddenly, Wren felt very tired. He let his anima dissipate, and started systematically stripping the corpses of anything he might find useful. There wasn't much—a few handfuls of jade, a waterskin, some rations and little more. The weapons and armor he left on the corpses, and he briefly considered a pyre. Expediency prevailed, however, and he settled for stacking bodies like cordwood behind the tree's massive trunk. One, the leader, was still alive, but resisted any attempts made to revive him. At first Wren considered simply dispatching him, but ultimately decided against it. He was curious as to what had sent such an inexperienced huntsman so far out into the Threshold, and the opportunity to have his curiosity satisfied was worth losing a few hours.

That decided, he still felt no obligation to treat the man gently, and slung him off to the side with the corpses of his companions.

The corpses' mounts he sent on their way, thankful they hadn't bothered to defend their riders. They went cantering off to the west, while Wren sat in the shade of the tree to wait, and practiced his skills at plucking unwary flies out of the air.

• • •

It took something on the order of three hours, while the sun climbed the sky and Wren took slow sips of water. Late-season flies buzzed around the corpses, and he shooed them away when it seemed worth the effort.

A single groan was the first evidence he had that his long wait was over. He smiled, stretched lazily to his feet, and walked over to the pile of bodies. There was another moan, and then a violent clatter as the pile shook and collapsed. Corpses fell to the left and the right as the leader of the troop of Dragon-Bloods crawled out, his handsome face covered in blood. Loose ribbons of flesh hung from his jaw where Wren's blow had connected, and flies crawled through his hair.

"You bastard," he said, and spat blood onto the ground. "The dishonor…"

"Honor is what comes out of the back end of a well-fed pig," Wren interrupted. "I don't want to hear about your precious honor. It only seems to matter to you when you need an excuse for a lost fight. Well, piss on that the way I pissed on you."

The man staggered to his feet and charged, but Wren simply kicked out his kneecap and down he went again, groaning. "Stay down. It's safer for you. Now, what's your name?"

"I won't tell you anything."

Wren squatted on the ground next to him. "Funny, that's what I said this morning, and you wouldn't leave me alone. I think it's time for me to return the favor." He grabbed the man's face with one hand, his fingers digging into the raw and torn flesh. "Listen, little Dragon-Blood, the only reason you are alive is that I've got a use for you. It's not that important a use, however, so don't push your luck. Now, for the last time I ask you, what is your name?"

"Peleps. Peleps Tonot."

"There, that wasn't so hard." Wren released the man's face, and he fell into the dust. "Well, Peleps Tonot, tell me what you were doing out here. Four Dragon-Bloods, even young ones like yourself, riding out into the Threshold? It doesn't make sense. Your parents must be worried."

"We... we had a mission."

Wren nodded sagely.""I figured as much. Well, what was it?"

"I can't tell. I've been sworn to secrecy."

"Ah." Wren stood, pacing back and forth in the shade of the tree.""So you've been sworn to secrecy about this mission which you and your three friends—all dead, I might add—were supposed to undertake in the middle of nowhere, and if you tell someone, what might happen? Grandfather Peleps will dock your allowance of shiny jade? Your favorite whore might be taken away and given to your brother? You might even be—dare I say it—killed? Oh, they'll be very proud of you back home when, after a suitable number of weeks they decide you're dead in any case." He stooped down next to the Dragon-Blood's head and whispered, "Better to stay alive."

"They'll kill me," Tonot whimpered.

"I'll kill you now. Make your choice."

"Fine." The Dragon-Blood rolled over onto his back and stared up at the overhanging canopy of leaves. Tears glistened brightly in the corners of his eyes. "We were sent, along with others, officially on a Wyld Hunt. But there were secret orders. We were supposed to find a priest who's gone missing. We split off from the main Hunt six days back because we thought we'd have better luck that way. Left our servants behind with the main train." The man coughed congealed blood onto the ground. Dull red stained his lips.""The orders came directly from the Palace Sublime."

"A priest…" Wren's voice trailed off, then exploded into fury. "Damn it all, can't any of them leave me alone? You'd think all Creation would collapse if dear old Eliezer Wren weren't there to pick up after it." He whirled, so quickly that a shower of dirt landed on the prone man. "You listen to me, Peleps Tonot, and you listen well. I want you to go back to the Isle. I want you to go to the Palace, and I want you to demand an audience with Chejop Kejak. I don't care that you don't know who he is; most people don't. But use my name and he'll see you. And when he does see you, tell him that Eliezer Wren is done. Tell him not to send anyone else after me. Tell him to forget I ever existed. He and I are finished. What you do with your life after that is your business, but don't cross my path. Do you understand?"

"But—"

Wren kicked him, hard, in the shoulder.""The next one is in the jaw. Do you understand me? It is a yes or no question."

"Yes."

"Good. Get up." He stepped back and let Tonot drag himself to his feet.""You know, I should have killed you, but I think sending the message is a better idea. Start walking before I change my mind."

Tonot stared at Wren, naked hatred in his eyes, then turned and stumbled off. Wren watched him until he vanished in the distance, then adjusted the daiklave at his back and rummaged among the waterskins. Carefully, he poured a little of the water of his hands and scrubbed away the blood. In the treetops, he could hear the carrion birds gathering, waiting. Graciously, he departed, and left them to their feast.

It might be worthwhile, he decided, to see where young Peleps actually went. It wasn't too far off his intended route, anyway, and a couple of days' delay wouldn't matter much to Rhadanthos in any case. He rubbed his hands against his thighs and set off after the Dragon-Blood with no expression on his face.

Chapter Nineteen

It took perhaps two days' travel for the Prince of Shadows to decide that Bonecrack was not, in fact, a wolf spirit. He may (and the prince could not help but think of the spirit as a "he," despite any evidence one way or the other—the beast's hunger and swagger seemed arrogantly masculine) have looked like a wolf, but that was simply the shape that he wore.

Rather, the prince decided, Bonecrack was a spirit of all the things that were associated with wolves. He was a spirit of ravenous cunning and night-born cleverness, a force of fear. The wolf's shape he wore was an expression of his true nature, a way to spread the terror he championed without a single word or action.

It also meant that Bonecrack's breath was exceptionally foul. Still, the prince reflected, there were compensations. Traveling with Bonecrack had taught him much. The spirit was garrulous in the extreme, and the stories he told of his encounters with the savage man-child Yushuv piqued the prince's interest. The boy's guardian interested him less. He'd heard of Dace and taken his measure from afar, and was not worried by him. The boy, on the other hand, was intriguing. Too many pieces of the puzzle *almost* fit together, and the sense of near-understanding was maddening.

He glanced to his left. A dozen yards from the main body of the prince's troupe, Bonecrack loped along, his red tongue lolling at the side of his mouth. His good eye caught the prince looking at him and he returned the gaze with a wolfish smile, then trotted ahead easily.

The prince, for his part, rode in the van of his party. A handful of hand-picked warriors rode around him, while the bulk of the survivors of the initial encounter with the spirit trailed uneasily behind. The whole party moved at a good pace, far faster than the pace they'd made moving north from the prince's citadel.

Behind them, the sun hovered just above the horizon, turning low bands of cloud into streamers of bright red and gold. Ahead, the first few timid stars had already made their appearance, and a sharp wedge of moon was visible in the deepening gloom.

"Sire?" The prince turned his head as Pelesh cantered up on his potbellied little steed, its hooves striking the ground seemingly twice as often as those of any other beast in the party.

He looked down his nose at the Exchequer, blinking in mild astonishment. "Pelesh, I do not recall speaking to you. Why, then, are you speaking to me?"

Pelesh gulped visibly.""My prince, I humbly beg your pardon, but—"

"You have my permission, then."

"To speak?" The crabbed little man was visibly relieved. "Sire, I wish to know if—"

"No," the prince interrupted.""To beg my pardon."

The Exchequer blinked. "My liege? I don't understand."

"My pardon," the prince said mildly, the reins held loosely in one hand.""You said you were going to beg it. You haven't, not yet, anyway. You do, however, have my permission to do so."

Pelesh opened his mouth, but no intelligible sounds came out. Sweat beaded on his brow and his eyes grew comically wide.

"That doesn't sound like begging, Pelesh. Of course, if you wish to renege on your offer, I can assure you that I would not be *too* terribly offended. After all, for your long years of service I think I can see clear to forgiving one little betrayal such as this…" He let his voice trail off speculatively and looked straight ahead, a half-smile playing at the corners of his mouth.

"No, no, my prince." Hastily, Pelesh reined in and slipped from the saddle. He prostrated himself, his face dangerously close to a ground-hugging thorned vine, and began babbling apologies. Pelesh's horse watched him with some curiosity. The rest of the column rode on, splitting around him if they were feeling generous, barely missing trampling him if they were not.

"When you are finished, Pelesh," the prince called back over his shoulder, "you may rejoin our company, and ask your question. I think another hour or so will prove sufficient. We are well pleased with your devotions." And with that he put the spurs to his horse's flank and cantered forward into the dying light.

Alone on the prairie, Pelesh looked up. The prince's party was already vanishing in the distance. For a moment, he considered faking his groveling, trusting in distance and disinterest to hide his lax performance from the prince. With a shudder, he decided against it, and again mouthed inane apologies.

It was no good lying to the prince. The prince knew. When it came to things like that, the prince *always* knew.

It was full dark by the time Pelesh finished, and his face was coated in pale reddish dust. He stood and stretched, wiping the dirt from his face as best he could, and stared off to the southeast. There was no sign of the prince's traveling party. Either they'd stopped beyond the range of his vision, or they were pressing on all night.

That, Pelesh thought bitterly, was all he'd wanted to ask the prince about in the first place. Since Bonecrack's arrival, the prince had been both a better and a worse master. He'd been more himself, more decisive and stronger. He'd also become more vicious, less solicitous of his servants and more likely to discard them on a whim. Pelesh in particular had suffered the brunt of the prince's new humor, a situation which left the Exchequer ruefully comparing his situation to that of his ancient rival, Ratcatcher.

Up ahead in the dark, a horse gave a terrified whinny. Pelesh recognized the sound. It was his own steed. It had stayed, more or less loyal, while he'd performed his obeisance, but now something hunted it.

Reaching to his belt for the stiletto he always carried when traveling, Pelesh hurried forward. The fact that anything that could hunt a horse could hunt him, too, was not lost on him, but without the animal he was doomed. Besides, he'd envenomed the dagger daily.

The horse cried out again, closer now, and something large growled behind it. Pelesh put on as much speed as he dared, feeling every one of his years as he ran.

He'd taken another dozen steps when the horse gave what sounded like a final, desperate moan that was cut off. A split second later, Pelesh heard the sound of something heavy hitting the ground, and a low, hungry growl.

He stopped, the dagger held before him. It seemed useless and tiny, but it was all that he had. If the beast that had taken his horse wanted him as well, it would feel his sting first.

"Little man, come here." The voice rolled out of the darkness like fog on a riverbank. Pelesh recognized it. It was the voice of Bonecrack.

"So you can gut me like you gutted my horse? Not likely. Come and get me, spirit," the Exchequer replied. He raised the stiletto so that it might catch whatever moonlight there was, and hoped the beast saw it.

"Your horse is fine," said Bonecrack, a tremor of irritation in his voice. "I have no need to feed tonight. My hunger is sated. Your prince feeds me well." There was just the slightest emphasis on the word "me," enough to let

Pelesh know that Bonecrack didn't think the prince took quite such good care of anyone else.

"I don't believe you."

"Believe me or not. Here is your proof." There was a meaty thwack, and the horse screamed, this time in shock and pain, not terror. "Your horse is as yet able to walk. Continue to try my patience and you may not be able to say the same."

Pelesh walked forward cautiously. His eyes were adjusting to the darkness, and he could see the hulking wolf-shape up ahead. One paw rested on a bulky, struggling shape against the ground: his horse.""Did the prince send you to look for me?"

Bonecrack chuckled.""The prince did not command me such, nor would he find me willing to play such a part. I am here because I will it, and because you and I have something to discuss."

"We have nothing to discuss, unless you wish to be paid for your service to the prince."

The spirit roared with laughter. Somewhere nearby, a covey of birds burst from cover at the sound, flapping away into the night sky. "Oh, little man, you should have been a jester. I'll take my payment when I chose, in the form I chose. Your jade does not interest me. It's the boy's soul I want."

Pelesh edged closer. "Then I do not know what we have to discuss."

Lazily, the wolf spirit ambled forward until it was face to face with Pelesh, its foul breath in his face. Behind him, the horse stayed down.

"Pelesh the Exchequer, you and I share one thing and one thing only: We both serve other masters besides the prince. Do I lie?"

Pelesh's thoughts raced. *How could Bonecrack have known? The messages from beyond the locked and barred door had been discreet, his own actions cautious and certainly not treasonous, and his intentions all for the prince's greater glory. Even the damned puppeteer that the voices in the dark had told him to summon had done nothing save amuse the prince on the rack. Surely the prince himself couldn't know…*

"I don't know what you're talking about," he finally said. "I serve the Prince of Shadows, and through him the greater darkness."

"Don't bother with denials. For a man of coin, you're a poor liar." Bonecrack growled deep in his throat, his muzzle bare inches away from Pelesh's face. "You serve other powers. So do I, though our masters are not the same."

"I serve the prince. Whom do you serve?" Pelesh said, perhaps a trifle too boldly.

Bonecrack roared and Pelesh stumbled back. "I do the will of the Fair Folk in this thing, for they have given me sweet dreams to gnaw on and nightmares on which to sup. They want the boy. So do I. Your prince wants something else, something connected to the child, and your other masters want both the boy removed and his treasure seized. I think there is room for an understanding between us. Do you agree?"

"What do you want?" Pelesh whispered. "I will not betray my prince."

"No one is asking you to. I simply wish for you to invoke your patrons to aid me in bringing down the boy, when the time comes. It will please them greatly to do so. In return, I will help your prince get what he thinks he wants. Do we have an understanding?"

"Yes," Pelesh said, looking into Bonecrack's eyes. "Lords of the Abyss help me, yes."

"I knew you were a sensible man," Bonecrack said, and licked Pelesh's face with his great, foul tongue. "Tend to your horse and come back to camp. The rest are about five hours ahead. You should make it easily, and have time to rest before sunrise." He laughed then, and turned to trot off.

"Wait!"

"Yes?" Bonecrack cocked his massive, scarred head." "Does the deal displease you?"

"No." Pelesh fell to his knees, his hands still on the stiletto. "If the prince discovers what you know, he'll have me killed. Worse."

"Oh, your secret is safe with me. You're little use to me dead. There's not enough meat on you."

"But how did you know?" Pelesh's words were a cry of despair.

"Silly man. Your kind always serves another master." With that, he loped off into the dark.

It was a long time before Pelesh rose from his knees. It was longer before he took the poisoned stiletto blade from his wrist and resheathed it. There was still life, after all. There was still hope, and the spirit's demands did not seem to demand that he betray either of his masters in any way.

The hollow feeling in his gut, however, told him that it was only a matter of time.

• • •

Pelesh rode into camp six hours later, not five. The gashes on his horse's flank had long since stopped bleeding, and the animal seemed almost calm by the time they rode past the sentries and into the circle of firelight.

The prince was sprawled out across a camp chair made of canvas and wood, just as Pelesh had known he would be. Various other members of the party were sprawled out around the fire, sleeping. A few tents had been pitched at the edge of the firelight, but not many.

Across the fire from the prince, Bonecrack lay sprawled out, his massive head resting on his paws. A low rumble in his throat indicated that he, too was sleeping. Indeed, of all the company by the fire, only the prince seemed to be awake.

"Pelesh," he said airily as the Exchequer rode up. "You certainly took long enough."

"It was dark, my liege. I did not wish to have my horse stumble and break a leg, which would have delayed my rejoining you even longer. In all things, I am your prudent servant."

"In all things?" The prince raised one delicate, thin eyebrow. "Yes, I suppose you are. Consider your apologies accepted, and the quality of your service very much appreciated."

"I thank you, my prince." Bonecrack growled in his sleep, and Pelesh barely resisted the urge to shoot a panicked glance in the spirit's direction." "Do you wish me to attend you, or may I sleep?"

"Attend me for a moment, Pelesh. Get off the horse. Sit. Find some wine."

"Yes, my prince." One of the sentries led Pelesh's horse off an instant after he dismounted, and another pressed a skin of warm wine into his hands. He took a healthy swallow, then wiped his mouth with the back of his sleeve and sat at the prince's feet. "How may I serve you?"

The prince leaned back languorously, looking incongruously catlike as he did so. "You can answer a question for me, Pelesh. Just one, and it's simple."

"Of course, my prince. Anything."

"Or course indeed." The prince leaned forward. "Tell me truthfully. Why were you really so eager to get me to leave my citadel and engage on this," he gestured away from the fire," "this ludicrous adventure?"

Pelesh looked up. His eyes met the prince's. "My liege," he said truthfully," "it was because I thought it best. And I am, in all things, devoted to your welfare."

"Ah." The prince sat back, apparently satisfied. "I appreciate your solicitous nature, then, though you should presume less in the future. It is a grand adventure. You chose well. Should things turn out as I hope, you will be suitably rewarded."

Pelesh's eyes dropped. "I thank you, my prince. My duty is its own reward."

"Mm." Long fingers reached down and tugged the wine-skin from Pelesh's nerveless grip. "I suppose it is, at that."

Chapter Twenty

For a man whose lower jaw had just been splintered, the huntsman made good time. He set a steady, loping pace, occasionally looking back over his shoulder to see if he was being followed and cutting a zigzag trail intended to sow confusion about his real direction. He took advantage of the cover afforded by lone buildings and clumps of trees, and frequently spent several minutes at a time wading upstream through small creeks in an effort to cover his tracks.

Eliezer Wren, who had been forced to take similar measures himself on many occasions, followed at a safe distance and decided, after a few hours' observation, that he approved of the man's technique. Most of the Dragon-Blooded he'd met disdained the fine art of covering one's ass, relying instead on equal parts raw power and pure arrogance as their shields. Many, he'd discovered, couldn't even conceive of the need to run. That, he supposed, had partially been his fault. After all, the Immaculate Order had told the world for centuries that the Dragon-Blooded were the next best thing to gods. Who was to blame them for believing it?

Peleps Tonot, however, had just gotten a rather rude reminder of his own mortality, and he seemed to be taking the lesson well. As Wren watched from behind the cover of a dilapidated farmhouse, his quarry paused to lay a false trail leading to a patch of particularly boggy ground, then carefully backtracked and skirted the sump before heading off almost due east.

Wren waited until he'd vanished behind a low hedge of junipers before sliding out of his place of concealment. Moving silently, he located the beginning of the false trail, and cast it over with a critical eye.

It was good work, he thought, but amateurish. Tonot had emphasized the depth of the prints he had left here, making them a little too deep, a little too obvious. Most hunters probably wouldn't notice the difference, and would charge straight ahead into the boggy morass just ahead. Wren grimaced at the stench. Even if the bog proved to be no more than a minor annoyance, it would cost incautious pursuers plenty of time, and there was always the chance that the sump was more treacherous than it looked.

Even if he hadn't seen the ruse being created, though, Wren still wouldn't have been drawn in. He could see the lighter tracks that Tonot had made—*shoes reversed, clever boy,* he thought—on his true path, and set out to follow those instead. Fifty yards on, the prints reversed themselves and grew more widely separated. Tonot had picked up his pace here, apparently, and Wren imitated him, determined not to let the Dragon-Blood get too far ahead.

A fast trot brought him to the edge of the line of junipers, and there Wren halted. The row of trees was not quite thick enough to be called a wood, but dense enough to make blundering straight through an unappealing prospect. Tonot's tracks, of course, went straight into the thickest part of the vegetation.

"Perfect ambush ground," Wren grumbled to himself, and sidled to the left. The dry leaves showed prints poorly, but to Wren's eye there was no evidence here that Tonot had headed lengthwise through the thicket, at least not in this direction. Shifting to the other side of the obvious trail, he repeated the process and came to the same conclusion. With a deep breath and a sigh of resignation, he plunged in.

So intent was he on the faint traces of Tonot's passage that he almost didn't notice the trap. It was simple, a loop of twig bent back on itself and tied with a strip of cloth torn from Tonot's shirt. Another, larger branch was tied to the loop and bent down to the ground. Covered by dried leaves and pinned down only loosely, the trap was designed to seize an unwary traveler's ankle with malicious intent.

Wren's foot was halfway into the snare before he noticed it. Cursing at his own carelessness, he threw himself forward into a shoulder roll. His foot brushed the ground and caught on something even as his shoulder hit the carpet of dead leaves. The trap snapped up and away, but he was already past it, coming to rest on the ground beyond and turning to see what had just happened.

There, dangling in the makeshift noose, was his sandal. He looked down and discovered, to his mild surprise, that his right foot was bare. "Closer than I thought," he said, and gingerly stepped forward to examine the trap.

It was good work for something so hurried, and Wren found his respect for Tonot climbing a notch. The trap wouldn't have been fatal—Tonot had neither the tools nor the time for that—but it was clever, and would most likely have snapped the ankle of anyone caught in it.

That's one way to slow down anyone following you, Wren thought, and examined the trap for further surprises before retrieving his sandal. There were none. Grimly aware of how much time little misadventures like this were costing him, Wren took back his footwear and put it on. Another moment's work rebuilt the trap, and then Wren added another one a few paces on. That one would unleash a bent-back branch at eye level when tripped, hopefully blinding anyone who stumbled into it.

It was best to be cautious, the former priest decided. Just because he was following the huntsman didn't mean that there wasn't someone following *him.* With a final inspection of his handiwork and some artful mussing of the carpet of dead leaves, he moved on.

•   •   •

The chase, or at least the first leg of it, petered out at the end of the second day. Wren watched, crouching behind a massive, weathered tree stump, as Tonot jogged across what might have been a plowed field once. As he reached the far side, the sound of hoofbeats echoed in the air, and he stopped. A pair of riders, both with House Peleps banners affixed to their saddles, burst into view, galloping hell bent for leather.

Tonot immediately began waving both his arms frantically, and Wren could hear his faint shouts of desperation. They had an immediate effect. The riders abruptly changed course and closed on Tonot. He stood his ground, no longer waving now that he was sure that he had been seen.

The riders reined in when they reached him, and Wren could only guess at the content of the conversation that followed. Whatever was said was brief and to the point, as the smaller of the two riders reached down and hauled Tonot up into the saddle. The wounded man clasped his arms around his rescuer's waist, and the three rode off to the north and west. A trail of dust rose up after them, one which rapidly extended as they galloped for what Wren assumed was home.

Frowning, he tested the straps on his sandals. They seemed tight, which was good. He didn't want to lose them, not now. After all, it seemed like he had some running to do.

Chapter Twenty-One

"So where did you get the knife?"

"Dagger," Unforgiven Blossom corrected him, and shifted infinitesimally so her back was against a tree trunk. "It is a dagger."

"If you say so." Yushuv shrugged. "That's the sort of thing Dace worried about." He was standing, looking out onto the plain at regular intervals to see if the rain was still coming down. It was, as the thunder of water on the canopy of leaves overhead attested. "You still haven't told me where you got it."

Unforgiven Blossom blinked, the only sign of her annoyance. "I have told you. I stole it."

"Who'd you steal it from?" The boy was, she noticed, keeping a reasonable distance from where she sat. He hopped from foot to foot unconsciously and circled from side to side, but never sat and never turned his back on her. *A sensible precaution,* she thought, *but one that makes conversation extremely difficult.*

"I stole it from the Prince of Shadows," she said evenly, "and since I can see from your face that you have no idea who that is, I will tell you that he is a servant of death and the things that come after. Stealing from him is not something you do lightly."

"Then why did you do it?"

She shrugged, delicately. "Because I had to. And because I thought it might be best if the weapon were not in his possession. It is better off in yours, I think."

Yushuv drew the dagger and looked at it. "I guess so. I found this, you know. It was in the tunnels underneath the village where I grew up."

"You have not yet finished growing up," she said reproachfully, and Yushuv's face turned bright red. He jammed the dagger back into his belt furiously and turned away.

"I'm old enough," he said. "Old enough to have killed a lot of… things. And people."

"But young enough that you still have much to learn."

He whirled around. "Don't tell me you want to teach me, too," he spat. "I've had about enough of teachers and messengers, all of them telling me what I have to do. All I have to do is to stay alive. Everything else seems to find me."

"I have no desire to teach you. You are a spoiled child, and I have no desire to aggravate myself to the extent that lengthy contact with you would entail. And as for fate finding you, that is exactly what is happening, my little rescuer. Set your mind to thinking about it. How many square miles of empty grassland are there out there, and yet we managed to stumble across each other. Aided, of course, by the efforts of those buffoons, whose racket drew you to me."

"*I* found *you*," he said sullenly.

"Either way. This is not coincidence. You were meant to have the dagger back, no doubt. That is the reason—the only reason— fate let us find one another. That is why teachers have discovered you, instructed you, and then allowed you to leave. That is why you are still alive." She sniffed, and her brow furrowed.""I am reasonably certain that my role in all this was not simply to serve as your courier, but the thought has cost me some sleepless nights."

"I think you're crazy," Yushuv said, his arms folded across his chest as he held himself tightly.

"That is fine. I think you are ignorant."

Yushuv shook his head. "It doesn't make sense. Everyone keeps on telling me that they're making tremendous sacrifices for me, that I have this incredible destiny. I've seen miracles, and all I ever expected to see was my village." He looked down at his hands. "I guess now I have to believe it, but… I still don't understand."

"Understanding would render you incapable of acting. Be who you are. Go where the spirit moves you. You will no doubt find yourself in the right place at the right time. Either that, or you'll miss your destiny and something catastrophic will happen, but I find that unlikely. You won't be permitted to do such a thing."

"You're very comforting," he said, frowning. "Who won't let me?"

"The Unconquered Sun, among others. You do bear his mark. That means your destiny would not be entirely your own regardless, even were you not marked for greater things." She ran her fingers through her immaculately groomed hair, then gazed at her fingertips. "You have the sun on your brow, in case you have forgotten. It does mean something."

Yushuv rubbed his forehead, as if finding the brand there for the first time. "I guess it does. So, are you going to go with me?"

She laughed, and laughed again at the startled look on his face. "Of course not. I have no desire to spend any more time with you than necessary. I despise children, and I doubly despise children who don't know their place. No, I will not be traveling with you, and with luck I will see neither you nor the Prince of Shadows again."

"Oh." Yushuv seemed almost hurt. "What will you do, then?"

"I do not know," she said, and was surprised to discover that she meant it. "I have thought of going to Nexus, and perhaps opening a shop there. I would tell fortunes and brew medicines, and young lovesick girls would come to me for philters that would make young foolish boys fall in love with them. It would be a pleasant change from being caught up in the affairs of the great and mighty."

"You're making fun of me," Yushuv said accusingly.

"Yes, I am. It is a privilege afforded to those of us who do not have many years left to live, to make fun of those who do."

Yushuv's eyes narrowed. "You're not that old. You look it, but you're not."

Unforgiven Blossom blinked. "Most do not realize that. You're cleverer than you look."

"Everyone keeps saying that, too." He grinned, and his hands fell to his sides.

"As well they should. No, I am not that old, but in the end, it does not matter. My body thinks it is old, and so does Time, and they cast the deciding votes in such affairs." She unfolded herself from where she sat and climbed to his feet.

"I think the rain is slackening."

Yushuv cocked his head to listen. "Maybe. But it's going to be dark soon. You should at least stay here until morning."

She pursed her lips. "Perhaps. But no longer."

"No longer," he agreed, occupying himself with over-busy attempts to find some dry wood for a fire. She cooked, and when she saw he looked askance at what resulted, she carefully tasted each portion first. She fell asleep not long after, huddled in a wool cloak from the pack Yushuv retrieved for her; she'd dropped it when the bandits first became serious in their intentions. He, for his part, stayed awake most of the night, crouched over the fire and watching vigilantly for enemies of any sort. A few hours before dawn, he too finally fell asleep, curling up near the remnants of the fire.

And true to her word, when he awoke, she was gone.

• • •

Yushuv left later that day, after burying the ashes of his fire. With no idea of where he wanted to go, he left it to fate. Reaching for the dagger, he pulled it out and contemplated it for a moment.

It was as breathtaking as ever, showing no signs of ill wear despite its travels. Now that she was gone, Yushuv found himself wishing he'd asked other questions of Unforgiven Blossom. He wanted to know where the dagger had been, and how it had come into the possession of the Prince of Shadows. Surely there were stories to be told there.

He also found himself curious about Unforgiven Blossom herself, and what had happened to her. The woman had not liked him; that much had been obvious. But she fascinated him, as much for what she had not said as for what she had.

That, however, was work for another day. He hefted the dagger in his hand, then threw it straight up. It spun end over end as it flew, cutting through overhanging branches with frightening ease before reaching the apex of its flight and then descending once more. Yushuv took a hasty sidestep to ensure that he wasn't impaled on his own decision-making device, then watched as it hit the ground with a surprising amount of force.

It lay there, half its blade sunk into the cold earth. Carefully, Yushuv positioned himself behind it and judged the angle the point seemed to be seeking.

"South-southeast," he said, and yanked the dagger out of the ground. The dirt fell away from it of its own accord, but he took care to wipe it against his leggings in any case. Dace had taught him to show weapons proper respect.

He looked around. The rough camp had essentially been annihilated by his morning's labors. There was little sign that anyone had ever been there, and what evidence there was would soon be swallowed by the elements. Unforgiven Blossom had left no trail when she had gone, and there had been no sign of her in any direction when he'd searched for her. Out on the plain, scavengers had gotten to the dead bodies of the bandits. Of the survivors, there was no sign. Either they'd run off during the night, or something partial to killing its own meat had found them. It didn't matter; they weren't waiting in ambush for him so far as he could see, and that was the important thing.

One last time, he held the dagger up before his face. "South-southeast," he said. "Are you sure?"

With a gesture of resignation, he shoved the dagger back into its makeshift sheath and slipped his pack back on his shoulders. The bow he held in his left hand, strung and ready for use. Nodding to himself, Yushuv stepped out onto the plain, now slightly marshy from the previous night's storm. He looked back over his shoulder, at the last outpost of the forest that had sheltered him for so long.

"Thank you," he said, not knowing why he did so but feeling it was important. "I'll be back."

And with that, he turned his back on the verdant wood and strode off, following the direction that had been given to him by the dagger.

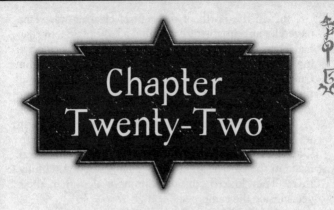

Chapter Twenty-Two

Even Eliezer Wren had to admit that when the Wyld Hunt settled into an encampment, it did so in style.

Crouched just below the crest of a ridge some five hundred yards from the sentries the huntsmen had posted, Wren took in the site below him and whistled. What he saw was no field camp. Instead, it was a small city. Broad avenues separated the individual enclaves within the camp, which were marked with prominently posted banners. Dozens of small tents clustered around larger, more ornate ones, reminding Wren somehow of newborn piglets trying to suckle from their mother. Armed guards were posted at each intersection within the encampment. They were kept in constant motion, bowing to the endless parade of gaily clad and armored Dynasts who rode or strolled by. Runners dashed from one tent to another, bearing scroll cases, packages or sometimes just urgent tidings. Immaculate monks walked to and fro, some ducking into this tent or that while others conducted martial arts exercises in the campsite's central clearing. Beside them, pairs of armored fighters practiced and dueled. Occasionally, a geyser of light would surge into the air as one combatant or another lost his temper and unleashed a storm of pure power at his foe. The spectators generally found this amusing. Even from where he had situated himself, Wren could hear the cheering.

Just to the north of the central clearing was what passed for an administrative center, a large plain tent that had a constant stream of functionaries and monks scurrying in and out of it. There was no central mess, each of the Dragon-Bloods having apparently decided they preferred their own personal cooks, and each of the sub-encampments had its own small, rough corral.

dAround the perimeter was a raised wall of earth. It was perhaps six feet tall, and in places surmounted with sharpened logs. At the cardinal points, breaches had been made in the barrier, and pairs of guards stood watchfully there. They looked considerably more alert than their peers inside the camp.

All of this, Wren suspected, had been set up in the past few hours. It looked for all the world like a legion encampment on the frontier, which was in and of itself odd. Wyld huntsmen, on those occasions when their duties stretched for days or even weeks, were notoriously unfond of any sort of manual labor. They rode to hunt and they rode to kill, and generally they trusted to their reputations to keep their quarters safe.

What that told Wren was that a professional had been at work here. Anyone who could whip those on the Wyld Hunt into this sort of labor, and do so while keeping the peace—Wren had counted the banners of most of the Great Houses while he scanned the grounds—was a force to be reckoned with.

The sheer size of the Hunt also raised his hackles. He'd seen Wyld Hunts before; every Immaculate had, but never one on this scale. This was not a Hunt. It was a small army, a bandit kingdom turned loose upon the Threshold. There were dozens of Dragon-Bloods here, and their entourages might number in the hundreds.

Sneaking in, he decided with a sad shake of his head, was not going to be easy.

•   •   •

Finding the camp, on the other hand, had been easy enough. Wren had simply followed the dust trail left by the riders who'd picked up Peleps Tonot as they galloped back

to camp, and the course it indicated was as straight as an arrow's flight. Overly conscious of arrows, however, and what they could do to his unarmored person, he'd taken advantage of what cover he could, and made sure to avoid even sighting the riders ahead. Assuming his jaw still worked, Peleps Tonot had by now undoubtedly told his rescuers about the man who had assailed him, and they'd be wary.

And so Wren had followed at a considerable distance, moving as fast as he dared without letting the shape of his anima billow out behind him. The run had been surprisingly short, no more than half a day's labor before the dust trail suddenly stopped. Ever cautious, Wren had moved off the trail and sought cover, in case the riders had made an encampment. Slowly and patiently, he'd wormed his way to the top of the ridge and peered down at what looked to be the entire graduating class of the House of Bells.

As Wren watched, a pair of riders left the camp via the western gate and started a slow circuit around the perimeter, clucking to their mounts and calling playful obscenities back and forth as they rode. Both carried unsheathed swords and full armor, and as Wren observed them he saw just a trace of reddish light flicker into existence behind the larger of the two.

Dragon-Blooded sentries. Wren gave a low whistle. Whoever sat at the heart of that camp was indeed a power, if he could get the Dragon-Bloods to perform such a lowly duty. For a moment, Wren fought back panic at the thought that Kejak himself might be the one commanding the display below. Then reason reasserted itself. Kejak was not there; the young huntsman had not recognized his name.

A flurry of motion in the camp below caught his eye. It was Tonot, his armor unmistakable, being led into the command tent by his two saviors. They exited almost immediately, but Peleps Tonot stayed inside for several minutes. Meanwhile, the mounted sentries continued their leisurely canter around the perimeter of the camp, reminding Wren of how exposed his position on the ridge really was.

Wren had seen enough. Without waiting for Tonot to reemerge, he slid back down the minute slope of the ridge that concealed him. Picking a likely stand of bushes from the few nearby, he flowed from the exposed hill face to the relative safety of cover. A squint up at the sky told him that it was still several hours until nightfall, and nightfall was when he would make his move.

•   •   •

The glow of firelight merged with the fading glow of twilight, but it was the smell of smoke that woke Wren from a short nap he'd allowed himself once he'd made certain his hiding place was secure. Again he crawled to the top of the ridge, and nodded in approval at what he saw.

With the coming of night, the sentries had been pulled back within the palisade. Torches blazed at intervals around the earthen embankment, and more lit the makeshift streets of the encampment. Someone had started a massive fire toward the south end of the central clearing, and the firelight cast strange shadows of the figures who comported themselves around it. Other, smaller fires burned throughout the camp, each attracting their own crowds. The largest of the tents glowed from within like silk lanterns, and the sounds of merriment drifted out into the dark.

"There. Up on the ridge. Did you see it?"

The voice came from the direction of the camp, mixed with a sudden thunder of hoofbeats. Shocked at his carelessness, Wren threw himself to the earth and listened. Even as he did so, the hoofbeats stopped.

Another voice called out of the night.

"I didn't see anything. You're just trying to make this seem exciting, and it's not. It's dull!"

"Hush. Use your eyes, not your mouth." It was the first voice again, and Wren slowly began inching himself back down the hill before the faceless watcher got lucky. *Thank the Sun he didn't have a bow,* Wren thought, and slunk down into the shadows.

"I'm telling you, there's no need for us to go this far out." It was the second voice petulant and shrill. "Everyone back at the camp is having a good time, and it's not fair that we have to be out here riding patrols instead."

Off to the right, Wren thought. *They're off to the right, which means along the crest of the ridge. They won't be silhouetted against the campfire as they approach, but if I keep retreating, they'll be framed by the light if they come at me. Better yet, they'll be blind.* He tensed himself against the necessity to flee, and listened again.

There was a long moment's pause, and Wren could almost convince himself he heard a sigh of exasperation. "We're out here because you got too drunk to stand nice, comfortable guard duty inside the perimeter yesterday, and the Most Revered Hunter of the Ancient Enemy T'fillit caught you. Pardon me; *you're* out here because of that; I'm out here because Mother would be very upset if you got yourself eaten by a wolf spider or some such and I don't trust you not to fall off your saddle and break your neck in the dark. Now stop complaining and ride with me. We're out here until midnight no matter what, so we might as well do this properly. Who knows, it might prevent us from ever having to do it again." This speaker's voice was deeper and more assured, and in him Wren recognized something of a kindred spirit.

The petulant rider muttered something of a reply. Wren didn't catch all of it, but what he heard sounded suspiciously like "My father has more land than your father," and then the whining was cut off by the sound of a hearty blow striking home.

He scurried to the right, and was rewarded with the sight of two armored and mounted figures. One was considerably burlier than the second, and the smaller shape was rubbing the back of its helmeted head.

"Ow! What did you have to do that for?" It was the first voice again, higher pitched and whinier than before, if that were possible.

"Because you're being an idiot," came the sensible reply. "Now ride with me."

"No." Wren could almost imagine the look of petulance on the face that could produce such a childish denial.

"Broken Serpent gave me a wineskin before we went out on patrol and I'm going to stay right here and drink it. And because you've been such a bastard to me, you don't get any."

"Suit yourself then." The larger of the two flicked his reins, and his steed—a black shape against the darkness—started forward.—"I'll check on you on each circuit. Try not to fall off the horse."

With relief, Wren noted that his path would take him in front of the ridge, not behind it, and watched the man go. This, perhaps, was an opportunity, and a better and less risky one than sneaking into the camp would have been.

•   •   •

The name T'fillit was vaguely familiar to Wren from his days serving Chejop Kejak. She was an Immaculate, one of dozens he had met, and he'd gotten the impression that she was high up in Kejak's councils. That meant that she was old, and powerful, and that younger priests were supposed to pretend not to notice when she dripped water on the temple floors they'd just painstakingly polished.

That she was out here, commanding this expedition, meant that Kejak was very concerned with finding him. Indeed, he was mildly startled that Tonot's story hadn't whipped the camp into a frenzy of activity. He could not imagine what they were waiting for.

Alone, he would have risked a confrontation with T'fillit, but he was not going to dare one when she was surrounded by a small and extraordinarily potent army, all of its members eager to shed his now-tainted blood. Fortunately, the reluctant sentries had given him a better and, he hoped, safer idea.

Pressed low against the earth, he crawled to his left, down the ridge lengthwise. A hundred yards further, it merged once again with the flat grassland the encampment rested on, and there he stopped. From where he crouched, he could see the path the sentry's horse had made in the dead grass, and he judged it to be perhaps thirty feet from where he was. He frowned. Twenty would have been ideal,

but thirty it would have to be. He'd just rely on his new gifts and pray they made up the difference.

It was nearly half an hour before the sentry came around again, his route punctuated by another argument with his unruly sibling. Even from where he was, Wren could hear the latter's slurred words, and he grinned mirthlessly. Things were going well.

When the debate finally ended, Wren froze in position and watched as the man rode past. He did so shaking his head angrily, oblivious to the crouched figure lurking so close. As he passed, Wren nodded. It was possible. If the other sentry continued to drink, and the watchful one continued to be distracted by his foolish sibling, if the two of them were not relieved or joined by other guards, if the accursed run of bad luck that had been following Wren for years didn't rear its idiot-grinning head—then it was possible.

The alternatives, however, were less appealing. Wren had spent the bulk of the rider's first circuit analyzing and discarding them; he did the same with the second and third transits as well. Finally, on the fourth pass, Wren acted.

The recalcitrant sentry was completely drunk now, his shouts at his brother echoing loudly through the night. It was a pity, Wren thought, that his self-absorbed idiocy would actually work to save his life, at least for a little while. Moments later, the dutiful sentry rode out of the dark and past Wren's position. Both hands were on the reins, and the hook-bladed sword the man carried was sheathed against his back.

With a whispered prayer to the Unconquered Sun, and to anyone else who looked out for ex-priests on the run, Wren gathered himself and leapt noiselessly. He landed with a soft thump behind the sentry's saddle, and immediately pressed himself against the man's back.

"What?" was all the rider had time to say before Wren's left hand clamped itself over his mouth. He reached back to seize his attacker, but even as he did so, Wren's other hand found the dagger he carried at his belt. With brutal efficiency and inhuman speed, he turned it on its owner.

The first blow skidded off the armor protecting the man's gut; but the second found the seam between leg and hip and punched into flesh. The third and fourth followed, and in an eyeblink the man sagged weakly in the saddle.

Taking the reins from the corpse's dead fingers, Wren gently steered the horse around to the rear of the ridge that had served him so well. There he slid off of the hose and examined his handiwork.

The dead man still sat in the saddle, his feet secure in the stirrups. His body slumped forward over the horse's neck, and a slow trickle of blood ran down the horse's flank onto the ground. It snorted nervously and stamped the ground.

"Easy," Wren said to it, "you'll be free soon enough." It seemed reassured by his voice, but Wren put no faith in its goodwill. Carefully, he shoved the cadaver forward in the saddle, then removed the dead man's feet from the stirrups. Irritated by the necessity, he tore a strip from the hem of his own robe, and used it to tie the corpse into the saddle. One or two jolts would be enough to make the body tumble onto the ground, but Wren didn't need it to hold any longer.

Satisfied, the former monk swung himself into the saddle behind his victim, reaching around for the reins. At a walk, he guided the horse around behind the ridge, to come out on the opposite side of the last place he'd heard the other sentry's drunken bellows.

With luck, Wren thought, *the fellow wouldn't be unconscious quite yet.* Then the absurdity of the statement struck him, and he suppressed a snort of laughter. When was the last time he'd hoped a sentry would stay awake?

Still chortling to himself, he came out from behind the ridge, exactly where he'd hoped he'd be. One hand still held the reins, while the other was fixed behind the dead man's gorget to hold him upright.

The other rider was framed against the glow from the camp, a flaccid wineskin in one fist. He weaved in the saddle, and Wren thought he heard off-key singing. The sounds of the camp's evening pleasures behind him had not abated, and the glow from the flames lent the figure an entirely undeserved sinister air.

Taking a deep breath, he urged the horse forward another six paces.

"Hey! Brother!" he shouted, molding his voice into the best approximation he could of the dead man's. "Come over here. I need your help!"

"Don' need anyone's help, an' I'm... *half* brother. Don' forget that." The reply was barely intelligible, and when the sentry shook a fist to emphasize a point he nearly launched himself out of the saddle.

"Please," Wren called back. "I've got some wine back in camp I've been saving. It's yours if you help me now."

The drunken figure straightened at that. "Wine?"

"Wine," Wren affirmed. "From the vineyards by the Lap."

"Damn good stuff." There was a pause, and then another cry, loaded with suspicion. "You don't have any in camp. You said you didn' bring wine! I know, I looked."

Oh shit, Wren thought. He's so stupid he's actually clever. His brain raced for a moment while he pondered a suitable response. "I had one of the Peleps hide it for me," he said with what he hoped was suitable confidence. "For a special occasion. It was supposed to be a surprise after we killed the Anathema."

"Which Peleps?"

Wren had a ready answer for that one. "Tonot."

"Hate him. Ab'slutely hate him. Glad he nearly died." There was the sound of exaggerated spitting, and the rider nearly pitched over again.

Wren gave a silent sigh of relief. If Tonot had died since returning, the deception would have evaporated in a heartbeat. "That's why I had him hold it. Now would you please hurry?" He grimaced. The saddle was sticky with cold, drying blood, and the scent of it was thick in his nostrils. The deception couldn't last much longer. With luck, though, it wouldn't have to.

The other rider considered the request for a moment, then lurched forward and clung to his horse's neck. "Good horse," he said. "Take me over there." The animal shook its head in distress, but after a few more drunken encouragements, finally started forward.

Wren released the reins, hoping to every god he'd ever worshipped that the horse didn't take advantage of the opportunity. With his free hand, he slowly eased the man's dagger out once again and hefted it to throw. He'd get one cast, he knew, and that was all. The weight was comfortable in his hand, the balance good. One throw was all he thought he'd need.

"S'dark," the drunken sentry said as he approached.

"Too dark to see anything." His horse snorted, smelling blood, and the man kicked its sides savagely to urge it forward.

Another two steps, Wren prayed.

Just two more steps.

The horse took another two steps forward. "Are you awright?" the drunk asked, peering forward. "You don' look good."

"No, he doesn't," Wren said in his own voice, and let the corpse drop forward.

"Wha?" said the drunk, even as the former monk let the dagger fly. It flew through the air hilt-first, catching the man between the eyes. He moaned softly, fell off the horse backwards, and landed in an awkward pile on the ground.

Wren wasted no time. Leaping from his commandeered horse, he snatched the reins of the second one before it had time to flee. The first just stood there and watched him, and he mentally revised his opinion of the entire species upwards, at least for the moment.

Still holding onto the reins, he bent down to examine the unconscious man on the ground. He was still breathing, though badly bruised, and there was a sizable puddle of vomit on the ground next to him. He was also emitting the faintest of snores.

Wren cursed the luck. He groped in the dark until he found the dagger, then used it to saw the reins of the drunkard's horse at one end. Tying the loose end to the other animal's tack as best he could, he stooped and caught the unconscious figure under the armpits. He was heavier than he looked, and it took Wren several tries before he could shove the figure back into the saddle.

Without hesitation, Wren cut another strip off his robe and used that to tie the second man more securely than the first. The horses looked at him, bemused, but he ignored them. The plan wasn't much, but it was almost ready. He twirled the dagger once, then ran down the remaining procedures in his head.

He was headed southeast, he knew. He was going to see Rhadanthos and then he was going to find the boy whom the daiklave supposedly belonged to, and then he was going to vanish. What he did not want was Kejak's latest catspaw riding herd on his adventures with a Wyld Hunt the size of the Imperial Deliberative. The further away from his destination the Dragon-Bloods were, the happier he'd be. That meant sending the notable and dangerous T'fillit off in another direction, and then running like hell.

With a few gentle nudges, he oriented the horses to face north. Both riders, the living and the dead, sagged in their saddles but did not fall. The dagger was a comfort in his hand, the only element of his plan he had faith in.

"Hopefully, the Unconquered Sun has a sense of humor," he muttered to himself, and then very deliberately jabbed the drunk man's horse in the buttocks with the tip of the dagger.

It reared up, whinnying, and as it did, he slapped the other one on the rump. It took off at a gallop, dragging its companion with it before it, too, caught the pace. The bodies bounced in the saddle as the two vanished into the darkness.

Wren coughed. The horses had certainly left a wide and obvious enough trail. With luck, the horses would keep running for some time yet. The dead man would fall off within a league, further enticing any who followed the track, and if fate truly smiled on him, the entire Hunt would go chasing off after it. It was nothing he could count on, but it certainly was superior to the possibility that the entire Hunt would backtrack Tonot's route and find him.

He shrugged. There was still a full night's journey ahead of him if he wanted the ruse to do any good. Throwing the dagger into the thicket that had sheltered him, he set off to the southeast at a careful trot. The sound of laughter from the camp hid his footfalls, and silently, he vanished into the night.

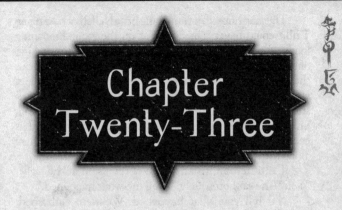

Chapter Twenty-Three

"We found the other body, Revered One." Mnemon Palap reined in as she rode up to where T'fillit sat on her mount, waiting. "He's just over that hill, there. The trail continues on beyond it."

"Is he dead as well?" A sharp wind blew, whipping her robes around her. She fought the urge to shiver. To do so in front of the others would be to show weakness.

"No, Revered One. Badly hurt, though, and there's puke on his breath. The whole thing is a mystery to me."

T'fillit nodded. "Bring me to him."

"Of course."

They rode forward, the rest of the traveling party flowing out and around them. While the whole Hunt was not here, a significant fraction of it was, a display of power. Whatever Anathema had ambushed the sentries the night before—for surely nothing short of one of those monstrosities could have done so without raising an alarm—had left a clear trail to follow, and if this was a trap, T'fillit intended to overwhelm it by sheer force.

The slope they rode up was gentle, the other side of the hill less so. It was easy to see how the man had been thrown from the saddle. Many a skilled and sober rider would have had difficulty with the hill in daylight, let alone at full tilt in the dark.

The man himself, an annoying little Nellens whose name T'fillit could never remember, sat on the ground moaning loudly. One of the party's Immaculates hovered over him, offering suggestions and attempting to see to his health, but the small figure on the ground shooed him away. His helmet was gone, and his shaved head was covered in short black stubble. A massive welt rose from the center of his forehead, just above the bridge of his hooked and narrow nose. His complexion was pale and he was sweating, and somewhere along the way various bits of his armor had gone missing.

T'fillit felt an instant surge of revulsion at the sight. "You," she said brusquely.""Tell me what happened."

"I'll tell you what happened. We were ambushed. Attacked! We were riding our circuit when they came out of the dark at us!"

"They?"

The little man nodded. "At least four of them. Anathema. We fought them back to back, Sayas and I did, but they were too strong for him. Then I got angry, and scared them off. When they ran, I chased them, but they had a trap waiting for me." He rubbed his head.""Which is how I ended up here. I guess they were too frightened to finish me off."

Palap nudged his horse closer to T'fillit's. "We found evidence of only one steed on the circuit last night, and no evidence of any fighting outside the compound except for a small trail of blood that led behind a hill south of the camp to where this track started. It continued until we found Nellens Sayas' body this morning. The blood was his. The other sentries reported no struggle and no signs of any massive incursion, and there were no other footprints on the ground that we could see."

"In other words, he's lying?" A half-smile quirked at the corner of her mouth. "I could have told you that."

"Anyone who knew him could have," he replied.

T'fillit straightened up in the saddle. "Are you quite certain that is exactly how the last night's events happened? Are you sure you're not… missing a detail?"

"Quite certain, Revered One." His eyes shifted nervously back and forth. "I don't suppose you brought any wine with you, as a restorative?"

She sighed. "Flog him," she said to Palap, "and then bring him to me when he's ready to tell the truth. Something here stinks." She looked around. "Where exactly is here, anyway?"

"If I remember the maps at camp correctly, we're south and a lot west of Sijan. Not entirely friendly territory. We're too close to the River Province for my liking. There's a small town about two hours' ride west of here. It might be worth heading there to see if anyone's seen or heard anything."

T'fillit nodded. "An excellent suggestion. When you finish with Nellens, we'll go."

"Yes, Revered One." Palap nodded, and crooked a finger at the man on the ground. "This won't take long, I assure you."

And true to his word, once the screaming started, it didn't.

•   •   •

The collection of buildings which Palap had referred to as a town was barely worthy of the name. It was really a trading outpost with a ring of homes and a low wall around it, a place where homesteaders gathered for gossip and protection against the barbarians that occasionally swept over the plains.

There was an inn at the center of town, a crude one that doubled as a temple, a trader's den and a stables, and it was to this establishment that T'fillit and her companions went when they rode into town. Children peered at them from around corners or behind windows; adults either prostrated themselves or hurried inside and bolted their doors.

"Not friendly territory, you said?" T'fillit was amused.

"So it would seem." Palap did not share her smile. "I was expecting more than this."

"The Threshold is under attack," she gently reminded him. "That is why we are here. Now, let us conduct our business and go."

Palap nodded. "Of course, Revered One. May I have the pleasure of facilitating our departure?"

"If you wish. Don't hurt anyone," she said, and called the company to a halt. Palap dismounted and walked into the rough inn. His voice could be clearly heard in the street outside, mellifluously asking if there had been any incursions of the sort his companions might be equipped to deal with of late.

The response was low and lengthy, interrupted several times by expressions of disbelief. A moment later, the Dragon-Blood emerged from the inn's doorway, a thoughtful expression on his face and a scrap of dirty parchment in his hand.

"Well?" T'fillit's tone had the merest hint of impatience.

"It's very odd. They have seen something. Everyone has. They're all talking about it." He swung back into the saddle. "But not what you'd think."

"I think," she said, "you had better tell me what they saw."

"Apparently there was an Anathema in the vicinity, and not long ago. The story, if you believe it, is that it— sorry, she, it's supposed to have been a woman—fought an Immaculate priest at a tavern a few days' travel from here. The fight supposedly lasted all night, with doom raining down from the heavens and so forth. In the end, they say the priest killed her magically but was gravely wounded himself. The details are suspect, of course. Both of them were supposed to be nine feet tall and fart fire, but the core of it is something they all agree on, and I must say, if it's fiction, it's certainly an odd ending for it."

T'fillit pursed her lips. "Fascinating stuff. And the parchment you're holding?"

"A map, of course. Not a good one, but a map. It should be good enough to get us there, if you decide to investigate." Palap shrugged. "They all told the same story. They're quite excited about it, actually."

A sudden thought struck T'fillit. "The monk. Did the man describe him?"

Palap furrowed his brow. "Vaguely. Big, of course, and bald. He also said the man had a beard, which made me scratch my head. There aren't many monks with beards, are there?"

"Only one who matters," she said distantly. She shook her head, and her attention snapped back to the present. "Give me the map. Choose five others to go with me, and then take the rest back to the camp and wait. Reward the innkeeper and then move. Hurry!"

Palap blinked. "Revered One?"

"You heard me," she hissed.""Move!"

And then, more gently, "I think we've just found Holok."

Chapter Twenty-Four

The stumps of the mountain laurel trees were still there when Wren picked his way down the path. The stream that they had flanked was not. Where once had been a muddy but sizable flow of water was now a flat, empty gully, paved in cracked mud and pockmarked with stones. Dry, yellowed rushes grew along where the waterline had been, and a few hardier weeds had pushed their way into the channel proper.

They looked, thought Wren, like the last scraps of flesh on a well-gnawed skeleton. Swiftly, he brushed through the reeds and dropped into the streambed. He knelt and pinched some dirt between his fingers. It was bone dry and crumbled easily at his touch. Parchment-pale dust shifted away on the breeze, and he frowned. Still frowning, he hopped over to a nearby rock and overturned it. The soil underneath was dry as well, and curiously devoid of the sorts of small crawling things one would naturally expect.

"This is odd," he muttered to himself, and cocked his head to listen. Overhead, the sun was high and the sky cloudless. A steady breeze blew from the west, rattling dried leaves and dead reeds as it went. But other than that, there was no sound. No insects buzzed in the bushes, no birds called from the trees upslope, no frogs complained from hollows beneath stones.

The stream, and all that had lived in it, was gone.

With a small sound of displeasure, Wren rose to his feet. He looked behind him, but there was nothing downstream except more dirt, baked hard by the weak winter sun.

It would be upstream, then, he decided. The answers he sought would be found there, and with luck, Rhadanthos would be, too.

•   •   •

An hour later, any watching eyes would have seen a slightly frustrated Eliezer Wren sitting on a rock in the middle of the empty stream bed, cursing in most unpriestly fashion and rummaging in his pack for some dried fruit he'd bought a week earlier. The walk upstream had brought no answers, only an ever-deepening mystery set amidst rocks stained with dead algae. There was no sign of water anywhere, not even a trickle, and in Wren's rough estimation there hadn't been any in the channel for quite some time. Old erosion showed in the occasional patterns of sediment, but even the rare deeper pools showed no sign of moisture. Whatever had dried up the stream had done so thoroughly. Furthermore, it had done so some time ago. The water weeds and moss were long gone, as were the corpses of any fish that might have dwelt here. Empty shells filled with sand showed that freshwater shellfish and snails had lived here once, but not any more.

At sufficient intervals, Wren had stopped to test the soil. Everywhere, it was the same—fine, crumbly and dry. No answers magically revealed themselves, no voice whispered the story of what had happened here. There was only a dry streambed, and no sign of those—natural or unnatural—who had lived in it.

Frowning, Wren found the fruit and opened the leather pouch it was carried in. The dates were dry and leathery, the apple strips even worse, and after a few bites he found himself in the midst of a coughing fit. Spitting out a hunk of something that might once have been a stem, he found his waterskin and took a long pull from it.

It was nearly empty, he saw, and that was going to be a problem. He'd been counting on being able to refill it at the stream, and if he didn't find more water soon he'd be in serious trouble. A look at the sky reminded him that no help would be coming from that quarter; the few clouds that had masked it earlier had evaporated, leaving only the benignly smiling sun to dominate the heavens.

"Fat lot of help you are," Wren muttered, and took another pull from the skin. Another coughing fit took him, and a spray of water burst from his lips. It landed on the ground in dark traceries, and disgusted with himself, Wren sealed the skin and turned to pack it away.

Instead, something on the ground caught his eye.

The water he'd accidentally lost, those precious few drops, had not stayed where they'd landed. Instead, they'd crept together, pooling themselves into a tiny puddle and then stretching themselves into the shape of a single word.

It read, "Help."

Wren stared at the script on the ground for a long instant. Then, with a hiss, the water sank into the ground and was gone.

He slid to the ground and ran a finger along the place where the moisture had been seconds previously. It was, as he expected, utterly dry.

The nearly empty waterskin was still in his left hand. Looking at it, Wren estimated that he had perhaps another day's worth of water if he was careful, two if he was penurious. He looked at the ground again, and made his decision.

Unstoppering the skin, he turned it upside down and let the last of his water trickle out onto the creekbed. It splashed against the dirt, gurgling away and swirling into the dust.

As the last few drops spattered out, Wren dropped to his hands and knees. "Where are you?" he whispered fiercely. "Tell me where you are or I can't help you."

The water shimmered, then spun. A miniature whirlpool formed in the tiny puddle.

"Tell me!"

Beneath the stones, the water spelled out one glyph after another. *You will find me beneath the stones.* Then the empty waterskin slipped from Wren's fingers, and the words vanished as if they had never been.

• • •

He found the stones, such as they were, a little further upstream, and gave a low whistle at the sight.

The last time he had been here, the stream had issued from a burbling, reasonably cheerful spring. Ice-cold and clear, the waters had welled up from within the mouth of a small cave. Now, the cave—and the spring—were gone.

Instead, someone had gone to great trouble to bury both the stream and its spirit. A massive pile of boulders had been erected on the site where the spring had once flowed, reaching nearly twenty feet into the air. Some of the stones, Wren saw, were easily the size of a full grown man, and bore signs of having been hacked ungently out of a cliff face. Smaller stones filled in the gaps between the large ones, and someone had begun an effort to cover the entire enterprise in loose soil. The attempt thus far had been unsuccessful, but it gave the impression that the earth itself was reaching up to take the impromptu monolith to its bosom.

The base of the mound, Wren noticed as he got closer, was less solid than the mound itself. The spring may have been buried, but it had not been entirely choked, as the area around the rough hill was marshy, wet and dank. Reeds poked up through intermittent puddles, and squelching noises accompanied Wren's every step. Here and there patches of incongruously dry land appeared, baked as hard and dry as the rest of the riverbed but sitting cheek by jowl with seemingly bottomless pools and massive puddles of unbroken mud. A will-o-the-wisp, more ambitious than its fellows, burned bright over the muck for a second, then winked out.

He paused to pull his left foot out of a particularly boggy patch, and regretted not having bought (or stolen) better footwear. Already the mud was caking on his lower legs and feet, and the slight itching it inspired was a harbinger of far worse discomfort yet to come. There were flies here, too, and a loud croaking somewhere nearby told Wren that the local frogs were clearly not keeping their mind on their work.

In the distance, he could see the ominous shape of Talat's Howe. The top of the hill had been sheared off by some unknown catastrophe, but even so its brooding silhouette was unmistakable. No trees grew on that hill, indeed, from where he stood Wren could see no life at all. Then again, that was appropriate. It was a dead place, left to dead things, and Wren found himself devoutly hoping that he'd never have to set foot inside its confines again.

The last time he had done so, he'd earned the enmity of both Ratcatcher and Ratcatcher's master, the Prince of Shadows, and that had set his foot on the path that had taken him to the bowels of the Underworld and beyond.

Life would have been easier, he reflected, if he'd been able to refrain from trying to be clever. Instead, he'd laced the empty tomb—for his desecration of it had yielded but a single coin and the awareness that the entire construction was a massive joke played on would-be tomb robbers like himself—with traps of varying lethality. One had caught the prince's favorite, and the prince been displeased enough to have Ratcatcher hunt Wren down across the breadth of a continent.

What had followed, Wren reflected grimly, had not been pleasant. He finished pulling his foot out of the mud and, lacking a better idea of what to do, started climbing the cairn under which Rhadanthos was presumably buried. A few seconds' scrambling brought him to the top, and demonstrated to him precisely how difficult his task was likely to be. The stones he climbed over were massive, far too huge for him to move on his own. Even with the power he'd been granted, there was no way he'd be able to shove aside half the boulders that made up Rhadanthos' prison, and it struck him as unlikely that he'd get the inhabitants of any of the villages he'd passed through to help.

Temporarily baffled, he sat. The evening was pleasant enough, with a cool breeze washing down from the heights behind the Howe. The sun sank at a leisurely pace, and Wren found himself scanning the nearby woods for a good place to camp. He recalled wolves and less palatable things haunting the woods nearby from his last visit, and had no desire to make their acquaintance. The problem of Rhadanthos' entombment might be easier to tackle come morning, but not if he spent the night dodging ghosts and teaching wolves painful lessons.

It was the sudden silence of the frogs that snapped Wren out of his reverie. Something large was crashing through the underbrush in the woods off to his left. Whatever it was was slow-moving and clumsy, and Wren had no desire to be seen by it. He slithered down the pile of rocks, keeping its bulk between him and whatever was making the sound, and listened.

In a few seconds, the noise resolved itself into the tramp of heavy feet, many of them. The pace of the footfalls was slow but their frequency spoke of numbers, and over the din Wren could hear a man's voice shouting orders liberally sprinkled with Nexus dockside profanity.

Wren scrabbled to his right and peered out around the edge of the hill. There was an instant when he could see nothing, and then the source of the noise emerged from the forest. It was a long column of shambling, shuffling figures in rags. The stench of the grave hung over them, and even at this distance Wren could see places where pale bone shone through holes in paler skin. Looking almost ghostly in the late evening light, each was weighed down with a heavy yoke linking two buckets. The buckets held overflowing loads of dirt, which trailed out behind each staggering figure and plopped into the soft mud a handful at a time.

"Walking dead," Wren said softly. "This is their doing?"

Another figure burst from the trees as he watched, one with considerable more animation than the shuffling cadavers he tended. The shape was armored in gleaming black, a barrel-shaped figure marked by spikes and excresences which gleamed with an oily shine. For a moment Wren thought he was staring at some sort of monstrous beetle, and then recognition dawned. He'd seen this figure before, once and long ago. From the cover of the woods on the south side of Rhadanthos' creek, he'd seen this man in the entourage of the Prince of Shadows.

A second look brought more details. The man was stocky. Friends would have called him burly; enemies would have called him fat. He moved slowly and ponderously, and the clack of the joints of his armor echoed over the marsh like the clacking of insect jaws.

It was not Ratcatcher, then, but one of his friends. Wren nodded. Heo 'd somehow been half-expecting to meet his former captor here, and it was a bit of a shock to discover one of the prince's other servants. Still, anyone in service to the Prince of Shadows was unlikely to be a weakling or a coward. The beetle-shaped figure, whoever he was, would no doubt be an enemy to be reckoned with.

Was the prince still here? Wren thought not. Piling stones was the sort of thing the prince entrusted to servants, and not particularly bright servants at that. This beetle-man had not struck Wren as the cleverest of the prince's servants, and so he was the perfect choice to remain behind and work the prince's will. That the prince's will had included the imprisonment of Rhadanthos was the bigger, and more worrisome, surprise.

The long column of figures emerging from the wood finally ended. Wren counted a dozen, plus the armored taskmaster, and noted with some alarm that they were clearly headed in his direction. Silently, Wren berated himself—of course that's what they were doing, what other reason would there be to have corpse tote heavy loads of earth? It was time for a retreat. Walking dead were less of a problem for him than they might be for some others, but the presence of the prince's henchman tipped the scales. Wren wanted nothing to do with him for now, not until he had a surer idea of the man's capabilities. Nodding to himself, the former priest began a slow, quiet descent from the rockpile on which he was perched.

Behind him, he heard a low growl. He turned his head and then silently asked the heavens, *"Why?"*

A wolf sat at the base of the pile of stones, its ragged fur marked by scars. Its eyes were bright blue, and they stared into Wren's own with a look of more than animal cunning.

"Good dog," Wren said, desperately ransacking his memory as to whether or not he'd stored any dried meat among his provisions. He didn't think he had.

The wolf snarled deep in its throat, and bared an impressive palisade of teeth. Its eyes held Wren's, daring him to make a move.

With agonizing slowness, Wren turned his left hand so that the palm was flush against the rock face. The wolf, by itself, was no problem. The help that a howl might bring, on the other hand, was. And if he needed a reminder of this, the splashing of the approaching dead men was getting closer.

Carefully, he extended his fingers, searching for a stone that would fit neatly into his palm. His hand closed on a clump of dried mud that exploded in his grip, and then a loose agglomeration of pebbles. "Nice dog," he said, a bit more urgently. It padded forward a step. On the other side of the hill, the black-armored man bellowed something about moving faster.

Wren moved faster. He splayed his right hand out and found a fist-sized lump of schist, held fast in a matrix of dried mud and grass. The wolf loped forward, to the base of the hill and stared at him.

He pulled the rock free. It fit in his palm the way a child's ball might have, just heavy enough to throw. The wolf threw back its head and closed its eyes.

Wren hurled the stone. From his awkward position, he didn't get quite as much on it as he would have wished, but it took the wolf in the jaw, and turned what would have been a full-throated howl into a whimper of pain. The beast shook itself as the stone splashed into the mud, and in that instant Wren leapt off the hill.

It barely had time to turn its head to face him as he descended, his foot connecting with the back of its neck and driving it down into the dirt. There was a sharp, vicious cracking sound, and the light went out of the wolf's eyes. Curiously, its tail wagged once, and then it was dead.

Carefully, Wren stepped off the carcass' neck, feeling rather pleased with himself. No other wolves leapt out of the reeds and scrubby brush to assault him and no alarm had been raised. Now, all that remained to do was to negotiate the tricky semi-swamp that surrounded Rhadanthos' resting place without attracting attention, and he could hide until morning and better options presented themselves. Gingerly, he stepped forward onto a tussock of firm-seeming ground.

Something in the grass moved. Wren saw a flash of green and then felt a sharp, stabbing pain in his heel. He lifted his foot and saw blood oozing from twin puncture wounds. A thin, ribbon-like tail vanished into the depths of the grass, and Wren felt his blood run cold with fear. Surely it was too late in the year for serpents, he thought, and carefully put his foot back on the ground. Nothing else struck at him, and hesitantly he put his weight on the wounded heel.

Despite himself, Wren screamed. It felt like his foot had been immersed in liquid flame, so intense was his agony. The pain crawled down the sole of his foot to his toes, and up his calf. He nearly stumbled, but caught himself and forced himself forward.

The sound of hurried footsteps through shallow swamp told him that his shout had not gone unnoticed. He took another step and gritted his teeth against the agony. The venom had flowed further now, the pain lancing higher up his leg.

A chorus of low moans came from around the hill, and the dead men shambled into view. They moved quickly for their kind, dropping their yokes and lurching forward with their hands out, grasping. Behind them strode their beetle-armored master, who exhorted them on with shouts that seemed more for his benefit than for theirs.

Wren took another step, and nearly collapsed into the mud. Another couple of hopping half-steps convinced him that flight was no longer an option. Behind him, the corpses were getting closer. The stench of them overwhelmed his nostrils.

Face set in a grim mask, he hobbled to a small rise and knelt down on it. His bad leg he tucked beneath him, his good one he leaned on. Drawing the daiklave from his back, he bared his teeth in a grin the dead wolf would have envied and waited. Three of his pursuers, he noted with grim amusement, had dropped off the chase, and were busy tearing hunks from the dead animal's carcass with their rotting fingers. Their taskmaster strode among them, striking with the flat of his blade and urging them forward, but they paid him no heed.

"You need a better class of slave," Wren called, and swung the daiklave in a broad, flat arc. It took the first of the cadavers in the midsection, spinning it around as its half-rotted guts snaked out of its torn belly. It caught at them with slow fingers, staring in amazement as they poured onto the ground. Another shambled forward on the left, and Wren reversed his swing. There was a moment of agony as he put undue pressure on his wounded leg, but his blow struck true. It took the figure just above the knees, severing one leg and nearly taking the other. The corpse fell on its side like a child's suddenly forgotten toy, its arms still waving madly.

"Forward, damn the lot of you, forward!" the man bellowed. "He's one man, and he's hurt!" He stalked back and forth behind the line of his advancing minions, brandishing a heavy curved sword with a basket hilt, yet seemed oddly unwilling to engage Wren himself.

Wren, for his part, found himself unable to take the time to analyze this strange behavior, being too busy fighting for his life. One of the corpses reached below the surface of a puddle and brought out a dripping hunk of wood that would serve as a club. It raised the makeshift weapon, and Wren took its arm off at the elbow. Another one rushed him as he did so, and he was forced to butt it in the gut with the sword's pommel. Dirty claws raked his face even as it folded in something approximating pain, and then he brought the blade around and made an end of it. Two more converged on him, and as he held them at bay, a third crept around behind him and raised clasped hands over its head, intent on delivering a crushing blow. Wren reversed his grip on the blade and thrust straight back between his arm and torso. The daiklave caught on something that was probably a rib, and Wren gave it a sharp twist to the left. There was the sound of rotten bones breaking, and then he pulled the blade free before the two in front could take advantage.

In the end, they all fell. Wren stared at his opponent across a sea of torn body parts and severed limbs, not a few of which were still moving blindly and without guidance. His entire side was aflame, but thankfully his leg had gone numb. The first fingers of fire had crept past his shoulder into his arm, and he didn't know how much longer he could hold the daiklave.

With luck, he thought, his opponent didn't know, either.

"You can run now," he called out, trying to keep the pain out of his voice. His cheek bled from four parallel cuts inflicted by the nails of one of the walking dead and his legs were soaked up past the knee. Old, black blood dripped from the end of the daiklave, spattering into a puddle one drop at a time.

"I can. You can't," the man called out, and advanced. His sword made a blur in the late evening light, the hum of it cutting the air an insistent nagging in Wren's ears. "You've got a big sword for a little man."

"And you've got a big mouth for a man behind corpses." Wren made a first, probing thrust, and it clanged harmlessly off the man's breastplate. In response, the man brought his sword down in a savage two-handed stroke, one that nearly wrenched the daiklave out of Wren's hands.

"I'll cut you a second smile instead, and then we can compare," he gloated. "You can tell the other ghosts that Pandeimos sent you, and you'll have a lot of company." He struck again, and again Wren barely parried. The strength behind the blow was staggering. Another blow came at his head, and as Wren ducked, the man stomped one booted foot onto his wrist. Wren cried out at the blow and his wrist turned, and the daiklave lay flat on the ground. Before he could pull it away, the grinning Pandeimos brought his boot down again, this time on the sword itself. It sank deep into the mud under his weight, and Wren was unable to pull it free.

"Having a problem with your sword?" Pandeimos spun his blade once, theatrically, and then rammed it point-down into the mud as well. Laughing at his own joke, he lifted off his helm to reveal a broad face that might have been ruddy if it weren't suffering the first stages of decomposition. Black hair gone to gray framed the man's face, matted with moisture that might have been sweat. Most of his teeth, his grin attested, were still present.

"What's your name?" he asked. "I hate killing people I don't know. It makes for boring stories afterwards." He flexed his fingers, the metal of his gauntlets clacking softly.

Wren gave another surreptitious tug on the sword. It didn't move. The pain in his side made him feel like his muscles had turned to water. There was, he decided, only thing he could do.

"My name," he said, "is Eliezer Wren."

It had the desired effect. Pandeimos gasped "You?" and shifted his weight. Wren shifted his as well, throwing himself backwards and willing the power in him to do something, anything, to heal the terrible pain. The daiklave came with him, whipping up and into the air, narrowly missing the underside of Pandeimos' jaw as the man ducked out of the way.

Wren landed on his back and rolled. Warmth flooded through him, not the harsh burning power of the venom, but rather the gentle heat that came with healing. He came up, covered in mud but smiling, the daiklave held in good form in front of him. A tattered cloak of light trailed out behind him, catching and snapping on an invisible breeze.

To Pandeimos' credit, it didn't take him long to recover. "The prince will be very happy to hear I killed *you*," he snarled, and charged. His helm fell, unnoticed, into the mire.

Wren cut low, then when his opponent parried, brought the daiklave up in a slow swing at the man's head. Again, Pandeimos parried, and Wren took the opportunity to plant a solid, flatfooted kick in the center of his chest.

The bigger man went over backwards with a loud grunt, landing on his back on the low rise that Wren had defended against Pandeimos' servants. His sword came forward in a wild cut that would have taken Wren's ear had he not snapped his head to the left by instinct. Another swipe came, one-handed, as Pandeimos planted his left hand on the ground in an attempt to hoist himself upright.

Wren saw this, avoided the wild swing, and jabbed at the joint at the elbow of the man's armor. The point penetrated, and with a hiss Pandeimos sank back to the ground. Wren pulled the daiklave back, its tip bloodied, and brought it up to fend off another wild blow. This one clanged harmlessly away, and Wren riposted by planting a kick under his enemy's chin.

"Not so much fun when you're the one on the ground, is it?" he asked, even as the sword flew from Pandeimos' fingers. He leaned forward, and rested the point of the daiklave against the man's throat. "Now, I have a question."

Pandeimos laughed, a thick, choked sound. "I won't answer you."

"Oh? And why not?" Wren let the blade swing back and forth. It cut the skin, and blackened blood welled forth.

"Because all you can do is kill me, and that's nothing anymore. I'll be back for you, Wren, and I'll tell the prince, too. I'll see you in one of the hells."

With that, he threw himself forward, driving the point of Wren's blade into his windpipe and beyond. There was a sickening, brief crunch, and then nothing more.

• • •

It took three tries for Wren to pry the daiklave out of Pandeimos' throat. Somehow it had gotten wedged between a few of the neck vertebrae, and seemed almost unwilling to relinquish its hold. At the last, Wren had to plant one mud-encrusted foot on the corpse's face and then pull.

The sword he'd wiped carefully on the tallest reeds he could find, and then tucked away again. The bodies he gathered as best he could and dumped them a ways down the channel, the better to distract any wolves that might come along. As for fresh water, he found precious little. Most of the puddles and pools had been fouled, one way or another, by the afternoon's exertions, and with the sun going down there was no time to search. Finally, in desperation, he dug a hollow into the ground and lined it with strips of cloth torn from his trews, in hopes that they might serve as something of a filter. Then, exhausted beyond belief, his heel still throbbing from where the serpent had bitten him, Wren climbed to the top of the cairn that imprisoned Rhadanthos and lay down in hopes of finding a few hours' sleep.

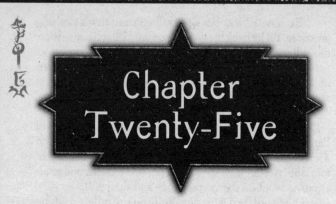

Chapter
Twenty-Five

"It's not the sort of place you would expect to find anyone interesting," said one of the riders doubtfully, and four of the other five murmured their agreement.

The six sat, mounted, outside the grounds of a small inn. The main building was a cut above ramshackle, but the outbuildings were on the brink of teetering into disrepair. A sprawl of untidy fields surrounded the central building, and they in turn were surrounded by a low wooden fence. A few members of the staff bustled across the central courtyard, some leading animals to what looked to be the stables. A heavyset woman emerged from the rear door of the main building and spent several minutes pursuing an equally heavyset chicken, then seized her prize and stomped back inside. A pair of wagons sitting outside the stable had blocks placed before and behind their wheels, but there was no need. The ground here was flat, and there was no danger of anything rolling away under its own power.

T'fillit shot a glance filled with annoyance at the woman who'd spoken, and she—a girl, really—had flushed and turned away. The others muttered inanities and subsided, and all was silent except for the soft whickering of the animals they rode. There were seven of those, one for each rider and a saddled but riderless beast tethered to one of the junior riders' mounts. That particular animal, which some foolish optimist had named "Thunderbolt of Wrath," was heavy and slow, which made it perfect for the task that lay ahead. It possessed a personality that kind riders called "gentle," which was another way of saying that it was exceptionally stupid even by the undemanding standards of beasts of burden, and that was precisely why T'fillit had called for it to be saddled and led out with her expedition. She was here to bring someone back, someone who might not be in the best condition to ride, and when it came to mounts for her esteemed guest, the gentler course seemed the wiser one.

T'fillit took in the panorama for another minute while the other riders sat silent and shamed behind her. Finally, one—a young noble of House Iselsi with a fraction more courage than most of his companions, spoke.

"Are we going in to get him?" he asked anxiously, his left hand on the reins while the right rubbed his exceedingly unpleasant-looking mount's neck. "It doesn't seem terribly well defended."

The priestess held up her hand.""Wait. Remember the story we heard—that there had been some kind of fight between a monk and an Anathema here, and that the monk had triumphed but been wounded. Does it sound like the situation demands that we ride in with fire, steel and naked power?"

"Well, no." The young Iselsi hung his head.""I just thought—"

"You thought what? Did the story not make our fearless monk out the hero? Why exactly do you think we would need to do anything more than ask where his chamber is, and then bring him home? We are here to eliminate Anathema. We are also here to make sure that the people know we are here to eliminate Anathema, so that they might remember their duty toward the Immaculate Dragons. Slaughtering innkeepers and stable boys for the crime of being bystanders when an ancient and venerable monk brought down this reborn evil, not to mention the heinous act of caring for him while he recovered from his wounds, is not the sort of act calculated to further our goals."

"Oh. So what do we do, then?"

"You—and by you I mean all of you—will ride into the courtyard and attempt not to burn, kill or pillage anything. I will go into the inn and see if their guest is in any shape to travel. If he is not, you will stay here with him until he is. If he is, then we will leave, after rewarding the innkeeper and his family handsomely for their good deed. Understood?"

The young Dragon-Blood nodded, then his head came up and his brow furrowed.""Reward them? With what?"

T'fillit's lips curled back in something that only a kind man would call a smile."'You have a purse, yes?"

"Well, yes."

"Then you have answered your own question. Enough of this. Let us ride." So saying, she flicked the reins and her heavy, coal-black mount surged forward. With a whoop, the others followed, startling even the mild-mannered Thunderbolt of Wrath into motion. Behind them all came the foolish Iselsi, who rode with one hand on the reins and the other on his purse, wondering why he'd chosen to join the Hunt in the first place.

•   •   •

The inn's hostess, her apron stained with fresh chicken blood, had already scurried to the front door when T'fillit dismounted. She bowed as best she could, her smile showing a half-set of yellowing teeth, and gestured to the interior of the inn. As T'fillit strode up the three steps that led inside, the other riders circled the courtyard, scattering the few fowl that remained there and generally discomfiting the hired help.

"Your Reverence," the woman said as T'fillit reached her, and curtseyed. "To what do we owe the honor of this visit?" Her hands, T'fillit noted, were also still bloody.

"It is you who does us the honor," T'fillit replied, trying not to gag at the odor emanating from the figure before her. "I have heard tales of a great battle that was fought here in recent nights against the forces of the ancient evil which we hunt, and we have come to praise you for your part in it."

The woman blushed and fluttered, her hands knotting up in the stained apron. "Oh, you're too kind," she said. "We did nothing, really. Just a few swings here and there." She demonstrated, and T'fillit was left with no doubt that a blow struck by this creature's meaty arms would indeed lay anything short of an Anathema out on the ground. "It was the priest that did all of the real fighting, though. He and his lady friend."

"Lady friend?" T'fillit did her best to control her curiosity.

"Oh, yes, yes. They took a single room together, and were here several days. Then one night the whole inn was awakened by a terrible clamor from their room. At first my husband and I—we own the place, we do—thought it was just the two of them squabbling, which we hear often enough, running an inn like we do. But then there was this tremendous crash, and a pretty young thing dressed all in black ran through the kitchen. Roused the staff, who set upon her. We could tell she was evil, you know, so we gave her what for." The woman's head nodded down into her wattled chins sagely.

T'fillit barely kept herself from laughing. Of *course* this woman could tell Anathema just by looking at them, she thought. She was also quite certain that the number of blows the staff had struck against the interloper had been exactly zero, in large part because there were no fresh graves to be seen. Scullery maids armed with skillets who fought sun-tainted monstrosities tended to turn into cadavers with alarming regularity. It seemed highly unlikely that the staff of this particular hostel was skilled enough at hand-to-hand combat for things to have gone otherwise.

All she said, however, was "You are very brave. Pray, tell, what happened next?"

"Ooh!" The fat woman threw her hands up in the air. "Well, this thief—for that's what she was, a common thief— had just about fought her way through the kitchen when in though the door from the common room burst the priest. He looked angry, I tell you, as angry as I've seen a man in many a year. The thief took one look back at him and ran like a rabbit who wakes up to find she's been cuddling up to a snake. She was out the back door like a stone from a sling, and that's no lie."

T'fillit nodded. "The priest—what did he look like?"

"Well, he looked a lot better then than he does now, begging your pardon. He was tall and broad and wore gray, and he had a great bushy beard like you don't see on too many priests. I'm glad it wasn't me he was angry with, let me tell you. There was some kind of light shining from him, too, though no one here seems able to agree on just what they saw. We just know it was some kind of light. A symbol of favor from the Elemental Dragons, no doubt."

Smiling benignly, T'fillit reached out and patted the woman on the shoulder. "Yes, that's exactly it. You are perspicacious as well as brave. Well done."

The hostess looked befuddled but pleased, and needed no further prompting to continue her story. "In any case, he chased her out the back door. We didn't swing at him, no not at all. You don't swing a kettle at a priest, I always say, on account of it being bad luck. So we held our ground and he ran out the back, and then the rest of us came to the door to watch."

"What did you see?" the priestess prompted with an inner sigh. The woman clearly wanted to bask in her moment of glory, and that necessitated a little bit of nudging.

"That's the curious thing, you see. She just fell down. Then the priest went out and whispered something to her, and carried her body back, and the priest's lady friend met him at the door. My husband and I felt it was none of our business any longer, so Wise Ox—that's my husband—went to try to fix the door on their room, and I shooed everyone else off to bed." She nodded, and added a prim, "It seemed proper," with the clear implication that while she was very thankful to the priest in question, she did not at all approve of his choice of traveling companions.

T'fillit ignored her moralizing. Something about the story—above and beyond the obvious bits of fiction the woman had injected to make herself look more important— bothered her. "The priest was not hurt when he brought the body back?"

"That was the"*other* curious thing, now. He didn't look hurt, but come morning we could all hear him shouting bloody murder—and bloody murder it damn near well was. Blood all over the place, let me tell you, and his companion long gone. He must have been hurt and not known it, that's all I can say, but how he made it up the stairs with those cuts I'll never know." T'fillit stared at her until she continued. "Across the back of the ankle, they were. The sort of thing a man shouldn't be able to walk on, even if he is a priest. My Wise Ox made him some crutches so he could get around, but the things he had to say, oh, they were terrible Just terrible!"

"I suspect I will be able to forgive him," T'fillit said dryly. "I would like to speak to him, if I may."

"Oh, of course. He's up the stairs." The woman gestured authoritatively into the darkness behind her. Past the wave of the flabby arm, T'fillit could see a long common room with a stairwell at the end of it, leading up to a catwalk that ran the room's length. "First room on the left. It's the one with the new door. You can't miss it."

"I am in your debt," the priestess said.""Young Iselsi Harrah," and she pointed at the sullen figure in the center of the courtyard, "has generously announced that you should be rewarded for your bravery. Go to him."

"Of course, Revered One," the heavyset woman said, and flounced out into the courtyard. Harrah saw her coming and blanched, but by then T'fillit had already gone inside. The hostess' shrieks of delight followed her, faintly, as she did so.

• • •

The stairs, like much of the construction on the inside, was surprisingly solid. A mended table sat just below the catwalk, while heavy, hand-carved furniture filled the room. None of it was decorative but all of it was functional.

T'fillit suspected the hand of the woman's Wise Ox in this. He was apparently a talented man. It was a pity, she thought, that he weren't wiser about his choice of a cow.

Two of the steps creaked loudly under her tread, a standard form of burglar alarm in the hinterlands of the far Threshold. So, too, did the dark wood of the catwalk, and T'fillit took care to step lightly as she came to the door the hostess had mentioned.

It was indeed new, pine wood that had not yet been subjected to the indignities of a constant cookfire smoke and thus was still light and unmarred. There was no peephole, nor was there a knocker of any sort. The handle was a simple knob, with a simpler lock below it. Both were cast from bronze.

She raised her hand as if to knock, but then thought better of it. Instead, she turned and put her ear against the door, to listen for any sound within. There was nothing, only silence. The floor underneath her creaked as she shifted her weight, her concern rapidly growing. The fat woman had said that the mysterious priest was here, and yet there was no hint of his presence. Frowning, she bent her head to the door again and shut her eyes, the better to concentrate on any noise she might hear.

What she heard this time sounded like a clap of thunder inside her skull, as something exploded against the door on the other side. With an involuntary shout, she turned, hands before her face, and prepared to kick down the door to do battle with whatever lay on the other side.

Instead, the door opened. Standing there was Holok, though a thinner, grimmer Holok than she remembered. He leaned heavily on a pair of rough crutches, and his expression was one of disdain. Burns in the shape of withered hands marked both his cheeks, and she suppressed a shocked gasp at the sight. "You shouldn't listen at doors, woman. It'll get you surprises you don't like."

"Holok?" T'fillit breathed. "Is that you?"

"Of course it's me. The question I have is, what are you doing out here, and how did you find me?" She started to answer, but he held up a hand. "No, no, not out here. Come inside and tell me, and I've got a few things to tell you, too." He turned with surprising agility, leaving her to follow and close the door.

The room smelled faintly of antiseptic herbs and old blood, despite the fact that the window was open and a cold breeze swirled through the chamber at intervals. There was a bed, unmussed, in the corner, and a cot on the floor. One table stood next to the doorway, and a half-eaten bowl of rice sat on it next to an empty teacup. Two wooden stools were placed next to it, both obviously the innkeeper's handiwork. A bundle of rags that, on closer inspection, proved to be Holok's clothes sat in the corner, but otherwise the room was bare.

Holok threw himself onto the cot and folded the crutches across his lap. "So," he said, "tell me how you knew to look for me in the middle of all this splendor."

"You're famous," she replied, settling onto one of the stools. Something told her that the bed was not to be touched.

"I am?" He gave a snort of laughter. "That's a disappointment after all these centuries of anonymity."

"It's true. The story's everywhere now, the bold tale of a noble priest fighting off a three-headed Anathema at a tiny little inn."

Holok frowned and looked intently at her. "You're making that up."

"The part about the three heads, yes, but the rest is true. Everywhere you go, you hear another version if. Your landlady had her own, which involved whacking the Exalt over the head with a frying pan."

"No, the only one she would take a skillet to would be her husband. I hadn't realized the story had gotten so far." He cast his eyes down at the floor.

"It's everywhere, I assure you. We just followed it back to its source to find you." She didn't mention that the reason she'd been in position to hear the story had been that she'd been utterly fooled by the false trail that someone had laid for her. There was no sense confessing to Holok that her brilliant work in tracking him down had in fact been an utter accident. "If you hadn't fought the Exalt, I expect we never would have found you."

"I expect I wouldn't have let you find me, if I hadn't fought her." He coughed once. "Rather, if I hadn't been sloppy after the fight. She's buried beyond the fields on the north side of the inn, if you want to see what's left of the body. There was nothing on it of worth. She was a thief, nothing more."

T'fillit nodded. l"But she led us here. Thank the heavens for happy accidents. I'm glad you were still here," she added after a short pause, and immediately wished she hadn't. Of course he was still here; his ravaged legs were not going to allow him to go anywhere under his own power any time soon.

He grunted by way of reply, then shook his head. "I'm sorry about the rap on the door," he said, "but I didn't know who was out there, and I don't like strangers listening at my door."

"How did you know I was there?" she asked.

"When Wise Ox put the new door in, I had him cut a section of the bottom an inch off the floor. He also hung a lamp in such a way for me that anyone standing in front of my door casts a little bit of a shadow. So when I saw the shape on the floor, I knew someone was at my door, and when it didn't move I knew that someone was listening." He patted the crutches. "That's where these came in. If you hit a pine door with one of them, they make a lot of noise."

"So they do," T'fillit said, wincing. "You'll have to try that one on Kejak some day."

"Kejak?" Holok snorted. "He turned me loose. Don't tell me he did the same to you. I thought you were snug as a tick on a hound at the Palace Sublime, playing Dragon-Blood for all the world to see. I can't think of another reason you'd be out here away from the comforts of home."

"I understand you were traveling with a female companion," she retorted. "Don't talk to me about comforts."

"Don't you talk about her!" Holok slammed his crutches down on the floor and lurched to his feet. His hands were balled into fists, and his face was red with anger. "I never laid a *finger* on her."

"I'm sorry," the priestess said softly. "I... misunderstood."

"So did I," Holok said, and collapsed back onto the cot. A thin line of red showed in the bandages wrapped around his ankles. "So why are you here, and who are the young idiots outside?"

"Wyld Hunt," she replied, answering the last question first.""The cover for the whole expedition is that we're following up on the events at Qut Toloc. It won't stand close examination, but it won't have to."

"And the real reason?"

She leaned forward.""To find you, and bring you home. He didn't trust anyone else to do it."

He snorted.""Poppycock. Kejak has other ways of finding a man than sending every lame-brained Iselsi by-blow who can ride off into the Threshold on a Hunt."

"Kejak hasn't quite been himself of late. Things are happening at home, odd things. You're needed there."

"That's funny," Holok mused. "I was told that I was needed out here. He never used to change his mind this often back in the old days."

"These aren't the old days, Holok."

"The way things are going, they might be the very old days," he said softly, so softly she barely heard.

"Dragons preserve us, I hope not." She lifted the teacup and sniffed it. "Still drinking sycamore leaf squeezings, Holok?"

"I drink honest workingman's tea," he replied, and bent to retrieve his crutches. "And don't swear by the Dragons if you don't mean it. It's unbecoming."

T'fillit nodded, feeling shamefaced despite herself. Holok's reputation had always been that of an honest man, regardless of his other quirks, and a devout one. While it was unusual, to say the least, for one of Kejak's cronies to adopt the figures and strictures of the Immaculate Order, Holok had done so, and without any apparent irony. She'd met him a few times over the centuries and had always found him, if not dull, then at least straightforward. But the man who sat before her now spoke with an uncomfortably bitter edge to his words, and his massive hands flexed constantly as if he were looking for something to crush. There was a light in his eyes, too, one which she'd not seen before. It made her uncomfortable, and she found herself being almost thankful that he was crippled.

"I beg your pardon," she said as formally as she could, and put the cup back down on the table with a click.""So I've told you why I'm here. You tell me why you are. These aren't your usual haunts."

"I didn't intend to stay," he said with undisguised sarcasm. "Kejak sent me out here to find two things. The important one was the boy from Qut Toloc. I trust you've heard about him?" T'fillit nodded, and Holok continued. "No luck there. The other was to find Kejak's errand boy, Wren. I failed at that as well."

"That's odd. Wren is supposed to be dead. That's what Kejak told me before we set out."

"But?"

"But one of my huntsmen apparently ran into him not too long ago. He's changed, it would seem. Been touched by the Unconquered Sun."

"Ah." Holok accepted the news with equanimity. "I find that hard to believe. The Unconquered Sun doesn't Exalt those of Wren's age too often, and the idea of taking one of Kejak's servants smacks of bad epic poetry. More likely that your fresh-faced huntsman got himself into trouble and made something up. Wren had acquired something of a reputation. He makes a good bogeyman."

"It's possible," she said noncommittally. "He's certainly been roughed up by something, and his companions are dead."

"Hunh." Holok sat back.""Send him home to Kejak and let him interrogate the boy. If there's some truth to the story, he'll find it, and he'll leave your huntsman mostly intact when he's done. All I know is that I didn't find Wren. I did find, however, some other interesting things. An orichalcum dagger, for one, of obscure provenance. For another, a very persistent Nemissary who gave me these," he pointed to the scars on his face, "before I knotted him into a tree. A few other things that I'm sure Kejak will find fascinating."

T'fillit whistled. "It sounds as if there's nothing he can find fault with there. You've had an interesting journey."

Holok waved her sympathy away. "He can always find fault. It's woven into him like green thread in a tapestry. That's not the issue."

"So where's the dagger?"

"Gone."

"Gone?" T'fillit blinked in surprise. "Stolen? From you?"

"I never really had it to begin with," he said heavily. "She took it when she left."

"And you let her." It came out sounding like an accusation.

"I couldn't exactly follow," was his answer, laced with a bitterness so pure that T'fillit found herself recoiling. "She made sure of that."

"Ah. I see."

"No, you don't. But it doesn't matter. You don't have to." Angrily, painfully, Holok rousted himself to his feet. "Take me back to the Isle, T'fillit. And while we ride, I'll tell you everything I know about Unforgiven Blossom and the thing she carried, and maybe, just maybe, you can find her. I think it's best if I don't try ever again."

Chapter Twenty-Six

"I've been here before."

Ratcatcher looked out over the low, rolling hills before him and squinted. The late afternoon sun turned the stream that wound its way across the landscape into a ribbon of molten fire, making it hard to see exactly what lay ahead. Still, he was struck by the nagging feeling that this place was familiar.

Behind him, Mushroom and Mold exchanged wordless glances fraught with meaning. One looked down at the ground, the other gazed off at a bank of thin, wispy clouds and offered a diffident, "You have been more places than most men, Lord Ratcatcher."

If he'd hoped that would be the end of the matter, Mushroom was disappointed. Ratcatcher half turned in the saddle and glared back at him. "I am well aware of that, thank you very much. I've got more decades of travel in my memory than you have chins. What I want right now, however, is an explanation for why this misbegotten stretch of earth tells me that I should know it."

Mushroom shrugged apologetically. "I do not know, noble one. There is certainly nothing here of note, nor within a few days' ride. There are a few villages here and there, some ruins that may once have been of interest—surely nothing that could command your attention. Perhaps you are just tired from the day's ride, and we should make camp?"

Ratcatcher's steed snorted impatiently, and its rider did the same. "'I am not that tired," he said, "nor am I prone to imagining things. Don't patronize me. You're no damn good at it."

So saying, he dug his heels into his mount's flanks, and it trotted down the gentle slope toward the creek. Panicked expressions on their faces, Mushroom and Mold belatedly kicked their mules into motion. With much snorting and excitement they trotted after him.

They caught up at the edge of the creek, their mounts lathered with the exertion. Ratcatcher had already dismounted, and he stood, stroking his horse's mane with odd gentleness as it dipped its head to drink.

"So," he said without turning to look at them. "Do you have a better idea of why I might remember this place now? I thought perhaps a different angle might jog someone's memory. Maybe even mine."

Wheezing, Mold dismounted and led his exhausted mule forward.

"An excellent idea, Lord Ratcatcher. Perhaps other changes in perspective will offer more insight."

Mushroom, still seated on his mule, gave his partner a horrified look. Abruptly, Mold's eyes widened, and with a whistling intake of air he clapped both hands over his mouth. Mushroom shook his head as subtly as he dared, indicating that Mold should cease the display immediately, but it was too late. Ratcatcher stooped to pat his horse's head, then glanced back over his shoulder with a bemused expression.

"You really shouldn't do that sort of thing where I can see your reflection, my little friend. It's one of the more useful aspects of streams, I think. Now, do me the great and good favor of explaining that little performance. Please." He spoke the last word with an intonation that left no doubt that, if his polite request were not heeded, impolite ones would soon follow.

Mushroom slumped in the saddle. Mold scurried around behind his mule, risking a kick, and peered out over the saddle with frightened eyes. "Milord, I can explain," he started, but trailed off as Mushroom raised a cautionary hand.

"My brother is right," he said, shaking his head. "Other changes might make this place more recognizable to you, Lord Ratcatcher."

Ratcatcher set his lips in a thin smile. His voice was brittle with false cheer. "Well then, let's play a game. Suppose, for argument's sake, you told me what those changes might be. Then I could imagine them, and we could see if I'm clever enough to figure out what you're trying to hide from me."

Mold whimpered. Mushroom spared him a pitiless glance, then slipped out of the saddle and calmly led his mule to the waterside.""If milord Ratcatcher wishes, we could do that."

"Your lord does," Ratcatcher replied pointedly. "Tell me. Now."

With a sigh, Mushroom pointed to the sky. "Do you see clouds there?"

Ratcatcher's gaze followed the direction of his servant's finger. "None worth mentioning, except off to the north. The creek's low. I doubt they've had rain here in a week."

"Certainly." Mushroom's tone was flat. It was as if the least Ratcatcher could do, having forced the secret out of him, would be to do him the courtesy of paying attention while it was revealed.""If, however, you imagine this place at night, and smothered in rain, it may seem more familiar to you." He shrugged his round shoulders, and slumped within his tunic. "Then again, it may not."

Ratcatcher frowned. Rising from the water's edge, he turned in place, taking in the whole vista as quickly as he could. His mind's eye painted it over with the colors of night and washed it clean with rain. *Spring rain*, his memory told him, and he wondered why. It had been cold rain, though. He remembered that much, and remembered being miserable and damp inside his armor. The others had been laughing at him the whole time, he was sure of it, especially the prince....

He shook his head to clear it. "Nothing," he said stubbornly.""I can't remember."

"Of course, Lord Ratcatcher," Mushroom replied smoothly, his tone showing every awareness of the lie. His mule having finished drinking, he led it away from the bank. "Perhaps we could discuss the matter further, if you wish."

"No, no." Ratcatcher waved him off, and stared into the water. "That won't be necessary. We should make camp here, though."

"Here?" Mushroom peeked around the side of his mule. "But milord… why? We're close to the water, and if it rains, we could be flooded."

"And if we are flooded, I'll be sure to cling to you and your brother, and thus be assured of floating away," Ratcatcher snapped.""Now do it."

"Yes, milord," the two replied in resigned unison, and scurried about their tasks. Ratcatcher watched them go with no small degree of irritation, then turned away and stalked along the creekside. Old reeds crunched underfoot as he went, dry and brittle beneath his boots. A few insects, bold survivors of the late season, buzzed over the water's surface, but he paid them no heed.

Why was this place so damnably familiar? His mind cast back over his recent travels, searching. He had not stopped here with Wren on the journey south, nor had he passed this way alone. No, it had been when he had ridden forth with the Prince of Shadows, and the rest of the prince's entourage had gone with him. But when? Which journey?

"Damnation!" he bellowed, and turned on his heel to return to camp. Downstream, he could see Mold and Mushroom industriously laboring away, one fetching water from the creek and nearly falling in as he did so.

Nearly falling in…

A memory leaped to mind, unbidden. Ratcatcher, off his horse and weary, leading it carefully along the muddy riverbank. He was bringing up the rear, of course, and had spent the last dozen leagues staring at the southern end of

Pandeimos's northward-bound horse. The ground was slick and soft, and the progress of the column was slow. He'd argued with the prince that they should keep to the hilltops, but Sandheart, damn her eyes, had said something about lightning, and the prince had agreed with her. The prince had *always* agreed with her.

And so, her argument had won out, and they'd trudged along the creekside, when suddenly Ratcatcher felt the mud beneath his boots give way. The stream was not wide, but it was swollen with rain. In the dim light, it looked fast enough to carry him off. Desperately, he'd clutched at his horse's reins, hanging on for dear life as his feet slid off the bank and into the chilly water. The horse had snorted and shuffled its feet, straining against the sudden weight as it backed away from the stream.

Pandeimos had chosen precisely that moment to turn around. He'd seen Ratcatcher there, clinging with all his might to his horse's reins while his feet dragged in the swirling, muddy water, and he threw back his head and laughed. The others had stopped and turned, even as Ratcatcher found footing and extricated himself as quickly as he could from his predicament. The laughter had spread up the straggling chain of men and mounts as he'd stood there, shivering and defiant. Eventually the prince himself had come trotting back down the line to see Ratcatcher standing there, blinking in the rain.

"Why Ratcatcher," he had said mildly, ""are you delaying us *again*?" Pandeimos had bellowed anew with laughter at this, and the slap of the rebuke had twisted in Ratcatcher's gut like a hot iron knife. It had not been his fault, the other riders had worn away the bank he led his horse upon, he had not delayed anyone save by their damnable laughter… it was no use.

"No, my prince," was all he could say, and bowed his head.

"Good," the prince had noted with an approving nod.""I'd be irritated with you if you had. We've still got many miles to go before the next town. Hopefully they'll have some news of Talat's Howe. It's like we're chasing a ghost."

He'd chuckled at that as he walked off, and the others had chuckled dutifully after him. But Ratcatcher had simply stood there, hands clenched into fists, and swore that someday he'd have revenge on them all, after they found Talat's Howe.

"That's it," he whispered to himself, equal parts elated at the discovery and furious with himself at having been fooled for so long. "Of course."

Careful of the water's edge, he sprinted back into the rude, half-finished camp. The two servants had looked up at him, surprise on their faces. "My lord?" said one, quizzically. "Is everything well?"

"Of course it's well, you idiot, now that I know where you're taking me." He kicked over the pot full of water that sat beside the carefully constructed campfire. The water doused the flame with a hiss. "Pack it up. Pack it all up. We're leaving."

"But night is coming on!" protested Mold, as Mushroom carefully set the pot upright. "We've started making camp."

"Night does not bother me, nor should it bother you, my fellow servants of the Abyss. Now do as I say, or I'll leave you and your camp behind. I know where I'm going now."

"Do you, lord Ratcatcher?" Mushroom's smile was patronizing.

Ratcatcher smiled back."Talat's Howe," he said.

"Ah," said Mushroom, as Mold simply stared. "We should pack up the camp, then."

"Yes," Ratcatcher replied."Yes, you should."

Chapter Twenty-Seven

Every door in the village was shut, and every window barred. Yushuv passed through at dusk, when the bustle of suppertime should have had the village alight, and instead saw nothing. Even the animals were silent, herded into pens or tethered inside barns whose doors were tied shut with lengths of rope. The smoke from a few cookfires trailed from chimneys, but most of the houses were cheerless and quiet. Yushuv could not hear any children's voices raised in play; indeed, he could barely hear any voices at all. Those few whose tones carried beyond the heavy wooden doors were hushed and anxious.

Near the southern end of the village stood the ruins of a house, one which had been destroyed by fire. No effort had been made to finish the work the fire had begun, pulling down burned timbers or moving hearthstones. Instead, the few pieces of the home that still stood jutted up into the air like the teeth on a blackened skull. The houses around it had all been abandoned, and they showed the first signs of neglect. Here the doors gaped open, unafraid of the night.

Yushuv frowned. He remembered some new homes at the north end of the village when he'd entered, ones that had been built even more securely than the older ones that were still inhabited. Something had happened in the burned house, it seemed, something horrible enough that the entire village had made a concerted effort to wipe it from their collective memory. But still the remnants of the burned house stood, waiting for time and weather to finish what fire had started, and until they did the village would be afraid.

Overhead, the sky was growing dark. Yushuv stopped, and looked back at the village. The land here was wild, steep hills and mountain laurel, and it promised to get worse if he kept going. The path to the village had been bad enough, and he didn't relish the thought of attempting anything beyond it in the dark.

"Here it is, then," he said, and scanned the village. The houses were short and squat, each built like a miniature fortress. It was almost surprising that there was no palisade around the central compound, and Yushuv wondered at that. What he didn't wonder at, however, was how all of the windows seemed to face in on the central square. It would make for a murderous field of fire on any interloper, assuming the residents of the village could handle bows. Out here, Yushuv decided, they most probably could.

Another look overhead revealed the speed at which daylight was fading. Yushuv looked from house to house, selected one at random, and scurried to its doorstep. Its door was heavy wood, painted with sigils, presumably intended to protect those who dwelt within against evil. A faint smell of cooking drifted out under the door with the light from the hearthfire; faint sounds of worried discussion drifted out as well.

Yushuv knocked. Instantly, the voices were stilled and he could hear the telltale rasp of a blade being unsheathed. There were no voices, though, only an urgent hiss and then the explosive release of a long-held breath.

He knocked again. "Can I buy some supper and sleep in your stable?" he called through the door. Again, there was silence, and a sense of expectation.

Somewhere in the distance, something howled. It sounded a bit like a wolf, but not much. Yushuv hammered on the door again. "Please," he said. "It's getting dark out."

There was the scraping sound of furniture moving across a stone floor, and then a voice very near the other side of the door. "We know, boy—if boy is what you are. Someone else in this village opened their door in the dark once. No more. You can sleep in one of the houses down at the south end. Stay out of the burned one, or the ghosts will take you. You'll get food in the morning, if you're still here." Then there was silence.

Yushuv turned his back on the still-closed door. He hadn't expected anything else, really. Selecting the abandoned building furthest from the burned wreck, he peered in through the doorway. Cobwebs and not much more greeted his eye in the failing light, and, praying that there would be something that would pass for kindling, he passed inside. The door he closed behind himself, and nailed shut with the orichalcum dagger.

The place was small, he saw, but dry. Some wrecked furniture on the floor would serve for firewood if he was careful, and he put it in the hearth. Drawing on a tiny bit of the power within him—the first he had used since meeting Unforgiven Blossom—he set the wood alight, and it burned merrily. Then, his back to the wall and his face to the fire, he settled in for the night.

•　　•　　•

In the morning, when the cautious villager came, against his better judgment, bearing a bowl a gruel, Yushuv was long gone. "Good riddance," he muttered. "Things haven't been right around here since Bold Hare died." He walked back to his home, set down the gruel, and then set about rousing his neighbors. By sundown, the houses surrounding the burned wreck were gone, their timber hauled off to feed evening fires and their thatch scattered to the winds. The lone ruin, however, they left standing, as a reminder. Well satisfied with their labors, they went home to their own suppers and families, and thought no more of the stranger who'd passed through their midst. "The ghosts got him," some said, while others doubted he had existed at all.

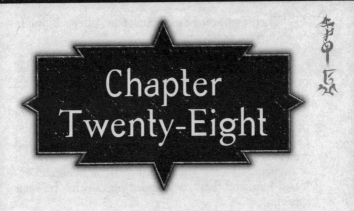

Chapter Twenty-Eight

Bonecrack did not wake Pelesh the Exchequer gently by anyone's standards save Bonecrack's own. With one swipe of his paw he tore asunder the tent the little man was sleeping in, the tearing of the fabric loud enough to rouse Pelesh from his slumbers.

"What?" he said groggily, sitting up from beneath the small mountain of blankets that served as his bed. He had no time to say anything else as the wolf spirit closed his jaws firmly over Pelesh's head and then, making some cursory effort to avoid doing undo damage, dragged him off into the night.

A few guards watched, their hands tight on their weapons, but they made no move to assist Pelesh, nor to threaten his abductor. "Do not interfere with his pleasures," the prince had warned them of Bonecrack, and they were only too happy to heed his words. Pelesh had never been popular among the prince's other servants in any case, and they were not necessarily sorry to see him go.

"We'll find what's left of him when we move out," the first guard said, sheathing her sword as she watched the spectacle.

"You will, maybe. I won't waste the effort looking," the second retorted. His partner snickered, and turned away.

"There's going to be screaming now," she said. "Just in case you were wondering."

• • •

There was, in fact, already screaming, although muffled by the spirit's huge maw. Pelesh had begun shrieking his panic the instant Bonecrack's jaws closed over his head, and did not stop. He screamed as Bonecrack dragged him out of the wreck of his tent, screamed as the spirit hauled him beyond the borders of the prince's encampment, and screamed more as he was bodily hauled off beyond any hint of firelight. He even screamed, briefly, as Bonecrack released him, and then backhanded him so that he went sprawling.

His mouth full of dust and his hands bloody from where they'd been dragged along the ground, Pelesh looked up. "Are you…" He paused and spat.""Are you going to kill me now?"

In response, Bonecrack batted him again, and again Pelesh went sprawling. "You've stopped screaming. That's good, for the moment. You're going to have to start again in a minute, though."

Pelesh hauled himself up to his knees. "You won't get the satisfaction from me."

Bonecrack chuffed laughter.""Please. You'd scream from a hangnail, let alone what I could do with you. Now be quiet."

"Fine." Pelesh crossed his arms across his chest and huddled there. The wind that blew over the grassland was chill, and he found himself thinking for a moment as to how he'd be able to repair his tent. Then his eyes caught Bonecrack's glowing red ones, and all thoughts save those concerned with immediate survival fled. "Just tell me what you want of me."

"I require your help in preventing your prince from getting himself killed. Is that enough to know?"

"Of course." Pelesh blinked.""But why not tell me back in the camp? Why…" He touched his neck gingerly. "Ah. The prince will not appreciate the help, I take it?"

"You're a clever little fellow." The wolf spirit sank down onto his haunches and regarded Pelesh through half-closed eyes. "And your prince is a bold one. Bold enough to get himself killed, perhaps, if he rushes in once we arrive at our destination."

"Where is that? You haven't told anyone where we're going."

Bonecrack growled with what Pelesh hoped was amusement.""Oh, your prince knows. He keeps his own council. He knows how dangerous the place is for his kind, and yet he's still willing to follow me there. It's fascinating."

Pelesh nodded. "So what do you want me to do?"

"When the time comes, delay him. A moment is all it will take, and it will save his life. And that, after all is what we humble servants wish, is it not?" The spirit's tone was mocking, and colder than the wind. Pelesh shivered.

"How will I know when to act?"

The great shaggy head nodded. "Oh, you will know. By all the spirits of river and field, you will know."

Pelesh nodded, and eased himself to his feet. Overhead, the thin crescent of a new moon gave him just enough light to see Bonecrack's bared yellow fangs, gleaming. His sleeping robe was tattered and dirty, and his legs and arms were marked with scrapes. A quick glance to the left and right told him that he had no idea where the ruins of his tent might be, though the trail the spirit had left dragging him offered a strong hint.

"What now?" he asked, afraid of the answer.""If you kill me, I can't delay the prince."

Bonecrack nodded, slowly. "True. But we can't have anyone back at the camp, least of all the prince, thinking you and I share a purpose. It would make things… awkward."

"There are other ways to do this, you know," Pelesh said, despairing.

"I know." Bonecrack smiled. "But this way will be more believable. And more fun."

• • •

With an elbow to the ribs, the first sentry jostled her companion. "Listen," she said, and pointed out in the direction in which Bonecrack had vanished.""Just like I told you."

Chapter Twenty-Nine

The first beams of the rising sun woke Eliezer Wren from an unpleasant slumber, and for that he was most thankful. He'd been dreaming that he'd been trying to roll the rocks away from Rhadanthos's tomb, but that each time he removed one, another rumbled back onto the heap. He could hear the water spirit beneath the cairn bellowing at him to hurry, but no matter what he did, the stones piled themselves up faster than he could remove them. Eventually, in desperation he took to hacking the stones apart with the daiklave, while the heavens bellowed disappointment in him for using it so unworthily.

He sat up, blinking, and realized that his back was wet, the fabric of his traveling garb soaked through. "Curious," he muttered. "I've been sleeping on high ground. There's no way..." Understanding dawned on him and he nodded to himself, once. Somehow, Rhadanthos knew he was there. The water had been an attempt to make contact, though what the spirit had been trying to say was beyond him.

Yawning, Wren set off down the rough hill he'd spend the night upon and looked for a reasonably clean pool of water to wash in and drink from. Bits of decomposing bodies from the previous night's swordplay littered the landscape, and reluctantly he decided to do something about that. As unhappy as he was with the notion of hauling and stacking the rotting flesh, the idea of drinking from water it had fouled was considerably less appealing. It would be a good morning's work, Wren decided, and then in the afternoon he could consider the question of how to start rolling rocks off of Rhadanthos's resting place. He glanced back over his shoulder, guiltily, at the daiklave, but shook his head at the notion. The warnings of dreams were not to be trifled with, he'd discovered, at least not that dream. The recent dreams he'd been having about women of his acquaintance, however, he felt he could safely discard.

Unenthused despite the necessity of his task, Wren stripped to the waist to avoid befouling his tunic with liquefying cadaver. He hung the shirt on a tree branch with the daiklave, then stooped down to the mud and retrieved the first few severed limbs that he could find. A hodgepodge of arms shorn off at the elbow and legs hacked off at the knee, they were dead weight in his arms. Staggering, he found the path they'd used while hauling dirt, and in a fit of inspiration dumped the pile in the middle of it. Grinning at his own cleverness, he turned around and repeated the process. The dead, for their part, didn't complain at the rough handling.

• • •

It took all of the morning, and a good portion of the afternoon, before Wren finished hauling the bodies to their resting place. He'd been forced to stop several times, either to cleanse himself of the foul muck that positively dripped from the bodies or to give his nostrils a rest from the up-close stench of decay. Pandeimos had proved problematic in the extreme, as well as time-consuming. He'd been forced to strip the man's armor off his weighty corpse, then haul the body off. He'd dumped most of the armor as well, though the helmet he'd kept. It looked as if it might make a useful makeshift shovel. The rest, however, was with its owner, and Wren felt that was good riddance. If he were particularly lucky, the local wolf population would feast on the dead bodies and drop dead of some rot-induced disease, but that was probably asking the Unconquered Sun for too much.

Sighing, he washed his hands in one of the puddles that rested where downstream ought to be, and considered his new problem. Much to his chagrin, the pile of stones had not gotten any smaller while he'd toiled around it.

Briefly, he tried digging out the mud around the pile, but quickly abandoned that approach. For one thing, anything he removed was quickly filled back in again, and for another, success would likely topple a significant portion of the pile on top of him. Neither outcome looked promising.

It would have to be, he decided wearily, done by hand. He'd pick at the smaller stones—the ones he could handle—and hope that the gaps he created would be enough to encourage the larger stones to tumble down on their own. It wasn't necessarily a good plan, but it was the best he could come up with at the moment.

He craned his neck back and looked up. The sun was already hurrying toward the horizon, and a rumble in Wren's belly reminded him that he hadn't eaten that day. He'd have to start trapping soon, he realized, if he didn't want to starve. There was enough food in his pack to last a few more days, however, and right now he had no great urge to wander far from Rhadanthos's mound. "Tomorrow," he muttered to himself, and made the weary climb to the top of the cairn. Selecting a rock the size of his head at random, he hefted it, and then threw it as far as he could, off to the east side of the hill. It hung in the air for a moment, then crashed into the mud with a satisfying thump. The crickets and frogs stopped their noise for a shocked instant when it hit, and then redoubled their efforts.

"Damn," Wren said. "I was hoping that would shut them up once and for all." He reached for another rock, grimly.

• • •

Wren had taken a good two feet off the top of the hill when he heard the child's voice behind him. "Why are you throwing rocks at the mud?" it said.

It was a boy's voice, high and clear, and it came from halfway up the side of the hill. Wren turned, a hunk of white stone the size of a money coffer still in his hands, and peered down at the one who'd spoken.

It was a boy, that much was clear, unless the Hundred Gods had taken to disguising themselves as ragamuffins. He was slender but well muscled, with dark hair and dark eyes. His hair was short, and it gave the appearance of having been cut by the boy himself, and without the aid of a mirror. A bow was slung across his back, along with a makeshift quiver and a small pack. Both his hands were empty, but a short blade was belted at his waist, and he moved like he had another weapon hidden, uncomfortably, somewhere inside his shirt.

He also, Wren noticed, had a strip of cloth tied around his forehead, just above his eyes. Unconsciously, Wren tugged his hat down lower with one hand, and took a step forward.

"That's an impolite question," he said, hefting the rock awkwardly. "You're supposed to assume that I'm older and wiser than you, and thus undoubtedly have a brilliant and sensible reason for hurling rocks into the mud of a swamp that never should have existed. Show some respect, boy."

The boy laughed at that, and Wren caught himself nodding. *At least he didn't get offended*, he thought.

"I've known too many who were older who weren't wiser," the boy replied, and continued picking his way up the slope. "Do you need help? Or can I just watch?"

Wren tossed the rock aside. It hit a puddle with a loud splash and an equally loud comment from an outraged puddle-dweller. Dusting his hands, the ex-priest gave a noncommittal shrug. "It depends, I suppose. Let me know who you are and what you're doing here, and then we'll see. I've had bad luck with strangers lately."

The boy surged up the last few bit of hillside without apparent effort. "Me too," he said sadly, and took in the view. "What's that?" he said, pointing off to the east.

"Talat's Howe," Wren replied before he realized what he was doing. He shook his head.

"You're safer here, believe me."

The boy's eyes met his, and suddenly Wren felt extremely uncomfortable. "I guess you're right," the child said.""My name is Yushuv. I'm looking for someone."

Unconquered Sun help me, not another one, Wren beseeched the heavens wordlessly. They made no reply, and so the former Immaculate found himself looking at the boy's face for any signs of dishonesty or, worse yet, any tendency to make Wren out as a potential foster father. Seeing none, he nodded slowly.

"I'm Eliezer Wren. I'm trying not to be found by anybody. How do you feel about moving rocks?"

The boy shrugged. "It'll do for the time being. Do you have any food? Otherwise, I can go out and hunt while you move the rocks." He gazed critically at the massive tumulus they both stood on. "Some of them are a bit large for me."

Wren found himself resisting the sudden, appalling urge to tousle the boy's hair. "You do that," he said. "Tonight, we'll talk about how to move big rocks in the morning. Just be careful out there. There's a big pile of dead bodies in the woods over there, just inside the tree line, and I expect it's starting to attract scavengers."

"I don't have anything to worry about from carrion birds," Yushuv said, and skipped off down the hill. Wren watched him go. The grace with which the boy readied his bow even as he bounced from rock to rock was uncanny.

"Exalted," Wren said to himself. His mind was suddenly full of questions that he had somehow failed to think of before inviting the boy to share his labors and campsite. Angry with himself, he kicked at a large stone, which obligingly tumbled down the slope. Even as he watched, the boy faded into the foliage, not at all far from where Pandeimos's body was moldering.

Wren shook his head. The boy wouldn't be gone long, and he had all night to get answers. And until he got those answers, he decided, he wasn't going to allow himself to sleep. The boy was undoubtedly trouble. It just remained to be seen for whom.

● ● ●

The meal was a good one, fat squirrels stuffed with some of the last of Wren's dried fruit and roasted over a small fire. Out of deference to Rhadanthos, Wren moved the campsite off the hill, just beyond where Pandeimos had dispatched himself. Fire, Wren felt, was not something the water spirit would appreciate.

Yushuv ate with fierce appetite, and Wren often caught himself simply watching the child as he attacked his portion. It was only after the boy had licked the grease from his fingers that Wren felt it was appropriate to ask his young guest some questions. Had he done so previously, he suspected he'd have gotten no answer but the gnashing of teeth and the sound of flesh being ripped off squirrelly bones.

He tossed a neatly cleaned bone onto the fire, and was rewarded when the cloud of sparks that shot skywards drew Yushuv's attention. "So," he said, "I was wondering about a few things."

Yushuv nodded, his eyes enormous in the firelight. "I was, too. You don't often find a man rolling rocks down a hill in the middle of nowhere."

"You don't often find a boy, even a boy with a bow, wandering around that same wilderness either. I think I'm owed something of an explanation as to what you're doing out here."

Yushuv looked down and into the fire. "I'll tell you my story if you tell me yours," he said slowly.

Mentally, Wren ran down the list of all the things he'd have to edit out of any tale he told the boy. The list was surprisingly long, and he found himself wondering if the story would make any sense without them. Still, he'd withstood the interrogation of golems, dead gods, and Chejop Kejak. Hiding details from one small boy, even one touched by the Unconquered Sun, couldn't be that difficult a task.

"All right," he said, and nodded. "You first."

Chapter Thirty

"There," Bonecrack said, pointing awkwardly with one paw. "Between those two hills is the pass we need to take. From there, our path should be easy."

The prince nodded. Pelesh nodded too, though more slowly. The respect for him among the soldiers had gone up a notch, but the wounds Bonecrack had given him were slow to heal. He shivered, and hugged himself tightly.

"What's through the pass," the prince asked languidly. "Any villages?"

"One, but it's barely worth mentioning." Bonecrack's voice was a snarl filled with recollection and hunger. "We could stop there if you like."

"No, no, unimportant." The prince waved the spirit off. "It's best that we get there fastest, don't you think?"

Bonecrack nodded, a string of drool dripping from his muzzle. "Oh, yes."

The prince waved and strode off. "I am so glad to see we agree," he said over his shoulder, then vanished into his tent. For the first time since the morning Bonecrack had awakened the exchequer, the two of them were alone.

"You're in a hurry, Bonecrack," Pelesh said mildly. The wolf spirit growled in reply.

"Yes. Look there. A track. One traveler." With a wolfish smile, he lowered his face to Pelesh's. "I smell the boy."

• • •

Something stirred outside the door to Chejop Kejak's chamber. It was not a large thing; a large creature would have been noticed and dispatched with ruthless efficiency. But it was small and kept to the shadows. It had been seen, but those who had seen it were judged weak and foolish, and so it had survived. And now it crept, ever so slowly, into Kejak's bedchamber.

The man himself was asleep, it saw. It paused to stroke its long, ratlike whiskers before advancing. Its pink, fleshy tail coiled on the wood of the floor once, then twice, and then the creature was moving as its claws scraped along the floor.

It crept up to the edge of his bed. Ever so slowly it advanced, barely daring to breathe. It had been born for this moment, created to do just this task. Kejak's throat lay inches from where it crouched. It could see now the faint hints of age that were inevitably catching up to the man. The wrinkles, the sagging flesh, the muscles that had lost the first hint of their magnificent tone—all of the evidence was there to see.

The creature's lips curled back, exposing sharp, yellowed teeth. Its red eyes gleamed with willful madness. For an instant it considered not going forward with its appointed duty. Time would soon enough render anything done or not done here today moot. But it was dutiful, after a fashion, and crept forward once again. Its first foot sank softly into the pillow by Kejak's head, and for a long moment it waited, terrified that the man would awaken. But Kejak did not awaken. His eyes stayed closed and his breathing remained regular, and after a dozen heartbeats that felt like a thousand, the creature took another step forward.

It was a single step too far. Like lightning, Kejak's hand closed around the beast. It squealed in terror and flailed frantically with its claws, but to no avail. Craning its neck as far as it could, it sank its fangs into the fleshy part of Kejak's thumb. Blood flowed, but Kejak neither loosened his grip nor dropped his prisoner.

"Well, well," he said, sitting up. "What have we here?" His grip tightened fractionally. "Another assassin? An omen? Or just another vermin trying to take a bite out of a sleepy old man?"

In response, the creature went limp. Kejak was not fooled. "I can feel your heart beating, you know," he said. "If you can speak, tell me who sent you. If not, prepare to have your brains dashed against the wall. The choice is yours." He stood, and in three strides was at the doorframe. "Last chance, little creature."

"Wait!" it squealed.

"Ah. You can talk. I thought you might. Excellent." Kejak peered into its eyes, and for the first time, it knew fear.

"I was not sent to kill you." The creature's voice was high and thin, grating like a flute played by an untalented child.

"You weren't, now, but you thought you might take the opportunity? I had wondered what was creeping around and frightening my acolytes, and I am very disappointed to find it's just a miserable little sending like you. Who sent you?" To punctuate his question, Kejak squeezed. The beast hissed explosively as he did so.

"Please! I cannot tell you!"

"Then I'll take the pleasure of feeling your ribs crack between my fingers." He paused for a moment, and thoughtfully added,""Prepare yourself."

"Wait!"

"Yes?" Kejak paused, arm in mid-swing.""Do you have something to say?"

"Only a warning." The creature could feel its ribs cracking. Forming words was a struggle now, and a red haze rimmed its vision. "I come… from the heavens. Many are… displeased… with you. Prepare to be judged for your works."

"Oh." said Kejak.""That." He clenched his fist convulsively, and the creature's back snapped in a half dozen places. Dropping the lifeless corpse to the floor, he examined the bite marks in his thumb. Painful, he finally decided, but not serious. It could wait.

He rang for his attendants. A slender acolyte with startling green eyes stood at his doorway almost instantly. "Yes, Excellency?"

"Dispose of this," Kejak said, and dropped the dead rat-thing in the boy's hands. The acolyte did not flinch, and Kejak noted this. *Good, very good,* he thought. *This one may have a use.* "And when you are finished with that, have my scrying chamber sealed."

"But Excellency," the boy said, shocked. "After all the effort to maintain it?"

"That's been rendered rather pointless now, trust me." He shook his hand absently, and drops of blood sprayed the room. "Do it. And bring me a bandage. It would seem that I am bleeding."

•   •   •

It was the carrion birds that finally lured her south. The day after she'd sent Holok by litter back toward the Isle, she'd seen the cloud, dozens of raitons and other flying vermin wheeling off in the distance. Too many for a single corpse, she'd thought, and sent a rider out to investigate. He'd found dead men in the livery of a servant of the Abyss, their bodies gnawed on by more than just crows.

The rider had also found clear evidence of a track leading away to the south and east, and offered his humble suggestion to T'fillit that they follow it. A chance, the man argued, to ambush one of the Prince of Shadows' patrols was a rare opportunity that must be seized.

T'fillit found herself agreeing. The Hunt had been exceptionally fruitless thus far, apart from the discovery of Holok, and her troops were becoming fractious. The chance to hunt down the servants of darkness was tempting, and it would give the seventh and eight sons gathered under her banner something to brag about back home.

Besides, she thought, killing that sort was always a good idea.

"South!" she called out to her heralds. "South!" they relayed the order to the rest of the camp. Tents came down.

Steeds were saddled. Servants ran too and fro, packing up goods or abandoning them in the hurry. "South!" went the cry from one end of the camp to another

T'fillit watched it all through narrowed eyes. "'South," she whispered, "and to the end of that trail, no matter where it goes. We *will* find you, my friends. Rest assured, we will."

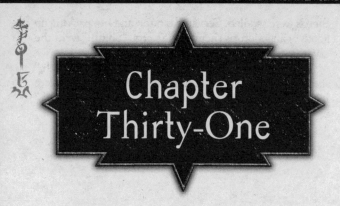

Chapter Thirty-One

"I believe I have something that belongs to you," Eliezer Wren had said when Yushuv finished his story. Originally he'd been planning to edit his adventures heavily, but the boy's tale caught him by surprise. It filled in gaps in what he had heard, made sense of many of the mysteries he'd experienced. And so, when it came his turn, he told Yushuv everything—about the Guild and the Order, about Talat's Howe and his capture by Ratcatcher, and even what happened beyond the door to the Underworld. Through it all, the boy sat there, occasionally offering a nod or an encouraging word, but never giving the slightest expression of disbelief.

For that, oddly enough, Wren found himself grateful.

When he finally finished, the former priest looked at his companion across the fire. "What do you think?" he said, not really expecting a response.

"I think you've done very well," Yushuv replied.

Wren laughed. "I've done very well. That's one way to put it, I suppose." Abruptly, his laughter died. "Wait here," he said, rising to his feet. Without another word, he walked off into the dark. Yushuv squatted by the fire, motionless, his eyes on the patch of darkness into which Wren had vanished.

When the former Immaculate returned, he was bearing the daiklave, which he set carefully on the ground in front of him. "It's a bit big for you, I think, but it never suited me. I'm glad to be rid of it, to be honest."

Reverently, Yushuv lifted it. "Is this…?" he asked, raising his eyes to meet Wren's. The man nodded.

"It is," he said. "I've been carrying it for you for a long time. It's seen some hard use, but I think none that was dishonorable." He blinked twice, then frowned.""I almost got the feeling it was glad for the work."

"I'm not surprised," Yushuv said softly.""Thank you."

"You're welcome," Wren said, and settled back onto his haunches. "I must confess, I had no idea how I was going to find you. My thought was to come here first and keep my word to Rhadanthos, then ask him for help."

Yushuv laughed.""And instead it's going to be the other way around."

"Hmm?" Wren looked up in surprise.

Nodding, Yushuv held the blade up so the firelight could play off it. "I think it's only right I help you free him. A water spirit helped me, after all. I think it's important somehow to keep the balance."

"Is that really it?" Wren's eyes held the boy's, and this time Yushuv looked away.

"It's part of it," he said. "It's most of it. Dace taught me to honor that sort of debt."

"What else did he teach you, Yushuv?" Wren eased himself to his feet. He'd felt something out beyond the firelight, something that made the hairs on the back of his neck stand on end. "Tell me quickly."

"Swordplay, the arts of war, hunting, honor, tactics— as much as I could learn." Then, more quietly,""And how to draw out my enemy by aiding those whom he has made war upon."

Wren, distracted, nodded. "I thought so."

"You feel it too." It was not a question.

"Yes. I don't know what it is, but it's in the trees near the bodies, and then again to the west a bit. Have you ever felt anything like this before?"

"I have," Yushuv said, putting an arrow to the string of his bow.""It's the Fair Folk."

•　　•　　•

They stayed like that through the night, backs to the fire and eyes on the darkness while the fey moved through the trees. They made no move to attack, nor did they retreat. Instead, they were a constant presence just beyond the firelight, daring Yushuv and Wren to come hunt them but offering no aggression themselves. For their part, the two Exalted stayed close by the fire, aware that they were silhouetting themselves but unwilling to offer battle in the darkness.

Just before dawn, the uneasy feeling vanished. A few mocking calls issued from the forest—calls of birds that Wren remembered from his youth, ones that had no business singing here—and then there was silence.

"They're gone," Yushuv said, and let the arrow slide from his bowstring. "I'm sure of it."

Wren yawned hugely.""Good. Get some sleep. I'll sit up and watch while you do."

"I can stay up," Yushuv protested. He started to add something, but a huge yawn overtook him, and he sat down, hard, on the dirt near the dying fire.

Wren chuckled.""I think you need it more than I do. One of the first tricks they teach you in the Immaculate Order is the art of staying awake for several days straight. You're supposed to do it in order to meditate upon one's insignificance in relation to the Elemental Dragons, but I've always found it more useful in avoiding being ambushed. So you go on and sleep. I'll be fine. Yushuv?" He looked down.

The boy was asleep, wrapped around his bow and snoring gently. Smiling, Wren took a blanket and draped it over the child's frame, then settled in to watch. "Apologies, my friend," he whispered to Rhadanthos, and then, with one eye on the sleeping boy, waited.

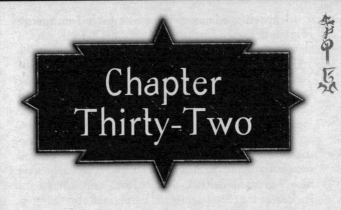

Chapter Thirty-Two

"I wonder where, in all these trees, Wren hid." Ratcatcher rode, slowly, through thick stands of pine and mountain laurel. Mold and Mushroom rode behind him, glancing uneasily from side to side as they went. Exposed tree roots here and there threatened to catch at the ankles of their mounts and slowed their progress to a crawl. More than once, Ratcatcher had been forced to hew down particularly persistent greenery that barred their way, and when he did so it felt like the whole forest shuddered.

"We could have gone around the wood, gracious one," Mold offered tentatively, but Ratcatcher waved him off.

"We're almost there," he said. "I can feel it." He urged his mount forward, carefully. It picked its way up a gentle slope and then, suddenly, broke through the treeline. Blinking, Ratcatcher reined it in and waited for his followers to catch up. He could hear them, huffing and puffing in the trees, and a momentary surge of disgust swelled up in his gut. What had he done, how far had he fallen to have servants like *these*?

The feeling passed, as it had the innumerable other times he'd felt it twist at his gut. To distract himself, he averted his eyes from the forest and instead looked out over the scene of his first humiliation at Wren's hands.

It had changed, he saw. The stream that had run through here was nothing more than a memory, and its sandy bed was slowly being colonized by grasses and weeds. But the path he and the others had taken was still there, and the route to Talat's Howe still led upstream. He could see it from where he was, a narrow track winding parallel to the empty creek, and he imagined what it must have been like for Wren to see the long column of armored figures go thundering by in the dark.

"Idiot." Ratcatcher pounded his fist onto his thigh. "Stop daydreaming. He was glad to see you go, and gladder you were walking into his little nest of traps. He probably stood here laughing himself sick." Irritated with himself, he turned back to see the two pudgy figures astride mules breaking out of the woods. "About damned time, you two!"

"My apologies, noble one," Mushroom wheezed, and Mold nodded agreement. "Shall we stop here?"

"No!" The answer came out sharper than Ratcatcher had intended, and the two servants shared a troubled look. "We're almost at the Howe. We'll stop there."

"As you say, lord Ratcatcher," Mold said doubtfully. Mushroom just nodded.

Ratcatcher didn't spare them another word. With a shout, he spurred his mount down towards the creekbed, and what lay beyond.

Mold and Mushroom watched him go. "It ends here, does it not?" Mold's tone was neutral, but his voice was leavened with despair.

"For some, brother. For some." Mushroom reached over and patted Mold's hand. "We have served our purpose. Take comfort in that."

"Every night, brother," Mold replied, but his voice cracked with fear. "We will die without his even knowing our names. This... bothers me."

Mushroom nodded sagely. "It is all part of the bargain. Now, let us ride. We cannot allow him to get too far ahead of us." A faint smile touched his flabby lips. "Without us, he might get hurt."

• • •

"Someone's coming."

Wren looked up from his labors, sweat pouring off him despite the chill of the day. He stood, once again stripped to the waist, and his hands rested on a massive boulder he was trying to roll down the side of the hill. With Yushuv's help, he'd made what he hoped was significant progress toward destroying the tumulus over Rhadanthos' prison. In their three days of work together, they'd settled into an unconscious rhythm. Wren would move the stones and tend to the camp, while Yushuv would hunt, assist and keep watch. Every night since he'd arrived Wren had felt the Fair Folk's presence, but they had made no attempt to come closer. "They're waiting for something," Yushuv had said, and Wren was inclined to agree.

Yushuv, for his part, sat on what was left of the slope, his bow on his knees and the remnants of a bored expression on his face. "Horses," he said. "Can you hear them?"

"Not with you talking," Wren snorted, but he ceased pushing at the rock and listened. "One horse," he corrected, "or something very much like it. Get on the other side of the hill."

"I can shoot better from here," Yushuv objected as he rose to his feet.

"We still don't know what you might be shooting at," Wren replied. "Come on."

Without waiting to see if he was followed, Wren dropped down behind the crest of the hill. Reluctantly, Yushuv followed, and hunkered down next to him. "He's getting close," the boy said.

"Or she," Wren corrected. "And he's got someone following him."

"Two someones," Yushuv said, a little stiffly.

"You're right." Wren nodded. "Good thing sound carries so well up the stream bed, otherwise, we'd never have heard them coming."

"Maybe *you* wouldn't." Yushuv sounded unconvinced. Wren opened his mouth to rebut his young companion, but Yushuv hushed him. "Here he comes."

Moving silently, Wren eased himself forward, his eyes barely cresting the top of the hill. The sound of hoofbeats was loud now, and getting closer. "Any second now," Wren whispered to himself, and found himself wishing for Yushuv's bow. "Any second."

And then the figure rode into view, and suddenly Eliezer Wren found himself wishing for something entirely different.

• • •

The smell struck Ratcatcher before the sound did. It was the scent of rotting plants and stagnant water, and considering the utterly dry state of the creekbed, it was something of a surprise.""What in all of the hells…" he said, and then nearly tumbled out of the saddle as his mount's front hooves sank into soft, wet mud. Barely catching himself, he dismounted under his own power and strode carefully forward. He sank in up to his ankles, the weight of his armor serving to press him a little deeper into the mud with each step.

Another half step convinced Ratcatcher that if he continued toward the strange mound in the center of the swamp, he'd sink long before he got there. As he didn't trust Mold and Mushroom to arrive in time to rescue him if he did, he carefully began backtracking toward where his mount waited, patiently. The shape of the Howe loomed off in the distance, reminding him of his real destination, and he suddenly wanted to be far away from this miserable, mysterious swamp. Glancing up at that odd central hill, he took a step back, and then another. Behind him, he could hear the sound of the servants' mules clomping along the path. In another moment, they would be here, he would be free of the swamp, and they could continue on their way. He thought about their arrival, red-faced and shifty eyed, and decided that he'd had enough. Enough of their sly glances, enough of their half-truths, enough of the game they were trying to play with him. It was over, and it was time they knew that.

Taking a deep breath so he could greet them with an appropriate bellow, he turned. He could see them, Mold looking pensive and Mushroom worried, and he relished the thought of the terrified looks that would soon be on their fat faces.

And then he saw Wren's shirt, hanging from the branch of a tree.

• • •

"Shoot, boy, shoot!" Wren hissed the command as he threw himself backwards. "Don't ask questions, just shoot!"

"Who is it?" Yushuv asked.

"It's your friend from the catacombs. Damn, damn, damn, where did I put Pandeimos' sword?" Wren looked at his hands helplessly, then reached down and picked up a fist-sized rock.

Yushuv's face curled into a mask of hatred. "He killed my father, you know," he said, and rose up, bow already drawn. Over the crest of the hill he saw the armored figure of Ratcatcher, recognizing instantly the man's arrogant carriage. A half second to aim was all it took, and then Yushuv loosed the arrow. Even as it sped through the air, his fingers were already closing on the fletching of the next one, pulling it from the quiver and aligning it on the bowstring.

"One arrow would almost be too fast," Yushuv said, and loosed again.

• • •

Perhaps it was the hum of a single loose feather in the fletching that alerted Ratcatcher. Then again, it may have been the whisper of the arrowhead slicing through the air, or the faint thrum of Yushuv's bowstring, or perhaps all three. Ratcatcher himself did not know, nor did he spend any time wondering.

Instead, in a single fluid motion he reached across his back and drew his sword, then whipped the blade down in front before his face. There was a split second where he could see his eyes reflected in the black sheen of the flat of the blade, and then it shuddered as the arrow hit. There was a sound like a temple chime, and splinters of wood exploded through the air. Wasting no time on surprise, Ratcatcher dropped the blade a handspan, and felt the shock of another arrow.

"Milord!" Mushroom shouted, riding hell for leather up the dried creekbed behind him. Mold followed a half-length behind, uttering a weird ululating cry.""Up there, on the hill!"

Ratcatcher grunted a reply, swinging to knock yet another arrow out of the air.""I see," he said, then paused as he watched an arrow arc over his head. Lifting his sword in challenge, he prepared to charge the rough hill when the sudden"*thwok* of an arrow hitting its target filled the air. He turned.

Mushroom sat there, a gray-feathered arrow protruding from his throat. He clutched at it frantically for a second, eyes bulging, then toppled slowly out of the saddle. "For… give… me…" he gurgled, and lay still.

For an instant, time seemed to stand still. All of the colors were too bright—the red fountain gushing from Mushroom's mouth, the defiant green of the plants low to the ground, the iridescent black of the mud. Sounds were too loud—Mold's anguished scream, the sound of his footfalls as he stumbled from his mule, the whirring of the arrow that even now flew towards its target. Ratcatcher blinked, and it took an eternity. Until this moment, none of it had seemed real. His unholy resurrection, the bumbling efforts of his two guides to lead him—all had seemed like a game. For the first time, he realized that he had not honestly expected the quest to lead anywhere, and that in an odd way he'd been content simply to meander without dead gods or live masters looking over his shoulder. But that was all gone now, and the battle was in deadly earnest.

All of this took less than a heartbeat, and then he was flinging himself sideways out of the saddle. He tumbled in midair and landed heavily on his feet, the sound of the impact masked by the heavy thumps of a trio of arrows plunging into his horse's flank. It screamed once, a horrible, thin sound, and then collapsed to the ground. Even as it fell, Ratcatcher was moving again, leaping high into the air as a series of shafts sped underneath him to impact in the mud.

For the first time, he could see his opponent. The figure that crouched on the top of the hill with drawn bow was tiny, fine boned and grim faced. Either a woman or a boy, it seemed; garbed in leather and furs, dark-haired and dark-eyed. A boy, he decided as he began his descent, sword held high for an overhand slash.

The boy looked up, eyes locking with Ratcatcher's. Naked hatred was there, and so was a terrible recognition.

Not a boy. The boy.

Ratcatcher felt his lips curling back in a savage grin. The wind whistled past his ears as he swooped down, a messenger of death from the heavens. The boy, the same boy he'd left for dead in the tunnels under Qut Toloc, stared up at him. The child's hand fumbled in his quiver for an arrow, but both he and Ratcatcher saw it would be too late. The first hint of fear blossomed in the boy's eyes and Ratcatcher began his swing.

And Eliezer Wren threw himself between sword and child, and knocked the boy away.

Yushuv hit the ground, arrows spilling out as he did so. He rolled down the slope, hands scrabbling for something to hang onto. Behind him, Wren twisted desperately in midair as Ratcatcher's blade came down. It missed him by a handbreadth, continuing down and cutting deep into the rock Yushuv had been standing on even as the man wielding it landed with a thunderous clatter. Wren's hands hit the ground first, and he tucked himself into a roll that somehow ended with him on his feet downslope, brow blazing with light and anima streaming out behind him.

Ratcatcher pulled his sword from the stone effortlessly and turned. Below him, the boy lay sprawled out on a pile of talus, his hands bloodied and his weapons scattered. A shirtless figure stood over him, crackling with light and his hands raised in one of the basic stances of the Immaculate martial arts. The figure's hair was ragged and his face drawn, but the silhouette he made was unmistakable.

"Eliezer Wren?" he whispered softly.

"Both of you in one place? Oh, this *is* going to be a good day after all."

"I wish I could say I was surprised," the former priest said grimly. To the boy, he added, "Yushuv, get the sword. Defend yourself if necessary, but leave him to me."

"He killed my father!" Yushuv's face was a mask of anguish as he climbed to his feet.

"He'll kill you, too. Get the damned sword. Defend yourself if he kills me, but otherwise, stay out of this. I owe him as much as you do."

"I can kill him," Yushuv insisted, clutching a bloody fistful of arrows.

"I know," Wren said softly. "It's what I'm afraid of."

Eyes downcast, Yushuv ran. Ratcatcher watched him go. "Very touching, Wren. I didn't know you knew the boy."

"You have a way of bringing people together," Wren replied, and shifted his feet infinitesimally.""Are you going to stay up there all night?"

"I thought I might make you come to me," the dead man, said, and twirled his blade. "I've learned a few things since the last time we faced each other, and this time Unforgiven Blossom's not here to save you."

Wren stooped, and took a pebble between two fingers. "You remember that fight differently than I do," he said lightly, and tossed the stone in the air. It tumbled, and came down in his palm. "I seem to recall Unforgiven Blossom not laying a finger on you while I was there, though I'm not surprised to hear she was unhappy with you for what you did to her orrery." He flipped the stone again and assumed a waiting pose.

"You're trying to buy time for the boy," Ratcatcher said flatly.""It won't work."

He raised the sword and, rather than charging, kicked at the stone his sword had sunk into. It split in half, and a chunk easily twice the size of a man rolled downhill at Wren. Smaller stones tumbled after, rattling and clattering down the slope.

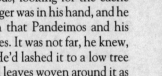

Wren dodged to the left, laughing. "That's the best you can do? Pandeimos put up more of a fight."

Ratcatcher's pale face reddened. "Never compare me to him. Never!" He kicked another stone, and Wren leapt over it, advancing up the hill.

"Earn it," Wren replied.

Ratcatcher gave a wordless howl of rage and dove forward, his sword seemingly drawing in the late afternoon light as it sliced through the air. Wren waited until the last minute, then slung the pebble in his hand sidearm at Ratcatcher's eyes. Involuntarily, the dead man's hands came up to block it, drawing the sword with it, and in that instant Wren launched himself, low. His shoulder hit Ratcatcher's knee, and then they were both falling.

• • •

Yushuv dashed into the woods, looking for the cache where he'd left the sword. The dagger was in his hand, and he followed it along the rough path that Pandeimos and his minions had hacked out of the trees. It was not far, he knew, just a couple of dozen feet back. He'd lashed it to a low tree branch with a bundle of sticks and leaves woven around it as camouflage. Wearing it while helping Wren had proven impractical, but he didn't want to simply toss it on the ground, so this had served as a compromise. Each night, well before sunset and the return of the watching Fair Folk, he'd retrieved it. Now, he cursed himself for having hidden it so well.

He came around the last curve before the tree he'd chosen as that day's hiding place, a lightning-scarred cedar with a trunk twice as thick as Wren's torso and a tangle of exposed roots surrounding it. The sword was bound with leather thongs to a broken-ended branch, high enough off the ground to be safe from animals but low enough that Yushuv could reach it.

Panting with exertion, he could see the tree now. Ducking inside its cloak of leaves, he took three fast steps clockwise around the trunk and looked up. The branch was there. The sword wasn't.

Yushuv gaped for a second, then leapt straight up in the air. He landed on the branch even as the sword whistled through the air where his head had been a second earlier. Looking down, he saw a sight that was almost comical. A fat little man stood there, sides heaving with exertion and the sword wobbling in his hands. His face was red, but there was implacable purpose in his small, pig-like eyes.

"You're looking for this, I think," the man said, and swung again, awkwardly and overhand. Yushuv sidestepped along the branch, but realized too late that he wasn't the man's target. Instead, the sword hewed through the thick wood itself, sending both tree limb and Yushuv tumbling to the ground. Somehow, Yushuv hit first and the branch landed on him, its weight knocking the wind out of him and pinning him to the ground.

The man looked down at him and nodded sadly. "You should stay there," he said. "You won't get hurt that way." Then he turned and ran off as fast as his thick legs could carry him, back toward where Wren and Ratcatcher were doing battle.

• • •

Ratcatcher's momentum carried him forward when Wren hit his knees, sending him airborne and down the hill. He landed hard on his right shoulder, and the shock of impact nearly tore his sword from his grip. Resisting the urge to tuck and roll, he instead spun so that he'd land on his belly, his sword slamming into the ground beside him. With a snarl he leapt to his feet, only to discover that Wren had flung himself back downhill, feet-first. Both of Wren's heels slammed into Ratcatcher's chest, and he went over backwards. His sword struck sparks from the stones as he slid downhill, even as Wren bounded after him.

He came to a stop at the bottom of the hill, feet in the air and sword firmly in his grasp. With a shout of rage, he forced himself into a flip, and came up five feet from the crumbling hill. Wren stood before him, hands weaving in an intricate dance of light. They regarded each other for a moment.

"We really should finish this in the Howe," Wren said lightly.

"So I could end up like that bitch Sandheart? Not likely," Ratcatcher sneered in return. "You killed Pandeimos, too, I see. Piling stones was about right for his talents. The prince should thank you for purging the fools from his retinue."

"Then he'll thank me even more when I've taken you down." Grinning, Wren feinted high and launched a short kick at Ratcatcher's knee. Ratcatcher avoided it easily and brought his sword up in a whistling arc that, had it connected, would have sheared off the top half of Wren's skull. Wren, however, was no longer there to receive Ratcatcher's benediction, having already dropped to a crouch as the sword screamed overhead.

"I'll be sure to remind your ghost you said that." With a grunt, Ratcatcher reversed his swing and brought the hilt down on top of Wren's head. The former priest saw it coming and tried to slide out of the way, but the pommel still caught him a glancing blow on the side of the head. He staggered back, helped along when Ratcatcher planted his foot in the man's chest and shoved.

Wren fell back against the base of the hill, blood trickling down his forehead. Ratcatcher reared up before him like a titan, sword held over his head. "Goodbye, Eliezer Wren," he said, and brought the sword down.

Wren tucked and rolled forward, somehow passing between Ratcatcher's legs. The sword came down behind him, biting deeply into stone and staying there. Ratcatcher cursed and tugged at it, but even as he did so Wren came to his feet and struck him a spinning blow to the back of the head. Ratcatcher sagged forward, only to be struck again, and stumbled. His fingers loosened their grip on his sword, and it slipped from his grasp. He half turned in an attempt to defend himself and Wren struck again, catching Ratcatcher on the jaw with a savage kick.

Ratcatcher retreated, shaking his head to clear it. Wren did not follow. Instead, he stopped and placed his hands on the hilt of Ratcatcher's sword. With only the barest visible effort, he tugged it from the rock. Ratcatcher lunged forward, but pulled up short when the tip of his own blade suddenly lined up with his throat.

"I think the advantage," Wren said, "is mine."

• • •

To say that Yushuv flung the branch aside would be inappropriate. Rather, it seemed to explode upwards, disintegrating into splinters as it flew. Tiny daggers of wood pierced trees and shredded leaves as they flew before settling back to earth as a haze of sawdust. Of the branch itself, there was no sign.

By the time the dust settled, Yushuv was gone. A few stray cracklings of energy marked his passage, lost bits of lightning flaring along tree trunks or snaking along the ground before finally guttering out. The sound of his footsteps faded as he sprinted towards the fray, his anima twisting and dancing behind him as the mark on his brow flared into new life.

Up ahead, a fat little man carrying a stolen sword heard the thunder of Yushuv's passage. For an instant, he looked back over his shoulder. Then, with new determination, he put his head down and ran like he had never run before.

• • •

"I think the fight will be fairer without this," Wren said as he tossed aside Ratcatcher's sword. The asp-headed blade clanged to rest among the rocks, point down. It quivered there for a moment, and Wren dusted his hands.

"I don't need that to kill you," Ratcatcher snarled. "Try more of your tricks; I've seen them all. I've seen things in the depths of the Underworld that you can't imagine."

Wren smiled without mirth. "Try me," he said, and leapt to the attack. Ratcatcher dodged his first leaping kick, ducking to the side and landing a solid blow from an armored fist to Wren's side. The former priest spun to earth, landing on the balls of his feet and bounding away even as Ratcatcher sought to press his advantage. Instead, the dead man's fist struck cold stone, splintering it into a thousand sharp-edged fragments. They rained against his armor, and as he turned away Wren landed an open-fisted punch to the side of his head. Ratcatcher stumbled back as Wren sought to press the advantage, raining blow after blow down on his opponent. Somehow, blindly, Ratcatcher parried them all, catching them on his bracers or taking the punishment on his forearms.

"You only… have to slip… once," Wren grunted as he struck again and again, each strike coming faster than the last.

"So do you." Abruptly, Ratcatcher let himself fall backwards, gambling his head wouldn't find a rock. Wren saw the maneuver too late, but he had already committed to the next blow and overbalanced for just an instant.

It was all the time Ratcatcher needed. With both legs, he kicked straight up. The impact caught Wren in the gut and flung him backwards. Even as Wren was landing, Ratcatcher sprang to his feet. "Armor's a useful thing at moments like these, Wren," he said, and stalked forward. A half dozen paces ahead, Wren hit the ground with a heavy thump.

Ratcatcher heard a low growl, and was surprised to discover that it came from his own throat. In two steps he reached Wren, and raised his fists for a crushing blow.

At the last instant, Wren rolled to the left. Ratcatcher's fists came down on the stone behind him, crushing it to powder even as Wren scissored the dead man's legs out from beneath him. Ratcatcher fell thunderously, arms flailing. More stones split as he landed, facedown, and Wren scrambled to his feet.

Before Ratcatcher could react, Wren brought his left heel down on his enemy's splayed hand. There was a sickening crunch, even through the metal of the gauntlet he wore, and Ratcatcher howled.

"Like that, Ratcatcher?" Wren's tone was grim as he raised his heel for another strike. "I thought you might like learning about pain for a change."

"The student should not presume to instruct the teacher." With his good hand, Ratcatcher dug a stone out of the muddy hillside and hurled it at Wren. The lapsed Immaculate ducked away from the throw, but Ratcatcher took the opportunity to roll downhill in an attempt to cut the legs out from under his opponent. Wren leapt straight up and over the tumbling Ratcatcher, but realized too late that his enemy's action had destabilized the entire hillside. He landed amidst a swarm of tumbling stones and sliding mud. For an instant he kept his balance, then slipped and fell.

Ratcatcher looked up as he rolled, giving a triumphant laugh as he saw Wren fall amidst the tumbling stones. Then his shoulder hit soft mud—*Wasn't this hill taller than this?* he wondered fleetingly—and the stones that had claimed Wren's footing also tumbled over him.

• • •

Mold ran. Behind him came death, implacable as a child's hatred, and so he ran. The daiklave was too long and too heavy for him to carry comfortably, so he had tucked it under his left arm as he went. His arms ached from the weight and his breath was short, but the sound of footsteps behind him banished any thoughts of rest from his mind.

At first he'd thought to steal the sword and bring it to Ratcatcher, but he'd somehow gotten turned around in the mazy windings of the wood. Now he found himself lost, scrambling along a path that vanished and reappeared at its own whim.

Up ahead, the path forked at a fat cedar stump that had been blasted by lightning. The stump was familiar—he was certain he'd passed it before—but he was just as certain that he'd not come to any forks in the path. "'There must be a great many cedars in this forest," he wheezed, and chose the left fork at random. It was the darker of the two paths, and scarcely any sunlight punched through the leafy canopy to illuminate it.

Two steps past the dead cedar, and the light vanished. Mold found himself in almost total darkness. He stumbled, barely catching himself in time against a tree branch and nearly dropping the daiklave in the process. He stopped, hands clutching his precious burden and his sides heaving.

"Easy there," he told himself. "Give yourself but a moment, and your eyes will adjust. Just a moment."

An arrow tore through the leaves just over his head, trailing a streamer of almost pure white flame. It thudded into a tree trunk less than a foot from where Mold stood and quivered before the flames consumed it. Smoldering bits of detritus dropped to the forest floor, where they sent up thin spirals of pungent smoke.

Mold stared at the spot where the arrow had impacted, his mouth open in a catfish look of surprise. "Oh," he said, and then screamed.

Another arrow whirred past, this one so close that he could feel the heat of its passage before it zipped off into the underbrush. Mold bit his tongue, then, to keep from screaming again. He could taste the odd, metallic flavor of blood in his mouth, could feel his muscles begging for permission to stiffen so that he couldn't move. The animal instinct to freeze in hopes that danger would ignore him was almost overwhelming.

Instead, he ran. Spotting the path dimly in the dark, he sprinted forward as best he could. His first footfall hit leaves, the second the dirt of the path, and the third hooked under a jutting tree root. With a high shriek, he fell forward, hands out to protect himself. The daiklave clattered to the ground as he pitched forward.

And as he fell, a dozen arrows screamed through the place where he had been.

The sudden realization struck Mold that had he not fallen, he would have been punctured in six different places, and he nearly sobbed with fear. Wide-eyed, he crawled forward, one hand at a time stretched out to reclaim the precious sword, while overhead a veritable storm of arrows whipped past.

."You can't hide from me forever!" The voice that called out those words was high pitched and young, yet steeped in menace. The last word coincided with another arrow, this one merely wickedly sharp, slamming into the bole of a tree a half dozen feet from where Mold huddled against the ground.

Oh yes I can, little boy, if I have to, Mold thought. His hand found the grip of the daiklave, and slowly, carefully, he lifted it up. "Don't shine," he whispered to it,""not here, don't shine." Much to his relief, no stray sunbeam peeked through the forest canopy to reflect from the weapon's golden blade. With infinite caution, he rose to a crouch and, tucking the daiklave back under his arm, slipped off the trail into the brush. The arrows came less frequently now, and Mold speculated that he was running out. That cheered him a little, and he pressed forward, even as the shouts of rage and frustration behind him grew louder. Up ahead, the forest was surprisingly lush for so late in the year, the shockingly green leaves of the shrubs and plants inviting him to take cover behind them. With a fearful glance back at the path, he stumbled into their embrace.

All around him was impossible greenery, so thick that light could scarcely penetrate. Trees rose up to impossible heights, heights he had not seen from the outside. Flowers bloomed at his feet, and climbing vines rendered everything ludicrously, unbelievably green.

"This can't be…." he said, letting the daiklave's point droop to the ground.

"You're right," said a voice, and a figure separated itself from the greenery. "It's not."

Mold did not have enough time to bring the daiklave up before the figure was upon him, but quite enough time to scream.

• • •

Yushuv stood, knee deep in dying ferns, and frowned. He'd found the fat little thief's trail easily enough. The man had taken a dozen steps toward the place where Yushuv had left Wren, then abruptly reversed field and plunged into the thickest part of the forest. He ran full tilt through brambles and old, desiccated briars, his headlong careening so cocksure that Yushuv for an instant thought the man had found a long lost path. But no, there was only greenery both living and dead, and the thief had burst through it like a stone from a siege engine.

Behind him, Yushuv heard the sounds of combat grow fainter. He'd stopped here, in large part because he didn't want to get too far away from Wren, and in part because he thought he'd seen the gleam of his daiklave up ahead. He'd loosed arrow after arrow in an attempt to bring down the thief, but the sound he longed for, the solid thwack of a shaft hitting flesh, never came. Warily, he let the bow drop the slightest bit, and scanned the woods from left to right. The trail ahead seemed obvious enough. There was no woodcraft to the fellow—a blind man could have followed the trace he left behind—but Yushuv found himself suddenly, unaccountably wary. The forest was dark and quiet, and Yushuv realized he'd been holding his breath. He let it out explosively, and stepped forward.

Then came the scream. It was brief, cut off after a second and replaced with a strangled, gurgling cry. A thunder of birds took flight from the branches above, startled into fleeing by the sound. Yushuv brought his bow back up, his arrow aimed straight for the clump of trees from which the sound had issued and the rest of him stock still. He waited.

After a few interminable seconds, the bushes rustled. "Come out," Yushuv said, and took a step forward. "Come out where I can see you."

The bushes a hundred feet ahead exploded outwards. It was the fat man, Yushuv saw, with the daiklave raised high over his head. Even at this distance, Yushuv could see that his eyes were mad.

The boy loosed his arrow. It took the thief in the chest, just below the breastbone. He staggered, looked down, and then charged again. Yushuv nodded, drew and fired. Another hit, and the fat man barely stumbled. Alarmed, Yushuv stepped back and fired again, hitting his target in the thigh. The man howled, tripped and fell, then rose again. Blood pumped from his wounds but still he came on. He was within thirty feet now, and still coming.

Yushuv reached back to his quiver and counted the arrows by feel. Six were left, and he had time to fire one before the staggering figure was on him. He could recover a few, perhaps, from the wood, but that was time spent away from Wren. There was nothing for it. He would have to end this now. Feeling the surge of his anima behind him, he drew an arrow and poured his energies into it. Crackling with power, it leapt from the bow, even as a shout of primal bloodlust tore itself from Yushuv's throat.

The arrow caught Mold in the throat with such force that it flung him backwards. He went down in the low brush, somehow still clutching the daiklave. His legs kicked, feebly, in the air as he struggled to right himself, struggled against the pain of the arrows that pierced him.

Yushuv drew his dagger and sprinted over to where his foe had fallen. The man lay on his back, hands clutching the sword possessively even as red foam flecked his lips. He looked up, and his eyes focused on Yushuv.

"Not for you," he whispered. "It was not supposed to be for you."

"Mine," said Yushuv, and took it from him.

A cry of loss rang out over the wood, and in the bushes and dark places, the Fair Folk echoed it with laughter.

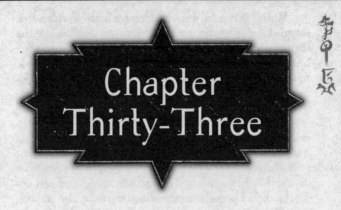

Chapter Thirty-Three

Stones geysered upwards as Ratcatcher freed himself from the rubble. Of Wren, there was no sign. Warily, he strode to the top of what was left of the hill and marveled at it. The peak from which Yushuv had fired on him was nearly gone, its boulders tumbled down and its earth scattered. It now was perhaps four feet high and twice that across.

A splashing sound caught his attention. He looked down, and was surprised to see a small spring bubbling from the top of the mound. A small pool had formed at the center of the tumulus, and from there a small rivulet tricked into the marsh. "Hunh," he said, and waggled one wet-soled boot. Drops of cold water flew from it.

"What in the name of the Abyss is water doing flowing uphill?" he wondered, and kicked at the pool. Water splashed out, but was almost instantly replaced. If anything the flow was faster now.

A shrill scream cut short Ratcatcher's ruminations. The sound came from the woods on the west bank of the river, the same woods into which he'd seen the boy disappear while he was engaged in dueling with Wren. A look of satisfaction crossed Ratcatcher's face. With luck, he thought, the sound meant that the boy was dealt with as well. Presenting the Prince of Shadows with one more trophy would simply be a matter of finding the body.

With a shrug, he went looking for both Wren and his sword. Of the former he could find no sign amidst the scattered stones and rapidly swelling pools, but the sword he could see. Miraculously, he could see it resting on its side in the mud, a few yards downstream. With a last cautious look around for Wren, he covered the distance to his blade in a few short strides.

Carefully, he lifted it out of the mud and wiped both sides of the blade on the grass. Already, he could feel cold water pooling around his ankles. A quick look told him that a small stream had formed, and was inching its way down the dry creekbed. A quick hop moved him onto marshy, if not dry, land, and from there he scanned the area. The mounts, at least, had demonstrated the good sense to get out of the way of the rising waters; he could see them grazing further downstream. Mushroom's body lay right in the course of the waters, and a cloud of mud swirled around him as he lay there. Even as he watched, Ratcatcher saw the waters slowly lift the corpse up and gently carry it downstream.

"My gracious lord."

The sound of Mold's voice was weak, barely carrying across the increasing gurgle of the waters. It took a moment's search and a repeated cry for Ratcatcher to locate his servant, and another moment to recognize him.

Mold stood across the shallow stream, at the entrance to the forest path. Broken arrows of various lengths protruded from his torso and legs, making him look like a poor and bloody hedgehog. Dried blood caked his lips and stained his garments, and thorns and brambles had torn his face. "My lord," he said again, weakly. "Please."

With a single leap, Ratcatcher bounded across the stream. "What happened?" he asked, sword drawn and eyes wary.

"I have failed you." Mold sank to his knees. "I just wanted to find you… to tell you…"

"Tell me what?" With quick strides, Ratcatcher was upon him. His hand found the garments at the man's throat and lifted him into the air. "How did you fail me?"

Mold's legs swung weakly. "Lord Ratcatcher... I am in such pain..."

"Then speak quickly, and I'll end it."

Mold looked into Ratcatcher's eyes with an expression comprised of equal parts pity and terror. "I took... the boy's sword. Took it from him. Tried to bring it to you."

Ratcatcher was taken aback. The boy's sword must be orichalcum, the companion piece to the dagger that had begun this so long ago. To think that it had nearly been in his grasp...

He shook his head. Nearly in his grasp meant that it was in someone else's. "What happened to it? How did you fail?" he demanded.

The dying man's face showed genuine confusion. "Lost... in the woods. Then he found me... took the sword from me. I am sorry. I am so sorry."

"He took it from you?" Furious, Ratcatcher flung his servant aside in disgust. Limp as a sack of flour, the man flew through the air, only to crash heavily against the ground. "Idiot! You had it in your grasp, and you got lost? I should have killed you and your brother when I first met you. You *lost* it, like it was a trinket for a fat man's whore." Still raging, he strode over to where Mold lay.

"Lord Ratcatcher," the man whispered, his voice a ruined croak. "There is... one more thing."

"Yes," Ratcatcher hissed, leaning in. "What"*else?*"

Mold grinned, revealing his blood-caked and misaligned teeth. "We both... hated you," he said, and with that, he died.

With a wordless roar, Ratcatcher brought his sword up over his head, then hewed down at Mold's corpse. It cut through flesh, fat and bone, sending a fountain of blood in the air. Still the dead man grinned up at him, though, and so he brought the sword down again. With a wet tearing sound, Mold's head half-severed from his neck, lolling gruesomely to one side as the thickening blood flowed down over the rocks. Again and again, the sword came up and swung down, until the corpse was unrecognizable.

Spatters of crimson marked the ground for yards around, mingled with gobbets of flesh and splinters of bone.

"You were supposed to fear me," Ratcatcher said sadly. "It's what good servants do."

• • •

Yushuv watched Ratcatcher from the cover of the trees. What the relationship had been between the dead man who'd stolen his sword and the rather more animated one currently defiling the first one's corpse was still unclear to him, but it was nothing he desired to learn more about. Reaching back, he felt the reassuring weight of the daiklave. His bow was in his hands, an arrow on the string, and he wondered if he should let it fly.

He was losing the light, he knew, and the possibility of fighting Ratcatcher in the dark was not one he relished. On the other hand, he knew that he might not ever have a better chance. The man was clearly exhausted and hurt, his energy at a low ebb. He leaned forward on his sword as if it were a staff now, and looked unlikely to be able to repeat the arrow-deflecting feats of earlier in the day.

But the memory of fear from the tunnels beneath Qut Toloc was still strong. Yushuv remembered being trapped there beneath the bones, remembered Ratcatcher's voice echoing through the tunnels. If he missed...

Not yet, he finally decided. Not until he knew what had happened to Wren. Certain that it was going to be a long vigil, he settled in, bow drawn, to watch.

• • •

The trickle of water in the streambed swirled around the feet of the Prince of Shadows' mount, then continued on its way. The prince himself leaned over in the saddle and looked down with some displeasure.

"This stream is no longer supposed to exist," he announced to the world with an air of general annoyance.""If Pandeimos has failed in the task I have set him, then he'll be buried alongside Wren's pet water spirit as a lesson in obedience. It shouldn't take him that long to rot away completely, I think, assuming the spirit doesn't deal with him first."

"Of course, my liege," Pelesh said reassuringly. "Though I think he would not dare to fail you."

"You're being sycophantic again. Stop it" The prince yawned hugely. "Go find out what the wolf is up to, and tell him we are getting impatient."

Obediently, Pelesh nodded and rode toward the front of the column. Bonecrack was there, ears flattened and fur bristling.

"The prince would like—" the Exchequer said, but got no further as the spirit turned its baleful gaze on him.

"I am well aware of what the prince would like. More so, perhaps, than he is himself. Go tell your master that what he seeks is very, very near. I smell the boy."

Pelesh nodded. "Is there anything else I should tell him? Should I ask him to alert the men?"

"The men won't matter," Bonecrack said brusquely. "But you can tell him that he may want to put on his armor. I smell blood here, too, and the death of dead men."

"Pandeimos?" Pelesh ventured. "Do you smell him?"

"I don't know what he'd smell like, but there's old rot in the air." Bonecrack paused. "And fresh meat. Now is the time, Pelesh. Delay him. Delay him as long as you can."

Pelesh stared at the wolf spirit, eyes wide. "Now?"

"Now!" Bonecrack roared, and swatted at Pelesh with one paw. The Exchequer scurried off, and Bonecrack watched him go. "Just delay him a minute, old man," the spirit said, "that's all I ask. And then the boy will be mine."

• • •

"Well?" T'fillit demanded. "How close are we?"

"Much closer, Revered Hunter of the Enemy," the tracker said from where he knelt on the ground. "These are a few hours old, no more. If you get off your horse, mind where you step. It's that fresh."

"They're moving more slowly than we are, then. Good." T'fillit's face showed grim satisfaction and little else.'

"And they don't know they're being followed."

"They're making a good pace, but ours is better," the tracker agreed. He was fair-haired and young, and wore only some well-seasoned leathers for clothes. The huntsmen mocked him, but T'fillit had discovered that no one among here company—least of all the arrogant noble children of the Isle—could be trusted to find a trail better than he could. "There are some strange prints mixed in there. Maybe that's slowing them down."

"What kind of tracks?"

"All sorts." The tracker shrugged. "Most are horses, or things like horses. There are a few with claws, one round set of prints I don't recognize at all, and something that looks like a wolf but can't be."

"Can't be?" T'fillit inquired softly. "And why, pray tell, is that?"

"Because they'd belong to a wolf the size of a beef cow, if not bigger, that's why." He stood and bowed, stiffly. "Do you want me to go on ahead?"

T'fillit pursed her lips. "No," she decided. "The way seems clear enough. Take point, but the Hunt rides now. All of the Hunt rides."

Chapter Thirty-Four

Another stone went tumbling into the water, and still there was no sign of Eliezer Wren. Ratcatcher spat in disgust, dusted his muddy hands ineffectively, and stared at the scattered mounds of stone. "If you're dead, you miserable bastard, you could at least have the decency to let me know where your corpse was. Better that I find it than the dogs."

There was no answer, not that he'd expected any. Muttering imprecations against Wren's ancestry and hypothetical descendants, he leaned his shoulder into a particularly hefty stone and pushed. It rocked forward, then stuck in the mud and stopped. Grunting with exertion, Ratcatcher shoved again, and again the stone rolled forward just enough to provide a hint of hope before grinding to a halt. He held it there for a minute, and was rewarded with the sensation of cold mud seeping into his boots.

"Blast!" Ratcatcher evaluated his position for a moment. All things considered, the rockfall had not been that large. There weren't too many places for Wren's body to be hidden, if it were still here. That being said, it made sense to leave no stone unturned, literally or figuratively. With a growl, Ratcatcher pushed again.

Something caught at his ankle and tugged. Ratcatcher had just enough time to look down and see the pale white arm reaching from underneath the stone. Then, with a shout, he was falling.

•　•　•

Yushuv heard Ratcatcher's cry and saw the man fall. *Wren's alive*, he thought, and a surge of relief washed over him. He eased to his feet, his muscles tensing to leap into the fray.

"Wait," a voice whispered, its words barely distinguishable from the wind.

Yushuv looked around in a panic. He could see no one, only the trees. Nothing moved in the forest save the breeze-stirred branches. No figures advanced, no shadows loomed.

"Wait," said the voice again, echoed by a dozen others.

Yushuv blinked. Suddenly, he could see shapes among the trees, shapes that terrified him. They could be misshapen branches, moved by the wind. They could be deadfalls and shadows, cloaks of leaves and bushes warped by the lack of sunlight.

Yushuv's blood ran cold. "The Fair Folk," he said softly.

"Yes," the voice said. "Wait, and we will wait with you."

•　•　•

"My prince!" Pelesh hurried toward the Prince of Shadows, who sat leisurely in the saddle. He wore his riding clothes, his armor having been stowed on one of the pack animals against the day's mild heat. His mace sat in his hand, and it caught the light as he hefted it this way and that.

"Yes?" The prince drew out the word, to make sure the full impact of his annoyance registered. "What did our friend have to say?"

"He suggested that you take the time to put on your armor, as there is some sort of conflict up ahead." Pelesh paused to pant a little bit. "He also said that he smelled blood."

"He did, did he? That's very interesting." The prince drummed his fingers against his saddle. "Alert the others. We go forward, now."

"But my liege, your armor!" Pelesh was shocked. "The chance of you getting hurt—"

"Is minimal," the prince responded. "Who can stand before me and my troops? And with our new ally, surely there is nothing in this place that can cause us harm. Ride!" He kicked his mount's flanks, and the beast reared up before dashing forward. Around him, the other men charged, chanting "The prince! The prince!" as they rode. A whirlwind of dust and spray rose up as they did, choking Pelesh and obscuring his vision. "My prince," he called out one last time, despairing, and then there was nothing but the sound of hooves clattering into the distance.

Shaking his head, Pelesh slid out of the saddle. "Go, boy," he whispered in his mount's ear. "Go far away." It took a few tentative steps, then trotted leisurely off downstream. Pelesh watched it go until it faded into the distance, then turned.

Snarling, Bonecrack stood in the thinning cloud. "I am not happy with you," the spirit said. "I am not happy at all."

•   •   •

Bonecrack faced Pelesh, who stood, shivering and defiant. A thin blade was in his fist, and he held it before him like a charm against evil. The others were long gone, having surged forward toward the sound of the fighting. Only the two of them remained.

"You did not delay him long enough," Bonecrack growled. "I am displeased."

"Of course you are," snapped Pelesh. "While I, personally, am ecstatic that he rushed into battle against an unknown foe without bothering to armor himself. It could be an ambush. It could be a—"

"Silence."

"No." Pelesh glared at the wolf spirit. "You be silent. The servants of the dead gods asked me to protect the prince. To see to his welfare. To make him ready for greatness. This," and he waved his hands, "is not greatness. This is a mistake. This needs to be corrected as soon as the prince deals with whatever ruckus is up ahead. And you, you should be thankful I'm here and not at the citadel. I have sources, you know, and powers that I can turn to.

We'd soon see who your real masters are. I do serve the prince, you know."

The spirit regarded him through narrowed eyes. "You are clever," Bonecrack said,""but you are not clever enough to say these things from a position of strength. You are not at the Prince of Shadows' citadel. You have no friends or allies here, no powers to call upon. And for my part, I am in league with the Fair Folk, who promised me a pretty toy in exchange for a young boy's heart. Your prince, fool that he is, is just a convenience. I allied myself with him so that he might feed me, and so that his surviving servants would eliminate any defenders the boy might have. I do not fear him. And you, my friend, you are now useless."

"The blade is poisoned," Pelesh warned.

"So's my heart," Bonecrack replied, and pounced.

•　　•　　•

Wren pulled Ratcatcher down, and then immediately wished he hadn't. The dead man was stronger than he was, and in the confined space under the rockfall brute strength was all that mattered. Once Ratcatcher stopped struggling and started trying to grapple him, the fight got very serious indeed.

What Wren did have, however, was cunning. Coated in mud, he slid from Ratcatcher's grasp and emerged from under the stone. Ratcatcher's face appeared behind him, and he gave it a swift kick before staggering off into the gathering dark. Behind him he could hear Ratcatcher scrabbling up from the hollow, and Wren found himself hoping that Yushuv had shown the sense to flee.

"Damn you, Wren!" the dead man called, and lurched forward. "You can't get away from me that easily!"

Rather than reply, Wren saved his breath for running. He'd been unconscious for some time, and had no idea what had transpired while he'd been under the pile of stones. What he did know, however, was that Ratcatcher was still apparently well enough to try to kill him, and that was enough.

He loped around behind the mound, cursing the softness of the mud. Water was everywhere now, and the ground sucked at his feet as he ran. *So much for moving silently*, he thought as he pulled one foot after another from the mire. *But at least Ratcatcher can't sneak up on me, either.*

Wren sighed. He felt drained, empty of power and strength. Hopefully, Ratcatcher was weakened as well, but that was nothing to wager on. He took a few more steps, then ducked behind a large boulder on his right. It would be, he decided, the best ambush point he'd find, and to spend too much more time searching for another one was just to invite trouble. He took up his position and tried to recall the Immaculate breathing techniques that had served him so well at moments like this. What he needed now was calm, and calm was the one thing that was escaping him.

Footsteps squelched on the mud nearby. Wren froze into a crouch. The footsteps slowed as Ratcatcher approached, perhaps scenting the trap. Wren bit his lip and willed himself to be still. *Another step*, he found himself mentally pleading Ratcatcher. *Just one more step.*

Ratcatcher strode forward. His sword was out, his helm was off and his armor was muddy. He stood there for a moment, then slowly turned to the left, scanning the marsh for his enemy.

Never in his life had Wren wished so devoutly for a rock in his hand. None was within reach, however, so he contented himself with leaping down upon his foe, silently.

At the last moment, Ratcatcher, warned by some whisper of sound, half turned. Unable to get his blade around in time, he still managed to bring up his elbow, and what Wren had planned as an elegant attack became an ugly collision of bodies. The two tumbled down onto the ground, Wren pummeling Ratcatcher's face even as the dead man struggled to bring his sword to bear. They rolled together in the muck, each striking at the other as best he could, and then Ratcatcher slammed the two of them against the rock Wren had used for concealment. A resounding clang rang out as Ratcatcher's armor hit the stone, but Wren's shoulder had no such protection. At the shock of the impact, his entire arm went numb.

With a sinking feeling, Wren realized it was dislocated. Fighting a rising panic, he dropped his good elbow onto his enemy's throat as hard as he could, then tore himself from Ratcatcher's grasp. The two foes separated and slowly rose to their feet.

"This is where it ends," Ratcatcher said, his sword cutting the air in intricate shapes.

"Yes," replied Wren, and prepared himself for the final assault.

• • •

Bonecrack bounded past the prince, his muzzle bloody. He easily overtook the prince's riders, even the swiftest, and he howled as he ran. "Mine!" he called out, "mine!"

"Damned fool," the prince muttered, and whipped his mount's flank with the flat of his hand. "Let's see what he's so interested in keeping for himself, shall we, Pelesh?" he called.

There was no response. "Pelesh!" the prince shouted, more urgently, and looked both left and right. Again there was no response, and a nagging worry rose in the prince's mind.

There was blood on Bonecrack's lips, he realized. *And the rest is no doubt on the ground.*

Suddenly, irrationally, he felt the desire for vengeance. "I did not give *him* to you," the prince shouted.""Bonecrack! A price will be paid!"

And with his men bellowing war cries behind him, the Prince of Shadows rode into the marsh that marked Rhadanthos's tomb, and found nothing.

• • •

Ignoring anything else, Bonecrack charged up the stream. He pounded through the rapidly shrinking marsh, sniffed the air once, and then turned to face the forest. "There you are," he said, and sprang forward once again.

The spirit burst through the screen of trees and leapt straight for Yushuv. "I have you, boy," he bellowed, heavy branches crashing to earth before him.

Yushuv raised his aim and fired as Bonecrack leapt towards him. The arrow sped through the air and took the wolf in the throat. Bonecrack's threats turned to a long howl, but he kept coming, crashing through the underbrush and leaping forward. Even as Yushuv fell back, he was firing again.

The wolf spirit roared, and Yushuv's arrow flew straight into his open mouth. "Talk less and fight more," Yushuv catcalled. Bonecrack waggled his head back and forth in an effort to dislodge the arrow stuck in his palate, then abandoned the idea and closed his jaws with an arrow-splintering snap.

"You should run more and fight less," the spirit retorted. "It might keep you alive longer." Even as Bonecrack spoke, he pounced. Yushuv dove forward, going underneath the massive wolf, but even as he came to his feet Bonecrack had landed and turned. "You can't pull that stunt too many more times, boy," Bonecrack growled. "Old dogs learn better than you'd think."

"You should have learned to stop following me, then," Yushuv replied, and drew another arrow. Bonecrack's fur bristled and he snarled, coiling himself for another leap.

"Enough." The voice came from everywhere and nowhere, and it echoed from every tree.

Yushuv and Bonecrack both froze. "Who said that?" the spirit asked, his head swaying from side to side and his eyes narrowed with suspicion.

"You know who," Yushuv replied, his hands steady and his arrow still sighted on Bonecrack's good eye. "You told me you worked for them."

"Them? Here?" Bonecrack's ears flattened against his skull. "Show yourselves!" he demanded.

"We are here," the voice replied, and abruptly the wood was full of shapes. They were green or brown or dying-leaf gold, and bent like old, weathered wood. Their eyes were yellow and their fingers were long, and it was impossible for Yushuv to tell where their skins ended and their garments—if they wore garments at all—began. "Enough," one of them—or perhaps all of them—said again.

"The boy is mine," Bonecrack snarled. "You cannot gainsay me this!"

"We do what we please," came the reply.""There is no point to your hunt any longer."

"No point?" The spirit's voice rose to an ear-splitting shriek.""He is here! He is mine!"

"He can destroy you," the Fair Folk replied sadly, "and you him. You are evenly matched, now. You've taken too long, Bonecrack. He is too powerful, and suits our purposes better alive than dead. Attempting to destroy him would rid us of two useful servants."

"I'm not your servant," Yushuv spat.

"You will be," came the unperturbed response. "As our brother told you, one way or another you will be."

"No," Yushuv said. "I'll die first."

"Life is sweet, Yushuv. You know that already. And this is the last you will see of us, unless you wish it." One of the figures looked over at Bonecrack with a look of something approaching affection.""Help him, Bonecrack. For the moment. Then you are free for a hundred years."

Bonecrack looked back and forth from the elf to Yushuv, hatred in his eyes.""You cannot be serious," he hissed. "I want his blood."

"The Prince of Shadows will have yours unless you help him. The choice is yours." And with that, the Fair Folk faded back into the forest. In seconds, it was as if they had never been there.

Yushuv looked at Bonecrack. Bonecrack looked back at him. "Someday, boy, I'll have your heart."

"Perhaps. But not today."

The wolf shook his head. "No. Not today." He cocked his head to one side.""Listen. Do you hear hooves?"

•   •   •

They leapt out of the wood together, the spirit and the boy. Yushuv emptied his quiver within seconds, the arrows trailing streaks of light as they took one after another of the prince's men out of the saddle. Bonecrack's approach was more direct, as he leapt upon the nearest rider in the prince's livery and tore the man limb from limb. He turned and leapt for another one, but found the prince in his way.

"I thought you were better trained," the prince said mildly, and swung his mace. Bonecrack dodged, only just, and the prince caught him with a savage backhanded blow. Where the prince's mace struck Bonecrack felt his flesh sear with cold, and he backed away with new respect for his opponent.

"You don't want to play?" The prince brought his weapon up over his head.""And here I thought you were such a *bad* spirit. Idiot. I've been waiting for this."

"And I've been waiting for this!" Bonecrack hurled himself at the prince, who brought the mace down on the top of the wolf spirit's skull. Bonecrack crashed to earth, his eyes unfocused and his fur matted with blood. He attempted to rise, but the prince struck again, and the crunch of bone could be heard even over the din of the battle.

"The boy... is still mine," Bonecrack said, and sank down into darkness.

• • •

Yushuv heard Bonecrack's last, despairing howl, and knew what it meant. He was heavily outnumbered and out of arrows, and now the Prince of Shadows was riding towards him with blood in his eye.

The prudent course, Yushuv decided, was to run. Concentrating for a moment, he filled the daiklave with something that was half Essence, half hope, and flung it at his foes. Then, before it could strike even one of them, he turned and ran.

The blade sailed into the nearest of the prince's soldiers and took an arm from him, then boomeranged to the next and then the next. Men dove from their saddles as the blade whirred through the air, and panicked mounts fled in terror. When a half dozen men had been struck down, the blade sailed off after the boy, and left a rain of crimson behind as it did.

The prince watched it all impassively, then let himself down from his saddle. "I am going after the boy," he said. "None of you should do so. You're too much trouble to replace." He looked around. "Defend this place against any who try to take it. I shall be back shortly, with a new sword."

So saying, he sprinted after Yushuv.

It was not lost on the prince, as he followed the trail, that Yushuv had instinctively headed for higher ground. Here, higher ground meant Talat's Howe.

"It comes full circle, then," the prince told the uncaring wind. "And this time, one of the Unconquered Sun's children dies."

•　　•　　•

Bonecrack roused himself to find a circle of the Prince of Shadows' men staring at him, weapons drawn. "You did not attempt anything foolish," he growled, hoping he could keep the dizziness that afflicted him out of his voice.""That was wise. Stand aside." He pushed himself to his feet.

One of the prince's men, bolder or perhaps more foolish than the rest, stepped forward. "We should kill it here and now," he exhorted his comrades. "It attacked the prince."

"I attacked the prince and lived," Bonecrack corrected. "Do any of the rest of you feel like making another attempt?"

There was silence, as the men looked from one to the other, or down at the ground. Then, majestically, an opening appeared in the circle. "Go," the ringleader said bitterly. "Go now, before I can make them change their minds."

Bonecrack said nothing. He merely chuckled wolfishly as he strolled out of the circle of his captors, then trotted leisurely across the stream and into the woods on the far side. He howled, once, and then he was gone.

Most of the prince's men agreed that this was a very good thing.

Chapter Thirty-Five

The prince caught him at the top of the hill.

They faced each other across the field of broken stone that marked the top of Talat's Howe.

The prince's mace was in his hand, and he twirled it as easily as he might spin a child's toy. His stance was loose and limber, and he was smiling. "You don't know what you're facing, little sun child," he called mockingly. "Go away. Train for a few decades. Learn what hate really means. Then you can come see me, and perhaps we'll have a duel."

"I've learned enough," Yushuv replied, his voice even. The daiklave was light in his hands, and it reflected the pale starlight as if it were the noonday sun. He advanced, cautiously.

"Idiot boy," the prince said. "Someone trained you poorly." He flung his left hand forward and dark light flared out behind him. A bolt of violet lightning leaped from the palm of his hand and struck the stones at Yushuv's feet, exploding them up in a blizzard of sharp fragments. Yushuv cried out as the slivers scored his face and hands, his left arm flying up to cover his eyes.

"You should have been expecting that," the prince continued, and struck again. The ground in front of Yushuv blossomed upwards with a sound like thunder, and the boy took a staggering step back.""You can't do anything to me, you know. This little charade goes on as long as I want it to, and then it ends." The prince laughed then, and raised his hand for another strike.

Anticipating the shock, Yushuv threw himself to his left. His hand found the dagger at his waist, even as another explosion kicked up dirt and stone where he'd been standing seconds before. He flung the dagger forward in desperation, then leapt forward after it. The cloak of his anima rose up behind him, making him appear as a phoenix swooping in upon its prey.

It may have been the sight of Yushuv's power revealed that distracted the prince, or perhaps the sound of his battle cry. In either case, for an instant the prince's eyes flicked upward, and in that moment the dagger caught him in the belly.

It was a weak cast, and the wound was not deep, but the pain of it shocked the prince. He stumbled back, one hand dropping to his gut as the other raised the mace before him.

Yushuv's daiklave came down like thunder, all the force the boy could muster behind it. The blade met the mace with a sound like the collapse of a mountain. Metal ground against metal for a long instant, then the prince went over backwards. Light exploded from his fingertips, and then suddenly he was falling backwards, down into the dark of a cavern that had not been there a second before.

Yushuv stared for a second, his gaze on the ragged hole that had appeared where the prince's blasting fire had touched the Howe. A dim light, the color of the power that served the prince as a cloak, emanated from the pit and filled the twilight. No sound could be heard from the pit, and the air that flowed from it was as stale and as cold as death.

Behind him, in the distance, Yushuv could hear horns blowing. They were loud and raucous, the horns of hunters who have found their prey. Faintly, the sounds of battle filled the air.

"Wren told me this was a tomb," he muttered, and leapt down. In the darkness, the Prince of Shadows was waiting for him.

•　　•　　•

Water splashed around the hooves of the Wyld Hunt's mounts as they charged up the stream. Battle-horns were blown, one after another in a cacophony of bloodlust and joy. The Prince of Shadows had left two sentries behind him to guard his rear; these were swept away like chaff as the Hunt rode upon them. T'fillit herself beheaded one; a grim Peleps Tonot took the other with a sword to the eye. Before the bodies slumped to the ground, the Hunt rode past them, and turned the final bend toward the place where Rhadanthos rested.

The prince's men were not fools. At the first sound of the horns, they had fallen back into the depths of the unnatural marsh, the better to take away the enemy's advantage of cavalry. They peered out from behind positions among the rocks Ratcatcher's wrath had shattered. Here and there, some glowed with power as they marshaled their Essence for the coming fight; arrowheads and spearpoints caught the colors of the approaching riders' animas and reflected them back like a rainbow of steel. Behind them, the remnants of the mound loomed up, and they chanted their lord and master's name as if it were a talisman against the light.

T'fillit saw this as she led the charge around the bend, and for an instant the Hunt faltered. The charge slowed, the cries of the horns grew less certain. She could feel the momentum ebbing away, could see the cost in blood of the coming fight.

Her face set into a grim smile. "Kill them," she said softly. "Kill them," she repeated louder, her voice a commander's once again. "Kill them all!"

Like a single hound held too long at the leash, the Wyld Hunt charged forward.

•   •   •

The impact of the Wyld Hunt's crash into the defenders' position was enough to shake the earth, but Ratcatcher didn't care. He stood, blade out and face bloody, halfway between the hill and the Howe, and Eliezer Wren stood before him.

"You're not going to help him," Wren said grimly. His lips were bloody, Ratcatcher could see, and his left arm hung useless at his side. A gash crossed Wren's forehead, nearly obliterating the pulsing sunmark that rested there. "I'm not going to let you."

"You don't have much choice in the matter any more." Ratcatcher's blade flicked out, and Wren barely spun away from it. "You're hurt. Tired. Slow." He tried a quick thrust, and Wren dodged it clumsily.

"Alive, which is more than I can say for you," Wren replied. He tried a leaping kick, but Ratcatcher swatted him out of the air with the flat of his blade, then drove the point down at Wren's head. Wren rolled to the side just in time.

"Not for much longer," Ratcatcher laughed.'"Idli's waiting for you, you know. I don't intend to disappoint him." Another overhand swipe cut the mud where Wren had been an instant before, and it stuck fast.

Wren saw his opportunity. He threw himself forward, inside Ratcatcher's guard. Even as the blade came up out of the muck, Wren was on his opponent, his fist drawn back for a blow at Ratcatcher's unprotected throat. Ratcatcher's eyes widened, and Wren saw fear there. He yelled in triumph, a wild, wordless cry.

Too late, he realized that Ratcatcher was smiling. He slammed into the dead man, and a sudden, tearing pain ripped through his gut. Looking down, he realized that only one hand was on the serpent-bladed sword. The other was on a short parrying dagger, which Ratcatcher held blade-out at his belt. The hilt was plain and lacquered black, Wren noticed; the blade was sunk into his belly.

"Miscalculated, didn't you, Wren?" Ratcatcher asked, and gave the dagger a twist. Wren gasped in pain and tried to pull himself free, but Ratcatcher dropped the sword and held his enemy to him. "You're not going anywhere."

"Bastard," Wren gasped, and shuddered.'"I'll still kill you."

"I don't think so," Ratcatcher replied.'"I, however, am going to kill you, and I'm going to take my time finishing the job." He yanked the dagger upwards and felt the hot gout of blood that spouted from Wren's torn gut. "That was for escaping the prince's dungeon." Wren could only whimper wordlessly. Ratcatcher tugged the blade left until it scraped against bone.""And that is for our little duel on the orrery. It hurts, doesn't it? Let's see how many more humiliations I can remember."

Wren tried to scream, but his throat was flooded with blood and bile. All he could see was Ratcatcher's face, rimmed in a red haze. The pain was unbelievable, as if someone had stuffed his belly with hot coals and then stoked the flames.

Flames…

An image of fire filled his mind, of tongues of flame as hot as the sun, and he took refuge among them. The flames would keep him safe. The flames would shelter him. The flames would give him vengeance.

Somehow, he found the strength to move his right hand. Weakly, he raised it to Ratcatcher's throat. The dead man felt his touch and laughed. "You can't choke a dead man, Wren," he said. "Don't waste your strength trying."

"I won't," Wren gasped, and shut his eyes. He saw nothing but flames now, and in the middle of them he imagined Ratcatcher's face. In his mind's eye, he saw the handsome features running and melting like wax, the flesh underneath crisping like pork on the spit. The heat built up inside him, the pain from his ruined belly spreading to every inch of his being.

"Burn," he whispered, and let the power go.

Ratcatcher's face exploded into flames. With a shriek, he staggered back, his head wreathed in incandescent tongues of fire the color of the sun. He howled his agony and dropped to his knees, even as the proud shape of his armor melted away. His arms were burning now, too, and through the scent of his own blood Wren could smell the nightmarish odor of burning flesh.

"No more," Wren said softly, and toppled forward. His cheek rested in a puddle of cool water, and it was somehow soothing. All of the pain had gone away, and he suddenly lacked the strength to hold his eyes open. A sudden warmth spread through him, as if he were resting in a meadow beneath the summer sun, and with his last strength he smiled.

So this is dying, he thought. No more errands for Eliezer Wren. And then, *I'm sorry, Rhadanthos. One debt left unpaid.*

And with that thought, Eliezer Wren died.

•   •   •

Ratcatcher did not see Eliezer Wren fall. His eyes blinded by flame, he pounded the ground in his agony. Mud baked to clay at his touch, and puddles steamed away at his glance. "Water," he howled. "For the love of the Abyss, fetch me water!"

A shadow fell across him. He turned, but could see nothing other than a blurry shape. "You seek water?" a deep voice said.

"Dead gods, yes," Ratcatcher begged. "Please."

"You'll have water enough, I think," said Rhadanthos, and brought his fists down.

Chapter Thirty-Six

The darkness turned to day as Yushuv fell, and the inside of Talat's Howe was lit by the colors of flame.

He landed on the stone floor and immediately threw himself forward. Behind him, he heard the whistle of the Prince of Shadows' mace cutting the air, and then the sickening crunch of it shattering the flagstones. "You can't run in here!" the prince roared, and raised the mace as he leapt after Yushuv.

The Howe was larger inside than he expected, Yushuv noted with a start. He could see a pair of corridors leading off from the pillared chamber in which he stood, and he guessed that an equal number lay behind him. The stonework was simple but elegantly done, and the pale stone seemed to drink in the light from his anima. But the floor was littered with wreckage, and great hunks of stone torn from the walls littered the floor.

All this he saw in only a second, and then Yushuv was in motion again. The prince's mace hummed past his ear, and he dodged forward. Wrapping one hand around a pillar, he swung around until he was facing the prince dead on.

He stood there for a moment, his weapon halfway through a swing and his shadow monstrous behind him. His fist was bunched in his stomach, Yushuv's dagger turned and clenched between his fingers. Slow drops of blood fell to the floor, one at a time. "Come to me, boy," he hissed. "No fair hiding among the pillars."

"I think I like where I stand right now," the boy replied. "Or are you afraid to face me?"

"Stupid boy. Before this ends, I'll teach you what it means to be afraid." He feinted forward, and Yushuv flinched back. A delighted snicker burst from the prince's lips. "Oh, that was very good, very brave. Shall we try again?" Again he feigned a swing, and again Yushuv took a half step back.

A tiny click registered at the edge of his consciousness, and Yushuv threw himself to the floor. A dart whirred overhead, its tip smeared with a vicious-looking unguent. It slammed against the wall behind where Yushuv had been standing and fell to the floor, even as the boy slid away from it.

"Oh, did I forget to mention that?" The prince advanced now, all playfulness gone. "Your friend Eliezer Wren thought it might be amusing to litter this place with booby traps the last time he came here. They're all lethal, as someone very dear to me found out. You might want to watch out for them. I thought I'd gotten them all the last time I was here, but it seems I was mistaken." He swung, and the impact of his blow cracked a pillar in half. A shower of pebbles rained down from the ceiling, and with a dying man's groan, the pillar collapsed.

Yushuv spun out of the way, putting another pillar between himself and the prince. He made a thrust past the pillar at the prince's knee, but the mace swatted it aside with ease. Yushuv gasped at the stinging in his hands and fell back again. *Think, boy, think*, he told himself. *What would Dace do?*

"This place is too small for you to hide for long," the prince said as he reduced another pillar to powder. "You'd do better to surrender the sword and let me make your death painless."

"I think not." Yushuv darted past the remains of a statue, the head and torso of which were long gone, and hacked with both hands at the prince's ankle. The angle of the swing forced the prince to divert his mace, and when he did Yushuv jammed the tip of the daiklave into the ground. Even as the mace swooped back up, Yushuv pushed down against the floor and used the daiklave to lift himself into the air. His feet caught the prince on the chin, and the man reeled from the blow. His arms flailed as Yushuv landed, pulling the blade behind him and spinning into a savage cut at the prince's midsection. The prince retreated, the tip of the daiklave tearing the fabric of his shirt.

"There's no place for you to run, either," Yushuv said, and pressed the attack. He jabbed forward, and the prince pirouetted away with astonishing grace. Again he tried, and this time the prince riposted with a blow from the mace that made the daiklave's blade ring like a bell.

"That's for your arrogance, boy," the prince said, and stepped inside Yushuv's guard. Before Yushuv could react, the prince's boot took him in the chest, and he tumbled backwards onto the ground. "And that's for your technique, which is piss-poor. Who trained you, the village idiot? A drooling priest with one good eye and a wooden leg?"

The mace came down and struck Yushuv a glancing blow on the side. He rolled with it, but the breath exploded out of him in a rush, and his side felt like it had been struck with a hammer.

"Not so fast," the prince called, and hammered the floor again. Yushuv barely caught himself from rolling into the blow. He raised the daiklave before him, but the prince swatted it out of his hands with arrogant ease. It skittered across the floor and off into the shadows. Yushuv tried to rise, but the tip of the mace pressed down against his breastbone. "No, don't move," the prince said. "I like you right where you are."

Yushuv froze, his mind racing. *What would Dace do now? Fight, obviously. Not surrender. Take the battle to the enemy.*

"You're not the first one to try to kill me," he said, trying to sound braver than he felt.

The prince smiled nastily. "No, but I trust I will be the first to succeed. It's a pity you had to find the sword so soon. A few more years, and you might have presented something of a challenge. I meant what I said about your teachers, by the way. They way you fought, I'm surprised you lasted this long."

"Dace is an excellent teacher," Yushuv yelled, surprised by his vehemence. "If he were here…"

"He's not." The prince jabbed downwards with the mace for emphasis.""Now tell me, how did you get the sword? It doesn't matter, really, but I'm curious. The dagger I'm familiar with. Unforgiven Blossom took it from me, but I'll be taking it back now." He prodded Yushuv again, but the boy kept his lips sealed.

He's armed, Yushuv thought. *I'm not. That has to change.*

"Ah." The prince's smile vanished. "You've learned discretion. Too late, though. On your feet." Slowly, Yushuv stood. "Good, good. Give my regards to the Unconquered Sun when you try to explain to him why you failed.

The prince's words seemed very far away suddenly. Dace's voice came into his mind, a lesson the man had taught him one day while they were fishing.

"Souls like ours don't go away, Yushuv," he had said. "Even when you and I die, whether it's tomorrow or a thousand years from now, our souls will live on. And they'll come back. They belonged to others before us, and that's part of what we're doing. Our souls have unfinished business. Fortunately," and he had glanced in the direction of the camp where Lilith was cleaning hides, "they also have friends and remembrances. Sometimes a sword or a helm sits for centuries in a rubbish heap, waiting for the right soul to come back for it. And it will. Never doubt that the soul will."

Dace had given him an odd look then, but before Yushuv could ask any questions Lilith had called them back into camp, and the subject never came up again. Now, though, Yushuv finally understood what Dace had been trying to tell him.

The sword. Yushuv focused on the blade, imagining it laying somewhere nearby.

My sword. Come to me. You waited for me. We were meant for one another. He imagined the way the sword felt in his hands, the gentle weight of it and the perfect balance. *Come to me*, he commanded it. *Come to me.*

"No irritatingly clever last words then," the prince said. "Fair enough. It marks you as wiser than your elders. Goodbye, boy." He raised the mace for the final blow, and started his swing.

"Come to me!" Yushuv shouted. As the prince paused for an instant, confused, the daiklave leapt into the air. Spinning, it flew forward. There was a wet slicing sound, like the meat of a roast pig coming off the bone, and then suddenly Yushuv stood with the daiklave in his hands.

The prince stood opposite him, staring in shock and disbelief at the stump of his arm. His hand lay on the floor of the tomb, still clutching the dented mace. Shockingly, he began to laugh.

"I must apologize to your teacher, when next I see him. Oh, that's a good joke to play on me, boy, a good joke indeed."

Yushuv lowered the daiklave until the point hovered just before the prince's eyes. "No more talking." He heard a dull clank, but ignored it. "Step back, against the wall."

"Anything you command, oh fearless warrior of the Sun." The prince jammed the bleeding stump against his side, and took a single stride backwards. "Is this sufficient?"

"Further," Yushuv ordered. "Against the wall."

"I fear that wall is booby-trapped," the prince said. "I'd prefer to stand here, if I may."

"No games," Yushuv growled. "Step back, and I might let you live."

"That's very generous of you," the prince replied. "It's also not enough."

Something caught Yushuv's ankle then, squeezing with hideous strength. Shocked, he looked down and saw the prince's detached hand clutching at him, blood still oozing from the wrist. Reflexively, he hacked at it with the daiklave, and in that moment the prince lunged forward with the dagger.

Yushuv tried to dodge. Instead, his foot caught on some debris and he tumbled backwards, his defensive swing turning into a wild, arcing swipe that sliced through the remaining columns on that side as if they were butter. The Prince of Shadows roared his defiance as he ducked beneath the blow, but even as he did so the ceiling over his head crumbled. He took a step backwards, then a heavy stone caught him from above and spun him into the wall.

In the midst of the roar of the collapsing ceiling, Yushuv heard a tiny click. Then the thunder of the rain of stones drowned out everything.

• • •

It took less than a minute for the roof of the Howe to finish falling in on itself, but to Yushuv it seemed like a great deal longer. When the last pebble had come to rest, he forced himself to sit and listen, though he was shaking like a twig in a stern breeze.

Nothing. There was nothing. No cries for help, no curses, not even a trail of blood from beneath the stones. The Prince of Shadows was gone and buried, vanished from the face of Creation as if he had never been.

"And he got to keep the dagger," Yushuv said, and sheathed his sword. Then, more tired than he had ever been, he began the long slow task of climbing out.

• • •

In the belly of the Howe, the Prince of Shadows felt the crushing weight of stone upon him and cursed Eliezer Wren. The stump of his arm throbbed, but the flow of blood had stopped enough that he didn't think he would die. *Not immediately, at least* came the unbidden thought, and he swatted it aside. He was the Prince of Shadows. He was Death's favored servant, and he would persevere.

He closed his eyes to preserve his strength. *Dead gods and masters,* he prayed, *lend me strength. Find me. Help me.*

WAIT.

The thought came to him faintly, as if from a long way away. The power of it was undeniable, but the force of the message was curiously muted. He remembered the oddities he'd noted on the Howe when Sandheart had died and shuddered. Even *they* would be weak here.

WAIT, the voice came again, stronger now. *THAT IS ALL.* Then, weaker, *SUCH WONDERFUL DREAMS OF DESTRUCTION HAD BEEN DREAMED FOR YOU.* After that was only silence.

"I will wait," he whispered, and smiled.

Chapter Thirty-Seven

"They're all dead, I think," said the blood-spattered youth in the colors of the Iselsi.""And the ones that were dead to start with are hacked up enough so that they won't be causing any more trouble." His right arm was in a sling, and T'fillit could see blood seeping through the white cloth at several points. Still, his expression was positively cheerful, and he held the reins of his mount with the loose assurance of a man who had learned, once and for all, that he could hold his own on the field of battle.

"Excellent," she replied. "How many losses did we take?"

"They're still counting bodies," the Iselsi said, using a curt nod to gesture back over his shoulder. "Nine was the last I heard, though two of those were inflicted by our own side. A couple of the stupider hotheads decided to rekindle some kind of argument from their training at the House of Bells. They ended up taking each other out, and a fair number of the enemy with them." He paused, and looked from side to side to see if anyone besides T'fillit could hear him. "If you ask me, it was an acceptable trade."

T'fillit nodded slowly, a great weariness filling her limbs. Around her, healers tended to the wounded and servants stripped the bodies of the dead. A trio of Immaculate priests wandered the battlefield, blessing those who had fallen in battle against the Abyss and singing solemn chants of praise. At the edge of the wood, trees were being felled for the sake of a pyre, and weary warriors were helped from their saddles.

It was, T'fillit decided, a satisfactory conclusion. "Discover the names of the dead and bring that list to me," she said. "We'll camp here tonight, so make sure the bodies are disposed of. I want a pyre—this place wants for wholesome light. Am I understood?"

"Of course, Revered One." He nodded quickly. "And may I say that I am deeply honored to have served under you."

"You may," she said, a smile tugging at the corner of her mouth. "But not more than once, and not loudly."

"Yes, Revered One," he said with a grin, and walked off. As he went, she noted with approval the fact that he did not run. *Good material, that one,* she thought. *The Empire could use more like him.*

A hullabaloo at the north end of the battlefield caught her attention, and she looked up. A single figure stood atop a small pile of tumbled rocks, a figure that was not at all human. It bore the rough proportions of a man, but its entire form shimmered with watery light, and a great beard of duckweed and moss hung down from its chin. Vines and reeds cloaked its limbs, and its torso was wrapped in strangling vines. It its massive arms, it cradled a body, and T'fillit found herself struck by a wave of sadness that seemed to radiate outward from where it stood.

Below it, swords and bows were raised, and those few huntsmen who had power remaining to them summoned it to themselves. "Stand and declare yourself," she heard a familiar voice call, and once again silently blessed the young Iselsi. "Another step, spirit, and we'll show you how small a god you really are."

"I come in peace," the figure rumbled.""I bring you my friend. I wish for you to take him home."

So saying, he knelt and laid the body down. Then, it slowly raised its hands in the air and backed away a few steps. Silently it waited, and its gaze moved over the crowd of huntsmen and their servants.

T'fillit spurred her mount forward. It splashed into the stream, struggling for footing on the bottom, but she urged it on. The hunters parted for her, and she thought she saw respect in the spirit's eyes as she approached.

"Do you command here?" it asked.

"I do," she replied.

"Who is your friend, and what do you offer us to take his body home?"

"His name was Eliezer Wren, and bearing his body should be its own reward. He did you great service this day, priestess, you and your dragons' children." The spirit's tone left no doubt that he was aware of T'fillit's true nature, and that he was contemptuous of the charade.

"Wren?" she breathed instead.

"Here? How?"

"Paying a debt," the spirit said with dignity.

"He has done much that is praiseworthy. Take him home, and have poets write songs to his memory."

"We shall," T'fillit said. "Prepare a stretcher!" she called out, "and have the healers preserve the body. Move!" Obediently, a swarm of servants scurried up the low hill and carried the corpse away. They bore it with reverence, and Rhadanthos nodded his approval.

"Excellent," he said. "And for that, you may drink of my waters freely."

"I thank you, spirit," she answered, "and we will burn the corpses of your enemies, so that their touch will not foul your stream."

"You are gracious." Rhadanthos settled into a sitting position.

"And also curious. What lies beyond this hill?"

"A wild place, full of wolves and not much else. Wren's slayer is dead, his corpse fed to the carrion beasts. You may continue past this place if you wish, but you will find the journey singularly uninteresting."

"I do not think that will be necessary," T'fillit said. "We will stay here tonight, and then disturb you no more."

"A wise decision." The great head nodded up and down. "I wish you restful dreams, and a safe and pleasant journey. For myself, I will sit here and watch the waters flow. It has been too long."

"As you wish," said T'fillit, and rode back down among her people.

•   •   •

True to T'fillit's word, the Hunt was gone within an hour of dawn the next morning. The pyre and the victory celebration had raged all night, and thus it was a subdued band of huntsmen who saddled up in the gray light. They left, horns at their saddles and songs unsung, and within minutes only a pile of charred bones hinted that they'd ever been there at all.

The day promised to be clear but chilly, and Rhadanthos could feel the first hints of ice coming on. He sat, cross-legged, on the mound that had once been his prison, and observed his domain. Below him, the waters of his stream flowed clear and cold, and already the marsh mud was being carried away in double handfuls. Rhadanthos had no doubt that within days, the stream would be stronger than it had been in years, and the valley around it would be renewed.

"Blood always did make the reeds grow better," he said to the morning air, and waited. Eventually he heard the sound he had been expecting, and without turning said, "It is done. They're gone."

"I know," said Yushuv. "I followed them through the woods a little bit. The Fair Folk are gone, too."

"That's a good thing," said Rhadanthos. "And soon you'll be leaving as well." It was a statement, not a question.

"Yes." He paused, and adjusted the rough scabbard that held the sword at his back." "Thank you for hiding me from them."

"Wren would have wanted me to." The massive shoulders shrugged." "Do not ask me how I know that, but I do.

I also know that the battle that would have ensued had they found you would have done great damage to this place, and enough has been done already."

"Still," the boy said, "I thank you."

"Where will you go now?" Rhadanthos asked, after the silence had grown uncomfortably long.

"I don't know," Yushuv said truthfully." "I don't think my work is done yet."

"You are very, very young to be pondering that sort of thing. A man's labors take decades, not hours."

Yushuv nodded. "But the Prince of Shadows is trapped, and the Fair Folk have been turned aside. It certainly seems like I've done enough."

"The only way to be certain that you have done enough for one life is to die, child. Never forget that." Rhadanthos chuckled to himself, a sound like water running fast over rough stones. "If you wish my advice, and I am quite certain you do not, I would tell you to hide yourself. Paint your sword black. Grow your hair long so that it covers your brow, and find yourself a hat. Practice, and teach yourself to sleep without dreams. Then, maybe, if the Unconquered Sun still needs you in ten years or a hundred, you'll live long enough to answer the call. Or have you grown too addicted to the thrill of danger to think of a quiet life ever again? If so, head east. There's challenge enough for you there, though I don't think you'll find it all to your liking among the trees."

"No," Yushuv said, shaking his head. "Wren and I talked a lot in the last few days. He told me what he'd done, and the people he'd done it for, and he said that the thing he wanted most in the world was for this all to be over so he could go home. But it's never really over, is it?"

"No," said Rhadanthos. "But it can pause for a while."

"I hope so," said Yushuv. "I think I'm going to go south, and then west. I'll get away from the trees for a while. If the Sun wants me, it will know where to find me. If not, I'll be just as happy." He paused for a moment, and looked thoughtful. "I'll come back some day, if you like."

"Someday," the spirit agreed. "But not too soon. I have labors to attend to."

"All right." Yushuv skipped down the low hill and splashed across the stream. "Someday it is," he said, and then walked off. At the bend in the stream, he turned and waved, and then with quick and quiet steps, he vanished.

•   •   •

In the depths of the citadel of the Prince of Shadows, a marionette slumped on a throne that was not its own. A tiny spark of light faded from its eyes, and it became, once more, a simple toy. With a vicious clatter, it fell to the floor.

Anyone looking closely at the puppet would have been appalled to know that when it had fallen, its right arm had broken off, just below the elbow. That piece lay on the ground, several feet from the rest of the marionette. The rest of the object, however, was quite intact, and all of its strings were still attached very tightly indeed.

Chapter Thirty-Eight

The wagon rolled to a dusty stop and the driver, a stocky man with an absurd shock of brown hair and a thin mustache, spat expertly from the side of his mouth as it did so. He leaned out, one hand shading his eyes against the noonday sun, and squinted back at the woman who stood by the side of the road.

She was old, he saw, but not frail. Her clothes were coated with road dust, and her shoes were worn. There was a staff in her hand that had seen hard use, though incongruously, it had a single green bud sprouting from it. Hair pulled back in a simple, severe bun, she trudged forward, head held high.

"Ho, Grandmother," the wagoner called.""You're a long way from home."

The woman stopped and her eyes met his.""Longer than you think," she said.

The man coughed. "Err, yes. Probably. There's no villages within a day's walk. You must have come a long way. Got a long way to go, too."

"Indeed." She leaned upon her staff. In the long moments as she did so, silence grew.

"I'm called Dreaming Tortoise," he said awkwardly. He reached down between his legs and scooped up a wineskin from the wagon's floorboards. "Can I offer you some wine, Grandmother?"

She smiled, and shook her head slightly. "I thank you, for your name and your courtesy. My name is Unforgiven Blossom, and I do not drink wine."

"Ah. I've got some water in the wagon as well, if you'd like." Abruptly, he smacked his forehead. "What am I thinking? Hop up on the wagon, Grandmother. I can take you at least as far as Stonebreak, if you're going that far." He slapped the wooden seat beside himself for emphasis.

"I do not hop," Unforgiven Blossom said, but the faintest hint of a smile creased her lips. "Will you give an old woman a hand?"

"Of course." Dreaming Tortoise reached out with one callused hand and hauled her up into the wagon. "Upsy-daisy, there you go."

With practiced ease, she settled in beside him and folded her hands demurely in her lap. "Where are you going, anyway, Grandmother Blossom?" he asked as he flicked the reins.

"Nexus, I think," she replied. "I am told that fortune-tellers do well there."

"Oh, certainly," he agreed, head nodding emphatically.

"A good fortune-teller can swim in jade in that town, they say. I'm going to Nexus myself, you know. Got a cargo of furs in back. If you want, I'd be happy for another pair of eyes on the trip. I've been told there are bandits on the road here."

"Bandits? I do not think you have to worry about bandits any longer," said Unforgiven Blossom,. Her laughter trailed behind the wagon as it rolled on to the west, and after a minute, Dreaming Tortoise 's joined hers.

"To Nexus," he said, toasting the journey from the wineskin.

"To Nexus," she agreed. "At least for a little while."

ACKNOWLEDGEMENTS

This novel would not have seen the light of day (or the dark of night) without the contributions of the following folks: Zach Bush, who cast his gimlet eyes upon it when it was still in 2000 word chunks; Philippe Boulle, who did a bang-up job editing it; Geoffrey Grabowski, who kept the continuity on track; Genevieve Cogman, for endless enthusiasm (in the form of constant questions as to what was going to happen next); the noble fellows of the Red Storm Entertainment Design Department, who helped keep the author sane and grounded (usually by suggesting that all of the characters get grenade launchers and use them on one another); and most of all, Melinda Thielbar, for constant support, suggestions, and an astonishing tolerance for one particular lunatic author.

ABOUT THE AUTHOR

Richard Dansky is a game designer and in-house writer for Red Storm Entertainment. He has worked on well over a hundred books for White Wolf, including **Wraith: The Oblivion (Second Edition), Guide to the Camarilla** and **Charnel Houses of Europe: The Shoah.** Richard lives near Raleigh, North Carolina, in an apartment he shares with a great many cooking utensils, worthless baseball cards, and books. For the record, they're not all books he worked on. Honest.

For a thousand years,
the vampire Lucita has
lived under the shadow
of her tyrannical sire, Monçada.

Now, the monster who defined her
existence is gone, destroyed
in no small part thanks to her efforts.

All she wishes is to
at last find a place for herself
in these Final Nights.
But to the rest of
Clan Lasombra,
she is a rogue and a killer,
a rebel who has assassinated
one of their greatest elders.

The hunt is on.

CLAN LASOMBRA TRILOGY™

SHARDS

BOOK ONE

AVAILABLE NOW

No Other Love

Isabel Morin

ISBN: 1482566729
ISBN 13: 9781482566727

No Other Love

Isabel Morin

My never-ending thanks to Abby Strom, whose support, advice and willingness to read draft after draft of this manuscript were never-ending. My thanks to Caroline Tolley, Katy Wight and Alexandra Mandzak for their crucial editorial help.

To my husband Michael, for coming along and inspiring me to finish this story.

CHAPTER ONE

May 28, 1841

The white three-story house sat gracefully atop a gentle rise, looking every bit the country seat of a wealthy Bostonian with its stable and carriage house, its pond and scattered trees. It was exactly what Rose had expected, yet dread filled her as she stood at the end of the long drive, facing Cider Hill for the first time.

For several long minutes she couldn't move. Her heart raced with nerves and she would have given anything to turn around and leave without looking back. But failing her father wasn't an option, nor could she stand there forever. The only thing to do was go forward.

She smoothed down her skirts and brushed the dust off her shoes. It wouldn't do to arrive dirty and disheveled from the long walk.

So focused was she on the house before her, she didn't hear the horse and rider approaching from behind until the thunder of hooves was nearly upon her. She turned around just in time to see a horse rearing above her, its legs flailing only inches from her head. She heard the rider trying to soothe his mount just before he was thrown backwards, landing with a thud on the packed dirt of the drive.

Instantly the horse calmed and returned to all fours, nosing the man as if in apology before wandering over to graze along the edge of the drive.

Horrified, Rose ran to the fallen man, dropping to her knees by his side as he struggled to a sitting position.

"I'm terribly sorry. I didn't hear..."

The glare leveled at her stopped her cold. Under normal circumstances she would have thought the man quite handsome, but today his curling dark hair, strong cheekbones and firm jaw were no match for her distress.

"What were you doing there?" he asked, grimacing as he tried to stand. "Trying to kill someone?"

This was an ironic accusation given the reason she'd come to Cider Hill, but Rose ignored it. The man had regained his footing and now towered over her, but it was clear from the way he favored his left leg that it was injured.

"Please, let me help you," she said, moving toward him instinctively, but he shrugged her off, his expression thunderous. Even in his weakened state he exuded power, his broad shoulders and muscled body evidence of his physical vitality.

"I'm perfectly able to walk on my own," he ground out, taking a step.

Immediately his leg gave out beneath him, sending him down on one knee. His eyes closed, his face tightening with pain.

Rose knelt beside him.

"At least let me help you to the door," she said, hoping to appeal to his common sense.

He said nothing for a time, and then a curt nod conveyed his acquiescence. Rose grasped his arm and helped him to his feet. When he was upright he draped an arm across her shoulders, the contact shockingly familiar as their bodies pressed together.

Without a word they began their labored way up the many steps leading to the door, Rose nearly staggering under the man's weight. Why had she not offered to fetch someone – a groom perhaps – to help?

The whole morning was a disaster. Not only had she hurt someone, but her entire plan was in ruins. Had he not arrived, she would have gone to the servants' entrance without notice from anyone in the family and been promptly assigned her new position. There was no chance now of a quiet entrance. Whether he was family or a guest, there was sure to be a great deal of fuss over him.

At last they struggled up the last step and reached the doorway. The man took his arm from her shoulders and leaned against the doorframe, relieving her of his weight. Rose stood beside him, grateful that her bonnet protected her from any sidelong glares. Without another word to her he reached for the doorknob.

Rose's knees went weak and her vision dimmed as she tried to catch her breath. The door would open momentarily, and then the plan she had set in motion weeks before would be real. There was no turning back now.

"De fumo in flammam."

It wasn't until the man looked at her sharply that she realized she'd spoken the words aloud.

"Out of the smoke and into the flame? Why do you say such a thing?" he asked, his dark eyes intent as he frowned at her.

Fortunately she did not have to answer, for the door was flung open by an older woman in a crisp gray dress and lace cap. Perhaps this was Mrs. Craig, the housekeeper with whom she'd corresponded.

"Good heavens, Master Luke! What's happened?" the woman asked, rushing to the man's side. Together she and Rose helped him into a room a few steps down the hall. With a groan of relief he collapsed onto the sofa where he sat, obviously exhausted, while the older woman settled him more comfortably.

"Thank you, Mrs. Craig. That will do."

"Shall I call Dr. Rhodes?"

Before he could answer, a distinguished-looking man and woman hurried into the room. Though older and stouter, the man was clearly the father of the injured man who now sat on the sofa, his leg propped up on pillows. Rose steeled herself at the realization that she was standing face to face with Jonas Fletcher, President of the Western Railroad Company.

Until that moment she'd been so wrapped up in thoughts of what Jonas Fletcher had done, she hadn't even considered that there might be others responsible. Now she looked at his son. Could it have been him? Was he capable of murder?

"Are you hurt? What's happened?" Mr. Fletcher asked, hurrying to his son's side.

Rose's chest tightened. As soon as Mr. Fletcher heard what had happened, he would blame her for the accident and she'd be turned away, her one chance over before it had begun.

Luke Fletcher frowned darkly.

"Neither my horse nor I were expecting to find someone standing dead in the middle of the drive. But there she was as we came around the trees. Arturo spooked and, much to my chagrin, I landed in the dirt. I seem to have twisted my ankle."

"I see," said Mrs. Fletcher. She wore an elegant, expensive dress and gleaming jewels. An elaborate costume given the country setting. Her gaze dropped deliberately to Rose's faded blue dress and scuffed boots, her expression full of disdain. She pinned Rose with a cold stare.

"Perhaps you could explain who you are and why you acted so foolishly."

The young Mr. Fletcher's mouth tightened and his shoulders tensed at this. Rose was about to reply, but before she could form an answer he spoke again.

"It wasn't entirely her fault, Charlotte. I was going far too fast as I came into the drive. It was careless of me," he said, much to Rose's amazement. "I'm only glad I didn't hurt Miss..." He turned to look at her, his brow furrowing as if only now realizing he didn't know her name. "She was kind enough to help me inside."

Just then a young maid appeared, holding the worn brocade satchel Rose had dropped outside and completely forgotten.

"Charlie's taken care of Mr. Fletcher's horse, but he found this," the maid said, placing it on the table before them for all to see.

"Thank you, Lydia," Jonas Fletcher said. He turned to address Rose. "I take it this is yours?"

Rose forced herself to look at Mr. and Mrs. Fletcher as a servant would – demurely, subserviently – even as the urge to accuse them all filled her. Behind that was the desperate urge to flee the house, so terrified was she of the plan she'd put in motion. A plan she had concocted with a beginning and possible end but very little notion of what would happen in the middle.

But it would have to be enough. Until the Fletchers paid for what they'd done, her own comfort was of little consequence.

Realizing she still wore the straw bonnet that hid her face from view, she untied the bow under her chin and lifted it off. Her hair was a damp mess after the long, hot walk from her friend's house in Boston, but she was not out to impress anyone with her looks.

"My name is Rose, Rose Stratton," she said. "I'm here because Mrs. Craig has promised me a position in your household."

"I see," said Mrs. Fletcher. "Well, that explains it. I wondered why a girl so poorly turned out would be here."

Rose bristled at being spoken to so rudely but managed to hold her tongue. Luke Fletcher shot the woman a piercing look, as if taking offense on Rose's behalf. Perhaps he felt that only he should be able to insult her, or perhaps he was regretting his earlier behavior.

"I didn't realize you were coming today," the housekeeper put in.

"I did write," Rose said. "My letter must have gone astray. I didn't mean to arrive unannounced."

Mrs. Craig shook her head. "That's of no consequence. We can certainly use you, if that's acceptable to Mrs. Fletcher," she said.

"Very well. I'll leave her in your hands, Mrs. Craig," the mistress replied, already losing interest. "Now if you'll all excuse me, I have other, more pressing matters to attend to," she said, exiting with a sweep of her skirts.

How odd that Mrs. Fletcher appeared so little concerned for her son. But then, he had called her by her first name, so they must be some other relation.

Jonas Fletcher turned to Rose.

"My thanks for helping my son," he said, his smile sincere. "I'm only glad you're unharmed. Hopefully the rest of your time here will be less eventful. In any case, we're pleased to have you."

"Thank you, sir," Rose replied, surprised that such a powerful man was taking the time to address her. He wasn't at all the imperious railroad czar she'd expected.

Picking up her bag, she glanced once more at the man sprawled on the sofa, his concerned father standing beside him. He looked back at her with something like curiosity or puzzlement, though why that should be she couldn't guess. Nor did it matter.

Only her father mattered.

"I'm afraid the only place I have for you is as scullery maid," Mrs. Craig began. "Normally I would give it to one of the less well-spoken girls and use you for serving and such. However, it was only fair that I let Dottie take the better position, as she's been with us for over a year now and has earned an advancement."

"I understand. I'm grateful for whatever you can give me."

They were sitting at the table in the servants' hall, a large room situated between the kitchen and laundry room. Mrs. Craig had commandeered a corner of it for use as an office. In front of her were lists and menus and an accounting of household expenses. She wore spectacles as she scanned her notes, but now she took these off and looked directly at Rose.

"Yes, well, Sally is a good judge of character," she said, referring to the housekeeper who'd referred Rose. "She tells me I won't be sorry." Here she paused for a moment, as if choosing her words carefully. "I am curious why a girl of your obvious education needs to work here."

"My schooling won't affect my duties, nor make me think myself above them," Rose replied. "I've been living on a farm for the past six years. I'm no stranger to hard work."

"Very well then. You'll room with Lydia. Through that door and up the stairs are the maids' quarters. Your room is the second door on the right. Put your things away but come right back down. There's plenty to be done in the kitchen."

Rose was so tired she could hardly think straight, but she followed Mrs. Craig's directions, ascending a narrow set of stairs to the silent, stifling hallway that ran above the servants' hall and kitchen.

There were six rooms in all, three on each side. Either the male servants resided in another part of the house, or they had rooms in another building. Not being familiar with how wealthy families lived, Rose could only guess at how many servants a house like Cider Hill required. The question was, how many Fletchers lived here? Was it only Mr. and Mrs. Fletcher, or did Luke Fletcher and perhaps others members of the family reside here as well?

She hesitated at the appointed door, irrationally fearing what lay on the other side. It would not be her bedroom on the farm with its familiar view of their fields, the cheerful yellow curtains her aunt had sewn, the quilt from her childhood bed.

Taking a deep breath she opened the door. Inside were two narrow cots with a rickety table between them. A half-burnt candle sat atop it, looking as lonely and dejected as she felt. A bonnet, dress and apron hung from pegs set into the wall. Beside the door stood a scarred chest of drawers, on its top a tangle of hairpins and ribbon and a tiny painting of a woman, her cheeks tinted a pretty, flushed pink.

How she would have loved to lie down, close her eyes and lose herself in sleep. Instead she comforted herself with the knowledge that she would not be here long. She was here only to find justice for her father, after which she would never set foot in Cider Hill again.

It took but a minute to hang her clothes on the pegs and tuck her unmentionables into the bottom drawer of the dresser. When everything was in its place she made her way back though the hallway, down the steep stairs, and into the kitchen where Mrs. Lynch, the cook, explained her duties. Before long she was armed with a pail of water and wire brush, scrubbing out the cookstove.

⌒

Luke sat across from his father in the quiet of the study, sifting through his survey maps and trying to concentrate. Unfortunately, all he could think about was Rose Stratton.

He'd behaved badly, too angry and embarrassed to act civilized. He'd not fallen off a horse since he was a boy of twelve, and it was damn aggravating to do so at the age of nine and twenty.

The trees lining the road had screened her from view, but he'd also been riding too hard. Nor did it help that he'd been worrying that the railroad line was going to take longer than he'd anticipated to complete, keeping him in Massachusetts far longer than he ever intended. He'd only been back for a few weeks and already he was itching to head west again. But his father needed him and he wasn't one to leave a job unfinished, so here he'd be until the line was completed.

Which meant he'd be seeing a good deal more of Rose Stratton.

She'd been far kinder than she needed to be, considering how beastly he'd acted. She'd even supported him all the way to the door, a fact that would mortify him for some time to come. Even worse, he'd laid the blame for his accident entirely at her feet. Quite the gentleman.

But how had she come to learn Latin, and why the reference to danger? Was she simply anxious about her new situation? Surely she didn't imagine that Cider Hill posed any danger to her?

She was full of surprises to be sure, but it was the moment she took off her bonnet that had left him dumbstruck. Until then he had caught very little of her features. Then suddenly the most beautiful woman he'd ever laid eyes on was standing before him, her face like a cameo with its delicately sculpted cheekbones, full and finely shaped mouth and small, patrician nose. Silky tendrils of hair the color of autumn leaves had slipped from her coil and tickled her neck.

This was the woman he'd leaned on as he sweated through his jacket. She'd looked too slender and fine-boned to have withstood the weight of a brute like him. Too refined to be working as a domestic.

So deep was he in his own thoughts, it took him several moments to notice that his father was asking him a question.

"Did Whistler's plan make sense to you?" Jonas repeated, looking at him curiously from behind his desk.

It took Luke a moment to regain his focus. "What? Oh, yes. I'm in favor of following his suggestions. He's the best engineer there is as far as I'm concerned. But we have to do our part and get the land issues settled first."

"I agree. I'll discuss it with Nathan again this week."

Luke nodded his head to show agreement, though in truth he was spectacularly uninterested in the railroad at just that moment.

"I wonder what Mrs. Craig has decided to do with the new maid?" he asked, unable to help himself.

"Why do you ask? Do you harbor ill feelings over the accident?"

"Quite the opposite," Luke replied. "I hope she doesn't think ill of *me*, after the way I behaved."

"I shouldn't worry," Jonas replied, donning his spectacles and turning his attention back to the documents before him.

"She struck me as capable and well-spoken," Luke went on, though it was clear his father had lost interest in the topic. "I only hope she's given a position that will make use of her abilities."

"Mrs. Craig will have it all well in hand," replied Jonas without looking up.

It was true that Mrs. Craig ran the household impeccably. But what if she didn't realize how unusual Rose was? It would ease his mind to look into the matter. Didn't he owe it to the new maid, given how badly he'd treated her?

He stood up abruptly, the pain in his ankle a sharp reminder of what happened when he moved too fast. A reminder he ignored.

Now his father did look up.

"Is there a problem, Luke? You've been distracted ever since dinner."

"It's nothing. I suppose I'm just a bit restless. I think I'll step out for a few minutes, if you don't mind."

"By all means. Go take some air."

Thus freed, Luke headed out into the hallway, limping only slightly.

As soon as Rose finished cleaning the cookstove she was put to work washing the myriad pots, pans and dishes that resulted from the several courses the Fletchers and their houseguests had consumed at the midday meal. The work was arduous and the kitchen sweltering, but it was not altogether unpleasant amid the chatter of Lydia and two other maids.

The girls were full of both gossip and useful information. Rose now knew that Mr. and Mrs. Fletcher resided in the house, and that Luke Fletcher had arrived only weeks ago to help see the railroad completed. None of them seemed to know exactly where he'd been before coming home. Apparently he'd been rather peripatetic, traveling in the wilds of the Territories for some years.

"He hasn't been back to Boston for ages, so no one save Mrs. Craig had ever seen him before," Lydia said, whispering loudly. "Imagine our surprise when the likes of him showed up. Mercy!"

"You'll pay him no mind and hope he does the same, if you know what's good for you," replied Abigail, a sullen, mousy girl who spent much of her time acting lady's maid to Mrs. Fletcher. It hadn't taken Rose long to discern that attending to the difficult mistress would turn even the sunniest disposition gloomy.

"You haven't had the pleasure of meeting Mrs. Fletcher's son, Mr. Byrne, but you will," added Dottie with a dark look. The youngest of them all at perhaps seventeen, she was a stocky brunette with a biting sense of humor and no-nonsense demeanor. "Mr. Byrne works for Mr. Fletcher too, but he has lodgings in Boston, thank goodness for everyone."

"If only Luke Fletcher came by as often as Mr. Byrne does," Lydia said longingly.

"Don't let Mrs. Craig catch you gossiping about the family," Abigail warned Rose. "She's been with Mr. Fletcher since before his first wife's death and won't tolerate that kind of talk."

Footsteps sounded in the hallway beyond and they all fell silent, fearing they'd be overheard by the housekeeper. But instead of Mrs. Craig, Luke Fletcher entered through the swinging door.

Immediately his gaze fell on Rose.

In the few hours since she last saw him he seemed to have grown even more handsome. Despite her intention not to feel anything but mistrust for the Fletchers, her face flushed with mortification to be caught hanging over the sink, her face damp with sweat and her hair in disarray. He looked at her and then about the kitchen, clearly displeased.

Mrs. Craig entered the kitchen just behind him. "Master Luke," she said, stopping in surprise. "What can I do for you?"

His reply was too low for Rose to hear, and the two of them retreated into the servants' hall where only the indistinct murmur of their conversation could be heard.

"What do you suppose has happened?" Lydia asked, eyes wide. "Did one of you break something?"

Abigail and Dottie insisted they hadn't done anything wrong. Still, they were all on edge, wondering if they'd inadvertently committed some terrible error.

Lydia broke the tension with a dramatic sigh. "Even angry he's the most handsome man I've ever seen."

"You'll be singing another tune if it's something you've done," Dottie countered dryly.

Lydia made a face at her, only to jump in surprise as Mrs. Craig returned, briskly giving instructions for the evening meal. She said nothing to indicate what her conversation with Mr. Fletcher had been about.

As soon as Rose finished cleaning up from dinner she and the cook, Mrs. Beech, began preparations for supper. As the family would have guests joining them, this entailed plucking ten hens, scrubbing and cutting piles of vegetables, and mixing egg whites until they stood up in stiff white peaks and her arm went numb. She had done all of this before for her own family, but never had she cooked on the exhausting scale required here.

As she worked Rose had time to consider things in more detail, and it hit her that although she had made it into the house, as scullery maid she would likely never see beyond the servants' wing. She would have no excuse to explore the rest of the house or move among the family.

It would be even riskier than she had anticipated proving the family's role in her father's murder. She would have to go into rooms in which she had absolutely no business being. And there was no telling when she would even have the opportunity to do that.

Was her effort to get here all for nothing, doomed before it even began? This thought left her so distraught she cut herself while slicing carrots and had to stop to staunch the flow of blood. Despair pulsed through her in time with the throbbing in her hand and it took all her willpower to hold back tears of frustration.

Early in the evening the staff sat down for their own supper. It was Rose's job to serve the staff, a task she wouldn't have minded but for the fact that she was dead on her feet.

This was her first chance to meet the two men on staff, a gardener and a groom. Both took their meals with the rest of the servants but, she learned, lived in a small cottage in back of the house. The gardener, a cantankerous older man named George, showed no interest in her whatsoever, but the groom, a young man of about eighteen named Charlie, was more attentive than was strictly proper.

"It's a real pleasure having a new face around here," he said, smiling familiarly at her. "Especially a pretty one like yours." This last was accompanied by a wink.

If she hadn't been so tired, his cocky attitude might have amused her. As it was, she only smiled wanly and asked if he wanted more gravy.

After the servants' meal was over and cleaned up, she scurried to keep up with the tide of dishes Lydia and Dottie brought back from the family's supper. For the next two hours she washed the never-ending stream of serving ware, a task that nearly undid her. How many courses could a person possibly eat? It felt as if she'd been washing dishes forever, and for an army no less.

All that separated her from the guests was the wall between the sink and dining room, and every time Dottie or Lydia came through the swinging door, a burst of conversation followed them. Rose burned with curiosity and sorely wished she were one of the serving maids. If she were able to listen to dinner conversation, she might learn something that would help her understand what happened to her father. Perhaps even now they were discussing the railroad.

Luke Fletcher's deep voice could occasionally be heard through the doorway. How would it feel to have his full attention for the length of a meal, those dark eyes focused on her once again?

Guilt at this errant thought immediately swamped her. What kind of a daughter entertained such ideas about a man she suspected of killing her father? And what would Will think of her? Her very first day and here she was thinking about another man.

If it had been up to Will, they would already be married, but ever since her father's death their courtship had stalled. At first she'd been too grief-stricken to want anything but a shoulder to lean on. Before long she was too intent on finding her father's murderer to think about anything beyond that, even her own future.

But she hadn't told Will her real reason for coming to Boston. He would never have understood. Instead she said she needed time away and would be going to her friend Vivian's until she felt well enough to face the farm and all its memories.

"At least promise you'll marry me when you return," he'd implored.

It was the night before she was to depart, and he had just taken supper with her and Aunt Olivia. He looked as if he wanted to hold her, or maybe shake her, but instead he thrust his hands into his pockets. He'd never been anything but proper with her.

She didn't have the heart to deny him her promise, but it felt wrong to make such a vow when her feelings were bent in an entirely different direction. Even so, the promise had been made. She had even let him kiss her.

Rose was jolted out of her recollection by the sound of chairs being pushed back and people rising from the table. The men were retiring to the library, the women to the drawing room. Rose was still cleaning when the guests departed an hour later and the family withdrew upstairs. Lydia and Dottie went to bed soon after.

The house began to settle around her, unfamiliar and disconcerting. She had just started her final mop of the kitchen floor, her last task for the night, when Mrs. Craig appeared, scaring Rose nearly out of her wits. The older woman gave Rose a tired smile.

"There's been a change of plans, Rose," she said. "Beginning tomorrow you will no longer be scullery maid. Instead you'll work in the main rooms and upstairs. Lydia will show you what to do."

"But why?" Rose asked, utterly bewildered.

Mrs. Craig looked reluctant to answer, but finally she replied.

"Master Luke asked that I reassign you. He doesn't feel we're putting you to good use back here."

"But why should he interfere with the servants?" Rose asked, incredulous.

"I thought perhaps you could tell me," replied Mrs. Craig, giving Rose a pointed look.

"I haven't the slightest idea. I only met him this afternoon," Rose said. Then a new worry occurred to her. "Who will take my place?"

Mrs. Craig frowned. "Dottie will once again be scullery maid," she answered, clearly unhappy at the prospect. And no wonder. Dottie had been in her new and better position only one day and would now, through no fault of her own, go back to her former duties.

"But that's terrible!" Rose exclaimed, the consequences of Luke Fletcher's demand sinking in. "Dottie will hate me. Everyone will hate me. Why must we do as he says?" she asked.

The housekeeper sighed, her expression softening. "Mr. Fletcher is a good man, if sometimes rough in his ways. And I have no desire to go to Mrs. Fletcher, as I assure you it would help none of us. Men will do foolish things for a pretty girl, and you're far prettier than most. But whether you brought this on or not, I advise you to be careful."

Rose was about to defend herself but thought better of it. The housekeeper had been kinder than she needed to be given the circumstances, and she was not blaming Rose for anything, simply warning her. A warning she would certainly heed.

"Yes, of course. I'm terribly sorry."

"Never mind that. Finish up and get some rest. The morning will come soon enough."

Rose stood in the middle of the kitchen after Mrs. Craig left, trying to make sense of why Luke Fletcher would care what she did. Whatever the reason, being accorded favors by the master's son would not sit well with the others.

She fumed as she swabbed the floor, heaving the heavy mop around the kitchen as she contemplated the trouble she was likely to encounter. But soon her indignation wore off and her movements slowed as she began to see that this was not such a bad turn of events after all. In fact, it was very much for the better, as Mr. Fletcher's interference meant she would be able to move throughout the house, a dramatic improvement in her situation.

As badly as she felt that her advancement came at Dottie's expense, her father was more important than anything else. She stood a better chance of finding his killer now, and that was all that mattered.

It was after midnight when she dumped the blackened water out the back door and put the mop away. Climbing the steps to the servants' quarters took the very last of her strength, and when she reached her room she had barely enough energy to undress. With great effort she shed her shoes and dress and stepped out of her petticoats. Taking care not to disturb Lydia, whose sleeping form was revealed by the pale moonlight, she set her shoes under the chair and her clothes atop it. A great sigh of relief escaped her as she unfastened her corset and took her first deep breath since early that morning.

Without even changing her chemise for a nightgown or removing her stockings, she fell back onto the lumpy straw mattress. But like every night since her father's death, she could not escape the vision that came to her as soon as she closed her eyes.

Her father lay on the ground, his face pale and clammy, his lips a faint blue. Blood soaked his shirt, turning it black.

Rose fell to her knees in the deep February snow, tears coursing down her cheeks.

"No, no. Oh, God, Papa," she sobbed, the sound echoing in the silence of the wood.

"Rose," he said, his voice weak. His eyes were open and direct, full of pain.

"It's okay, Papa. I'll take care of you," she choked out, her hands working frantically at his coat and shirt to get to his wound. Taking off her apron she pressed it to his chest. "I'll get Aunt Olivia. She'll know what to do."

"No, Rose," he gasped out, his voice so faint she had to lean down to hear him.

"I must get help," she sobbed, hardly able to see through her tears. "You've lost so much blood."

"Stay," he said, his hand reaching for her. He was so cold, his once strong grip too weak to hold on to her. Despair pressed down on her as she took his hand in both of hers, willing her life into him.

"Who did this to you?"

His face was relaxed now, as if he were already leaving her. "Fletcher..."

"What do you mean?" she asked, willing him to keep talking, to stay with her.

"My sweet girl," he said, closing his eyes.

The next moment he went utterly quiet, not even a breath moving through him. Rose held his hand in hers, unable to let go, still pleading with God to save him.

CHAPTER TWO

A cheerful humming wakened Rose after what felt like mere minutes of sleep. Opening her eyes she saw Lydia, already dressed, braiding her hair and pinning it back. Wishing for a few moments of peace, Rose said nothing, gazing out the window as the gray light of dawn lit the sparsely furnished room.

This had always been her favorite time of day. She and her father used to sit at the kitchen table in companionable silence, eating a slice of buttered bread with a cup of tea as the sun rose over the countryside and lit up the windows.

There was no stopping the coming of day. The feeling had once been a comfort to her. Now it just made her more aware of her burden.

Lydia turned as Rose sat up in bed, her round, freckled face brightening immediately.

"At last you're awake," she exclaimed. "I tried to stay up for you but I just couldn't keep my eyes open. Well, I daresay you won't be working like that again. Oh, the girls are just in fits about it, I tell you. You're not here a day and already you've created a scandal."

She went on, oblivious to the effect she was having on Rose. "So tell me," she said, her voice lowering to a conspiratorial whisper. "What did you do to make Mr. Fletcher so smitten with you?"

Rose's heart sank at the damage Luke Fletcher's foray into the kitchen had caused. Determined to correct Lydia's misconceptions, she spoke with more than usual force.

"Lydia, I don't know what everyone's saying, but it's all a terrible misunderstanding. I admit it's strange that Mr. Fletcher would have wanted to intervene on my behalf, but there's nothing at all between us. I spent only a few minutes in his presence when I arrived yesterday. Perhaps he was trying to do me a good turn, but it's nothing more than that. We've barely spoken to one another."

"But of course! You helped him into the house when he was injured, which is terribly romantic. Though it would have been more romantic had *he* helped *you*. Even so," she continued darkly, "when he's done with you, you'll have no one to protect you anymore."

"He won't be done with me, as he hasn't begun anything with me," Rose replied firmly, standing up to retrieve her corset and petticoats. "I mean nothing to him. Besides, I have my own beau at home. I'm not interested in anyone else."

"It's easy as pie to like two fellows at once, especially when one of them is far away," Lydia responded, her dreamy countenance suggesting she was recalling just such a scenario.

"I've only just arrived and everyone thinks ill of me," Rose said, thoroughly dismayed. "And I don't know how I'll face Dottie."

"Yes, Dottie's furious, and she's been known to hold a grudge."

Rose groaned at this and sat down heavily on the bed, her face in her hands.

"Don't worry," Lydia consoled. "They won't be too awful, as they all think you can get Mr. Fletcher to sack them. Anyway, I'll help you. I can see you're a good sort."

Rose looked up, smiling wanly at her new ally.

"Thank you, Lydia. That's very kind of you. I'm afraid you'll also need to explain to me what I should be doing from now on, as I haven't a clue."

"Oh, that's no trouble. You'll get the hang of it in no time. And now that you're a maid we can really get to know one another. It'll be fine, you'll see. Just make sure you don't get on Mrs. Fletcher's bad side. She doesn't forget anything."

Remembering Mrs. Fletcher's displeasure of the day before, Rose feared she had already managed to rub her the wrong way, but there was nothing to be done about it now except make sure the mistress of the house had no further reason to notice her. How difficult could that be?

"We'd best hurry down for breakfast," Lydia told her. "Mrs. Beech, our cook, makes a horrible fuss when anyone's late to table, though luckily we don't need to do much serving in the morning. We set food out on the sideboard and they come down and eat when they please."

Rose rushed to dress, but she struggled with her corset lacings. Aunt Olivia and she had always laced each other up, so she was grateful when Lydia came behind her and with a few tugs set her to rights. Hastily Rose donned her petticoats, dress and a new white apron she'd sewn expressly for this position. Her hair, which she would normally have plaited before bed, had completely fallen out of its pins. Pulling a brush out of her valise, she tidied it before twisting it into a serviceable knot at the back. The hair that framed her face was shorter, as was the style, but since this was not the sort of situation one curled one's hair for, she braided each side and pinned that back as well. Lydia stood watching her and sighed dramatically.

"My mother always said red hair was a sign of the devil, but yours is so pretty it's hard to believe that's true. Of course, the talk about you might convince people otherwise, but we won't pay them any mind, will we, Rose?" Lydia said, smiling and waving her hand dismissively.

How had *she* become a *we*? Bemused though she was by her new roommate, it was a comfort not to feel so alone. Grateful to have someone at her side, Rose followed Lydia out of the room and down to the servants' hall.

The entire tableful of servants ceased talking and looked up as soon as Rose entered the room. Throwing her a look of encouragement, Lydia took a seat on one of the long benches and Rose followed, squeezing in at the end.

Someone walked by and placed dishes on the table, far out of her reach. Glancing up, Rose found herself face to face with Dottie who, as scullery maid once more, was bringing all the food to the table before sitting down herself. This she soon did, sliding in directly across from Rose and fixing her with a look of contempt.

Rose concentrated on getting food on her plate, no easy task when most of the people at the table had no interest in passing food to her. But she had not come all this way just to be intimidated at the breakfast table.

Ignoring Dottie's constant glare, she asked politely but firmly for the buns, raspberry tarts and fried potatoes until her plate was full.

Eventually conversation started up again, though she could feel everyone looking at her with either suspicion or outright malice. Everyone, that is, except Lydia, who gave her arm a comforting squeeze.

As soon as breakfast was eaten they all scattered and left Dottie to clean up, but Rose lingered in order to apologize. She had barely begun before Dottie interrupted.

"If you're so sorry, why am I still scullery maid?" she demanded.

"This wasn't my doing, so I'm afraid I cannot undo it," Rose replied, all too aware that as apologies went, hers wasn't very impressive.

"That doesn't help me none, does it?" said Dottie before turning on her heel and heading into the kitchen.

Rose stood where she was, her face hot with shame. Never before had anyone disliked her so. To be hated now, when she was new and so unsure of herself, left her shaken. In all of her planning, she'd never considered outright hostility from the servants.

After a few deep breaths to settle her nerves she went in search of Lydia, who took Rose on a quick tour of the house.

The main part of the building, which was more or less a square but for where the ballroom protruded on the bottom floor, comprised the family living space. The library, ballroom and drawing room were on the left side and the morning room, dining room and billiard room were on the right. Upstairs were the master bedchamber, Mr. Fletcher's private study and three smaller bedchambers, one of which was currently occupied by Luke Fletcher. The topmost floor held still more guest chambers, though they could not be used in the full heat of summer.

The pantry, servants' hall, kitchen and laundry rooms were in a wing that extended off the back of the house from the dining room. Above the wing were the maids' quarters.

At Lydia's direction Rose cleaned and polished while committing to memory everything she saw and heard. She thought it best to wait until she knew the habits and patterns of both servants and family before she began her investigations, so she resolved not to do anything out of the ordinary for the first few days.

The other servants remained cold toward her, but even so it was good to be working in the general living quarters, as she would be privy to all manner of conversations. The family gave little thought to the staff, often speaking as if they didn't exist, so she was hopeful that sooner or later she would overhear something useful.

It was late afternoon on her third day when she entered the morning room. She cleaned the windows with a water and vinegar solution and carefully dusted the writing table, taking care to replace the pen, ink and sheets of paper exactly as they had been. Next she went around the room tidying books that were scattered about. It was not until she set the pile on a table that she noticed the book sitting on top.

Ralph Waldo Emerson's collection of essays had been a favorite of her father's since its publication earlier in the year. Even now she could hear him reading aloud passages to her and her aunt of an evening, after they'd eaten and all the chores had been done.

A smile curved her lips as she recalled the many times he'd referred to or quoted from it, so often in fact that she'd begun to tease him, making up silly quotes and insisting they came from Emerson himself.

She heard her father's laugh as if he were right beside her, and then her heart was breaking all over again. Silently she spoke to him, as she often did, once again promising she would not let his murder go unpunished. Tears coursed down her cheeks as she hugged the book to her chest, wishing with all her heart that she could have him back again.

She stood there for several long minutes until gradually she became aware of someone watching her. She knew without looking it was Luke Fletcher.

He was standing in the doorway, looking bigger and more intimidating now that he'd recovered from the fall. Dressed in a black jacket and trousers and gray pinstriped vest, he was unnervingly handsome.

"Why are you crying?" he demanded. Crossing the room in two strides, he gripped her shoulders until she was forced to meet his gaze. With an urgency that took her by surprise he searched her face, genuine concern in his eyes, so near he overwhelmed her. She could smell the clean spice of him, feel his heat as he waited for her answer.

"I – nothing. There's nothing the matter," she finally got out, bewildered by his concern.

"Did someone do something to upset you? Tell me what's happened and I'll take care of it."

Rose didn't know what to say. As much as she mistrusted him, she was also too aware of his attractions. But whatever her confusion, he was no friend.

"I was merely remembering something that saddened me. Please let me go," she said, pulling away from him. "I can't afford to be seen with you, not after your interference."

That did the trick. His hands fell abruptly from her shoulders and he stepped back.

"My apologies," he said, his voice cold and formal. "I had thought I was doing you a favor."

"Unfortunately, now everyone thinks I'm offering you favors in return."

As soon as this was out of her mouth, Rose could have died of shame. Mortified, she looked at the floor, her face burning. What had come over her to speak like that?

"I see," he replied, his tone changing from anger to something unreadable. "How unfortunate to be accused of a thing like that without the pleasure of it being true."

Rose's mouth fell open. Of all the detestable things to say. But what had she been expecting, an apology? Men of his ilk didn't apologize to servants. And what did it matter? After all, she was better off for what he'd done.

Yet she couldn't seem to stop herself from saying more. He was too sure of himself, too forward with her, and his attentions would only cause her trouble.

"I suppose it doesn't matter to you that I was hated within a day of arriving for something over which I had no control. No doubt you gave no thought to the girl whom

I replaced, but I assure you she isn't pleased to be back in the kitchen just because you've taken an interest in me."

"Well, I won't take back what I've done. Not if it means you slaving away in the kitchen."

"Someone has to do it. Why shouldn't it be me?" she countered.

"Because it shouldn't," he answered, his voice suddenly harsh. "A fool could see you're not meant for that sort of thing."

Rose stood rooted to the floor, staring at him.

"I don't understand why you care one way or another," she said at last, dropping her eyes.

"I don't know either," he said, a note of rough confusion in his voice. "But is it so terrible?"

She raised her eyes to his and immediately wished she hadn't, for in his intent brown gaze she saw a heat she couldn't help but respond to. Whether from anger or confusion, her cheeks heated and her heart pounded.

Will had never once made her feel this way. Why must this man, of all people?

Thoroughly out of her depth, Rose nevertheless knew she had to take control of the situation or risk disaster. Her voice was quiet and firm when she spoke, not even a quiver betraying her inner turmoil.

"I'm nearly betrothed to a man back home. But even were I not, I'm a servant in your father's house, Mr. Fletcher. If you insist on giving me unwaranted attention, you will only make things more difficult for me, and possibly cost me my position. I beg you to leave me be."

A bleak silence greeted this harsh speech. It was several seconds before Mr. Fletcher spoke.

"I see. I have no wish to cause you distress," he replied stiffly, his eyes shuttering. "I shall bother you no more."

With that he turned and left the room, his limp a silent accusation. As soon as he was gone Rose began to shake. Everything depended on her remaining in the Fletcher's employ, but she might very well have insulted Mr. Fletcher beyond endurance. For all she knew he was on his way to speak to Mrs. Craig about dismissing her. If only she'd explained things rationally, without goading him. It was unlike her to lose her temper so.

Looking down she saw that she'd dropped the book. Bending over she picked it up, gently set it on the table, and left the room.

⸺ꝰ⸺

"Luke," Charlotte called, her voice more command than greeting.

Luke stopped, one foot on the bottom stair step, desperate to escape to his own bedchamber. Biting back a sigh, he reluctantly turned around and faced Charlotte.

Not for the first time he wished his father had chosen someone more generous and less concerned with appearances to share his later years. Jonas seemed happy enough and Charlotte did no real harm, but just speaking to her put him on edge, and after the unpleasant episode with Rose he had no desire to engage in conversation with her. But they were living in the same house for the time being, and that meant they had to tolerate one another until his work on the railroad was completed.

"Yes, Charlotte?" he replied, forcing a polite smile.

Charlotte approached him, the skirts of her blue dress rustling with each step. With her dark, only slightly graying hair pulled back in a severe coiffure and her strand of pearls, she was every inch the mistress of the house.

"What's this I hear about you asking Mrs. Craig to change the new maid's duties? Please tell me you did no such thing."

It seemed there was no end to the fuss over what he'd considered a minor request. He tried to quell his impatience over having to account for his actions, and instead endeavored to answer her with as much equanimity as he could muster.

"Unfortunately, I can give you no such assurance. However, I meant no affront to Mrs. Craig or to you. I only thought she'd be better suited to something other than scullery maid. Surely no harm was done?"

Luke watched the indecision work in Charlotte's expression as she hesitated, as if unsure whether to be angry or to dismiss the incident as unimportant.

He sighed as Charlotte's mouth thinned. Bitterness had won out again.

"You needn't concern yourself with a servant girl. If you must have your sport with one, at least choose one from another household."

This was insulting on so many levels that Luke chose to ignore it altogether. Clearly he'd misjudged the consequences of his request. It wouldn't happen again.

"Much as I'm enjoying our conversation, I'm afraid I'm a bit weary. If you'll excuse me ..."

Charlotte opened her mouth as if to reply, but Luke gave her no time. Taking the stairs as fast as his ankle would allow, he made for his chamber. Once inside he fell back into a green brocade armchair, a cast-off from the drawing room that had been a favorite of his mother's.

He seethed for several minutes over his conversation with Charlotte, but before long Rose's accusations pushed their way to the fore. Now that he thought about it, he saw how people might misconstrue things, though surely that would blow over when it became clear there was nothing between them.

Then again, he did seem to be taking an inordinate amount of interest in her. She was a maid in his father's house, and just minutes ago he'd accosted her in the morning room.

What had she said? Oh, yes, she'd accused him of not considering the maid who'd been sent back to the scullery.

He'd always considered himself a liberal thinker, but the fact was he had not for a moment thought about how his request would affect the other servants. Aside from Mrs. Craig, whom he'd known since he was a boy, they remained in the background seeing to the family's comfort. Though he certainly never wished them ill, on the whole he didn't worry about their feelings. Why bother when he'd soon be gone?

Which made it even odder that he'd taken such an interest in the new maid. Or perhaps not so odd, given her extraordinary beauty and mysterious background. Still, it had been years since he'd gone out of his way for a woman. Not since Catherine, come to think of it.

Unbidden, the memory came to him of Catherine as she lay dying, her heart-shaped face pale, her eyes glazed over. As always, he pushed the image away before it could take root.

Catherine had died six years ago, and not once had he wavered in his decision never to marry again. He wasn't a man to make the same mistake twice. Nor had he felt more than casual interest in any woman since.

Of course, when it came to Rose Stratton, any man with eyes felt more than casual interest. But what did she mean, she was *nearly* betrothed? One either was or one wasn't. If he were betrothed to her, nearly or otherwise, he sure as hell wouldn't let her slave away in some stranger's house.

He picked up one of the rocks he'd set on the table near his chair, mementos he kept to remind him of where he'd been these past six years. He'd pulled this one, a rock of hardened red clay, from the ground on a foray into Mexico some three years ago. Just holding it brought back the heat of the day and vastness of the land, the absolute freedom he'd felt.

He felt anything but free here. Even now Catherine's death, and the death of their unborn child, weighed him down, haunting his every step. It was the reason he'd left six years ago, though he'd hoped that the years between would have dulled the memories.

But then, why should it be different? Guilt had just as tight a hold on him now as it did the day he left. But whereas out west he had only his own conscience to contend with, now he was back on the streets they'd once walked together. Boston had once been the town he called home. Now it was the scene of his greatest regrets.

For the last six years he'd gone weeks at a time without seeing or speaking to anyone, and he still wasn't used to the noise and commotion of Boston, to all the people and constant conversation. Oh, he could converse well enough in the course of his work, but that was with businessmen. Clearly he'd forgotten how to behave around other people.

Maids, for instance.

Also on the table was a bottle filled with rough little garnets he'd panned from the gravel of Sully's Creek. They'd need to be smoothed and polished before they looked like jewels, but even so the light from a nearby candle struck sparks in them.

All at once he remembered the brilliance of Rose's hair lit by the late afternoon sun streaming through the window, and his fist clenched around the little bottle, threatening to crack it.

⎯⎯⎯ᴄ

For the first few days after her encounter with Mr. Fletcher, Rose held her breath every time Mrs. Craig spoke to her, certain she was about to be dismissed. But when several days passed without incident she dared to relax and hope that she'd last long enough to finish what she'd started. That was all that mattered and all that kept her from despair, as she had never been so lonely.

Every morning at breakfast she had to endure the hostility of the staff, who either ignored her or made snide comments. Even worse than their dislike was the game they made of misinforming her. Several times Abigail or Dottie told her she was wanted in one of the rooms to serve tea or clean up a spill, but upon entering the room Rose found that no one had requested any such thing. Worse still were the times she ignored their claims, only to be scolded because they'd been telling the truth.

Luke often travelled out to the Berkshires on behalf of the railroad, leaving Rose to wonder how the line was progressing, and what it might mean for the farm. On the evenings he was present at Cider Hill she had no choice but to wait upon him, and each and every time she approached him her face flamed and her hand trembled with nerves. He was perfectly courteous, nothing more, but even so there remained a strained awareness between them that shook her.

Each morning after he left she tidied his bedchamber, her heart beating as if she were taking part in something illicit. Day after day she made his bed, though she was unable to imagine his powerful body subdued by sleep. Instead her willful mind pictured him lying beneath the sheets, bare-chested, looking at her with the hunger he'd shown before.

For those few minutes he was all around her – in the coat draped over a chair, the cluster of stones on his chest of drawers, the scent of his shaving soap and fresh linen. Even without his presence he overwhelmed her senses, until the act of smoothing his pillow and straightening the bedcovers left her flushed with awareness.

She countered this reaction with stern lectures to herself. She had no business feeling anything for him, least of all attraction. Her goal was the only thing that mattered, and all that kept her spirits from plunging too low as she dusted, cleaned, served and scurried from sun-up until sundown, all without discovering anything new about the Fletchers or her father. Even mealtimes were disappointing, as Mrs. Fletcher couldn't abide discussion of the railroad and had forbade it in her presence.

But as tired as Rose was, each night she added a bit to the letter she was writing Aunt Olivia. It was a comfort to compose her thoughts, and just the act of writing made her feel closer to the farm. Since she had no wish to burden her aunt, she kept her tone light and said little of what her days were like. Instead she wrote of the countryside, her chatty roommate and general observations of the house and family.

After a week of writing, she slipped the finished letters between the pages of a book of Shakespeare's sonnets. She would mail them on Monday when she visited Vivian. Most of the staff gave their letters to Mrs. Craig to post, but Rose couldn't let anyone connect her to her aunt's farm.

She knew better than most how damning a letter could be.

For days after her father's death she had replayed her father's last words over and over, unable to make any sense of the name Fletcher. It was not until going through some papers that she found several letters from Jonas Fletcher, president of the Western Railroad Company. They were addressed to Olivia Harris, as her aunt had inherited the farm, and contained an offer to buy her land.

"Why didn't you tell me about these?" she'd asked her aunt, holding out the letters.

Her aunt looked up from where she sat at the kitchen table, sorting through her seeds. It was nearly time for planting, though the threat of frost was not yet passed.

Aunt Olivia sighed and sat back from the table.

"They didn't seem important at the time. You knew I'd had an offer and refused it. Peter and I didn't think much of the rest of the letters, as they were no temptation to us, not with your uncle and mother buried here, and this land in our family so many years. I didn't tell you about them after your father died for fear of upsetting you."

"But we've got to tell the sheriff —" Rose began.

"I already have. He doesn't think there's anything to it. Or not enough to go chasing after a powerful Boston family."

Rose couldn't believe what she was hearing.

"Did he read these? He must see how urgently Jonas Fletcher wants our land. Why, he offers more each time he writes. In the very last one he says he'll send someone out to speak to you. How can the sheriff not see how important this is? It was written only two weeks before Papa was shot."

"I feel just as you do, but it's no use. According to the sheriff it's not enough to start an investigation."

"But what about what Papa said before he..." she trailed off, her throat closing up as she recalled the last few minutes of her father's life.

"Oh, Rose, I understand how this feels. Don't you think I want to know who did this to us? But if someone from the railroad did kill him, then we may still be in danger."

"I can't accept that the man who shot my father is still out there, living his life. If the sheriff won't do something, I shall."

"That's exactly what I was afraid you'd say, and the very reason I didn't mention anything to you. I can't lose you too, Rose."

But Rose couldn't bear the thought of never knowing, of such an act going unpunished. She spent weeks lying awake at night, considering and discarding ways to prove the Fletchers' guilt. Now here she was, despite her aunt's fear and protestations. After two months spent searching for a way to get near the Fletchers and another month exchanging letters with Mrs. Craig, her plan was in motion.

Perhaps she was as rash as Aunt Olivia said.

She missed the farm. While her life there was a far cry from her earlier life in Boston before her mother's death, still her father had been there to challenge her, to give her books and discuss her thoughts on them. Aunt Olivia was a well-read and curious woman, and the three of them would read aloud to one another or play word games in the evenings, a ritual Rose missed dearly.

But at least she had some of her books here to comfort her. In addition to the sonnets, she had brought *Oliver Twist*, a book both she and her father had always loved, and which he had assigned her to read as if he were still a teacher. She would have brought Emerson's Essays as well, had not her father's name been inscribed inside.

Homesick and eager to escape her own circumstances, at least for a time, Rose opened Dickens and read by the light of the wavering candle while Lydia tatted lace for a sister who would soon be married.

A few minutes later Lydia let her lace fall to her lap with a sigh.

"I guess you must like reading. You hardly notice anything when you have your nose in a book."

Rose held her place with a finger and looked up with a smile.

"Yes, I suppose that's true. Do you dislike reading?" she asked, wondering what had prompted Lydia's comment.

"Yes, but I suspect that's only because I do it so poorly. I was always so busy taking care of my little brothers and sisters, I wasn't in school enough to learn properly. But I love to listen to stories, so if ever you want to read something out loud from one of your books, you don't have to worry about bothering me."

Rose smiled inwardly at Lydia's eager, rather childlike way of asking Rose to read to her.

"I'd be happy to read aloud," she said. "In fact I'll start the book over so that we can begin together." She paused for a moment, turning an idea over in her head. "We could even take turns, if you like. That way you could practice."

Lydia flushed with pleasure. "Are you sure you wouldn't mind? I don't think I'm much fun to listen to. The teacher used to get awful cross and strike my hand with a ruler when I made a mistake."

"Well, I won't get cross. What do you think? Should we begin now?"

Lydia smiled with delight and nodded her head. Rose held out the book, which Lydia shyly took from her, and so their own nightly ritual began.

CHAPTER THREE

*R*ose was standing at the dining room table polishing an enormous pile of silver and working out the best way to get into Mr. Fletcher's study when Mrs. Craig stopped in the doorway.

"Rose, please take tea to Mrs. Fletcher and her guests in the drawing room. Mrs. Beech has a tray of food as well."

When Rose entered the kitchen for the tea tray, Abigail was giggling, her face bent toward Dottie.

"Well *I* could have sworn I heard her sneaking down the hall late last night, no doubt to meet him," Dottie said, before Abigail caught sight of Rose in the doorway and whispered urgently to Dottie. The two of them looked at Rose and laughed meanly before turning back to their tasks.

Rose's heart sank. She'd hoped the staff might be helpful in learning more about the family and its business, but that was impossible now. She would have to rely on her own ability to gather information, and it was time she got started. Sometime this week she would find a way to search the study.

Without saying a word to the other girls she moved about the kitchen, preparing the silver tea service, adding fresh baked scones and the little finger sandwiches Mrs. Beech had prepared. Shouldering the heavy tray, a task she had not yet mastered, she made her way to the back of the house. Her arms shook and the service started to slide as the tray tilted precariously, but just before everything crashed to the floor someone approached from behind and righted the tray.

"Allow me."

Rose's heart sped up at the sound of Luke's voice in her ear, and she nearly jumped out of her skin when his arm brushed her side as he moved to take the tray. Embarrassed to be caught in such a vulnerable position, she wanted only to maintain a safe distance from him.

"Thank you, but that's not necessary. I have everything in hand," Rose replied curtly, inwardly cursing her breathlessness and the visible trembling of her arms.

One eyebrow rose. "Of course you do. Humor me anyway."

And with that he plucked the tray from her arms and let her proceed him into the room.

Upholstered in shades of gold with flowered accents, the sofas, brocaded chairs and heavy satin drapes caught the late afternoon light and spun it into a warm glow that lit the room. Mrs. Fletcher sat with two women, a mother and daughter from the look of them, and a young man Rose had never seen before. After a moment's study it became obvious he was Mrs. Fletcher's son, Nathan Byrne. Both he and his mother had the same narrow face and rather pinched features, though Mr. Byrne's hair was dark blond. Rose felt his eyes on her as she stood awkwardly by while Luke set the tea service on a table.

Mrs. Fletcher looked on, none too pleased to see her stepson carrying a tray.

"I see you still need some training, Rose. I'll have to speak to Mrs. Craig about that. We can't have family waiting on the servants, can we?" she said silkily.

Rose was mortified to be rebuked in front of everyone and felt her face burn in embarrassment. Then Luke spoke.

"You misunderstand, Charlotte, " he said easily. "I insisted on carrying the tray as I could see it was quite heavy. I'm sure any man would have done the same."

Mrs. Fletcher's face hardened, her lips thinning, before she remembered herself.

"Of course. What a gentleman you are, my dear."

"Shall I pour the tea?" Rose asked, stepping forward to take hold of the pot.

"Thank you, no. We'll manage without you."

Turning to her son, who had not ceased his scrutiny of Rose, she began to pour. "Do tell us all about your trip to Albany, Nathan."

Rose was dismissed. Retreating from the room, she made sure not to look anyone in the eye, least of all Luke Fletcher.

Rose stood outside the study door later the next day, her heart pounding. She had been told to change the linens in all the bedrooms on the second floor, which made it the ideal time to search the study, but even the cleaning supplies she carried would not be enough to shield her if she were caught. Mrs. Craig had made it clear that Mr.

Fletcher allowed no one but her in there to clean, and even then it was only upon request.

But this morning was perfect. It was a lovely summer day and Mr. and Mrs. Fletcher had left for a riding party and picnic with their guests. The staff was making use of the unexpected leisure time to loll about in the shade out back of the house. She could hear them laughing and teasing one another from an open window.

She paused outside the door, nearly faint with anxiety as she listened to make certain no one was inside. Not a sound but the blood beating in her ears. Before she could change her mind she turned the knob, the squeak it made seemingly loud enough to bring everyone running. Slowly she opened the door and let herself in, her breath fast with fear, noting with relief that the heavy damask curtains were drawn on the bright day outside. She needn't fear being seen through the window.

The study looked very much as she had imagined it would, with two wing chairs set before a giant oak desk and bookshelves against the far wall. But what caught her eye were the pen and ink sketches that hung around the room. She had seen nothing of the kind anywhere else in the house.

The one nearest her depicted Cider Hill in wintertime, the starkness of the house at that time of year conveyed with simple yet compelling details. Moving closer, she saw by the signature that it had been drawn by Luke Fletcher.

Quickly, knowing she should not be wasting even this much time, she looked at the others, all bearing the young

Mr. Fletcher's name—portraits of children she guessed must be nieces and nephews, as well as one of a dark-haired woman in a garden. At first Rose thought her one of Luke's sisters, but on closer inspection she looked to be older than they would be even now, and the style of dress was far too out-dated. This, then, must be the first Mrs. Fletcher. Luke's mother.

She was lovely, and lovingly portrayed as well, particularly given how young Luke must have been when he drew it. And though Luke looked far more like his father, she could see something of him in her high cheekbones and the fullness of her mouth.

Moved by the affection evident in each drawing, she found herself wanting to study them more, to see others he'd done. But she could spare no more time now on the discovery.

She hurried to the desk, grateful for the carpet's muffling effect, and scanned the desktop. She didn't know exactly what she was looking for. A reference to running the railroad though Lenox, a letter on the subject perhaps? Taking care not to disturb anything, she read through the various papers on the blotter, her hands quick as those of a seasoned spy, though perhaps a trifle shakier. Next she opened the drawers and rifled through them. A thick file with Luke's name on it caught her eye.

Inside were letters from Luke to his father. She held her breath as she paged through them. Near the end she found a letter from Fort Laramie dated 4 April, 1841.

Dear Father,

I see that it took so long for your last letter to find me that you may as well have come yourself. There will soon be no need for letter writing, however, or for further requests that I come home to work for the R.R. I am finally persuaded by you to return to Boston, at least until we see the railroad over those blasted mountains. My work here is coming to an end and I daresay they can spare me now. Someone must help Whistler find a way over that range, and there is nothing like surveying in the mountains.

Having begun my task under President Harrison, it is strange indeed to be ending it under Tyler, though I expect he too will want to organize and tame the Territories as much as his predecessor. I only hope he is not too successful. I would hate for all the country to feel as civilized as my hometown. The irony is that my own work hastens the very thing I fear.

If all goes well I will set off from here in a week's time. As I will be passing so close to Woodstock, I shall stop for perhaps a week to visit with Annabelle. My niece and nephew must meet their uncle before they are too old to care that they have one.

I know you understand why I stayed away so long, and why I shall not remain in Massachusetts beyond the completion of the railroad. As much as I miss my family and my beloved Cider Hill, I cannot forget what I lost there.

I sincerely hope the frustrations you expressed in your last letter have passed. If not, I hope I may ease them upon my return. As ever,

Your faithful son,

Luke

Rose stared at the date on the letter, the import of it gradually sinking in. At the time of her father's murder in February, Luke was somewhere out west surveying for the government. He couldn't possibly have killed her father.

Earlier letters from Luke to Mr. Fletcher were filled with tales of his adventures in the wilderness and occasional frustrations with government officials, but nothing of relevance to her search. If only she could get her hands on the letters Mr. Fletcher had sent to Luke, perhaps she would get an idea of how desperate he was, what lengths he might go to in order to finish the line.

Quickly she skimmed through the rest of the papers, but there was very little in the way of railroad business. No doubt there was a good deal more at his offices in town. But at least now she knew Luke's role with the railroad. As a surveyor, he would be relied upon by his father, as well as the shareholders and engineers, for the best route through the hills.

She was putting the papers back in order when the sound of approaching footsteps broke the silence. Panicked, her hands trembling, Rose replaced the papers and closed the drawer. She had just stepped around the desk and grabbed the duster when the door opened.

Luke stared at her from the doorway, his expression quickly turning to a frown, and Rose feared he could read her guilt. Silently she ordered herself to remain calm.

"You startled me," she exclaimed, a hand going to her heart as she smiled at him with what she hoped was a convincing display of innocence.

"What are you doing in here?"

"I'm dusting your father's study. It looks as if no one ever has. Goodness, it's dreary in here!"

Walking over to the drapes, she pulled them open one by one until the dust covering the desk and bookshelves was satisfactorily revealed. With a flourish of the feather duster she commenced a vigorous attack on the offending dust.

Luke looked less than convinced.

"My father doesn't allow anyone but Mrs. Craig in here, and even then only when he specifically requests it."

"I didn't realize," she said. "Please don't tell anyone. I can't afford to lose my place here."

Rose bit her lip and clasped her hands in distress, playing on his sympathies and acting as though she were on the verge of tears. Indeed, it was hardly an act.

"You don't need to be frightened. I won't tell anyone," he said, clearly bemused by her overreaction.

Relief flooded through her, quickly followed by an overwhelming awareness of him. Now that she knew he was innocent, all the protection her suspicion had afforded her drained away. Her breath came fast and light, and she couldn't seem to look away from him.

In the blink of an eye his mood shifted. His gaze swept over her from head to toe and back up to her face, the heat in his eyes holding her where she stood. Neither of them said a word as the tension that had simmered below the surface now shimmered between them.

Then he moved, covering the space between them in two strides. For a moment he looked at her as if daring her to deny him, or perhaps he was giving her the chance to stop him. But a second was all it lasted, for in the next instant those big hands dove into her hair and he bent his head down to her, his mouth claiming hers.

She started at the hot rush of his lips on hers, her hands automatically rising to grasp his shoulders. Never had she been kissed so, without any time to think, only to feel the hardness and heat of him pressed against her. He said her name like a rough prayer and then his tongue was parting her lips, devouring her where she stood.

Rose went utterly still, shocked at this new demand. Part of her wanted to follow where he led, but it was too treacherous, too sudden. Tearing her mouth from his she pushed at his chest, her breathing fast and light as she stared up at him.

Releasing her, Luke backed way and stood with his hands on his hips, his cheekbones flushed and his breath ragged. Then he turned away from her, pressing a hand against the wall as if for balance.

The feather duster lay on the floor by her feet, a laughable reminder of the whole charade gone awry. Quickly she snatched it up along with her pail and rags and nearly ran for the door, desperate to get away.

"Rose. Please wait."

She stopped where she was, her back to Luke, unable to face him. The feelings were too new, her newly awakened body too inexperienced to contain them. She didn't understand what had just happened. Why had he kissed her? And how could she have kissed him back? She was terrified at how quickly she had let go of everything she knew of herself. When Luke was near it was as if Will didn't even exist. Even now she could not so much as summon his face to mind.

"Rose, please look at me," he said, and she felt his hand on her shoulder, urging her to turn around.

But she couldn't bring herself to speak to him. Her life had been turned upside down in the space of a few minutes, and she was very much afraid she would not be able to pretend otherwise.

So she ran. He called after her but she didn't slow down and she didn't look back. Out of the study and down the servants' staircase she flew until she was safe from him, if not from herself.

⌇

Luke ran a shaking hand through his hair. What had he been thinking? Nothing rational, that was certain. He was so utterly drawn to Rose, his reason fled whenever he was around her.

At first he'd just been startled to see her. But when she pulled open the curtains, the sun that flooded the room lit her hair and warmed her skin to a glow. He could see where a sheen of perspiration dampened the fine hairs on her neck, and her worn dress revealed her gentle curves.

And then, sweet heaven, the taste of her. He was so undone by that kiss he could have dragged her to the floor then and there. Even now he imagined Rose opening for him, her skirts up around her waist while he buried himself inside her. A moment of heaven for a lifetime of hell. It might have been worth it, come to that.

But of course it would never come to that. She had stopped him because she was not some strumpet who lifted her skirts for every man who couldn't control himself. He doubted she'd ever been kissed properly – if indeed she'd been kissed at all.

The last time he saw her she was telling him to leave her be, and now look what he'd done. It hadn't helped matters that she'd stood there, looking at him with naked hunger. She was so innocent she probably didn't even know what she was inviting, but he was no saint.

He needed to put some distance between them. He'd been planning a trip out to survey for possible routes over the hills, so he might as well leave now. When he came back, he'd have his head on straight.

That was the thing to do, but even so he felt an alarming pang at the idea of never touching her again. If only she were not so innocent, or not employed in his father's house.

If only he were not the man he was.

Rose tossed and turned all night, falling asleep only a few hours before dawn, her dreams a disturbing mix of her father and Luke Fetcher, desire and guilt. She woke feeling ragged and forlorn. Fortunately today was her day off and she would see Vivian.

It was a six-mile walk to the March's modest home just off Tremont Street near the Common, nearly two hours each way. But as it was virtually her only time alone, Rose didn't mind the long walk. She nearly ran the last few minutes, stopping only at the post office to mail her letter. Though she and Vivian had remained close after Rose's mother died and she and her father left Boston, the friendship had been conducted almost entirely through letters until Rose's return two weeks ago. Seeing Vivian once a week while working for the Fletchers was a treat she didn't take for granted.

"You look tired, Rose," Vivian observed. "Are you well?"

They were sitting on the front porch where the breeze slipped pleasantly over them, sipping lemonade made by Sally, the March's housekeeper. Sally was more like family, and in fact it was she who had helped secure Rose's position at Cider Hill.

Vivian waited patiently, her kind face inviting Rose's confidence. It felt like months since anyone had shown such concern for her. The thought flashed in her mind that Luke Fletcher had worried for her, but she quickly banished it.

"Oh, you needn't fret over me," Rose said, smiling at her friend. "It's not so very bad. In fact, most of the work is no harder than what I do on the farm. The difficult part is that most of the staff dislike me. But I have you, and that will be more than enough to see me through," she finished, trying to sound optimistic. Like Aunt Olivia, Vivian had been against the idea of Rose going to the Fletcher's, though her support never flagged once it was clear Rose would go through with her plan.

"We're always here for you, you know that," Vivian said. "If you should get into any trouble..."

"Don't worry, I'll come straight here if I find I must leave Cider Hill." Rose paused, trying to find a way to broach the subject that was most on her mind this morning. "There are complications that I hadn't expected, Vivian. Ones that are dangerous in an entirely unforeseen way."

"What do you mean?" her friend asked, frowning in puzzlement.

Taking a deep breath, Rose began to tell Vivian about Luke.

Vivian kept silent and let her speak without interrupting, though she leaned forward in her chair, her hands gripped tightly together. She squealed as Rose described the tension of searching the study, and let out a gasp, her hand flying to her mouth, when Rose described their kiss.

"So you see," Rose finished, "the work is actually the least of my worries."

"This Mr. Fletcher must be very compelling for you to behave so uncharacteristically."

"Yes, he is. He's terribly handsome and ...there's just something about him."

"Something Will doesn't have, I take it?"

"Next to Luke Fletcher, Will feels like a brother," Rose replied with dismay.

"Oh dear."

"I can't believe I said that, or thought it, but I'm afraid it's so. Will has never made me feel as Mr. Fletcher does. I've always wondered why I never got as excited as other girls do over their beaux. But if Mr. Fletcher were to court me..."

"Oh Rose, do be careful! There are so many things that could go wrong if you get mixed up with him. What if he's trifling with you?"

"He most certainly is trifling with me. What else could it be? But I'll be more careful. I'm sure someone in that family killed my father. Jonas Fletcher makes the most sense, though I confess I have difficulty believing it of the man I met. I must contrive to see his business correspondence."

Vivian looked alarmed. "How will you do that?"

"I have no idea, but I'll find a way."

Vivian reached out and took Rose's hand in hers.

"I admire you exceedingly, you know."

"Whatever for? I'm making a mess of everything."

"For your courage, your heart, your loyalty. Not to mention that perfect skin of yours," she laughed, lightening the mood with her smile.

"Oh, but you can't admire my hands. Look at them," she said, holding out her chapped hands for her friend to see. "No one could ever mistake me for a gently bred woman now. I never thought I was vain," she sighed ruefully, "but I must admit, I did set a store by my hands. I suppose I got that from my mother. Every night we smoothed salve over them and wore kid gloves to bed. I never stopped doing it, even after she died, though it doesn't seem to make much difference these days."

"I always thought the way your parents fell in love was the most romantic thing I ever heard," Vivian confessed.

"The way your mother gave up her family in England to live with your father here. I made my father tell me the story every night at bedtime for a year at least."

"They were very much in love until the day she died. I always hoped I'd find that sort of love myself."

"Yes, we all hope for that," Vivian murmured.

"Has Mr. Mitchell gotten up the nerve to speak to you yet?" Rose asked.

This elicited a telling blush from Vivian, who shyly told her about Mr. Mitchell's careful approach after church the previous Sunday. They sat happily for hours, enjoying one another's company, and Rose joined Vivian and her father, Edward, for an early supper. She left soon afterwards, promising to be careful and return the next week.

The town still held the day's heat, but once she left Boston proper the air cooled. Houses fell away and farmland took over, most of it bordered by low stone walls running along the side of the road. The soft light of early evening descended as she approached Fletcher land, blurring the landscape until it felt almost dreamlike. On either side of the road freshly tilled soil alternated with pastureland, the peaceful goats and cows bestowing an air of serenity. These gave way to the apple orchard Cider Hill was named for, the trees with their froth of late-blooming white blossoms stopping Rose in her tracks.

They looked so full of promise, so graceful in a week perilously short on grace. Rose stood and gazed at their long, arcing branches and delicate flowers, drawing strength from them before continuing on.

She was no more than half a mile from the house when she heard someone call her name.

"Rose? Rose, is that you?"

Startled out of her thoughts, Rose stopped and looked up to see Mrs. Fletcher's son, Mr. Byrne, sitting in a brougham watching her expectantly. A coachman sat atop it looking the other way.

"May I offer you my carriage the rest of the way?"

Rose began to object, but he would have none of it.

"I insist you let me convey you to the house."

Rose hesitated, unsure what to do. She had been enjoying her walk and wanted these last few minutes to herself before returning to the house. But it was not only that. There was something about Mr. Byrne that made her uneasy, yet in a way unlike his stepbrother did. Maybe it was his smile, which held no warmth, or the way his pale blue eyes traveled over her figure.

Still, it seemed ridiculous to refuse, and she didn't want him to make a greater fuss.

"Thank you. You're very kind," Rose replied without feeling, unsuccessfully trying to calm her misgivings as Mr. Byrne watched her climb in.

It was luxurious inside, far nicer than she would have expected, given that he did not have a great deal of money. It struck her as an affectation for a bachelor to keep a coachman, particularly as he did not have the means. But then, perhaps he had his mother's ambition for greater social standing.

He was smiling to himself as if terribly pleased. He had a dissolute look about him, his eyes bloodshot, his clothing wilted as if he'd been up all day and night in the same attire.

The carriage had just begun to move when he spoke.

"I cannot help wondering how you came to work at Cider Hill. You're much too pretty to be a servant."

Rose stared resolutely ahead, her hands curled into fists on her lap. How dare he speak to her so? She should never have accepted the ride. Though she had only to bear his company for a few more minutes, even that was intolerable.

"Cannot a servant be pretty?" she countered, more sharply than was wise.

"I suppose, but there are so many other things pretty girls may do if they like," he replied with an insinuating smile.

Rose shook with fury, but she could not afford to insult him. Though she'd once feared that Luke Fletcher would have her dismissed, she understood now he would never do such a thing. She had no such confidence in Mr. Byrne.

"I prefer an honest day's work. In fact I wouldn't have it any other way," Rose replied, refusing to look at him.

Mr. Byrne shot her a quick look and she worried she'd gone too far. Then he chortled as if amused.

"I guess you came to the right place then. Just remember, if you ever tire of it there are easier ways to make a living."

Mercifully, they had arrived at the house. Climbing out of the carriage, Rose hurried away without a word. She knew without looking that he watched her the whole way.

By the time she gained the servants' entrance she had moved Mr. Byrne up her short list of suspects. The fact

that he was a cad did not necessarily mean he was a murderer as well. But he was family and he clearly had a stake
in the railroad. Just how much she would have to find out.

Her pulse sped up as she made her way through the
servants' wing and up the stairs to her room. Of course she
didn't hear or see any sign of Luke, but just knowing that
at any moment she could run into him kept her on edge.

She spent the next morning in this state, her senses on
alert for Luke's voice or footstep. Her anxiety was soon dis-
pelled however when she overheard Mrs. Craig reviewing
the week's menu with Mrs. Beech.

"Master Luke left for the Berkshires this morning on
railroad business. That leaves us with just four for supper
tonight, though tomorrow..."

Rose lost track of what Mrs. Craig was saying. She knew
only that she need not face Luke for a while yet. It was a
four day trip on horseback, which meant he would likely
be gone at least two weeks. It was an unexpected reprieve.
Yet mixed with her relief was a sense of disappointment.

It was only then she admitted to herself that part of
her very much wanted to see him again.

CHAPTER FOUR

"*R*ose?"

Rose started at the voice behind her and turned from where she stood on tiptoe in the pantry, searching for the tea Mrs. Fletcher insisted must be served to her guests. Charlie, the lanky young groom, stood in the doorway, shifting his weight from foot to foot as he tried and failed to make eye contact.

Rose couldn't begin to guess the reason for his shyness. Normally he was quite confident, and though he was not as cold to her as were Dottie and Abigail, his manner when they had occasion to meet was familiar to the point of rudeness.

"Yes, what is it, Charlie?"

"I was wondering...that is...Lydia says you read real pretty and you're helping her read too. I don't need to read out loud to people or anything, leastways I don't expect I'll ever want to, but I was thinking maybe someday I'll want to do something besides take care of horses. So I was wondering if you could help me read better, and maybe even write better also."

He looked up at her hopefully.

Rose stared at him in surprise, turning the idea over for a moment before replying.

"Yes, I could help you," she said, glad for the opportunity to make another ally. Besides, she enjoyed her sessions with Lydia and could never turn down anyone who wanted to learn to read.

They had their first lesson the very next afternoon. It being too warm in the servants' hall, they settled themselves on a horse blanket under the shade of a maple tree near the carriage house. With a sheepish grin Charlie produced a bible given him by his mother.

Charlie was an eager student and Rose found that she possessed an endless amount of patience when it came to teaching. She didn't mind if it took ten minutes for him to get through a single paragraph, and she recited passages for him to copy, repeating herself as many times as was necessary.

Word of their lessons spread, and within two weeks several of the farmhands who worked at Cider Hill had approached her and asked if they might join them. Delighted, Rose agreed and soon had eight students she met throughout the week for lessons.

In the evenings, when not reading with Lydia, she read and re-read letters Vivian had given her from Aunt Olivia and Will. Her aunt wrote of how well the crops were growing, a runaway cow that had managed to travel ten miles before being caught, and the new schoolhouse that would be raised within the month. She had always loved the parties for raising buildings, when people from miles around ate and drank and danced after the walls went up. She missed laughing.

It was at just such an event that she met Will. He came from a good family with a thriving farm, was shy but not afraid to approach her. She enjoyed his company, found him sincere and comfortable to talk to. But whereas his eyes lit up every time he caught sight of her, she was never more than pleased to see him.

He was handsome and kind, with a gentle manner, and he genuinely wanted to know what she thought. Only she somehow could never talk to him about the things that mattered to her. When she spoke of her former life in Boston he seemed at a loss, puzzled and worried that her life did not already contain all she could want. The way he spoke of his farm she knew he loved the land, and she envied him the certainty he had of his place in the world.

When Will suggested they might one day marry, Rose went home to talk to her father. She found him in the barn, sitting on a bale of hay and mending a piece of tack in the sunlight from the open door. Though it was a story she knew well, she asked him how he and her mother had fallen in love, something she hadn't done since she was a little girl. But she listened now with a woman's heart and wondered if she would be giving up on that kind of happiness. And if so, would she find another kind in return?

"Everyone has to decide for themselves what they want, Rose," her father had said in that quiet, thoughtful way of his. "You'll know it when you find it, and it may not be the same as what your mother and I had. You may need to be brave enough to see it for what it is."

All she'd wanted at that moment was to remain in the warmth and safety of her father's presence, breathing in the sweet smell of hay as the goats shuffled in a nearby pen and cows lowed in the field below. But life did not stand still. Everyone had to grow up and make their choices.

Perhaps growing up meant giving up on childish ideas of love. Few people had what her parents had. They were lucky, luckier than most, but wasn't she lucky to have found a man like Will? Maybe it was foolish to expect more than that.

A couple of women told her she'd be a fool to pass him by, and that one day she'd regret it. She even overheard one woman say that Rose thought she was too good to be a farmer's wife, coming as she did from Boston with her city manners, her Latin and French. Rose didn't think she was too good for Will, but she wondered if maybe she had gotten foolish ideas in her head. She wasn't so special, and she could do a lot worse than marry him. But three weeks later her father was dead, and Rose asked Will to wait.

The questions she'd struggled with then loomed even larger now that she knew what she was missing. But Will loved her and was ready to share his life, whereas Luke Fletcher was an impossibility. Comparing the two men was ludicrous, and yet she couldn't seem to help herself.

Of course, she didn't have much to compare these days, as she hadn't seen him since that day in the study two weeks ago. Their encounter was beginning to seem like something out of her imagination, which was all for the better, as her imagination was dangerous enough.

Which was why she needed to find out who killed her father before things got even more complicated.

A rare opportunity finally came her way. She was on the second floor replacing rugs she and Lydia had enthusiastically beaten outside when she heard Mrs. Fletcher address Mrs. Craig.

"I need a message sent to Mr. Fletcher at the office. The Willoughby's shall arrive earlier than expected. Please convey this note to Mr. Fletcher as soon as possible so that he may come home early and greet them with me. I would hate for it to look as if he thought work more important than our old friends."

"Yes, ma'am. I'll send someone straightaway."

Rose caught up with Mrs. Craig as she descended the stairs.

"I hope you don't mind, but I overheard Mrs. Fletcher say she needed a message sent. Shall I go? I've just finished the carpets."

"Very well. I'll have Charlie bring the wagon around. Mrs. Beech needs some things for tonight's dinner as well. Get the list from her and you can stop at the market on the way back."

Quickly Rose retrieved her bonnet from her room before stopping in the kitchen for the list of ingredients. Mrs. Beech scowled at her, but then, she scowled at everyone.

It was a comfortable day for early July, hot but without the stultifying humidity they'd had all week. The sun shone and a soft breeze blew through the trees. Gratefully she sat on the rough wood seat behind Charlie, the two of them enjoying the break away from the house. It was good to be outside, good to be off her feet. It felt like she hadn't drawn a deep breath since her visit with Vivian several days earlier.

She closed her eyes for a moment and could almost believe she was back home, riding with her father to visit a neighboring farm or buy supplies. Though she and her father had always talked easily to each other, they had also enjoyed the quiet of their own thoughts, the creak of the harness leather and occasional snorts from the steady team of horses. If only she could keep her eyes closed forever and go on imagining her father next to her. But it was no use. It merely reminded her of his absence.

The houses stood closer together and traffic grew heavier as they neared town. Riders on horseback vied with carriages and pedestrians for the road, and the air was full of noise — greetings and shouts, stamping hooves and the more distant screech of one of the local trains braking.

Charlie maneuvered the cart through the crowded streets, just barely avoiding a collision with a cart full of chickens. Soon he pulled up before an impressive brownstone on Beacon Street. Next to the door a plaque read Western Railroad Company. For a moment Rose could not move. So long did she hesitate that Charlie looked over at her, one eyebrow raised in question.

"Something wrong, Rose? If you're nervous I can bring the message to Mr. Fletcher."

"No, I'm fine. I'll manage," Rose sputtered, moved to action by his look of concern.

Taking a deep breath, she headed up the brick walkway and mounted the steps. Pausing a moment before the door, she put her hand on the knob and turned.

The interior of the building was even more impressive than the exterior. The shiny wood floors with their plush Turkish rugs spoke of money and success, and bronze sculptures scattered about on delicate tables lent the room an air of elegance and sophistication. Behind a desk a young man in eyeglasses, brown vest and matching coat frowned down at a sheaf of papers.

For a moment, Rose was so terrified she could neither move nor speak. Then the clerk saw her and blushed furiously, standing up so quickly he upset a jar of pens. Somehow his nerves eased her own distress and she was able to approach his desk.

"May I help you, miss?"

"I've come to give Mr. Jonas Fletcher a message from Mrs. Fletcher."

"Of course. Yes. Do let me take it for you. I'll be sure it reaches him."

Rose had not foreseen even this simple obstacle. Quickly she recovered with a lie.

"Oh no. Begging your pardon, Mrs. Fletcher said I must deliver it myself and wait for his reply."

The young man came around the desk.

"Very well, I'll escort you to his offices."

Rose followed the clerk down the hallway, her heart hammering so loudly she feared he would hear it. Offices opened up on both sides, the low hum of voices emanating from inside. At the end of the passage they turned left into a room richly decorated in shades of blue and dark wood. On the walls hung maps of Boston, both older and more recent. The clerk gestured for her to sit.

"Please, wait here. It won't be long. Mr. Fletcher left half an hour ago for an appointment at Town Hall. He should be back shortly."

He hesitated, looking for all the world as if he longed to stay with her, before dropping a self-conscious bow and leaving.

On the wall to her left was a door that she guessed led to Mr. Fletcher's office. Surely a trip to Town Hall would require longer than half an hour, in which case she had time to search it.

Entering his office was terribly risky, but if she wasted this opportunity she would never forgive herself. When the clerk's retreating footsteps had died away she went and pressed her ear to the door. All was silent. Nearly faint with anxiety, she opened the door and stepped inside.

At one end of the large room sat a desk of heavy oak; on it were stacks of paper and what appeared to be ledgers. Tacked up on all four walls were maps detailing different sections of the railroad line. Scanning them quickly, Rose found one showing the most western part of Massachusetts. A thick black line traveled across the state from Boston, breaking right at the boundary of their farm.

She could see that they would have to lay track in another section entirely now that they couldn't run it through their property. She couldn't imagine how it was even possible to lay track through the those mountains, but these men seemed to think they could do it if only they had access through Aunt Olivia's land.

Going to the desk she paged through the ledgers but could make no sense of the figures. It would take much longer than she could spare to decipher them, so she quickly moved on.

Opening a drawer, she flipped through the files until she came to one marked "Land Offers." Inside were letters from landowners all along the route, some of them refusing to sell, others agreeing. She recognized a few names of farmers she'd met or heard mentioned, but there was nothing pertaining to their farm. Disappointed, she replaced the papers. Then her eyes fell on a file labeled "Harris."

With shaking hands and racing heart Rose opened the folder. Inside were copies of the letters Jonas Fletcher had sent to her aunt. Also enclosed were her aunt's replies, including her response to the last offer made for the farm. In it she thanked Mr. Fletcher for his generous offer and said that neither she nor her brother wished to sell. On it Mr. Fletcher had written a note indicating that Mr. Byrne would handle the matter going forward.

A hurried look through the rest of the papers revealed several letters from George Washington Whistler, the engineer responsible for finding a way over the mountains. Whistler mentioned the anticipated arrival of Luke Fletcher, noting that his expertise would be greatly appreciated on such a difficult endeavor.

How strange that all this mapping and planning and focus had been on their part of the world, and they had known so little about it.

Someone was coming down the hall. With her heart in her throat Rose replaced the files and slipped into the next room. She had just taken her seat when Mr. Fletcher entered.

"Good afternoon, Rose. I hear you have a message for me. What has Mrs. Fletcher to say?"

Rose stood and silently offered up the note, her eyes on the floor. Her thoughts were spinning so out of control, she was afraid something of her confusion would show on her face.

Mr. Fletcher read the note with a smile.

"Please assure Mrs. Fletcher that I shall return home by four o'clock."

Her task completed, she should have taken her leave. Instead she stood there, unable to move. She wanted to cry, wanted to demand he tell her what had happened to her father.

"Is that all, Rose?"

Schooling her expression, Rose forced herself to meet his gaze. "Yes, sir, that's all. I'll relate your message."

Dropping a curtsy, she left the room. The clerk jumped to his feet at the sight of her, but Rose merely walked passed him, her head down, a terrible weight in her chest. What was she to make of all this? Was Mr. Byrne the one responsible? And if so, would anyone care? The Lenox sheriff had already dismissed her once. Would the Boston police be any better?

Outside, the bright sun momentarily blinded her. She stood on the top step until her eyes adjusted, and when they did, she grew even more confused. Gone were Charlie and the cart.

"What the devil am I to do now?" she stormed aloud, not expecting a reply.

"Don't blame Charlie. He was merely following orders. I told him to go."

Rose's breath caught at the sound of Luke Fletcher's voice, and she turned to see him coming through the doorway behind her, her marketing basket in his hand. His hair had grown longer since she'd last seen him and now curled over the collar of his shirt. He hadn't shaved in several days and his hat and shoes were dusty. He must ridden straight to the offices without even stopping at Cider Hill.

Heat flooded her at the memory of their last encounter, and she grew too flustered to say anything. And yet she felt caught in that heated look, trapped by her warring emotions. Suspicion of his family and mistrust of his motives vied with an attraction she couldn't control. She could feel his nearness, the warmth emanating from him carrying with it the memory of that shattering kiss.

But she would not be made a fool of.

"Why did you tell him to go? How am I to get back to the house?" Rose demanded, the quiver in her voice betraying her reaction to him.

"When my father and I returned from Town Hall he was here, complaining that he'd been waiting for ages. So I told him I would take you back."

"How could you?" Rose exclaimed. "Already everyone suspects the two of us." She flushed at the realization that this assumption was no longer entirely inaccurate.

Luke ran a hand through his thick hair as if in frustration.

"I hadn't considered that, but no doubt you're correct." He gave her a piercing look. "Are any of the men in the house giving you trouble?"

"You and your stepbrother are the only ones who've made advances," she replied, hoping he saw the absurdity of his righteousness.

But he was not amused. Rather his expression turned thunderous. He approached her, stopping only when he was a foot away.

"What has Nathan done?" he ground out. "I'll kill him if he's laid a hand on you."

Rose stared at him, shocked at his unexpected ferocity.

"It was nothing you need worry about. Please promise me you won't say anything. It will only make things worse for me if you say something on my behalf."

Luke looked aggrieved that he couldn't defend her honor, but finally nodded in agreement. He continued to look troubled, however, and there was something pained in his expression. "I didn't force myself on you, did I, Rose?"

A hot flush raced over her at this, and she knew without a doubt that her face was flaming.

"No, of course you didn't," she replied, her voice nearly a whisper. "But it mustn't happen again."

"I'm well aware of that."

A man hurried by them into the building, looking at them curiously as he went by. Luke took a step away, breaking the unbearable tension.

"Come, let us take care of your errands," Luke said.

"Don't you have anything better to do than see me home?" Rose quipped, her nerves already frayed.

"In fact I don't," replied Luke, smiling down at her. "I'm completely at your disposal."

It wasn't fair. No man should be allowed to smile like that. His eyes crinkled and his white teeth flashed and he was so handsome it simply hurt to look at him.

At a loss as to how to respond, she took refuge in practicalities.

"Very well, then. I must stop at the market before we return. Shall I meet you back here?"

"No, you shall not. I'm coming with you. It's a lovely day for a walk to the market." So saying he placed her hand in the crook of his arm and started off.

Rose glanced up at him out of the corner of her eye. She didn't understand him. Here he was, escorting her through town as if he were her beau. There was nothing in her experience to prepare her for the likes of Luke Fletcher. Nevertheless, she swore she wouldn't let her guard down again. She simply couldn't afford to.

The streets grew more crowded as they neared Fanueil Hall marketplace, and Rose found she was grateful to have Luke by her side, as she quickly became confused in the maze of stalls and shouting vendors. He guided her to each item she needed – a sack of cornmeal, tea and honey – and carried the increasingly heavy basket.

He seemed in no hurry and led her through the commotion at a leisurely pace. So at ease did he make her that she soon forgot all about not letting down her guard, forgot who they were to each other and simply enjoyed the warm sun and pleasant conversation. He even began to point out buildings and explain their uses before she could tell him there was no need.

"Oh, I know the city well, though it's changed since I left. I lived here until I was fifteen years old. I attended the Temple School on Tremont Street."

"That explains it," he said, looking intently at her.

"What does it explain?"

"Why you're so well-spoken and poised, why you're not like any maid I ever knew."

"Oh, and have you known many?" Rose asked, giving him an arch look.

"Not in the way you mean, Miss Stratton, no," he replied, causing her to blush once again. "What happened when you were fifteen to make you leave here?" he asked.

"My mother died of consumption. My father couldn't bear to stay in Boston without her, so we moved back to the farm he grew up on. But now he's gone too."

"I'm so sorry." He paused a moment. "I lost my mother when I was seventeen, just before I went to university in England. I can't imagine losing my father as well."

They stopped in the street and looked at each other with understanding, and Rose felt another wave of awareness wash over her, this one more profound than before. Then Luke took her arm and they began walking again.

"Did you miss Boston?" he asked.

"I did miss it, very much at first," she reflected. "I missed my friends terribly, and there was always something new to see and do in town. But my father was much more at peace on the farm, and my aunt needed us after my uncle died, so it was best all around."

"Was it best for you?" Luke asked, his voice quiet and serious.

Rose thought a moment before replying.

"The land is beautiful out there, and I learned to love what it has to offer. I wasn't unhappy, but somehow I always felt that I wasn't meant for that life. I suppose I was like many girls who think they're meant for something greater. Farm life is much the same day after day, and one is so tied to it. I dreamed of getting away and seeing new places ..." Rose broke off, embarrassed at how much she'd revealed.

"No, you weren't meant to be a farmer's wife," he said. It should have sounded presumptuous, given how little he knew of her. Instead he sounded thoughtful.

"Meant for it or not, it's what I shall be one day," she said, knowing she sounded resigned to her fate rather than excited to be marrying the man she loved. She could feel Luke's gaze on her but looked straight ahead, unable to meet it.

How far she'd come from her ideas of travel and excitement. Her life would be spent working just to put food on the table. There was no shame in that. Maybe someday it would even bring her pleasure.

They were both quiet as they reached the livery, where Luke arranged for a buggy and team of horses. Before long they were on their way back to Cider Hill, the top down in order to enjoy the pleasant breeze. Rose settled back for the ride, conscious of the new ease she felt with Luke. How unexpected, this new sense of friendship between them. It felt strange to tell him details of her life, and yet not wrong. She hadn't given anything away, but more than that, she felt understood.

What a shock it had been to exchange the sights and smells of Boston for life on a farm. She could see it when she closed her eyes – how the woods bordered their spread on all sides, and in the middle the gold of fine hay, flecks of color from the vegetable garden, horses and pigs, the dairy cows and chickens. Even now it was a constant battle to keep the land clear. Always there was the forest wanting to take it back.

Yes, she had grown to love the land, but somewhere in the back of her mind she had always planned to leave it. Since agreeing to marry Will, the life that awaited her seemed more trap than blessing.

But she was too relaxed, too tired, to examine her feelings any further. Instead she closed her eyes and let herself sink into the seat, her body rocked by the gentle sway of the carriage.

⎯ᴄ

Luke let the horses slow to a walk when he saw that Rose had fallen asleep. There was something new and intimate in seeing her like this – the whisper of her breath, the unguardedness of her lovely face as she slept.

She stirred beside him, her body curling into the side of the buggy for a more comfortable spot. Her long auburn lashes fluttered against her cheeks, her soft lips turning down at the corners as if she dreamt of something sad.

She must be exhausted. Six days a week she worked from sun-up until sundown, and on the seventh day she walked for hours. He hated that she worked for his family, that she worked for anyone. Though her tasks now were better than what he had seen her doing the first day, that wasn't saying much.

It didn't escape him that his vow to stay away from her had already failed. He hadn't planned it, but Charlie had seemed in a rush, and without thinking he'd told him he'd make sure she got home. Come to think of it, Charlie had given him a queer sort of look, but he hadn't taken any note of it at the time. He was too pleased with the idea of seeing Rose to consider his actions.

He wasn't sorry either. Their outing had been pleasant and cordial, and he could almost believe they were becoming friends. He knew a great deal more about her now than he had before, though much was still a mystery.

Still, as much as he enjoyed knowing more about her, it was all he could do to hold his tongue when she mentioned the farmer waiting for her back home. Her expression had turned pensive, and everything in her seemed to dim when she spoke of him.

The fact that she was bound, more or less, to another man was reason enough to stay away from her. But she was far from her friends and family, and she needed someone to look out for her. Which left him, if only he could keep from being one of the things from which she needed protection.

He brought the horses to a stop a short distance from the drive so that no one would see them return together. Rose woke slowly, her eyes soft and unfocused as she looked at him. In that one moment between sleep and wakefulness she smiled the loveliest, most heartbreaking smile Luke had ever seen. His breath caught in his throat.

Who was going to protect *him* from her?

Then she looked around and, getting her bearings, came fully awake. He could see her blush even as she thanked him, and just like that a wave of lust and tenderness swept over him and pulled him under.

She gathered her basket and rushed off without waiting for him to hand her down, walking down the drive toward the back entrance. She was not even allowed to enter the front door of his father's house. Rose, who was finer in every way than anyone who walked through that door.

There was something between them. He was sure she felt it as well, though in many ways that was even worse than if it had been just his own foolish longing.

CHAPTER FIVE

Rose sat in Vivian's parlor, fretting over what to do with the information gleaned from Mr. Fletcher's office. It was possible her father had been shot before Mr. Byrne visited the farm, but Rose didn't believe it. Everything pointed to someone from the railroad, and that someone was probably Mr. Byrne. The question was why. Did he think it would make Olivia more likely to sell? It was a drastic measure to take for such an unpredictable outcome.

"If only I knew if Mr. Byrne did in fact ride to the farm that day, then I would know for certain. Someone would have to listen to me."

"But you've discovered so much already!" Vivian exclaimed. "You mustn't expect so much of yourself."

Realizing she was once again worrying away her cherished weekly visit, Rose made a concerted effort to change the subject to something more pleasant. As usual, she stayed for the evening meal, but she lingered a bit too long and in consequence found herself leaving town much later than she intended.

The sun was just beginning to set, the western sky a display of fierce orange and deepening blue. But though it was a lovely time of night, she would soon be walking in the pitch black. She suffered not a few hoots and hollers by day, even with her face completely obscured by her bonnet, so she had no desire to test the limits of Boston's male population after the sun went down. But it seemed she would have no choice.

She had been walking for only a short time and had just made the turn onto Beacon Street when she heard the easy canter of a horse coming up behind her, gradually slowing until it kept pace beside her. The sides of her bonnet acted like blinders, so she could see nothing without turning her head to look.

Resolutely she continued walking, hoping that by pretending the rider did not exist he would give up and ride away. Another minute passed and tension twisted itself inside her until she forgot the perspiration trickling under her chemise and felt only a rising sense of panic.

"Rose?"

Rose stopped in her tracks, finally looking around and up.

Luke. He smiled easily at her from atop his horse, looking far too handsome for anyone's good. She kept her voice modulated and a bit severe in order to cover the ridiculous elation she felt at seeing him.

"What do you mean, sneaking up on me like that? Why didn't you speak sooner?"

"My apologies, it wasn't my intention to frighten you. I was merely unsure if it were you. Now perhaps you might answer something for me. Why are you out walking alone at this time of night? It will be full dark before you reach Cider Hill."

"I was visiting a friend, as I do every Monday, and I lost track of the time. I don't particularly relish being out this late either, but you needn't trouble yourself on my account. I'm perfectly capable of getting back on my own."

Despite her reassurances he swung down from his horse.

"You must be tired. Let me give you a ride back."

"I can't ride on that horse with you!"

"I see. I suppose it wouldn't be proper, is that right? Well then, I'll hand you up and you can ride while I walk beside you."

Rose was too surprised to say anything for a moment, and instead stood pensively wondering what to do. Mounting a horse without a sidesaddle was enough to cause looks from everyone they passed on the street. On the other hand, it was getting dark, and no one knew her anyway. She had ridden horses astride often enough on the farm when she was younger, so it was not a question of ability. And she was awfully tired.

Luke stood patiently waiting, as if he knew she needed to come to the decision on her own. Finally she nodded.

"That's very kind of you," she said stiffly, uncomfortably aware of how generous his offer was.

"Think nothing of it. You'd have done the same for me, I have no doubt."

She had no idea how to respond to such a statement until she noticed the glint in his eye and realized he was teasing her. She couldn't help but smile at him. Walking to the horse's left side, she stepped into Luke's laced fingers and let him boost her into the saddle.

Once seated, she took a moment to arrange her skirts, trying in vain to cover her legs. There was nothing for it though; her ankles and calves were revealed, as were her dingy stockings, rolled to her ankles in deference to the July heat. She nearly jumped out of her skin when Luke moved her leg forward in order to shorten the stirrup leather.

Was it her imagination, or did his touch linger for a moment longer than necessary? She wished she had silk stockings like the ladies he must know. Then she caught herself. Why in the world should she care what sort of stockings she had on?

He adjusted the stirrup on the other side, his manner somewhat more subdued now. When he finished he looked up at her.

The sun had made its way down to the tops of the trees, taking the worst of the heat with it. He was standing near enough that she felt his warmth and could yet see his dark eyes as he studied her. For a moment she thought he would say something, but instead he gave a little shake of his head and wordlessly led the horse forward.

⟋

Luke tried to think of something other than Rose's legs. He set his mind on a problem he was having with one of his maps and when that didn't distract him, he mentally composed a letter to a cousin in New York.

All to no avail. It was the woman riding beside him who filled his thoughts. Just touching her leg had nearly filled him to bursting. He had to pretend to be unaffected, but he heard her quick intake of breath when he touched her, and it was all he could do not to run his hand up her long, shapely leg to where her skirts covered her, and then beyond.

His reaction to her was the very reason he spent so few evenings at his father's house. Instead he'd been taking many of his meals at a club in town, anxious to keep his contact with her to a minimum.

They said very little on the way to the house. The things he was thinking could not be said aloud and he could think of no small talk. Nor did she seem inclined toward idle chatter. He was glad just to be near her, glad she didn't have to walk home alone. But he wouldn't always know when she needed help. What if he hadn't happened along tonight? Who knew what might have occurred, who might have bothered her?

No, he could not be sure he would be around when she needed someone, and the chances were he would not be. He had no claim on her, he wanted none, and yet the fact that he couldn't ensure her safety caused a clenching in his gut.

If she were his, he'd make sure she never had to walk alone at night, or any other time. Nor would she have to lift a finger if she didn't care to. And she'd have a new pair of silk stockings for every day of the year. He would personally remove them every night.

His reaction to her was unprecedented. She'd done nothing to deliberately entice him and yet he had never wanted a woman more. So much so that all rational thought fled at the sight of her ankle. He had to pull himself together.

When they reached the house he made sure to stop where they couldn't be seen. Though it was clear Rose needed no help getting down, it was all he could do to keep himself from lifting her to the ground. Any excuse to put his hands on her.

"Are you not going in?" Rose asked, as he took the reins from her and swung up into the saddle. "I thought you were going this way, or I'd never have inconvenienced you as I have." Her face was solemn, her eyes anxious.

He had intended to return for the night, but now he was entirely too worked up to go inside. He'd ride until his blood cooled instead.

"You did nothing of the kind, Rose," he answered. "The distance is nothing on horseback. I daresay I'd go much farther than that for you."

He gave her a devil-may-care smile to let her know she should not think twice about it. An answering smile lit her face, though he could see her uncertainty. He knew he should go, and yet he hesitated still, unable to ride away from her.

"Thank you," she said, her voice low and husky. "You're very kind." But he didn't feel kind. He wanted that voice whispering to him in bed, telling him what she wanted, how good he made her feel.

She looked at him a moment, as if about to say something, before turning and walking away. He watched her slim figure, lit by moonlight, until she disappeared into the house. Then he urged his horse into a gallop, hoping to outrun his need.

⸺ ᕤ ⸺

The next Monday evening Rose managed to leave Vivian's house at a more reasonable hour. As she headed down Beacon Street she could not help replaying in her mind the previous week's trip back to Cider Hill with Luke. She could almost feel his hand on her ankle, see his strong profile as he led the horse.

He had walked beside her nearly six miles just to see her safely back, then turned around and left. She had not seen him since, but even now her thoughts were full of him, desire and guilt warring with each other. Why couldn't she feel this way for Will? The mild, comfortable response Will called up in her was no match for what Luke Fletcher did to her. In fact all thought of Will fled when she was in Luke's presence. It was only afterward that guilt descended.

Why must her heart beat uncontrollably for the absolutely most unsuitable man? How could she stay true to Will when she could barely conjure his face? Every time she tried, she saw Luke, his strong cheekbones and stubborn jaw, those eyes that seemed to notice everything.

As if materializing from this very thought, there he was waiting in a buggy at the very place he'd come upon her the week before. Grinning playfully, he jumped out of the carriage to stand beside her, his jacket off and his shirtsleeves turned up to just below the elbow. Just the sight of him sent a wave of giddiness over her.

But why was he here? Could it be that he'd paid for the carriage and waited for her just to see her back to his father's house? A thrill of hope and fear travelled through her at the thought. But perhaps that was presumptuous, and he was merely on some other errand and happened to see her.

She paused a moment to compose herself before crossing the final few yards to him.

"What are you doing in this carriage? You ride a horse."

"Generally speaking, yes. But I guess this is your lucky day, since I happen to be in this handsome contraption. I gather you're returning to Cider Hill. May I drive you?"

Rose hesitated, wondering what it meant that he'd been waiting for her. She knew with every part of her she should say no. There was no reason to ride with him, as she had plenty of time before sunset, and yet she couldn't refuse.

Luke watched her speculatively, and he looked relieved when she nodded her assent and allowed him to hand her up.

Once again she recalled with utter clarity his hands in her hair, his lips on hers. Mortified at the blush she felt burn her cheeks, she turned away for a few moments as if entranced by the passing scenery.

He kept the horses at an easy trot and they rode for a few minutes in what might have seemed to an outsider like companionable silence, but to Rose felt fraught with tension. Glancing over, she watched the play of muscles in his forearms as he controlled the team, and could not help noticing how the material of his trousers pulled tautly over his thighs. He was so big beside her, so overwhelming.

A muscle worked in his jaw and she wondered what he was thinking about. Was he angry? He didn't seem so, and yet he did not seem quite so easy with her as he had at first. Too soon they arrived in sight of his father's house and he helped her down.

"Thank you, Mr. Fletcher. Once again, I find myself in your debt."

"You don't owe me anything. It's for my benefit, really. It eases my mind to know you're not walking alone."

"I see. So it is I doing you a favor," Rose replied, a teasing note in her voice. "It would seem you should thank me."

"It would seem so," he said, his eyes crinkling at the corners as he smiled. "I thank you for the pleasure of your company, and for allaying my fears by allowing me to escort you. Perhaps you'll do so again."

And with that he made a low bow and stepped back into the buggy. The horses pulled away, their hooves a quick staccato as they disappeared around a curve in the road.

And so it went every Monday from then on, though before long he began waiting for her outside the March residence. She didn't ask why he came for her, but she was certain the carriage was purely for her benefit, as every other day he was on horseback. Each time he dropped her off well before the drive to the house in order to avoid being seen with her, then turned around and headed back to town.

Their drives amounted to only slightly more than an hour a week, yet it felt to her that every other day was merely a prelude to their time together. She could not help but notice that he seemed to enjoy the drives as well, even going so far some days as to take a longer route if they were in the midst of a conversation.

He was friendly, warm and cordial, but there was nothing in his manner that suggested he was hoping for something in return. Their previous charged encounters seemed like figments of her imagination, except that she felt the same thrill each time she saw him, as if her body had already learned what it meant to be near Luke Fletcher and no change in his demeanor, no truce or understanding, could convince her treacherous body that anything had changed. Despite her awareness of him, she was grateful he didn't force her to end those drives, as she would have done had he tried to kiss her again.

Before long they were talking about all manner of things. She learned about his travels across the country, surveying and mapping the western territories. He described trekking across the Rocky Mountains when a storm hit, how the dull browns of the desert bloomed with fiery colors in springtime, and countless other fascinating stories of places he'd been. One day he showed her rocks embedded with flecks of gold and others with strange crystals on them, and explained the geological forces that created such specimens.

Rose tried to tell him that her stories were not nearly so interesting, but he truly seemed to want to hear about her family and the farm. She couldn't help feeling a pang of guilt and doubt, for talking about her life only served to remind her that her connection to him was part of a pretense. Whatever truth came out of her presence among the Fletchers, her deception would cause pain to both of them.

Even so, she couldn't resist his genuine interest in her memories of Boston before she left, as well as stories about life on the farm. He even asked about Will, though he frowned all the while she spoke, as if it displeased him to know more.

"He lives on a neighboring farm. We met a year ago," she said, looking down at her hands. "He's good and kind, and he's been very patient. I haven't always known what I wanted, and even when I did, it didn't always sit well with him."

They were near to his father's house, but Luke took a turn to lengthen their drive. Rose smiled to herself, though she was not inclined to talk overlong about Will with him.

"You mean you didn't know whether you wanted to marry him?" he asked bluntly.

"I...there was a time when I didn't know what I wanted," she said. She didn't mention how her doubts had resurfaced since spending time with him. "Promising oneself in marriage is the biggest decision a person must make. It determines one's future happiness. But I did finally decide."

She looked at him then. Why should she be the only one answering such questions?

"Have you ever wondered what it would be like to live the rest of your life with one woman?" she asked.

There was a long pause before he answered. When he spoke he looked straight ahead, his voice betraying no emotion.

"I married when I was but twenty-one to a girl I met in England. I brought Catherine back to Boston but she took ill when she was with child. The baby died first and she not long afterward."

Rose looked at him in horror. She would never have guessed such a thing about him. But then, she hardly knew him, did she?

"Oh, Mr. Fletcher, I'm so sorry. How awful."

"It was quite some time ago," he said, and she could see that he didn't want to speak of it further. And no wonder. What could be worse than losing one's wife and child? Her heart ached for him, but she knew instinctively he wouldn't want her pity.

"And was it then that you moved out west?" she asked. She hoped this was a less sensitive topic and was pleased to see the tension leave him.

"Yes, six years ago now. I suppose I just needed to be somewhere else."

Roes said nothing for a moment. It was so like what her father had done when her mother had died. He must have loved his wife as her father had loved his.

"Will you stay here, now that you're back?" she asked.

Luke frowned thoughtfully and then looked over at her.

"You do get right to the point, don't you?" he said wryly, causing her to blush. "I'll stay at least until we get the railroad over those hills, but it was never my intention to stay beyond that. Most likely I'll get restless and want to be moving on again."

Rose tried and failed to imagine living the kind of life he described. Though she wanted very much to see new things, what he described sounded lonely rather than adventurous.

"It must be strange to start over again and again. I would miss my friends and family terribly."

"You get used to it. I don't depend on anyone for anything, and that suits me fine."

"But didn't you miss having people you could count on, and who counted on you?"

Luke scowled and she could see she'd made him uncomfortable.

"I didn't want to know anyone, and I didn't want anyone knowing me," he replied brusquely. "All I wanted was to be left alone." He stopped speaking for a moment and when he continued he sounded more thoughtful than agitated. "Lately I have wondered what it would be like to stay in one place long enough for it to matter. I suppose that's why I finally came back."

"And what do you think so far?" she asked.

"It has its attractions," he said, looking sideways at her as he steered the carriage to their usual spot near the stone wall.

Rose felt herself flush and dared not look at him until he'd handed her down, this time pressing a kiss to her hand before he bid her goodbye.

Rose had now searched Jonas Fletcher's desks at home and in his office. She could think of nothing else to do now but listen carefully and ask questions without inviting suspicion. Though she felt she had gleaned very little in her time at the house so far, she was more certain than ever that Mr. Byrne, and perhaps others, were responsible for her father's death.

Chills ran through her remembering that map on the office wall, the black line broken off at her family's farm. Something about that had shaken her. It felt as though everything she held near and dear was threatened, its fate decided in that plush room, far from the lives in question.

Until she knew more, all she could do was conduct herself as any maid would and draw as little attention to herself as possible. However, that became more and more difficult as Mr. Byrne came around more often. He was at the house nearly every day and without fail managed to find her. Often he stood watching her intently, paying her compliments that made her skin crawl. Ever since her ride in his carriage she had regarded him warily. Now her nervousness grew.

Late one afternoon she was laying the table for a large dinner party, her thoughts far away as she set the china and silver along the table. She was brought out of her reverie by the smell of spirits. Looking up, she saw Mr. Byrne leaning against the doorjamb, his waistcoat partially unbuttoned, his cravat askew. She flinched as his bloodshot eyes raked over her.

"Ah, so we meet again. Fate seems to throw us together, Rose."

"I would call it supper," Rose replied, unable to suppress her distaste.

Byrne entered the room to stand beside her. His proximity made her stomach roil and her nose wrinkled at the stench of liquor, but she continued her task, refusing to give him any sort of reaction, for that was what he seemed to crave.

"You'll turn your back on me but you'll accept rides from my stepbrother?"

Rose gasped and looked at him. What had he seen, and when?

"That's got your attention, hasn't it?" he said, moving even closer.

"I don't know what you're insinuating, but Mr. Fletcher did nothing but give me a ride home from town."

"That's not how it looked to me. You were riding beside him in a rented buggy. That speaks of more than coincidence, my dear. My esteemed stepbrother is going to great lengths on your behalf, leading me to wonder what favors he's receiving in return."

"Your imagination is getting the best of you. Mr. Fletcher passed me on the road and politely offered to take me the rest of the way here. I couldn't say whose benefit the carriage was for, but it wasn't mine."

"Either way, my mother will be most displeased to hear of it. I hate to think what she'll do."

"You can't mean you're going to tell her?"

"Indeed I do. Of course, I could be persuaded to keep silent were you to show me the same generosity you show Luke."

He was blackmailing her, his face glowing with pleasure as he watched her with predatory eyes, no doubt sure he'd trapped her. He drew even closer, so near now that were someone to see them, there would be questions.

Rose stepped away, bumping up against the table behind her in her haste. "You have no proof, and it won't be my word against yours, it will be yours against Mr.

Fletcher's. Do you think he'll stand by while you make your accusations?"

Mr. Byrne's mouth tightened, his nostrils flaring as he glared at her in fury. With great effort he reconfigured his features until they were fixed in a grim approximation of a smile.

"Of course I was merely jesting. There's no need to look at me so. But do watch yourself," he said, straitening his cravat with feigned nonchalance. "Mrs. Fletcher has no tolerance for antics such as yours. Of that you can be certain."

As soon as he left the room Rose sagged against the table, trembling with reaction. She had managed to outwit him this time, but it wouldn't be the last time she had to contend with him.

"Are you saying Nathan threatened you?" Luke asked, his expression ferocious.

They were standing beside the carriage outside Vivian's home the very next Monday, as Rose had refused to get in.

Rose nodded. "He's seen us. I don't think he'll tell Mrs. Fletcher, at least not yet, but I would put nothing past him. In any case, you can see why our drives must end. I can't risk losing my place."

Luke looked as if he wanted to tear something apart. Abruptly he turned and walked away, turning around after a few paces and walking back to wear she stood. His cheeks were flushed and he was scowling with such ferocity, the passersby regarded him warily.

"I'll be damned if I let Nathan threaten us out of something perfectly innocent. I see no reason why I can't continue to drive you, so long as we're more careful. We'll simply keep the top up so no one can see us. I'll let you out farther away from Cider Hill, as well."

Rose looked at him. "Why do you and your father put up with Mr. Byrne? It seems to me he must be detrimental to your work."

Luke sighed and rubbed his face in a weary gesture. "Because he's family, and we don't turn our back on family. No matter what."

A chill coursed down Rose's spine at this, for if this were true, might they not all close ranks around Mr. Byrne to protect him? She would need to be absolutely certain of his guilt, and have proof of it as well, before accusing him.

Of course, at the moment she was more worried about what Byrne might accuse *her* of, and whether riding with Luke was worth the risk. Her mind raced as she considered Luke's suggestion. The safest thing to do would be to end their drives. Then again, how would anyone know it was them if they kept the top up?

Later perhaps she'd examine the pleasure she felt at his solution. For now, she was only too happy to agree.

"Very well," she agreed. "Let us do as before, only more cautiously."

Luke looked relieved. "I'll speak to Nathan and ensure he stays away from you."

"Please don't. He hasn't done anything yet, and your interference will only make him more certain that we've been too familiar."

Luke stood with his hands on his hips, looking as if he would argue. Then he sighed. "As you wish. But promise me you'll let me know if anything else happens."

"I'm sure that won't be necessary."

He regarded her with an aggrieved expression, then shook his head, as if giving up. Without another word he moved back to the buggy and began raising the top. Rose waited, anxious that they might be seen, though they were on a small street down which no one from Cider Hill could possibly need to travel.

A few minutes later Luke turned back to her, his hand outstretched. "Shall we?"

They both settled into the buggy, the raised top enclosing them together in a whole new intimacy. He was so close, mere inches from her, and it was many minutes before her breath evened out and she could look at him again.

CHAPTER SIX

Each week Rose felt closer to Luke, but when at Cider Hill they acted as strangers to each other. Luke nodded and greeted her when they met in a hallway or room, and if she were serving him at mealtimes, he thanked her but paid her no more mind then he did the other girls. It was a strange, divided existence, and yet another deception she had to negotiate.

Her situation at Cider Hill took yet another turn as she was cleaning Luke's bedchamber one morning not long after Mr. Byrne threatened her.

"Rose?"

Rose started at the unexpected sound of Luke's voice. He was standing in the doorway of his bedchamber, looking at her with surprise and dismay. She stood up straight, letting go of the counterpane she'd been straightening.

"You startled me," she said, laughing to ease the tension.

He was frowning at her now, his gaze sweeping the room and taking in the fresh flowers in the vase, the clean towel and full water pitcher on its stand. Then he looked at her.

"Am I to understand that you come in here every morning and clean up after me?"

"Well, yes, but you needn't look so horrified. I tidy all the bedchambers."

Luke let out a groan and closed his eyes. Opening them again he came into the room until they were standing a mere two feet apart.

"This is untenable," he said, his voice pitched so that no one else might here. "I cannot abide you having to clean my chamber. If I'd had any idea ..."

"You mustn't make too much of it. It takes but a few minutes."

"That isn't the point, Rose." He was whispering now. "There must be another way. Perhaps one of the other girls could take your place."

Rose looked at him, horrified. "That's impossible. Suggesting such a thing will only make everyone suspect us."

Jut then a frigid voice spoke from behind Luke.

"What exactly is going on here?"

Luke and Rose turned as one to see Mrs. Fletcher looking at them, her eyes narrowed in suspicion. Fortunately Luke spoke up, as Rose's mind had ceased to work properly.

"I've lost the key to the offices. I thought perhaps I might have left it here, but it seems not."

Mrs. Fletcher was unconvinced. "Is that so? There was a good deal of whispering for something so mundane."

Luke's expression hardened as he faced her. "Yes, it's so."

Rose tried to quell the panic rising in her at the silent battle being waged between them.

Finally his stepmother broke eye contact, her mouth tightening in displeasure. "Very well. I'll mention your lost key to Mrs. Craig. Now why don't we leave Rose to finish in here? She's already taken far longer than she should."

Mrs. Fletcher stood where she was, waiting for Luke to precede her out. Rose turned away to finish making the bed, fearful something of her inner panic would show on her face. When she looked up again, they were gone.

⌐

Luke stood next to his father, the two of them studying the map on the wall and shaking their heads over the incomplete rail line.

"We'll have to decide soon. It's costing us money just to wait," Jonas stated matter-of-factly.

"We should never have built so far west without having that farmer sign the papers," replied Luke, unable to hide his frustration.

"Yes, yes, that's clear enough now. But I thought that was well in hand. Nathan told me as much."

"Nathan's a fool. He wants so badly to prove himself, he'll do or say anything. Anything, that is, except get to work on time and put in an honest day."

Jonas sighed. It was a discussion they'd had many times.

Luke pressed his point.

"Frankly, I fear his character is not all it should be. For several months now I've been hearing disconcerting news. I'm told he gambles, seemingly without control or sense. He incurs debts and takes too long to pay them off, an unpopular character trait to say the least, particularly for the crowd he associates with."

Jonas sighed and sat down, looking weary. "I hadn't realized it was so bad. I'd hoped he would build his character and reputation through the business. Charlotte thinks Nathan merely needs someone to guide him, though he's a bit old for such hopes. She sees him with a mother's eyes, I suppose. Be that as it may, I cannot give up on him just yet. We must both try to work with him, give him a chance to come through. He may surprise us yet."

Nathan had received little in the way of an inheritance when his own father died, and that had been frittered away long ago. He now relied exclusively on the salary Jonas paid him, whereas Luke had made his own living for years and also held substantial stock in the railroad. Nathan thus had every reason to put forth his best effort, and his failure to do so clearly troubled Jonas. But instead of looking to the source of the trouble, both Nathan and Charlotte resented Luke's return and the shadow he cast over Nathan.

"I hope you're right, but I fear you're too optimistic. He seems to be getting worse, rather than better. I've run into him a time or two in town and he's always in his cups. Not to mention the fact that he's late again today."

"Never fear, dear brother, here I am."

Nathan entered the room with a swagger and sat down heavily in the chair beside Jonas. It was not yet ten o'clock and already he smelled of spirits, his face an unhealthy pallor. Luke's jaw clenched as he took in Nathan's state of dress and bleary eyes. He looked as if he'd been up all night, and he smelled it too. The fact that this sad excuse for a man had a stake in their company infuriated him.

"It was good of you to show up," Luke shot back, immediately regretting his lack of control.

"I hate to disappoint you, but I have things well in hand."

"Is that right? By all means then, do show us where we are to lay track," he said, gesturing to the map on the wall.

At this, Nathan's skin paled and his eyes darted to the map and back again.

"Actually, I believe we've received a break on that score. Mrs. Harris's brother has been killed in some sort of an accident. I daresay we'll have no trouble buying the land now."

"I see." Jonas replied. "When was this?"

"Five months ago, I believe. But I only just found out."

Nathan's manner was curious and Luke watched as he shifted in his chair, his eyes not quite meeting theirs. If what Nathan said were true, things might turn around. Still, he had no desire to circle the women left behind like scavengers at a kill.

"Well done, Nathan. It's a smart man that keeps his ears open," Jonas said, his tone warm with approval. "We'll approach Mrs. Harris and make another offer, a little more generous than our last. That should suit her well if she has any notion of selling."

"Of course, it only makes sense to make one more offer," Luke put in. "But I think we ought to leave it at that. We've spent enough time badgering a family that has no interest in selling. Until we know, we should continue looking into other routes."

Nathan glared at Luke with true malice.

"Agreed," Jonas said. "Luke, I'd like you to ride out to the Harris farm and see what you can do. If Olivia Harris doesn't accept, we'll lay track to the north and get on with the business of building a railroad. Either way there will be more mapping and surveying to do. Nathan, once Luke returns you can ride to Albany and reassure interested parties there."

Luke expected Nathan to argue that he ought to be the one to go to the Harris farm, but in fact he looked relieved not to be chosen.

The three men discussed other business for a few minutes more before the clerk knocked on the door and poked his head in.

"Sir? Mr. Miller is here to see you about the coal."

"Oh yes, I'll be right with him. We're nearly done in here." Turning to Nathan, Jonas fixed him with a steady look. "I'll expect you to arrive promptly to work in the morning. We have a lot to accomplish if we want to get back on schedule."

Luke didn't linger after his father left. Without a word to Nathan he headed down the hall toward his own office, only to have Nathan catch up to him before he reached his door.

"I know very well what you've been up to with Rose," Nathan said, walking quickly to keep up with Luke's longer strides. "I can't fault your taste. We've had ourselves some nice little talks lately. In fact, I think she's grown rather fond of me. I know I'm quite fond of her," he finished, smirking at Luke in deliberate provocation.

Luke fumed. Nathan was like a spoiled child trying to pick a fight because things hadn't gone his way. Still, there was something threatening about his remarks. Was Nathan all talk, or would his fixation on her lead to more trouble? He'd assumed Nathan hadn't bothered Rose recently, but would she have told him if he had? It didn't sit well with him that he'd be away for several weeks and Rose would be left without anyone to protect her.

He turned around to face Nathan, standing closer than necessary to make his point clear. Nathan had to look up to meet his eye, a fact that pleased Luke greatly.

"I don't know what you're playing at, but if you harass or harm Rose in any way, you'll answer to me. Rest assured I would take great pleasure in teaching you a lesson. Your place with the railroad is already hanging by a thread. I won't hesitate to break it."

Luke didn't wait for a reply. Without another word he strode away, anxious to put distance between them.

⤚ᴄ

Vivian peeked out the parlor window.

"Of course he's there, exactly as he always is. Why would you doubt it?"

"Do come away from the window," Rose pleaded. "What if he sees you?"

"I shouldn't worry. He doesn't see anything but you, dear," Vivian quipped, stepping back and looking at her friend impishly.

"You haven't even met him, you goose," Rose replied, laughing.

"Perhaps not, but I've watched his face as you walk toward him."

Rose's heart squeezed at Vivian's observation, and she found herself both wishing it were true and hoping it were not.

Giving her friend a kiss on the cheek, she left the house, restraining the urge to rush toward Luke. Every Monday for the past four weeks she'd made this walk toward him, her heart beating madly, and each time she wondered what she was doing. And then she would answer her own question by reassuring herself that it was just one drive a week, surely nothing to lose sleep over. But the way he looked at her, the way she felt sitting next to him as his deep voice flowed over her, those things did indeed keep her awake nights.

It was getting harder and harder to write to Will, and harder still to read the earnest and devoted letters she received.

Luke smiled as she came closer, his eyes never leaving hers as he handed her into the carriage. It had been an uncomfortably hot day but now a faint breeze stirred, bringing with it some relief.

"I trust you had a pleasant visit with your friend?" he asked.

"Oh yes. Vivian and I talk nonsense and eat ourselves silly. It's wonderful."

Luke urged the horses on as she settled her skirts about her. There was something at her feet however, and she bent down to move it aside.

"That's for you," he said, his voice casual as he glanced at her and then back to the road.

Leaning over, Rose picked up a package wrapped in heavy brown paper and bound with string. Carefully she removed the wrapping to find her lap full of beautifully bound leather books. There were perhaps a dozen of them – books by Emerson, Dickens, James Fenimore Cooper, as well as Shakespeare and Marlow. All of them perfect new editions, the letters stamped in gold leaf.

Rose stared in disbelief at the treasure she was holding. "What is all this?"

"I thought perhaps you might like some new books for your lessons, or just to read yourself. One can only read the same thing so many times."

Rose was speechless. It was the perfect gift. Nothing, no jewel or flower could have touched her more. How had he known? She'd told him about the lessons, but never once had she mentioned needing more books. Tears swam in her eyes as she ran her hands over the smooth leather. But how could she accept such a gift from him? It nearly choked her, but she knew she must refuse them.

"I can't accept such a generous gift from you. It wouldn't be right."

Luke reined in the horses and turned to her, but she found herself unable to meet his gaze for fear that he would see how much they meant to her, far more than he could have intended them to.

"Rose." Luke's voice was firm but kind, and demanded she look at him. Tentatively she complied, looking up to find his expression serious and full of understanding.

"You owe me nothing in return for these. In fact, you need not think of them as gifts to you at all. They are meant for anyone who needs them, and you may keep them or give them away as you wish." Here he stopped and his expression grew thoughtful. "Charlie told me how much you're doing for him and the others. I know it can't be easy finding books to read. This is the least I can do."

He made it so easy. Nodding her head, she accepted his gift that was not a gift, finally allowing herself to smile, her joy in the bounty on her lap expanding until she could hardly contain herself. She ran her hands over each book in turn, admiring them all.

They drove on in companionable silence, and she could see him glancing at her every so often, a pleased smile curving his mouth. This time he stopped closer to the house in order that she not have to carry the books too far. There was no one else about, just the trill of birds delighted by summertime and the distant sound of a woodpecker hard at work.

"I'm afraid I won't see you for some time," he said, frowning as though the thought disagreed with him. He took one of her hands in his, his thumb brushing over her knuckles. "I have some business to attend to in the Berkshires that will likely take at least three weeks. Do whatever you can to stay away from Nathan while I'm gone. He said some things today that have me worried about leaving you."

"What will you be doing?" she asked, her heart beating fast as she tried to sound only casually interested.

"Oh, just dealing with some trouble with the route over the mountains," he replied with an aggravated sigh. "We thought we had a route but the landowners in Lenox wouldn't sell. It should have been sorted out long before I arrived, but that's another matter. We've been set back by months and a good deal of money, and now the shareholders are getting nervous, as are the people in Albany. They expect to connect our railroads next spring. If we don't keep up our end of the bargain there'll be serious repercussions. We've decided it's worth speaking to the owner in person, and as I have to go out there to meet with Whistler, I'll call on her myself."

"How badly do you need the landowners to sell? Enough to make things difficult for them to stay?" Rose asked, knowing she was taking a risk but unable to help it.

Luke looked at her curiously. "What makes you ask that?"

"I just wondered. If the stakes are so high..."

"We're offering a very generous amount, and I'll do my best to persuade the owner of all the benefits to her. We'll lay tracks over those hills, whether she agrees or not, so she may as well benefit from it. You can't stop progress, try as one might."

This last was said almost regretfully, as if he wondered himself about the price of progress. But if he were so ambivalent, why could he not leave her aunt alone?

"Some people have an attachment to the land that's greater than any price you could name," Rose said, angry now as she envisioned her aunt having to encounter Luke on her own.

Luke looked at her curiously. "I've upset you. Perhaps I sound callous, but I do understand loving the land. I have a job to do, and I mean to do it, but I have no intention of strong-arming anyone."

Rose didn't know what to feel. As much as she'd tried not to dwell on his connection to the railroad, it was impossible to ignore. He had no idea how much pain she and her aunt had suffered, nor how closely connected he was to it.

He looked at her, his expression teasing. "Will you promise to leave your friend's at a decent hour while I'm away? I won't be able to concentrate if I have to worry about you walking the roads in the dead of night."

"Yes, of course," she replied, but she couldn't match his teasing tone. She could no longer even meet his eyes. "I must go before someone sees us," she said, desperate to get away and think. He was frowning, clearly confused by the sudden change in her.

She didn't wait around for him to ask more questions. Thanking him quickly for the ride and the books, she hurried away, clutching his gift to her chest.

Back in her room, Rose paced the floor, trying to figure out how to get word of Luke's visit to her aunt. It wasn't long before she realized it would have to wait until her next visit to town. She could only hope her letter would reach her aunt before Luke appeared at her door.

She would have continued fretting had not Lydia entered the room and exclaimed over the new books sitting on the table.

"Where did they come from?"

"Vivian, gave them to me," Rose replied, knowing it was unwise to tell Lydia the truth. "They're for everyone. Won't the others be pleased?"

"We'll have the most beautiful reading voices in all of Massachusetts," Lydia declared, her face beaming so brightly Rose couldn't possibly regret accepting the books. Already she was looking forward to hearing the students read them, and she was thinking of other ways to keep the lessons fun. Perhaps they might even put on a play.

Rose threw herself into her lessons in the weeks after Luke left, and a curious thing happened. Staff who had until then been cold and difficult began to soften toward her. Whereas previously Mrs. Beech and Abigail had spoken to her only when absolutely necessary, and then with disdain, they were now almost kind. Even George was civil to her, and he was never more than civil to anyone. The one person who remained decidedly unfriendly was Dottie.

And then a rather remarkable thing occurred. It was a scorching day in August, the sun pounding down as Rose hung clothes on a line stretched between two oak trees. She bent over to pull a wet sheet out of the basket and when she stood up Dottie was standing in front of her. But instead of her usual scowl, Dottie seemed nervous, even embarrassed.

"Would you like some help?" she asked Rose. Without waiting for Rose's reply she began shaking out pieces of clothing and securing them on the line. Rose stared at her for several seconds, wondering what had come over her, before shrugging and continuing her task. Dottie would say what was on her mind in her own time.

The two women worked in silence for a few minutes before Dottie stopped and turned to her.

"I want you to teach me to read," she said, to Rose's utter astonishment. "I'm not like the others," she continued, a note of defiance in her voice. "I don't know anything besides the alphabet, and I'm not sure I know that too well either. But I'll pay you five cents a lesson to teach me."

Rose thought this over before replying, as this presented an opportunity she could not resist.

"I don't want your money," she said, and Dottie's face fell in disappointment. Quickly Rose continued. "I'm helping the others for nothing and will gladly do the same for you. What if I said I would teach you to read and write and all you have to do is be nice to me."

Dottie looked at her appraisingly. "How nice?"

Rose held her gaze and tried not to smile.

"At least as nice as George is," she said. George hardly spoke to her, but when he did, he displayed no feeling whatsoever. That seemed fair.

Dottie sighed.

"Your way sounds more complicated, but I suppose it's not a bad bargain. I can't promise to like you though," she said, and Rose could have sworn Dottie's mouth quirked up at the corner, as if she were trying not to smile.

But though relations with the staff had become easier, things had become more trying in a different corner, for Mr. Byrne appeared at Cider Hill every day that Luke was gone. And just as Luke had warned, he was even more aggressive in his attentions. Rose was careful to stay around other servants as much as possible, but the strain of avoiding him was wearing on her.

She was dusting the drawing room one afternoon, her thoughts far away, when she felt the presence of someone beside her. Looking up she saw Byrne standing before her, grinning with pleasure.

"What a treat to catch you alone. One would think you've been trying to avoid me."

Fury welled up in her, but it would serve no purpose to have him see it. Looking back down she continued her task. "I have a great deal of work to do, Mr. Byrne. And as you know, Mrs. Fletcher doesn't take kindly to servants conversing with family."

"You needn't worry about my mother. I can handle her," he said, moving closer. "Come, stop for a moment and look at me."

"Please let me work."

"What's the matter? Am I not rich enough to tempt you? I'll soon be wealthier than Luke, you can be sure of that. It's thanks to me the railroad is being completed."

"What do you mean, thanks to you?" she said, on full alert.

But Byrne wasn't listening to her. He was growing more agitated, his thoughts turned inward as he spoke.

"Jonas had no right bringing Luke here. He should have had more faith in me."

"Maybe he didn't understand how much you'd helped," she said, hoping he'd reveal more.

Byrne looked straight at her, his countenance tight with malice.

"Luke's been gone for weeks, and still I feel his shadow over me."

Without warning he took hold of Rose's arm, yanking her to him so that she fell into his chest. He was smaller than Luke, but still far stronger than she, and though she struggled she was unable to break his hold or pull away.

Grabbing the hair at the back of her head, he pulled until she was forced to look at him. Before she realized what was happening, his lips were on hers, hard and cruel. His tongue tried to force her mouth open and she nearly gagged. Now she struggled in earnest, with no thought but to break free. She kicked him hard in the shin, hard enough that his lips left hers. He looked at her in shock and fury, his face contorting as if he were about to do real violence.

Only the sound of several people approaching stopped him from whatever vile act would have come next. Rose was thrust away just before the door opened.

Mrs. Fletcher stood in the doorway, two matrons just steps behind her. Fury darkened her eyes as she looked at Rose and her son, and Rose could only imagine the picture they made – their clothes in disarray, their faces flushed.

As horrified as Rose was at being caught in such a position, she was more relieved at getting away from Byrne. Picking up her dust cloth she made a few more swipes at a side table for show before hurrying out of the room. Let Byrne stay and answer to his mother's wrath. Rose would feel it soon enough.

"Watch yourself, Rose," Mrs. Craig cautioned the next morning. "The mistress is in a foul temper. Why don't you do the ironing and keep out of her sight. I don't know what she has against you, but she seems to look for reasons to reprimand you."

"Thank you for the warning. I'll make sure to stay out of her way."

"Stay out of who's way?" asked Mrs. Fletcher, entering the kitchen.

Rose paled, but luckily Mrs. Craig answered for her.

"We were speaking of Mrs. Beech."

"I see," Mrs. Fletcher replied, unconvinced. "No, Rose," she went on, as Rose made to leave. "I'd like a word with you."

Rose reminded herself that she was acting the part of Mrs. Fletcher's servant and so must play her role convincingly. One day she would tell this woman exactly what she thought of her, but until then she must make sure she kept her job. Pride could come later.

The older woman's cold gaze pinned Rose where she stood, and for a moment she said nothing. Rose waited in silence for her to speak.

"I don't know what I interrupted yesterday, but I won't have scandalous behavior in my house. I insist that you watch yourself with my son and stepson. Men will be men, and that means they can be tempted. But do not think for a moment you'll better your situation by enticing one of them. You'll remember that if you want to keep your place here."

Rose's blood ran cold, and she remained silent, unsure how to respond. But Mrs. Fletcher wasn't finished.

"Nor will I put up with servants who put on airs. Don't play innocent with me," she remarked at Rose's look of confusion. "It's one thing to teach servants to read. But I've also heard you speak French and Latin. Under no circumstances may you do so again. Do I make myself clear?"

Rose forced herself to respond appropriately. "Yes, ma'am."

"Very well then, you may go."

Rose was shaking when she walked away from Mrs. Fletcher. She was lucky she hadn't been turned out directly. If servants were easier to come by so far from town, there was little doubt she would have been sent away this very day.

She'd have to be far more careful from now on. But that would only go so far, for how on earth would she stop Byrne from accosting her?

"Drat that Mr. Byrne," Lydia said. She and Rose were in their beds, the candle between them not yet blown out. "He's a bad one for certain. He's pestered others, but he's never been this bad. Then again, Mr. Fletcher took a liking to you. Everyone knows Mr. Byrne's envious and spiteful about anything his stepbrother has."

"But Luke doesn't have me. He's merely kinder than he needs to be."

Lydia looked at her, one eyebrow raised. "If you say so. But one thing's for sure. Mr. Byrne is in dire straits. His groom told Charlie that something's come over him lately. He was never a gentleman, mind you, but these last few months he's begun drinking and carousing. Mrs. Fletcher is beside herself. You know how much stock she puts in the family's standing."

Rose took in this further confirmation of her suspicions. Something had caused Byrne's behavior to change radically. If he'd murdered her father, as she thought he had, the timing of his decline made perfect sense.

Fortunately, whatever Mrs. Fletcher said to her son caused him to stay away from Cider Hill for the next week, allowing Rose some measure of peace. Now instead of jumping at the sound of Byrne's footsteps, she listened for those that heralded Luke's return. Maybe she would ask him about his stepbrother's behavior, though she'd say nothing of Byrne's violence toward her. Whatever Luke's response would be to the news, it was sure to inflame matters.

And yet along with her anxious anticipation of Luke's arrival rose an awareness of the dangerous line she'd been walking in continuing to let him drive her home each week. Mrs. Fletcher was watching her so carefully, anything between them was sure to be noticed. She couldn't control what Byrne did, but what about the danger she was bringing on herself?

For days she turned the dilemma over in her mind, worrying it until she could hardly think straight. She had come all this way to find her father's murderer. Why then could she not accept what must be done?

Because she loved Luke.

The truth of it came to her just as the sun disappeared from her window, ringing through her with a clarity bestowed by pain. All this time she'd wondered what made her go against all common sense to see him, but the answer was so simple, and so devastating.

Their weekly rides had come to mean so much to her. His warm voice, the way she felt around him. He eclipsed Will in every way. Yet there was no denying what she had to do. Tears streamed down her cheeks as she lay in bed, letting go of what she'd only just admitted wanting.

CHAPTER SEVEN

ose had just finished inventorying the contents of the root cellar when Mrs. Craig poked her head down the ladder.

"Rose, I need you to go into the garden and cut enough flowers to freshen all the vases downstairs before the guests arrive."

Grateful for the chance to wander in private, Rose snatched a basket from the kitchen and headed outside.

Screened from the house by a cluster of birch and maple trees, the flower garden spread nearly half an acre. Pathways wove between carefully tended daylilies, coneflowers and black-eyed Susans. The sun was just beginning to sink below the trees, casting long shadows across the beds

It was lush and bountiful, a balm to spirits brought low by both her painful realization about Luke, and the fact that she'd finally sent a letter to Will explaining she couldn't marry him. He would be hurt and confused, and she knew of no way to ease his pain. Nothing could help that kind of hurt. She ought to know.

But there was no going back, and no choice but to end it. She couldn't conceive of marrying him when she was in love with Luke. And Will deserved better. He deserved a wife who adored him, who would not think always of another man.

Slowly she made her way deeper into the garden, bending over to cut flowers as she went. Her basket was nearly full when she stood up and saw she was no longer alone.

Even silhouetted by the sun, she recognized Luke's large frame and loose-limbed gait. As he drew closer she saw his hands were thrust deep into his pockets, his head bent toward the ground. He looked lost in thought, a slight frown furrowing his brow. He was even more handsome, more powerful and compelling than she remembered.

Her heart beat frantically in her chest at the sight of him. Every day since her decision to halt their friendship she'd imagined seeing him for the first time, imagined what she would say. Yet now that he was before her she could scarcely breathe.

Everything in her wanted to be with him. Would she be able to turn him away?

⸺⟶

Why had he accepted the invitation for dinner instead of going to his club? He was still exhausted from the ride home and didn't feel at all inclined to make small talk with twenty people he hardly knew.

But it was hard to refuse when the invitation came from his father, and when there would be people who had an interest in the Western line – town officials and stock-holders as well as business people. And, if he were honest with himself, he wanted to see Rose as soon as possible, even if he couldn't speak to her.

The house was abuzz with preparations, servants hurrying about with table linens and polished silver, but Rose wasn't among them. The commotion and heat drove him outside for some air, and without thinking he headed down the garden paths he knew so well.

Even without seeing her, Rose was all he thought about. Though he'd maintained his resolution to keep his hands off her, their carriage rides had forged an intimacy at least as dangerous as his lust. He'd made things harder on himself by getting to know her and learning how much he enjoyed her company.

He barely looked up as he strode along, deep in thought. Just knowing he'd see her tonight made him restless, and he needed to master his feelings before returning to the house.

He was turning down another path when something caught his attention, something bright at the edge of his vision.

Rose.

She was standing on the outer garden path near the edge of the woods, a basketful of flowers clutched in her hands. Her eyes were wide and she stood unmoving as he approached, as if unsure what she should do. Her head was uncovered, her hair vivid even in the darkening air.

Quickening his pace, he closed the distance between them. But she didn't smile her usual smile. Instead she held herself stiffly and took a step away from him. He didn't know what he'd been expecting, but it wasn't this.

"Rose?"

"You're home," she said, her voice barely rising above a whisper.

"You don't look pleased to see me."

"It's not that. But I...I've been thinking about the way things are with us, our Monday drives ..."

"Yes, what of them?" he asked warily.

"They've been lovely, but it's too dangerous now. They must stop."

He flinched as if he'd been slapped, but in fact the pain went far deeper. It was as if he were losing something essential he'd thought always to have. A rib or a lung. Surely something had been torn from him, for he could no longer breathe as before, and his chest felt hollowed out.

Her lovely face was pale and her voice trembled, but she spoke with conviction. He knew what she'd been risking these months, knew she was right to end it, and still he couldn't stop himself from cajoling her.

"You know I wouldn't hurt you for anything," he said, desperate to change her mind, change her back to the woman who had so slowly and deliciously been opening up to him.

"You don't want to but you will. You won't be able to help it."

Her words sliced through him. She was right of course. The way he felt for her, their time together could not have remained innocent for much longer. He'd been telling himself for weeks that their drives ought to end, had reminded himself over and over of her place in his father's house. None of it had stopped him.

"So this is it?" he asked. Already she seemed unreachable, untouchable.

A fine tremor ran through her, as if they were standing out in the cold. Her eyes wide and somber, she nodded her head.

Weeks of restraint snapped at her silent confirmation.

Pulling her to him, his mouth found her soft lips as if it were his last moment on earth. For the space of three pounding heartbeats she resisted, and then the basket fell to the grass and her glorious body molded itself to his, her hands clutched in his shirt.

The heat of her radiated through him, scorching along his veins as he coaxed open her mouth, delving into all her secrets, secrets he had not even begun to know and would never again taste. Her scent surrounded him – the fragrance of her hair, the hint of musk that was her essence. There was nothing else but Rose, nothing but the need to keep her with him for as long as possible.

Fueled by her soft moans, dazed by her skin and heat, he dove his hands into her hair until the pins scattered into the dusky flowers at their feet. He wound his hands in it as he'd wanted to since the first moment he saw her, the silken strands tethering him to her, if only for the briefest of moments.

He pressed kisses along her jaw, the smooth curve of her cheek, kissed a trail down her throat to where her pulse beat madly. But his need for her was too fierce, too dangerous, and it was a few moments before he realized she was trying to push him away.

He pulled back and looked into eyes full of desire and confusion. He would have given up everything in that moment to have her, her lips passion-stung, her body trembling with feelings he'd stoked in her. But it was no use. Her gray eyes shimmered with tears and she looked at him as if he brought only pain.

Then she turned and fled. Her skirts rustled the plants like a storm wind, her bright hair brighter than the flowers that nodded at her passing.

He stood unmoving for long minutes as his blood cooled. He would never again know her thoughts, touch her skin, taste her sweet mouth. But it was best that it was over.

Best that he suffer rather than cause her more pain.

⸻

Rose took shelter in the laundry room, her thoughts racing, her body wracked by sensations she couldn't contain.

Ending it was the right thing, so why did she feel like she was dying inside?

She couldn't go out there and wait on Luke as if she weren't torn apart. The idea was impossible. But neither could she hide away all night. Dazedly she emerged from the room, praying she wouldn't crumble in front of the staff and guests.

Luckily, Mrs. Craig was too busy to notice her come in without flowers. It was nearly time for supper, so Rose headed into the dining room to help Lydia set the table. Lydia chatted non-stop for so long that it seemed she might not notice anything was wrong, but eventually she looked at Rose closely, a frown appearing between her eyes.

"You look positively peaked. Are you ill?"

"It's nothing," Rose said, waving her hand dismissively. "I'm simply tired and overheated."

"If you say so," Lydia replied, though she didn't look convinced.

Wanting a moment to herself before the meal began, Rose headed into the kitchen and continued to the back door for some air. She stopped cold before she reached the door.

Sitting on the floor was the basket of flowers she'd dropped. Luke must have gathered the blooms up and brought them back. Even this simple gesture filled her with longing and regret. Her eyes blurred with tears as she grabbed the basket and carried it into the kitchen.

"Very nice, Rose," Mrs. Craig said, entering as Rose stood staring at the flowers. "Hurry now and put them out. We haven't much time."

Quickly, feeling the eyes of Mrs. Beech and Dottie on her, she filled half a dozen vases with flowers that had always brought her such pleasure, their perfume like a taunt now. One by one she set the heavy crystal vases in the downstairs rooms, nearly lightheaded with the fear that she'd encounter Luke. Fortunately he wasn't in the drawing room with the rest of the supper party, but how in heaven's name would she get through the evening?

She didn't have long to wonder, as everyone began to file into the dining room soon thereafter and Luke appeared at the very last. There were sixteen guests in all, not counting the family. Fortunately only six of them were staying over, as the others hailed from Boston. Byrne was absent, preparing for a trip to Albany Rose was gratified to learn would last at least several weeks.

She'd hoped that if she refrained from serving Luke, Abigail or Lydia would attend to him. But it wasn't to be. The other girls left Luke for her, assuming on their connection, and Rose had no wish to create more speculation by entreating them to take her place. In the end she was forced to bring him each course, ply him with drink and remove his empty dishes.

To be so close to him after what had happened in the garden, what had happened in her heart, was nearly unbearable. She felt his gaze upon her but refused to look at him. When her hand shook as she poured wine into his glass, she saw him move as if to help before he stopped himself. She knew by his rigid posture that he found the situation as painful as she did, but he refrained from anything that might draw attention to them.

It quickly became apparent that all the men present had an interest in the Western Railroad Company in one way or another. Most of them had brought their wives, so polite conversation was required until the men retired to the library. A few stray remarks surfaced, however, and Rose heard Luke quietly tell one of the men that the original route across the Berkshires was not possible. It was no great matter, he went on, as they already knew the alternate route they would take and were even now mapping it out. The line would come to Albany only a few months behind schedule.

Relief flooded her. Her aunt's last letter had recounted how she'd refused Luke's offer to buy her land, but hearing it from Luke himself confirmed that the matter had finally been put to rest.

Her relief was brief compared to the endless meal. The strain of waiting on the table began to show in the second hour of her ordeal, and by the time the raspberry tart and lemon sorbet were served, she was lightheaded and visibly trembling.

Then she knocked over Mrs. Cabot's wine glass. Though it had been nearly empty, the dark red stain spreading over the white tablecloth was damning.

"How clumsy you are, Rose," Mrs. Fletcher said. She turned to her guest. "My apologies. I don't know what to do with her."

Mortified as well as furious, Rose righted the glass and mopped up as best she could.

"Don't trouble yourself, Mrs. Fletcher," Mrs. Cabot replied. "It's not easy finding domestics who know how to serve. One must get them from England, if at all possible."

At this Luke opened his mouth as if to defend her. Rose looked at him pleadingly and he subsided, jaw clenched.

"Yes, but would they be as pretty as this one?" asked Mr. Morris, one of the two young men who had come without wives. He sat to the right of Luke and was clearly in his cups. "I'd stand for a few spills now and then to have a pretty maid around day and night."

A shocked silence followed this remark, and Rose could have died. Now Luke did rise from the table, his cheeks full of hectic color, his body rigid with anger as he glared at Mr. Morris, a much smaller man who cowed in his seat.

"What precisely is that supposed to mean?"

Rose and Lydia exchanged helpless looks of alarm and the guests glanced about them, unsure what was happening. Fortunately Mr. Fletcher acted quickly.

"You'll understand that we take pride in treating our staff well," Mr. Fletcher said, looking around the table with a gracious smile. "I feel as strongly as my son that one should never take advantage of one's position. No doubt you all feel the same way."

Mr. Morris nodded his head rapidly. "But of course," he spluttered, his eyes darting up at Luke. "My apologies if I gave offense."

"Since you're already up, Luke, why don't you bring your maps to the library?" Jonas suggested. "I think the men are ready to see what we're up to."

Luke looked at his father with bemusement, his fury visibly leaving him, and the whole table seemed to sigh with relief when he nodded in agreement and left the room.

The rest of the men filed out shortly thereafter, all of them laughing again and perfectly at ease. Rose looked on, amazed at how Mr. Fletcher had conveyed both his principles and his support for his son, dispelling the tension in the process. It was a remarkable feat, especially as most men in his position would simply have apologized for Luke. Once again she was struck by his fair-handedness.

It was hard to believe that such a principled man could be responsible for her father's death. It seemed more likely that Byrne had acted alone. If that were the case, did anyone else know what he'd done? Perhaps Mrs. Fletcher? She certainly didn't have her husband's principles.

Mrs. Fletcher rose from the table and led the ladies out of the room. As soon as they had retreated to the drawing room Rose fell into one of the chairs, her head in her hands.

"Are you unwell, Rose?" asked Lydia. "Perhaps you ought to rest. We can handle the clean-up."

Rose looked up, grateful for her concern but unwilling to abandon her duties.

"Thank you, but I'll be fine."

"Go to bed, Rose," Mrs. Craig said, appearing beside her. "The other girls can handle this. It will do no one any good if you fall ill."

With an effort Rose stood and went up the back stairs into the heat of the servants' wing. Stripping off her sweat-soaked garments she fell into bed, grateful that she could, at least this one night, escape Lydia's questions.

But as exhausted as she was, scenes from the long evening ran through her mind. Luke kissing her in the garden, watching her through the meal. Ready to defend her honor.

Exchanging looks over the dining room table was as close as they would ever be now that she'd ended their friendship. Though she had finally done the right thing, nothing had ever felt so wrong.

⤴

Luke spent as little time as possible at Cider Hill after Rose's decision to part ways. He woke early, ate quickly and didn't come back until late in the evening. The few times he ran into Rose, he had to restrain himself from asking how she was, or worse yet, dragging her to him for another kiss.

He missed her. It was as simple, or as complicated, as that. More than anything he wanted to see her, and more than anything he could not endure seeing her and acting as if she meant nothing to him. He wanted to make everything right, and yet it was he who caused her pain. All he could do was stay out of her way and hope he could forget her.

Only once in those weeks afterwards did he see Rose for more than a few moments at a time, though she didn't see him.

He was on his way to get his horse when he heard loud voices and laughter coming from beyond the stable. Curious, he headed toward the commotion, and on turning the corner saw Charlie and one of the maids acting out a play in the shade of a spreading oak tree, a crowd of servants and farmhands watching them.

After a few lines it hit him that they were performing *Romeo and Juliet*, one of the plays contained in the Shakespeare collection he'd given Rose. He'd come upon them during the balcony scene. A wagon had been pulled around and Lydia played Juliet standing atop it. Charlie stood on the ground gazing up at her in the part of Romeo.

"See how she leans her cheek upon her hand!

O, that I were a glove upon that hand,

That I might touch that cheek!"

Luke watched, his casual attention changing to stunned awareness. Standing there watching his father's servants on their makeshift stage, he finally understood Romeo's moonlight declaration.

If only he could touch her cheek. If only he could be so unfettered, so pure of spirit, holding nothing back.

Drawing closer to the rapt crowd he looked for Rose, knowing she must be somewhere nearby. Then he saw her. Standing a few feet behind the actors, Rose herself had no part in the play except as prompter and director, discreetly whispering forgotten lines and stage directions, an expression of pride and delight on her face as she watched her students shine.

For people who had barely known how to read mere months ago, the performance was extraordinary. But though everyone else watched the actors, Luke had eyes only for Rose. Luckily, the audience screened him from her view, but in any case, her attention was only for the unfolding scene.

So devoted was she to these people she had only recently met, she let them enjoy all the glory. She was always tired, and yet she spent what little free time she had helping others. She had wanted more books not for herself but for them.

He had never met anyone like her, and he never would again. He would never again touch that fine skin, make her laugh or see her home. Sick at heart, he wished he could stand with the others, watching the play and cheering them on. Or better yet, declaring himself to her without hesitation or doubt.

Instead he walked away, leaving as unnoticed as he'd arrived.

⁓

Rose followed Lydia and Dottie through the woods bordering the house. The Fletchers were out for the evening and all their chores had been done, or at least those that couldn't wait. The unrelenting heat, so unseasonable for early September, had so enervated everyone that Mrs. Craig had taken pity on the staff and let them go early.

"Just you wait, it's heavenly," Lydia trilled. "Soon you'll be sneaking away every chance you get."

It was cooler in the woods, and Rose felt almost comfortable for the first time in days. If she could feel this good, she didn't care where they ended up. Lydia and Dottie ran ahead of her and broke through the edge of the woods to a clearing beyond, laughing and squealing in delight. Coming through, Rose saw why and broke into a run.

It was a small clearing of perhaps two acres taken up by a pond that shimmered in the late afternoon light. The sight of all that cool blue water before her nearly brought tears to her eyes. Riotously growing ferns, milkweed and tangled vines converged around it, but here and there were openings to the edge. Without wasting any time, Lydia and Dottie began to shed their clothes.

"Does anyone else come here?" Rose asked, hesitant to follow suit. She swam often in the pond back home, but she knew for a fact that no one else ever went there.

"This is still Fletcher land. Sometimes Charlie or George comes here, but since Mrs. Craig won't let them go until we return, we're perfectly safe from discovery," replied Dottie.

She and Lydia, dressed only in their chemises, rushed into the water shrieking with joy. That was all Rose needed. In no time she had joined them, her shyness lost in the delight of being submerged in water.

Then a thought occurred to her.

"Have you two been coming here without me?"

Lydia looked guilty.

"Only a few times, when I still hated you," Dottie replied matter-of-factly. "I told Lydia not to tell you. But that was before. We're all friends now, right?"

There was no use feeling hurt over what was already done, and Rose was too thrilled to be upset anyway. Instead she made do with splashing the two girls mercilessly until they were all laughing and making as much noise as possible.

Soon Dottie got out a cake of soap and they all bathed, taking their hair down and washing that as well. Finally they climbed out of the pond and sat on a patch of moss, letting the late sun dry them. Rose closed her eyes and let the other girls' chatter flow over her, feeling relaxed and renewed and yes, even peaceful.

A lavender veil dropped over the clearing, the first whisper of the shadows that would soon fall, and Lydia and Dottie stood up and began dressing.

"We'd best get going. The men will want to be coming here."

"I'll be along in just a minute," Rose said, reluctant to let go of her blissful state.

Lydia and Dottie made their way back along the trail, their cheerful chatter fading into the noises of the woods. Rose closed her eyes and drowsed as all around her toads croaked, insects whirred and birds flitted from tree to tree.

She must have dozed for a few minutes, for when she opened her eyes the shadows had lengthened and the sun no longer reached her. Standing up, she shook out her damp hair, combing it through with her fingers but keeping it down so that it might dry more. Her chemise still clung damply to her, but there was nothing to be done about that just now. Bending over to pick up her dress, she stood back up just in time to see Luke step out of the forest.

For a long moment Luke could only stand there, unable to take his eyes from her. Even in his wildest imaginings, he could not have conjured a more erotic picture.

Her hair flowed in molten waves over her shoulders nearly to her waist, and her arms and legs were bare. Her chemise was utterly transparent where it clung wetly to her breasts, hips and thighs. She stared at him with startled gray eyes, the crumpled dress clutched to her chest poor protection from his gaze.

It was two weeks since her refusal of him in the garden, and he had not yet made peace with the loss. Cursing his own weakness, he'd thrown himself into his work, barely sleeping, hoping that one day soon he would wake up free of her.

Now he saw he would never be free.

He had to have her. That was his only thought as he crossed the distance to where she stood, wide-eyed and unmoving.

"What are you doing here?" she asked.

But he was beyond speech.

Pulling her to him, he crushed her against his chest and slanted his mouth over hers. He heard the soft gasp as her mouth opened for him and a fierce trembling swept through her. She smelled like the forest, her skin sun-warmed and flawless as poured cream. Too far gone to bank down the force of his need, he gave it full reign.

Her dress slipped to the ground as her hands came up to grip his shoulders. With lips and tongue and teeth he traced the graceful column of her throat, down, down to where the wet cotton outlined her breasts and the tightened buds at their center. He wanted to know every inch of her, leave nothing untouched.

Bending his head he took her nipple in his mouth through the cotton, nipping and tugging until a tortured moan rose from her throat and her hands twined in his hair.

Rose's legs gave way as his mouth closed over her other breast and together they fell to their knees in the soft pine needles. Catching her against him, his mouth came back to claim hers, his hands on her hips bringing her into contact with his arousal. He was wild for her, his whole body pulsing with the need to have her, to press her to the forest floor where only the birds would bear witness.

The sound of voices in the distance brought him abruptly to his senses. Pulling away from her, he looked at Rose with lust-glazed eyes, unable to trust himself to move or speak. He was panting, his breath hoarse in his own ears. Rose was still smoldering, her eyelids heavy, her gaze unfocused.

He watched as awareness returned and with it visible horror at what they'd done, her expression so like the day in the garden that he could have roared in frustration. Wordlessly she stood up and began pulling on her drawers, petticoats and dress. She struggled with the lacings of her corset but when he reached out to help she pulled away. He could only stare helplessly as she armored herself with each new layer.

"Rose, look at me. We must talk."

But she said nothing. Only when she was fully clothed did she look at him.

He hated the hurt and confusion he saw there. She might look like a wanton goddess, but she didn't understand the passion they aroused in one another, nor her reaction to it. Which was no wonder, as he wasn't sure he did either.

"There is nothing to discuss, Mr. Fletcher. I won't ever let such a thing happen again."

He strove now to keep himself in control, though his senses were full of her.

"I still want you, Rose," he said, his voice rougher than he intended. "Forget about Will. You belong with me."

"Belong with you? What are you saying?"

"Let me take care of you. You won't need to work here or anywhere else," he said urgently, desperate to convince her.

"Are you offering to marry me, or just bed me?"

"I can't marry again, Rose. But I'm offering you all that I can. A home, my affection."

Her mouth opened but no words came out, and she flushed, though with anger now rather than desire. Luke watched the emotions play across her face and knew he was losing her.

"Rose," he said, moving toward her, needing to touch her. She took a step back.

"None of this should have happened. And it's not because of Will. That's over."

Hope surged in him. "Then what's stopping you?"

"I never felt for him as I do for you, but at least he didn't shame me. How can you care for me and ask me such a thing? I deserve better than this."

"I know you do," he said, full of regret and need, his desires utterly conflicting. "But I'd give you everything I have."

"And when you move on? What would you do then, leave me here? Or would I follow you into the wilderness?"

Her eyes looked wild as she stared him down, demanding answers he didn't have. He knew it was madness, knew he had no right to ask it of her.

"Let me think," he said. "Perhaps there's a way..."

Her voice had dropped to a whisper when she spoke again.

"I won't live my life in shame, or bring shame on my family."

The exuberant voices of men coming down to bathe came closer. They would be upon them soon.

"Let us talk about this somewhere else. We can't stay here."

"No, we'll finish this now," she said her chin coming up with fierce pride. "I don't understand what it is you do to me..."

"Rose, don't," Luke said, reaching for her.

"Leave me be. I can't do what you ask. Please don't ask it of me again."

Luke let his hands fall to his sides as despair shot through him. He'd never seen anything so lovely or heartbreaking as her face, lit by the dappled forest light, as she turned from him and disappeared into the trees without a sound, as if he'd only imagined her.

CHAPTER EIGHT

hank goodness Lydia wasn't in their room when she returned, for she couldn't have withstood her scrutiny. Sitting on the bed in her damp dress, her hair in a tangle down her back, she closed her eyes as the full weight of her sadness and crushing disappointment descended over her.

For just a moment she'd thought he was asking her to marry him, and she'd felt only elation. No fear or doubt or guilt. Never mind that the idea was impossible. Her heart knew nothing of right or wrong, what was possible and what was not. She hadn't thought she could be any sadder than she'd been after she turned him away in the garden, but this was worse. For just a moment it had seemed she might have the man she loved.

Her feelings in a constant turmoil, it was a relief to be back at Vivian's the next day, where calm and order reigned. Her friend looked at her with concern, but almost immediately presented Rose with a small package from Aunt Olivia that had arrived only the day before.

It was the first correspondence she'd received since informing her aunt about Will. Ever since sending the letter she'd worried that Aunt Olivia would think it yet another poorly considered decision. It was with considerable relief that she read her aunt's supportive reply.

I know you have not made this decision lightly, and that you have struggled with your feelings about Will for some time. I confess I was always fond of him, and liked knowing you would be well taken care of, but more than once your father expressed concern that you and he were ill-suited to one another. It seems he was right. I trust that someday you will find the right man, one who will bring you all the joy you deserve.

Tears came to her eyes as she read, and it seemed for a moment as if her father were smiling down on her, pleased that she'd made the right choice, however difficult it had been.

But the letter did not end there, for her aunt went on to relate shocking news. It seemed a farmhand had come across a glove buried in the dead leaves of their woods very near where her father had died. Immediately suspicious of the fine workmanship and singed leather, he connected it at once to Peter's murder and brought it to her aunt.

There was something in the parcel, something soft pushed into the back of the box. Reaching in, Rose pulled out the glove.

"What is it?" Vivian asked.

Too dazed to explain, Rose handed Vivian the letter. Vivian read it in amazement and looked up, her eyes wide. "Oh, Rose. What's to be done with it?"

"The name of the maker is sewn into the glove. Bailey and Sons. Have you heard of such a place?"

"Yes, I believe I have. It's very near the Common. We could walk to it from here."

"I must go at once. This could be the proof that I need."

"Yes, of course. We'll go now," Vivian said, standing up.

"I can do this myself," Rose told her. "You needn't worry."

"As if I'd let you leave on your own," Vivian replied, looking insulted at the suggestion. "I'm going to pretend I didn't hear that. I'll just tell Father we're going for a walk. I won't be a moment."

Unable to keep still, Rose paced the room while she waited for Vivian. This new evidence was just the thing she needed to renew her faith in her plan. She would find out whether Mr. Byrne, or any of the Fletchers for that matter, were customers at the store. If so, she would find a way to get the information she needed.

Looking down at the glove in her hand, she was suddenly overwhelmed by it, as if the glove itself were somehow malevolent and capable of harm. Her father's murderer had worn it, of that she was sure. Turning it over she saw the singe marks of which her aunt had written.

The room swam in front of her and she sat down heavily, waiting for the world to stop its sickening spin.

Dimly she heard Vivian return. "Rose? Rose, are you ill?"

"I'll be fine in a moment."

Vivian looked unconvinced, but Rose forced a smile.

"It's just such a shock," she said quietly. "All this time I've been looking for some kind of evidence, and now that I have it, I can hardly stand to touch it."

"Who could blame you?" Vivian said, squeezing Rose's hand in sympathy. "I'll put it in your reticule and you can keep it out of sight as much as you want."

The streets around the Common were full of mothers pushing babies in prams, and young men and women exchanging long looks as they passed each other. She and Vivian had been walking for several minutes when Vivian stopped. "This is it," she said with a nervous whisper.

They were standing in front of a storefront, its white and green awning flapping softly in the breeze. Rose looked at Vivian, who gave a smile of anxious encouragement.

Squaring her shoulders, head held high, Rose took a deep breath and opened the door.

The store was dim and warm, filled with the comforting smell of leather. The man behind the counter looked up as she entered. Rose judged him to be about Jonas Fletcher's age, a stout, balding man with a red face. She forced herself to smile as she approached him.

"Yes, miss. What can I do for you today?" he asked, his voice gruff but not unkind.

"I wonder if you can help me. My mistress would like a pair of gloves made for her son. He's forever losing the ones he has. He gets his gloves made here and she's hoping you keep records of past orders. Measurements perhaps, or the style," Rose finished, her chest tight with anxiety.

"Well now, as a matter of fact I do. At least, I keep them for a few years. If he's ordered anything from me in that time, I should have something. What's his name?"

"Nathan Byrne."

"Let me take at look in my files. You ladies have a seat, " he said over his shoulder, disappearing behind a curtain.

"Rose, that was brilliant," Vivian said excitedly, making an effort to keep her voice low. "I can't believe how clever you are."

"Let us hope he finds something. Otherwise my cleverness won't count for much."

The two of them sat down on a bench to wait, but Rose found she couldn't keep still. Getting up, she perused the goods on display – gloves, shoes and boots of all styles, riding whips and crops, fine saddlebags. At last the curtain parted and the proprietor came out, a sheaf of paper in his hands.

"Looks like I might have what you need. I have an order for a Nathan Byrne from a year ago. I have the measurements, so making another pair wouldn't be any trouble."

Rose brought the soiled glove out and laid it on the counter.

"Does this fit your record of it?"

Picking up the glove with a frown at its condition, he smoothed it out on the counter and began to measure it. Rose gripped Vivian's wrist below the edge of the counter but tried to appear unaffected.

"I'd say so. This is my work and it fits the measurements exactly. It's no wonder he needs another pair, if this is what becomes of them. I can start on them later this week and have a pair ready for you by Monday next."

"Oh, no, that won't be necessary, thank you," Rose said, the words tumbling out one after the other. "His mother insisted I check back with her before placing the order. But thank you so much for your time."

Of course this made no sense to the glove maker, but she couldn't worry about that. She had what she'd come for.

The shopkeeper frowned at her, confused by her sudden reversal.

"Whatever you say, miss. Come back again if you decide you want them made."

"Yes, of course. Thank you," Rose replied before rushing out of the shop.

Without a word Vivian followed her out onto the walkway, where the two of them stopped out of sight of the shop. Vivian grasped Rose's hands in hers, her eyes wide and pleading.

"I don't want you to go back to that house, Rose. It's too dangerous. Who knows what those people are capable of? Stay with us tonight instead and we'll figure out what next to do."

Rose understood her friend's anxiety, but this was something she couldn't run away from. If she walked away now, she risked failing her father for good.

"I must finish this, Vivian. Don't you see? I'm getting closer. I couldn't possibly back down now."

"But what will you do?"

"I'm not certain. But at least now I know the truth. My own doubts are satisfied."

They ate a subdued supper together, with Edward casting searching looks at Rose and Vivian but forgoing any questions. Rose made sure not to linger afterward, for she hadn't much time to get back before the sun went down.

Walking back to Cider Hill with the glove, she wondered if she were finally close to finishing what she'd come for. Soon, perhaps, she could go home. The thought no longer gave her the comfort it once did, for while she missed her aunt terribly, the one person she wanted most wouldn't be there. She couldn't act on her love for Luke, but she felt its pull on her regardless. She even thought she heard his voice, calling to her from somewhere far away, like the ghost of the happiness she'd so fleetingly known.

She was still immersed in these gloomy thoughts when she returned to the servants' quarters. Lydia leapt up from her bed when Rose entered their room, her expression stricken.

"Oh, Rose, thank goodness you're back!"

"What is it, Lydia? Tell me quickly," she demanded, grabbing Lydia's hands to still them.

"Not long after you left this morning a girl came by looking for work, and Mrs. Fletcher hired her on the spot. You're to be dismissed. She says you're more trouble than you're worth, and the supper party was the last straw.

Here Lydia paused to catch her breath. She stared at Rose imploringly, as if Rose herself could resolve the crisis.

Rose stood numbly as the news sank in. She felt no surprise. How could she, when every day she'd been expecting such a thing? The wonder was that she'd lasted as long as she had.

"I suppose I ought to find Mrs. Craig," she said.

Lydia was nearly in tears, but Rose felt nothing as she left the room. She couldn't let herself feel, for she couldn't bear the idea of failure. Absently she smoothed down her hair and dress, as if that could make any difference at all.

She walked through the downstairs rooms until she found Mrs. Craig in the foyer. The housekeeper stood with her hands on her ample hips, her back to Rose.

"Abigail, I believe I requested yesterday that you polish this banister. It looks as if you hadn't touched it."

Rose, thinking she had never heard Mrs. Craig sound so cross, stopped a few feet away. Abigail gasped when she caught sight of Rose. Mrs. Craig turned, her look of annoyance fading to one of something else, regret or resignation. But though her mouth was pressed into a grim line, her eyes softened as they looked at her.

"Wait for me in the servants' hall, Rose," she said, sighing. "I'll be in directly."

Rose did as she was told, feeling as if she were awaiting her own execution. Perhaps she should simply leave, pack her things and never look back. But what if there was still a chance to change their minds? She couldn't leave without trying, not when so much depended on her staying. But at least she'd been paid her week's wages this morning. That was something.

After several minutes Mrs. Craig entered and sat down heavily across the table from her.

"Do you know why you're here?"

"Only what Lydia told me when I arrived," Rose replied. "Mrs. Fletcher feels I'm more trouble than I'm worth."

The housekeeper seemed surprised by her blunt reply, but Rose saw no point in being circumspect.

"That's correct. I assume you understand her reasons as well as I."

"I don't suppose there's any point in defending myself?"

Mrs. Craig sighed and rubbed the corners of her eyes in a rare gesture of fatigue.

"I'm sorry, Rose, but I'm afraid there's no changing her mind. I don't know why things have been so difficult for you here. It doesn't seem to have been your doing, but my hands are tied. You're to pack your things and be gone within the hour."

Despair filled her as she stood to go, but it wasn't the housekeeper's fault she was dismissed. Mrs. Craig had done all she could for her from the beginning.

"Thank you for your kindness. I truly am grateful for your help."

Mrs. Craig nodded her head in acknowledgement and stood up as well.

"Good luck, dear," she said, enveloping Rose in a heartfelt embrace.

Lydia was waiting just outside the servant's hall when Rose left. Rose gave a quick shake of her head and watched as Lydia's face crumpled in tears. Together the two of them walked up the servants' stairs and into their room, where Rose began putting her things into her satchel.

The glove seemed to get heavier with every minute that passed. But as much as it meant to her, by itself it likely wasn't enough to convince anyone who didn't already believe in Byrne's guilt.

It was time to go. She looked around one last time, thinking how strange it was that this stark little room had become a place of friendship and comfort.

The two girls embraced, Lydia snuffling onto Rose's shoulder until Rose pulled away.

"Thank you for being such a good friend to me, Lydia. If not for you, I daresay I wouldn't have lasted even this long."

"But where will you go? What will you do?"

"I shall go to Vivian's and catch my breath. This has all happened so quickly, I haven't had time to think beyond that," she said, sounding lost even to her own ears.

"It's so unfair," Lydia said. "I don't want you to leave."

Rose reached into her satchel and drew out her good nib pen, a sheaf of paper and a bottle of ink. She handed them to Lydia. "So that you'll write me," she said.

"I wouldn't be able to write a letter if not for you," Lydia replied, sobbing in earnest now.

Rose was very near tears herself. She was going to miss Lydia, miss everyone far more than she would have guessed, but she mercilessly tamped down her feelings. There would be ample time to cry after she had walked out the door. Leaving in disgrace was bad enough. She would not let anyone see her fall apart.

Rose left their little room only to find Dottie, Abigail and Mrs. Beech waiting in the hallway for her, all of them furious on her behalf. Dottie gave her an ironic smile, her eyes shimmering with tears.

"Who would have thought I'd be so sorry to see you go?" she said, making Rose laugh despite herself.

After many well wishes and promises to write, Rose made it through the hall and down the stairs. She was intent on gaining the rear entrance without running into anyone else when she stopped cold.

A rising tide of cleansing fury swept through her at the injustice her family had suffered at the hands of the Fletchers. The devil take them, she had seen quite enough of the servants' entrance. Reversing course she made for the front door. She strode with purpose, determination building with each step. Somehow, she vowed, she'd find a way to finish what she'd started.

She was passing by the drawing room when Byrne stepped out in front of her. She hadn't seen him since he'd gone to Albany several weeks ago, and he was the very last person she wanted to see now.

"There now, what's your hurry, Rose? Have you some sort of engagement?" he asked innocently.

"I'm no longer in your family's service," she said impatiently. "Let me pass."

Byrne's face bespoke surprise, though whether it was feigned or sincere she couldn't tell.

"What will you do now?" he asked, refusing to move out of her way.

Rose's poise was wearing thin. She was furious, scared, and disgusted.

Her eyes narrowed as she answered him. "You needn't concern yourself with me," she said, an edge to her voice. "You've already done far too much."

"Not nearly enough. Come work for me," he said eagerly, deaf to her anger. "I guarantee the work will be much lighter and the accommodations more comfortable."

Rose said nothing, too stunned for a moment to respond. It was impossible. Just being near him filled her with revulsion. And yet, though there was danger in the prospect, working for him would bring her closer to the answers she sought.

Part of her couldn't believe she was even considering his offer. She didn't trust him for a moment, and she might not be able to keep him at arm's length. But it needn't be for long. She would talk to his servants and glean what information she could. If it became too treacherous, she would simply leave.

"Very well, I accept your offer," she replied.

"Splendid," Byrne crowed. "Wait for me by my carriage. I'll just be a moment."

Somehow Rose propelled herself forward. It appeared she would have a final scene with Mrs. Fletcher, for the formidable lady of the house stood rooted to the floor near the entrance, as if unable to believe Rose's audacity. Sensing the drama, the servants had appeared as well. Some peered over the railing from the second floor, others stood in doorways watching the scene unfold.

Mrs. Fletcher stood rigidly, her voice cutting.

"I see you go out as you came in, looking for trouble."

"*Audaces fortuna iuvat*," Rose replied, unable to resist a parting jibe in Latin for good measure. Hopefully what Virgil said was true and fortune did indeed favor the bold.

Rose watched as Mrs. Fletcher's complexion paled in fury and her eyes narrowed.

"Show me your satchel. I should like to see if you had the nerve to steal anything on your way out."

Rose could only stare at her, her face hot with outrage. Yet in the midst of her reaction she suddenly understood that Mrs. Fletcher was threatened by her. Perhaps because her son acted so shamefully around her, perhaps because Rose didn't fit her notion of a servant. The realization calmed her. Let Mrs. Fletcher do what she would. She couldn't hurt her any more.

With a poise that maddened the mistress like nothing else could have, Rose offered up her bag and smiled as if she were appeasing a difficult child.

"By all means, though I wonder you have time to bother with such things. I would have thought a woman in your position would leave such demeaning tasks to a servant."

Rose could hardly believe the things coming from her own mouth. Never had she spoken to anyone in such a manner, and yet she felt freer than she had since arriving.

"Get out of here this instant," Mrs. Fletcher ground out in fury.

Just then Byrne entered the foyer, oblivious to the tension.

"Oh, hello Mother. I hope you don't mind, seeing as how you sacked her, but I've decided to give Rose a place in my household. Say you're not angry," he pleaded childishly.

But Mrs. Fletcher could take no more. In an angry whirl of skirts she turned on her heel and marched upstairs. Whatever had buoyed Rose through the altercation deserted her as soon as Mrs. Fletcher was out of sight. Refusing to look at anyone, she made for the door and didn't stop until she was outside.

Byrne was right behind her.

"I'm pleased to see you're so anxious to get to my house. Fear not, we'll be there in no time. Now then, step on up."

But Rose refused his hand as she climbed into the carriage, unable to bear even so slight a touch. She tried to ignore her rising sense of panic, but now that she was on her way to Byrne's home, it would not be subdued.

Merely sitting next to him in his carriage made her feel ill. Her father would have hated that she put herself in such danger, and it was clearer with every step the horses took that she'd made a terrible mistake.

It was full dark but for the moon, and as the carriage moved toward its final destination, she felt as if she were being plunged into a darkness from which she'd never return.

"You can't imagine how happy I am you're coming home with me," Nathan said, breaking into her thoughts. "I've wanted this for so long."

A chill ran through her at this, but she stared resolutely out the window, saying nothing.

"There's something between us, Rose. I know you feel it too."

She turned and looked at him. "All I want is to work in your house. Nothing more."

"Once we're used to each other I feel certain you'll feel differently," he replied with absolute calm.

"Please stop the carriage," she choked out, sickened beyond bearing.

"There's no need to be frightened. I'll take care of you."

"Whatever scenario you've imagined for us, I assure you it will never happen," Rose said, her voice shaking now, her breath shallow with rising fear. "I insist you either take me to my friend's house in Boston or leave me off here."

"I know I can make you feel for me," he said, as if he hadn't heard her. "You'll forget all about Luke soon enough."

Rose couldn't believe what was happening. Surely Byrne had lost his mind. Truly panicked now, she reached for the door, more afraid of him than of jumping from a moving carriage. She was stopped by his vise-like grip on her arm.

"I can't let you do that, Rose. I've waited too long for this to let you go now."

Now Rose struggled in earnest, but he was too strong. Unable to break free of his grasp, she screamed for the coachman to stop. But there was no help to be found, for the carriage sped ever faster into the night.

⟶

Luke knocked on the door of his father's study before striding in. Jonas glanced up from his desk, a distracted look on his face.

"Have a seat, son. I want to finish this letter before I forget what I mean to say."

Luke stuffed his hands in his pockets and paced about the room, unable to keep still. As always, knowing Rose was somewhere nearby made him restless.

Jonas sighed and dropped his pen, looking up at Luke.

"Now then, what is it?"

"I've been thinking that I might find lodgings in town for the remainder of my time here. I don't mean to sound ungrateful, but I think it would suit me better to have a more private situation. I find I'm not used to having so many people around all the time."

"I'm sorry to hear that, but considering the state of the house tonight, I can't say that I blame you."

"What do you mean? Has something happened?"

"Charlotte's dismissed Rose Stratton. I don't know all the ins and outs of it, but Charlotte seems to think she caused too much trouble. The girl left not twenty minutes ago."

Luke froze.

"Where has she gone?"

"Well, that's even odder than the rest. Nathan offered her a position and she accepted."

"Are you telling me Rose means to work in Nathan's house?"

"Yes, that's exactly what I'm saying," Jonas replied evenly.

"Over my dead body," Luke ground out.

Within minutes he was at the stable and tacking up Arturo. Then he was off, charging up the road at a full gallop, fury and fear coursing through his veins. What had she been thinking? Was she so desperate?

The thought of Rose at Nathan's mercy nearly unhinged him. Urging his horse on to still greater speed, he road as if his own life depended on it. Four miles down the road he saw a carriage ahead, a lantern sputtering near the driver. He was fast approaching it when he heard Rose call for help. Urging his horse to still greater speed, in less than a minute he'd gained the carriage. Riding beside the team, he spoke to the terrified coachman.

"Stop this cursed rig this instant," he ordered, fully prepared to leap onto the carriage himself if necessary. But the driver immediately stood up and hauled on the reins, gradually slowing the team. Before they had even come to a stop Luke was off his horse and yanking open the carriage door.

Nathan crouched against the side of the cab, one arm circling Rose's waist to keep her still.

"Take your hands off her," Luke spit out, so enraged he could hardly see straight.

"She wanted to come," Nathan said, pressing back against the carriage wall as if to escape him. "Ask anyone at the house."

Luke looked at Rose. Though terribly pale and frightened, she seemed unhurt. He hated the fearful look in her eyes though, and her disordered clothes and hair were proof of an ugly struggle. He could have howled with rage, but that wouldn't help her.

"She's changed her mind. So help me I'll kill you if you don't let her go this instant."

Nathan blanched. After a brief hesitation, he released his grip on Rose and fell panting against the seat. Rose made her way over to Luke and he swung her to the ground.

"Are you hurt?" he asked her, tamping down his anger to attend to her.

Rose shook her head but said nothing, her gaze wide with shock, her whole body trembling.

"Take Arturo, darling, and bring him to the side of the road for grass. Give him a pet or two to calm him down."

The horse was fine, but it might help Rose to concentrate on the animal, and he needed to get her away from the carriage. Numbly she nodded and did as he suggested, looking back over her shoulder as she led the horse away.

Nathan had been trying to signal his coachman to move on, but the driver, still cowed by Luke's threats, refused to comply. Luke reached in and yanked Nathan out, his hand on Nathan's throat as he held him against the door.

"The only reason you'll be able to walk away from this tonight is that my father cares for you. It won't save you again. If you go anywhere near Rose there'll be no more talking. Understand?"

Nearly suffocated and unable to speak, Nathan nodded. Luke released him and he slid to the ground, gasping for air. Luke looked down at him in disgust. That such a man was part of his family was beyond revolting.

Reaching into the rig he grabbed Rose's satchel. Stepping back he signaled to the driver, who promptly climbed down from his seat, pulled Nathan to his feet and helped him into the carriage before taking the reins up again. Slowly and then with increasing speed the carriage pulled away and disappeared around the bend.

Luke walked toward Rose on the empty stretch of road. She was looking at him, wide-eyed and perfectly still. Then she shivered, whether from the cool night air or reaction, he couldn't tell.

Taking off his coat, he slid it over her shoulders and pulled her close, wrapping his arms around her. Gradually her trembling eased, and still he held her.

They were less than a mile from town. Trees interspersed with fields stretched away on both sides of the narrow road. His horse grazed among the short roadside grass looking for tender blades, a darker shape in the night.

An owl hooted nearby and then flew over them on silent wings.

Luke looked down at the woman in his arms and knew he couldn't lose her again. His hands came up to cup her face.

"Marry me, Rose."

The words came of their own volition, but as soon as he said them he knew he didn't want to take them back. Rose's mouth fell open in shock.

"You can't mean that. You don't want to marry me."

"I can't lose you again. Be my wife and let me take care of you."

"But you said…."

"Never mind what I said. I know how I feel about you, how I've felt these last weeks without you."

She only shook her head in bewilderment.

He had no other words to express what she meant to him, the terror he felt at the thought of losing her. Instead he kissed her, pouring everything he felt into it, his lips demanding but patient, hungry but unhurried.

She opened to him, her sweet mouth like honey, her lush breasts pressed to his chest in innocent abandon. He kissed her eyes, the sweet curve of her cheek and the hollow beneath. He wanted all of her, without limit. Sweet little moans sounded in her throat and her hands roamed over his shoulders, scorching him though the cloth, her movements restless and demanding. Breaking the kiss, her lips skimmed over his jaw before moving to his neck, nearly bringing him to his knees.

At last they stopped and looked at each other in wonder and fear, the power of their mutual need overwhelming them, as new to Luke in all his experience as it was to Rose in all her innocence.

Luke pulled her to his chest in a fierce embrace, one hand buried in the raw silk of her hair, his forehead resting against the top of her head in surrender.

"God in heaven, Rose, say you'll marry me."

For a moment, there was no sound but the beating of his heart. Then she spoke.

"Yes. Yes, I'll marry you."

He slipped his hands around her tiny waist and picked her up, swinging her around in a celebratory whirl before crushing his mouth to hers once more. They were both breathless by the time he put her down.

"Does this mean you won't want to move away again?" she asked.

"Wherever you are, that's where I'll be," he said, smiling down at her. "Right now I think we need to be inside. We can't stand on the side of the road all night."

"Yes, I ought to go to Vivian's house. I can stay there until..." She stopped and looked up at him uncertainly.

"Until we're married," he finished for her. He tucked a strand of hair behind her ear. "Whom should I ask for your hand?"

"You may ask Vivian's father, Edward March. Though I hardly know what he'll think," she said doubtfully. "I've scarcely said two words about you."

Luke laughed ruefully. "It has been a most unusual courtship. But I can be very persuasive when I want to be," he whispered, covering her mouth with a kiss.

They stood together catching their breath, and though it was time to be going, he couldn't bring himself to let her go. Even knowing he would have her forever didn't diminish his need.

Just then she started in his arms.

"Luke, what will you tell your family? They'll be totally against this. Good lord, I was turned out by your step-mother just hours ago, not to mention accosted by her son. It's too much."

"I don't live my life worrying about my family's approval, or anyone else's for that matter."

"Very well, but I'll be sorry if this makes things difficult for you," Rose replied, sounding doubtful.

"The only thing I can't handle is living without you," he said, pressing a reassuring kiss to her forehead.

Pulling his reluctant horse away from the grass, Luke led him over to Rose and then helped her mount. Her skirts rose above her ankles just as they had the last time she'd ridden astride, though she tried mightily to cover them.

Good God. The woman wasn't wearing stockings.

He stared at those few inches of smooth skin, unable to move or breathe. As if of its own volition, his hand slid under the hem of her dress and petticoats. He heard her gasp at the same moment his blood began to pound in his ears.

She was soft and silken, warm to the touch. For a few beats of his pulse he simply let the curve of her calf rest in the palm of his hand. But it wasn't enough. He wanted more. Her skirts rustled as he pushed them up, revealing her inch by inch, her skin as luminous as pearls in the moonlight.

Her knee was bared, then her thigh. She didn't stop him. Her hand was on his shoulder, fisted in the fabric, her breath ragged.

The horse snorted and stomped his foot, startling Luke out of his lust-induced trance. With trembling hands he pulled her skirts back down and silently led the horse forward.

"Is something wrong?" Rose asked, and he could hear the nerves and confusion in her voice. Still in an agony of desire, he nevertheless managed to smile wryly up at her.

"Yes, but it's my own fault. I can't touch you without driving myself mad, but I'll be just fine in a few minutes."

The tension in her eased and her lush mouth curved in a private smile of pleasure.

"I don't mind if you ride with me, now that we're to be married," she said after several moments of silence.

"That's a very fine offer, my sweet Rose, and one I'll take you up on as soon as I trust myself. In the meantime why don't you tell me what happened tonight. Why did Charlotte turn you out?"

With stops and starts Rose recounted how Nathan had accosted her while Luke was away, and how Charlotte had come upon them and subsequently threatened Rose with dismissal. Rage surged in him again and his hands clenched into fists at the thought of what she'd endured. If only he could strangle Nathan all over again.

But he was angry at himself as well, for it was clear that his own reaction at the dinner party had sealed Rose's fate. He'd utterly failed in protecting her. But Rose was smiling now as she told of her last words with Charlotte.

"I could not believe the things I said. Mrs. Fletcher looked ready to strike me when I spoke to her in Latin. It was quite thrilling," she said, sounding surprised and pleased with herself.

"I imagine it was, after everything you had to swallow working there," Luke said, smiling at the thought of Rose finally standing up to Charlotte.

"Of course, it's slightly less thrilling now that she'll be my mother-in-law. I can't quite wrap my mind around that. But things have turned out much better tonight than I thought they would. I must have lost my head to get in a carriage with Mr. Byrne. If it weren't for you…"

Luke stopped the horse and looked up at Rose, his stomach clenching at all the time he'd wasted, how close he'd come to losing her. To hell with his arousal, he needed to put his arms around her. Swinging up on the horse he settled behind her, her sweet bottom nestled close enough that he was immediately hard again. It was an agony he was happy to endure. Wrapping one arm around her, he held the reins in his other hand and they moved as one toward their future.

CHAPTER NINE

*R*ose knocked on the door at 35 West Street, rehearsing what she would say and hoping she could explain things so they wouldn't sound shocking. Then the door was opened and Sally was looking out at her with surprise. Hastily she stepped back and beckoned Rose to enter.

"Who is it Sally?" Edward called, emerging from the parlor.

"It's Rose, Mr. March."

Instantly Edward was beside her.

"Rose, whatever is the matter?" he asked, looking her over as if to assess any damage. "Do come in and have a seat. You look exhausted."

Rose smiled wearily at him, relieved to finally be somewhere both restful and predictable.

"I'm well enough, Edward, though it's been a strange sort of night."

Rose and Edward sat down in the parlor and Edward leaned forward in his seat, clearly anxious to hear what had brought her there at such an hour.

Looking at his kind face, Rose was suddenly nervous. She needed him to accept something that was still new and shocking even to her. She didn't know how or where to begin, so she started with the end of the story.

"Luke Fletcher intends to ask you for my hand tomorrow afternoon."

Edward stared at her in surprise. Finally he found his voice.

"I'm not sure what to say. Perhaps you could explain how such a thing came to be."

Perched on the edge of her chair, Rose told him about Luke in as much detail as she could. Which was very little, considering their forbidden kisses and the secret she carried. Instead, somewhat guiltily, she painted a picture of innocent courtship, emphasizing the kindness Luke had shown her.

"Tell me, child, do you love him? And does he love you?"

Rose bowed her head and looked at her clasped hands. With this question Edward hit on the aspect of her engagement to Luke that caused her real pain. For of course he had said nothing of love. But she loved him, enough to leave behind everything she knew, brave his family, and keep a secret that could someday tear them apart.

"He cares for me," she began, trying to put her feelings into words, explaining them to Edward even as she acknowledged them to herself. "He promises to make me happy. Perhaps that's love, perhaps his love will grow over time. But I love him, more than I thought possible. He's a good man, Edward."

She could see how the responsibility of looking out for her weighed upon him, and knew also that he would be glad to see her taken care of, if only he could be sure Luke would do so.

"You know I care nothing for class distinctions, but there is no changing the fact that you were a servant in his father's house. People will make things difficult for you."

This she couldn't argue, as she had the very same worry. Moreover, she couldn't even allow Luke to meet her aunt before she told him the truth. When that would be, she had no idea.

"No doubt you're right, but we're prepared to deal with the consequences."

"I don't envy the struggle ahead of you, Rose, but I'll speak to your Mr. Fletcher tomorrow. As stand-in for your father, I must see for myself what he's about. If he's all you say he is, I'll gladly give my blessing."

Rose squeezed Edward's hand, relieved he would hear Luke out but still anxious about the day to come.

The two of them stood and Rose kissed his grizzled cheek before dashing up the stairs to tell her oldest friend the news.

Vivian met Rose at the doorway to her bedchamber. She wore only her nightgown and her hair was in a braid down her back, ready for sleep.

"What's happened, Rose? Are you all right?"

"Yes, better than I've been in a long while. Come, let's get into your bed and I'll tell you all about it. I feel dead on my feet, and yet I'm not sure I'll ever sleep again."

Once in bed beside Vivian, the covers drawn up to her chin, she told her friend of the day's events. Vivian was appalled at the accusations against Rose, and terribly impressed with her showdown with Mrs. Fletcher. But when Rose described her ordeal in Mr. Byrne's carriage, Vivian was beside herself. By the time Rose had finished her tale, complete with swooning kisses, marriage proposal, and the ride into town sitting astride a horse with Luke behind her, Vivian was dumbfounded.

"But when will you tell him who you are?"

"Every moment I'm with him, I want to tell him everything. But I can't bring myself to do it yet. It's a terrible mess. But I love him, Vivian. Maybe if I give it some time, whatever we have will be strong enough to withstand the truth."

"I'm very happy for you, Rose. But I do worry. Everything seems so tenuous, as if it could all go terribly wrong."

Rose was surprised to hear such a dire assessment from her normally optimistic and supportive friend, and yet she couldn't deny the truth of it.

"It's possible that things might go very badly, but I'm willing to take the risk."

"But that's just it. Though it's you I care for most of all, you're not the only one who stands to get hurt. Mr. Fletcher is the one who will one day find himself wed to a wife who lied to him."

For a moment Rose couldn't speak. All this time she'd been thinking only of the risk to herself or her family, but she wasn't the only one with something at stake. Did she have the right to risk Luke's happiness too?

"I know I should tell him, but I can't risk losing him," she said, full of both anguish and resolve. "I have to believe we can all live with the consequences, whatever they are."

"And I will be there for you, whatever they are." Vivian whispered.

Long after Vivian fell asleep, Rose lay awake. She was so tired she could hardly keep her eyes open, and yet there was too much to think about, too much to feel.

She had always hoped to find the kind of love her parents shared, but until she met Luke she hadn't realized how powerful pure attraction could be. It burned through her childish views of love and devotion, a force all its own. Luke's desire for her was strong enough for him to go against all that he'd planned, all that made sense in his world. Could such feeling turn to love one day? And if it didn't, how long before it burned itself out?

Among all her doubts, one thing was certain. She must prove that Byrne killed her father as soon as possible. There was no future beyond that.

Rose sat at Vivian's desk the next morning, a blank piece of paper in front of her as she wondered how to tell Aunt Olivia the news. She had said next to nothing about Luke in her letters, and she was now faced with having to explain her reasons for marrying into the family of her father's murderer.

It would have been so much easier if she could see Olivia in person, but what if Luke offered to go with her, or visit while she was there? Given the problems with the line in the Berkshires, it was possible he would be out there again soon, and she would be forced into more lies.

Bending her head to the task, she began to relate how unfailingly kind and protective Luke had been. Pouring out her heart, she confessed how she felt about him, so much more than she had ever felt for Will. She would want for nothing. Most importantly, she trusted him with her life.

There was no way to know if she could convince her aunt she was making the right decision. Most likely Aunt Olivia would still be worried sick. But Rose couldn't help that. She could only hope that one day soon her aunt would understand. Hopefully by that time so would Luke.

Later that afternoon Rose nervously paced the upstairs hall as she strained to hear the sound of Luke's approach. Suppose he didn't come? Suppose he'd changed his mind?

"He'll be here, Rose. It's not yet three o'clock," Vivian said calmly from where she sat embroidering in a chair.

"He's probably used to rich women in fine clothes and I still look like a servant. I must have worn this dress hundreds of times," Rose said in dismay, looking down at her blue dress. The hem was fraying and the high waistline was several years out of fashion.

"You're as beautiful as ever. If I didn't love you so much I'd be green with envy."

Rose smiled at her friend's reassurances, though she wasn't convinced. A moment later they both started at the clatter of approaching hoof beats. Grabbing Vivian's hand, she listened anxiously as a knock sounded at the door. Sally answered and Luke's deep voice floated up as he was let in and led into the parlor.

"He came," Rose said with relief.

"Yes, dear, he did."

For the better part of the next hour, Rose waited anxiously upstairs, trying and failing to concentrate on the stockings she was darning. What if Edward didn't see what she saw? What if he didn't approve of the marriage after all?

"I wonder what they can be talking about all this time."

Vivian looked up from her embroidery.

"I'm sure Father is just getting to know him. I shouldn't worry if I were you."

Finally, after what seemed an eternity, Sally came upstairs to tell Rose she was wanted in the parlor. Heart beating frantically, her stomach in knots, she headed down the stairs. At the door to the parlor she paused, gathering her courage, but Luke saw her immediately. Standing up, he looked at her with an intensity that shook her, his eyes never leaving hers as she entered the room.

Edward came to her and took her hands in his, smiling warmly.

"It looks as if Luke and I both want the same thing, your happiness. You have my blessing. I feel sure your father would have given it as well. However, I do have one stipulation that I have already discussed with Mr. Fletcher. Your relationship to date has been most unusual. Because of this, I must insist that you announce your engagement immediately, and set the date of the wedding for a month from now. That will give Mr. Fletcher time to court your properly. You deserve it, and it will benefit you both to spend time together before your marriage."

One month. Everything had happened so quickly, she had given no thought to when they would marry. Now she found herself relieved to have more time to get to know Luke before the wedding.

"Yes, of course," she agreed, trying to sound calm and sensible.

Edward shook Luke's hand, kissed Rose on the cheek and then left them alone together, letting the door close behind him. All at once Rose felt terribly shy. To think he would soon be her husband, and she now had permission to see him openly. It was such a turnaround from their surreptitious meetings. All those days wanting just to catch a glimpse of him, and here she was, promised to him forever.

He moved to stand before her and cupped her face in his hands. "I can't believe I get to have you," he said quietly, a rough note in his voice. "I've spent so long trying to live without you, I hardly know what to do."

Rose could only smile, too overwhelmed herself to reply.

"God knows how I'll keep my hands off you for an entire month," he said, pulling her closer.

"Sometimes kissing you is all I can think about," Rose confessed.

"My dear, that is a dangerous way to talk when we're alone in a room together. I plan to kiss you, never doubt that. But I meant something a bit different. I meant that I would like to put my hands on you in the way that a husband may do with his wife. And that is all *I* think about. When we kiss as we did last night, I find it difficult to stop when I ought to."

"Then we must not indulge in those sorts of kisses until we are married. A month is not so very long."

"It's a lifetime, but you're worth the wait," he replied, smiling his devilish smile as he drew her closer. "How shall I kiss you? Like this?" he asked, pressing his lips to the back of her hand.

"Yes, that's perfectly acceptable," she replied, smiling her approval.

"Is this to your liking?" he inquired politely, dropping a chaste kiss on her cheek.

"Yes, that is most proper for a fiancé, though not in public," she responded archly, though she could not keep a smile from touching the corners of her mouth. She liked this teasing, light-hearted side of him and was now thoroughly enjoying herself.

She looked up at him expectantly, and his voice was rough and low when next he spoke. "How does my lady like this?" Rose's eyes fluttered closed as he bent to her, and she gasped, beyond speech, when he lightly kissed each eyelid, his lips soft as a butterfly. Kissing first one corner of her mouth, then the other, he brushed his lips over hers as if he had all the time in the world. So sweet was the seduction, a little moan escaped her.

Luke's nonchalance vanished.

Sweeping her into his arms, he carried her to the loveseat, where he sat down with her in his lap. Rose's eyes widened in surprise at being held so intimately. Curious, she moved tentatively over the evidence of his desire, and he groaned deep down in his throat, his eyes closing as a deep flush stained his cheekbones. Pleased with the reaction she drew from him and the answering pull she felt in her own body, she moved again. He opened his eyes and looked at her intently for a moment, as if trying to make up his mind.

Then he kissed her.

Though they had kissed before, this time was different. Now they were betrothed. There was no shame, no fear.

At first his lips were light and caressing, feathering over hers, his tongue coming out to tease her before retreating again. Rose delighted in this new side of kissing. Relaxing into him on a sigh, she dared to mimic him, teasing him with her own demanding kisses.

But though the kiss started out light and playful, soon she was restless for more. Kissing him back without reservation, she molded her body to his, wanting to be closer and closer still. Cradled in his arms, she felt his need match hers, felt the power he held in check.

In the back of her mind she knew that one of them must pull back, and yet she could no more do so than she could will her heart to stop beating. His mouth skimmed over her throat, his hand covered her breast. Rose's breath caught and she froze as he caressed her nipple with his thumb, his eyes intent on her.

Fire shot through her veins until she was saturated with desire, undone by her craving for him. His hard chest pressed against her tender breasts, the roughness of his jaw abraded her neck with delicious friction as he kissed his way down her throat until she throbbed at the juncture of her thighs. Her fingers tangled in his hair as his mouth again devoured her, his hands restless on her back and hips.

From down the hall she heard Vivian and Edward talking and slowly came to her senses. With a low cry she struggled off of him, desperately trying to right her hair and clothing.

Luke smiled tenderly at her and smoothed her hair away from her face. Leaning down, he picked a pin up off of the floor and deftly secured a wayward lock. Somehow that gesture was as intimate as the kisses they'd shared, and she trembled anew at the decision she'd made.

Regaining her composure as Edward and Vivian continued past the parlor and up the stairs, Rose allowed Luke to pull her close. There they sat side by side as her heartbeat gradually returned to normal. Too soon Luke sighed and sat forward, taking her hand in his.

"I'm afraid I must be off, much as I'd rather stay here with you. May I take you to a play tomorrow night?"

"That would be lovely."

"Excellent. I'll come for you at seven o'clock."

Edward was there to see him out, and he and Rose stood at the door, watching as Luke rode away. Edward turned to her with what seemed a knowing look but said nothing, only gave her an affectionate kiss on the cheek.

"All right, my dear?" he asked.

"All is right," she answered with a smile, fervently hoping all would indeed be right, someday.

Leaving Rose, Luke stopped at the shop of the most sought-after dressmaker in Boston, as he didn't intend for Rose to worry for one moment about her clothes. The seamstress raised not an eyebrow when he requested an entire wardrobe be created for his fiancée, from morning dresses to riding habits to ball gowns. After being assured she would get Rose's measurements straight away, Luke stopped next at the jeweler's.

Only after he was done there did he stop for supper at his club, so it was late evening when he returned to Cider Hill. He found his father reading in the library.

Too nervous to sit down, he roamed about the library, studying the titles without really seeing them.

"Is there something you need, Luke?" his father asked.

"I'm not sure how to say this, so I'll just come out with it." He paused a moment. "Rose and I are to be married."

Jonas stared at him.

"Do you mean to say you're marrying the maid Charlotte dismissed yesterday?" his father asked, incredulous.

"Yes, that's exactly what I'm saying. I've asked for her hand today and it was agreed we'd marry in a month's time."

"I see," Jonas said with admirable calm. "Would you care to explain how this came to pass? And what am I to make of the accusations against her?"

Luke scowled, thrusting his hands into his pockets as he paced a few steps away.

"Whatever Charlotte's complaints, they weren't of Rose's making. The blame can be laid squarely on myself and Nathan. I don't imagine she told you that Nathan attacked Rose while I was away, and yet Rose was blamed for attracting his attention. He attacked her again in the carriage last night. I don't like to think what would have happened had I not come upon them in time."

Jonas took this in, his expression grave and resigned.

"I hate to think she endured such treatment under my roof, but of course I believe you. What Nathan did was unforgiveable, and I'll have to give some thought as to what to do about it. But I'm troubled that you had some kind of relationship with Rose while she worked under my roof. You know very well my feelings on that subject."

Luke made himself look his father in the eye, though he was mildly ashamed on this point. Certainly his actions were not above reproach.

"I didn't dishonor her," he replied. "In any case, my intentions now are nothing but honorable."

Jonas looked thoughtfully at Luke and at last gave a nod.

"If this is what you want then you have my blessing. You'll understand if I feel far from enthusiastic at present. However, as you care for her, I will do all I can to make her feel welcome."

Luke didn't realize how much his father's blessing meant to him until that moment. Relief flooded through him.

"I know this won't be easy for you. The last thing I want is for this to cause a rift between you and Charlotte."

"No doubt Charlotte will find this difficult to swallow, but I'll deal with her myself." He sighed and rubbed his eyes, looking suddenly weary. "It hasn't escaped my attention that the two of you have never cared much for each other. You needn't deny it," he said as Luke tried to cut in. "I care for Charlotte, but I'm aware of her shortcomings. Perhaps I ought to have done more to ease the tensions between you, but it's not in my nature to intervene in such matters. Now the least I can do is show my support, and insist that Charlotte do the same."

"I'm afraid I can't imagine her welcoming Rose into the family. It would be a lot to ask even in less trying circumstances. But I won't let anyone hurt Rose. I told her I'd take care of her and I mean to keep that promise."

"The people in this town won't be as easily persuaded as I. Are you prepared for that? Is she?"

"I'm marrying her regardless."

His father studied him for a long moment before nodding to himself. "You're in love with her."

Luke started to speak but then stopped, unsure what he meant to say.

In love with Rose?

Certainly he cared about her. He wanted to keep her safe and make her happy. And God knew he wanted her in his bed as often and for as long as possible. But that had nothing to do with love. He'd sworn never to fall in love again and he had no intention of changing his mind. After all, he'd once loved Catherine and his feelings for her had bled away to nothing but regret.

"I don't know what to call it, I only know I've thought of little else since I met her, and I won't lose her."

Jonas nodded his head and smiled as if at a fond memory.

"I suppose it doesn't matter what you call it, if that's how you feel."

"I am sorry for whatever trouble this causes you. If there's anything I can do..."

"I believe you've done quite enough."

Luke turned at the sound of Charlotte's voice. She stood in the doorway, her face set, her mouth grim. Luke regarded her warily.

"You have some nerve coming to this house with such revolting news," she said, her eyes blazing with unconcealed fury.

"Charlotte," Jonas began, a note of warning in his voice, "as my son, Luke will always be welcome in our house."

Charlotte's face whitened at being chastised in front of her stepson. Her hands clenched at her sides, and she stood there, momentarily speechless. Much as Luke would have liked to give her a piece of his mind, he was determined to try to salvage things for his father's sake.

"I'm sure this comes as a shock, Charlotte. Perhaps we ought not to discuss it until everyone's had time to think things through," Luke replied, trying to be civil for his father's sake. "Things are not always as they seem."

"Of all the..." she began, but just then Nathan sauntered into the room. He stopped cold when he saw Luke and instinctively took a step back.

Luke's carefully controlled temper was in danger of erupting at the sight of him.

"Quite the little tableau," Nathan sneered, evidently feeling safe in the company of Jonas and his mother. "To what do we owe the pleasure?"

"We're discussing Luke's engagement," Jonas replied, in what struck Luke as a carefully neutral tone.

"What are you talking about?"

"He would have us believe he's marrying the very maid I was forced to turn out yesterday."

Nathan turned to Luke, his face contorted in rage and disbelief. "That's not possible. She's leading you on as she did me. Trollops like her will do anything—"

In one clean punch Luke knocked Nathan to the floor. Blood smeared Nathan's face as he stared up at Luke, momentarily speechless with shock and rage.

Luke stood over him, knowing he'd made things worse and yet not sorry for it. "If I ever hear you speak of her that way again, I'll do much worse."

Luke was so furious, he wanted to lift Nathan back up and knock him down again, but the worthless wretch lay where he was, looking pitiful. Charlotte crouched down beside him and held her handkerchief to his lip to stem the blood. She looked up at Luke, her eyes cold and unforgiving. Then her gaze shifted to Jonas.

"Do you see this? Will you still defend your precious son?"

"Nathan brought this on himself. I have a thing or two to say about his recent behavior, but that can wait."

Reaching down, Jonas grabbed Nathan's arm and pulled him to his feet.

"I expect you to take this like a man, and I suggest you start by riding home and sobering up. Now, if you'll excuse us, I need a word with Luke."

Luke followed his father out of the library and upstairs to his study. Silently, his father poured them each a whiskey and together they stood at the big bay window and looked out over the gardens. Even lit by the waning moon it was breathtaking scenery. Once upon a time his mother used to hold impromptu little picnics out in the garden. Even now he couldn't look upon that rich expanse without bittersweet memories of those days.

"I'm damned sorry about this," he said, turning to his father. "I'd hoped it would be different."

"Charlotte is my worry. As for Nathan...I confess I don't know what's gotten into him. He wasn't always like this.

"Whatever the reason, I don't think recent events will improve him."

"No, I don't suppose they will," Jonas agreed.

﹏৻

Rose was looking despairingly at the two dresses laid out on her bed when Vivian came in and stood by her side.

"What exactly are we waiting for?" she teased.

"I was hoping that they would turn into something I can actually wear out in public," Rose replied, near tears at the sorry state of her wardrobe. "What on earth am I to wear to the play tonight? I can't possibly be seen in any of these."

"Well, that's one thing you shan't have to worry about any longer. I daresay Mr. Fletcher will make sure you have the finest wardrobe in Boston."

"I suppose he will," Rose said, unable to take it all in. She didn't know what sort of wealth her fiancé had, but it was most likely enough to keep them both quite comfortable.

"I have an idea," Vivian exclaimed. "You can wear something of mine. We can let out the hem and sew ribbons and lace until it's as good as new."

Rose hated feeling sorry for herself, especially over something so inconsequential, but she was terrified of going out with Luke and didn't want to be an embarrassment to herself or him. Even so, she was not so small-minded that she would alter one of her friend's dresses just to satisfy her own vanity.

The door chimes sounded and a moment later Sally came into the room.

"There's a dressmaker here to see you, Rose. She says she's here to take your measurements."

Rose gaped at her in surprise. "There must be some mistake. I haven't arranged any such thing."

"I have an idea who did," Vivian said, smiling at her. "Let us go and see what she has to say."

A perfectly turned-out woman of perhaps five and forty sat, her back ramrod straight and hands clasped in her lap, not quite patiently waiting in the parlor. With her was an assistant, a young lady about Rose's age who sat meekly beside her. The dressmaker stood as the girls entered.

"Which one of you is Miss Stratton?"

"I am, but there's been a mistake."

"There has been no mistake," she said, her French origins unmistakable. "I am Madame Beauchamp and Mr. Luke Fletcher engaged my services. He has ordered for you as many new dresses and accessories as I deem necessary."

"But I can't possibly let him," Rose exclaimed.

"Of course you can," the dressmaker replied dismissively. "Now then, how many dresses have you at present?"

Rose was thoroughly cowed. "Three."

Madame Beauchamp did not blink.

"Well then," she replied briskly. "It's fortunate my services have been engaged."

Over the next hour Rose was measured within an inch of her life while simultaneously questioned at length about her likes and dislikes, in fashion as well as in her daily activities. Madame Beauchamp caught Rose glancing with confusion at Vivian after another of these questions.

"I create dresses that suit each particular woman. Therefore, I must become acquainted with you."

She had brought with her samples of silks, taffetas, muslins and wools in pastels, neutral colors and deep jewel tones. Rose stood still while Madame selected one after another and held them up to her, furrowing her brow in concentration. Every so often she muttered to herself as her assistant took notes.

"Yes, this one we must have for a ball gown," or "Absolutely not, it will make you look sallow."

Before she left, she turned to Rose.

"I have a dress that would suit you much better than the silly girl I made it for. I will alter it and have it dropped off before your play this evening."

Rose couldn't believe her good fortune. Inexplicably her eyes filled with tears. Madame Beauchamp looked at her and shook her head.

"Mademoiselle, you must get used to such gifts. You are marrying a man who is very generous with his money. It won't do to cry every time he gives you something."

With this the dressmaker took her leave, her assistant trailing behind.

Rose and Vivian looked at each other, eyes wide with sudden mirth.

"Well, it seems as if your prayers were answered," commented Vivian. "Have you wished for anything else?"

"A great many things, Vivian," Rose replied. "Though I cannot expect Mr. Fletcher to grant them all."

CHAPTER TEN

*R*ose stood in front of the mirror that evening, unable to believe what she saw. Madame Beauchamp had outdone herself. The gold silk dress she had brought earlier that evening complemented her coloring, and its drape and flares showed off her curves in a way that both pleased and embarrassed her.

Never before had she worn a dress that revealed her shoulders, and she couldn't help feeling it was improper. The sleeves, which ended at her elbow, were garnished with a fall of lace and ribbon. The skirt was full, the silk whispering when she moved. Madame Beauchamp had even delivered a pair of dyed kid slippers and gloves to complete the ensemble. She hardly recognized the woman in the mirror.

"Sit down, Rose," Sally commanded as she entered the room. "Mr. Fletcher will be here in twenty minutes and I still need to dress your hair."

"I feel as if I'm in costume, pretending to be someone else. What if everyone is able to tell I don't belong with Luke?"

"Just get that foolishness out of your head. What people think and what's true are two different things. You'll get used to your finery in no time."

Rose tried to relax into the soothing rhythm of Sally's brush. "I hope you're right," she murmured to herself, unable to imagine such a day.

Sally was just putting the finishing touches on Rose's hair when Vivian came in.

"Rose, have you seen..." Vivian began, stopping when she saw her friend.

"Oh my goodness. Rose, darling, if Mr. Fletcher hadn't already proposed, he surely would have tonight. You're absolutely radiant."

"Vivian, do stop, there's no need to exaggerate," Rose admonished, laughing at her.

"She's not exaggerating," Sally put in. "You are a sight to behold. And your hair looks quite nice, if I do say so myself," she added.

Sally had indeed done a wonderful job, arranging Rose's hair in a coil with a few judiciously curled pieces framing her face. She wove a gold ribbon through the knot and stepped back to survey her work.

"Do ladies wear such low-cut dresses?" Rose asked. "I feel as if one could see right down the front."

"Oh, yes," Sally replied with confidence. "I've seen *Goddard's and Ladies Home Journal*. This is just what they're wearing in Paris."

"Paris?" Rose repeated, even more nervous at this.

But there was no more time for questions, for all three of them stopped what they were doing at the sound of a carriage drawing up outside the house.

"That's he!" Rose cried, fully panicked. "What if the dress is too extravagant? What if it's not right for the play?"

Sally slipped a small, beaded reticule over Rose's wrist. "Madame Beauchamp specifically chose this for tonight," Sally reminded her. "She ought to know."

"Time to go downstairs," Vivian declared. "And don't you worry, Rose, I'll be with you the whole time."

Rose could hear Luke's deep voice coming from the parlor and felt lightheaded with nerves and anticipation. Taking a deep breath, she smiled gratefully at the two women and slowly descended the stairs with one hand on the banister for support. She was halfway down when Luke and Edward, drawn by the sound of footsteps, came out into the foyer and looked up. In an instant Luke's easy grin left his face and he looked at her with an intensity that had her flushing clear to the roots of her hair.

"Miss Stratton," he greeted her as she reached the bottom step. "You take my breath away." And he pressed a kiss to her gloved hand and bowed low over it. It was all very proper, and yet Rose felt sure the undercurrent of heat must be felt by everyone. Shyly she looked at him and met his penetrating gaze.

Edward cleared his throat meaningfully and Vivian appeared from upstairs to accompany them. She looked lovely, and Rose was grateful that Vivian so generously agreed to accompany them. Luke bowed over Vivian's hand as well and gave her his compliments, and the three of them proceeded outside to the carriage Luke had hired for the evening.

They chatted easily, Rose and Vivian on one side with Luke facing them. They arrived at the bustling playhouse where they were treated to an amusing comedy, the first play Rose had seen since leaving Boston six years ago. Her mind whirled at all the possibilities open to her now that she would be living in town. Once again she could go to recitals and plays, and enjoy all the things she'd had to give up so long ago.

And she would enjoy them with her husband. Rose sat between Luke and Vivian and was conscious all the while of Luke's powerful body next to hers. Several times she glanced over, only to discover he was already looking at her, a smile on his lips and warm appreciation in his eyes.

"You'll miss the play looking at me like that," she whispered teasingly in his ear.

"You act as if I have a choice," he whispered back, his voice a low growl. "You have no idea what you do to me."

Heat shot through her at that dark voice in her ear and she recalled their last passionate kiss, the feel of his arousal against her. She hardly took in the rest of the play, so aware was she of him beside her. She wanted to be alone with him again, and yet she was terrified by the depth of her feelings, the strength of her passion. Every moment with him taught her something new about desire.

What would her next lesson be?

They did draw the attention of some in the audience, though there were no cutting looks or snide remarks. After the play a number of people approached Luke through the crowd with smiles and warm greetings, obviously curious. Rose stood by Luke's side, anxiety streaking through her at this first test.

"I'd like you to meet my fiancée, Miss Rose Stratton, and her friend, Miss Vivian March," he said to each.

Her anxiety soon eased, for though there were expressions of surprise, everyone she spoke to was warm and gracious. To their questions of where she was from, she said only that she was originally from Boston but had been away for some years. When the three of them finally exited the playhouse to the fresh night air, Rose was jubilant over the night's entertainment and her first success meeting people in Luke's circle.

"That wasn't at all as difficult as I'd feared it would be," she said, smiling up at him. "Everyone was perfectly lovely. Maybe even some of them will become friends."

But Luke didn't look anywhere near as pleased as she was.

"Yes, everyone was utterly charmed by you. But I suspect things only went so well because Charlotte hasn't yet begun her campaign. Once she does, things won't be nearly so pleasant."

Rose was crestfallen.

"I'm sorry, sweetheart. I only want to prepare you. Perhaps I'm wrong."

But as soon as he said it Rose knew he was right. Of course Charlotte Fletcher would speak ill of her. It wasn't in her to do anything else.

Two days later when Luke called on her she came downstairs to find him in the parlor looking restless. His eyes twinkled and he grinned at her before taking her by the hand and leading her to the door.

She stood stock still on the front step, staring in surprise at the glossy black phaeton in front of the house, the pair of perfectly matched bay horses hitched to it waiting calmly. Rose looked at Luke in confusion.

"We can use them for our drives, but they're mainly for your use. This way you can go where you like when I'm not at home."

Rose flew down the walkway to the horses, greeting each of them in turn and running her hands along their warm sides and silky noses.

"They're an excellent team," Luke said, coming up beside her. "I tested them out myself and they're steady and reliable as well as fast. But if you find they don't suit you, we can look for another pair."

"Oh no, I wouldn't dream of it. I'm sure they'll be perfect."

"This one here is Samson and this lovely lady is Delilah," he said, sliding a hand down Delilah's neck. "You can saddle them up as well if you're of a mind to go for a ride."

"I don't know how to thank you."

"Consider it an early wedding gift. Come," he said, taking her elbow. "See what you think of the rest."

The cab was beautiful, with black lacquered wood and plush green velvet seats. There was room for herself and one passenger, and it had a top that could easily be folded down in good weather.

"Do you think you can drive it?" he asked.

"Oh yes, though it may take a little getting used to. I drove all manner of contraptions on the farm, and a buggy or two, but never on busy streets such as these. I'm only afraid I'll hit somebody."

"You'll do fine, I have no doubt. Let us go for a drive so you can get used to the feel of it."

Rose dashed inside to tell Edward she was leaving, returning breathlessly for her first lesson.

"I think I've found a house for us," Luke declared as soon as he entered the March's parlor several days later.

"That's wonderful," Rose said, a thrill of pleasure and nervousness going through her at the news. The days were flying by in a blur. In just two weeks they'd be married, so of course they must find lodgings as soon as possible.

"A man I met at the club is leaving town in several days," Luke explained. "He'll take most of the furnishings, but the servants will stay on if all parties agree it's to their liking. Shall we go see it?"

"Give me a moment to get my bonnet and gloves," Rose replied, dashing up the stairs in her excitement.

They headed out on foot, as the house was walking distance from Edward and Vivian's. That fact alone delighted her.

"I've been trying to imagine what my days will be like once we're married, and I must admit it's been rather difficult," Rose confided. "I think it will be much easier to picture once I know where I'll be sleeping every night."

No sooner were these words out of her mouth than she blushed furiously. Luke stopped in his tracks.

"We'll be doing precious little sleeping if I have any say in the matter," Luke said, his voice oddly rough. Rose's mouth fell open in surprise, both embarrassed and inflamed by his matter-of-fact reference to what they would do in the marriage bed. An act she thought she understood in a general sense but was very much ignorant of in the specific sense. After all, she'd thought she knew what kissing was, too.

She'd been holding onto his arm as they walked, and now even the feel of his flexing muscles under her gloved hand seemed intimate. What did he look like under his jacket? Would she watch him dress in the morning? Would he watch her?

He must have noticed her agitation for he smiled at her.

"Never mind, sweet. I just hope you like the house."

No more than a mile from the March residence they turned onto Walnut Street and stopped before Mr. Booth's house. A handsome three-story brownstone, it sat on a quiet cobble-stone street lined with similar houses, all of them neatly tended with small patches of lawn. The house before them had late roses blooming under the windows.

"It's wonderful, Luke," she said, turning to him with a smile.

She'd been afraid he would want to live somewhere more extravagant, and was thus relieved at the relative modesty of the house.

He grinned back at her. "Let us go see the rest of it."

A feeling of unreality came over her as they approached the front door. This would soon be her front door, her house. Her staff, whom she would need to oversee. Would they like her? Would she like them? What would she do all day when Luke went to work?

"It's a small staff. Mrs. Williamson cooks and looks after the place generally, and her son Jeremy does some of the heavier chores when not at school. A girl named

Martha helps with the cleaning and laundry. They live in the servant quarters on the top floor. Booth had no need for more servants, but we can hire whomever you like if you find you need more help."

"Goodness, I can't imagine what more I could need. There'll be nothing for me to do as it is."

"Good," he said turning to look at her as the reached the first step. "I don't intend for you to lift a finger ever again."

Luke hardly had time to knock before a stout, plump-cheeked woman with graying hair opened the door and let them in.

"Mr. Fletcher, so good to see you again. I hoped you'd come back."

"Thank you, Mrs. Williamson. Please meet my fiancée, Miss Rose Stratton."

"A pleasure, Miss Stratton," she said with a warm smile. "Do come in and look around. I'm happy to answer any questions."

Rose made certain she struck the right note with the housekeeper. If the house were to run smoothly without causing any of them undue worry, they two of them needed to trust one another.

"Thank you, I'm very pleased to meet you as well," she replied with a smile. "If Mr. Fletcher and I do take the house, I have no doubt I will come to rely on you quite as much as Mr. Booth did."

Mrs. Williamson smiled. "Shall I take you around, Mr. Fletcher, or would you prefer to show the place yourself?"

"I'll show her myself, thank you."

"Very well. I'll put together a tray for you to have after you've seen the place," she said before heading down the hallway toward the back of the house.

After this Rose met the other two servants – Jeremy, a gawky boy of about fifteen who blushed and could barely look Rose in the eye, and Martha, a sturdy girl of perhaps nineteen. Both of them seemed terrified of her, and she realized that they had much more to fear than did she. After all, she could make their lives perfectly miserable and there would be nothing they could do about it. She could even dismiss them this very day. Since she understood this as well as anyone she tried her best to put them at ease.

The house itself was well-kept and solid, though it was clear a bachelor occupied it. Many of the rooms had only the most necessary furniture, which made it all the easier to imagine how she might furnish and decorate it. All of the rooms pleased her, particularly the sunny parlor.

Then they came to Mr. Booth's study.

"I hope you'll forgive me," Luke said, "but this is the only room in the house you are not free to redecorate. While it might not appear so, it's quite perfect as it is."

Rose laughed, looking around the room and noting it was actually quite handsomely done in dark silk wallpaper and plain, though well-made, drapery.

"I wouldn't dream of it, Mr. Fletcher," Rose replied, batting her lashes at him. "Though I do think doing the whole room over in a scheme of pink and white would be just darling."

Luke grinned down at her, backing her up against the desk as he bent to kiss her, and it suddenly hit Rose that

Luke would soon occupy this room, and the desk would be filled with his correspondence and papers. Might she actually need to snoop through her own husband's study to solve her father's murder? It was a horrible thought, and she jerked away from him just as his lips met hers.

"What's wrong?"

"I'm just not sure we should be kissing here," Rose replied, trying to cover up her distress. "What if someone sees us?"

"Very well," Luke reluctantly agreed. "I suppose we should wait until we well and truly live here before shocking the servants."

There were three bedchambers upstairs as well as a sitting room, which Luke informed her she could have for her own use. The master bedchamber was the largest of them all, with several windows and a pleasing amount of light. The most dominant feature, however, was the enormous bed hung with deep blue drapery.

"Booth tells me the bed will stay, as it's far too much trouble to move," Luke said, walking into the room. Idly he ran a hand down the bed hangings and peered out a window.

Rose had stopped in the doorway, unable to venture farther. She now took several steps backward until she was in the hallway. Luke walked back toward the door in order to keep her in sight, and stood peering at her in confusion.

"Rose?"

"It's a very nice room," she said. "I'm sure it will do fine for us, I mean you, I mean, for whomever sleeps here," she said, knowing she was speaking too fast but incapable of stopping herself. "Thank you so much for showing me around. It's a lovely house. I'm sure it will do wonderfully."

Here she finally stopped talking and looked down, mortified beyond measure. Luke came to her and took her hands, dwarfing her smaller ones in his. Still she could not meet his eyes.

"Rose," he said quietly, and there was a note of tenderness in his voice. "Can you not look at me?"

Slowly she raised her eyes to his. He was so powerful, so overwhelming in every way. Standing not twenty feet from what would soon be their bed made her knees weak and her heart pound. With terror, yes, but also with anticipation.

"I apologize, Rose. I sometimes forget myself. If it makes you feel any better, I confess I'm not feeling so very calm myself."

"You're not?"

"No, far from it. I want to make everything perfect for you, including this house."

"You needn't worry on that score. I'm not so terribly hard to please. In any case, this house is perfect. I think we'll be very happy here," she added shyly.

"As do I," he replied, smiling down at her.

A week later Luke came to the door with a pleased grin on his face. He whistled happily as he handed her into the little buggy, the top down to enjoy the day. Rose sat beside him as he drove Samson and Delilah out of town, the reins easy in his hands.

The sky was a terrific clear blue, soft with clouds, the air warm but touched by the breath of autumn. All around them the maples and oaks were turning their brilliant colors – flaming orange, red and yellow. The first fallen leaves laced the ground, their colors as bright as her hopes.

Stealing a look at Luke, she almost wished he wasn't being such a gentleman. His strong profile and thick lashes, combined with the slight bristle of his jaw, left her weak with desire. So it was several minutes before she noticed the basket at her feet.

"What's this?" she asked. "Surely you haven't hidden more books in a basket?" she teased.

"Not this time," he grinned. "What do you think of a picnic?"

Rose opened the lid to the delicious aroma of fresh-baked bread, cold chicken, decadent squares of chocolate and a jar of raspberry jam that gleamed like jewels when she held it up to the sun. He had even included a bottle of Champagne.

"Edward would insist on acting chaperone if he knew you'd brought this," she teased.

"Edward knows I've lost my head over you. He's not worried."

Rose couldn't think how to respond, so she said nothing. Instead she reveled in the feeling she heard in his voice. Could it be that he loved her a little?

They followed the road for a ways until Luke turned onto a smaller lane that led along the Charles River, a sparkling swath moving lazily between clusters of trees. Stopping the horses in the shade, he pulled a plaid blanket from beneath his seat, took her hand and together they made their way to the bank. A few feet from the edge he arranged the blanket and set the basket down.

The sun shone down as if in blessing, the river flowed past, and Rose felt as if she'd wandered into a dream.

Luke stretched out, his long muscled body at ease as he leaned on an elbow, his shirtsleeves rolled past his forearms. It was all Rose could do to keep her eyes from wandering over the perfection of his body and his almost too-handsome face.

Luke poured them each a glass of Champagne and then watched as Rose took a sip.

"Oh, my. This is much better than whiskey." Happily she drank more and before long finished her glass. Laughing, Luke leaned forward and pressed a quick kiss to the tip of her nose.

Rose's mouth fell open. She'd never known a man could kiss a woman's nose. It was so different from what he'd shown her so far.

"We'd better eat some of this feast Mrs. Williamson so kindly packed, or you'll be feeling a little too good," he said, turning to the basket.

As they laid out the picnic he told her about his boyhood days picking apples and learning how to make cider. The sun moved overhead as they talked and ate, and Rose grew drowsy in the late afternoon heat. She curled her legs beneath her, her buttercup-colored cotton dress draped demurely over her ankles. A soft breeze blew the fallen leaves in shifting layers of color.

"If I could paint, I would portray you just as you are now," Luke said, watching her with an intensity that had her pulse racing. "You've no idea how lovely you look, with your yellow dress and your hair the color of the maple leaves behind you. I fear my poor sketches will never do you justice."

Heat shot through Rose's veins at this quiet declaration. Never had she felt more beautiful, more desired. They looked at each other for a long moment, the air charged with their mutual longing.

Luke moved closer and took her left hand in his much bigger one, holding it as if she might break.

"Even your hands drive me mad," he said, sounding bemused. He gave a shaky laugh. "I'd like to shower you with jewels, but this will have to do for now."

Rose watched without comprehending as he slipped a ring onto her finger.

A dozen small garnets were set like rose petals around a larger center garnet, all of them glowing with their own inner fire.

Too awed by the gift to speak, Rose simply looked at him, tears shimmering in her eyes.

Luke smiled at her, his expression filled with fierce tenderness. He kissed her hand. "Now there's no mistaking you're mine."

"As if I'd be anyone else's," she replied, her heart so full she wasn't sure what to do with herself.

Luke too looked caught in some inner struggle, watching her as if he might give in and kiss her. After a moment he shook his head and smiled ruefully, pouring more Champagne into their glasses.

"You must try this tart," Rose said, holding the confection out to him as she licked the raspberry from her lips. "It goes wonderfully with Champagne."

The look in his eye stilled her hand in midair. His body, a moment ago utterly relaxed, was now strung taut as a bow, his eyes dark with desire. With a low groan he leaned forward and slanted his lips over hers, his hand cupping the back of her neck. His tongue coaxed her open and Rose yielded to him utterly and immediately, drugged by the devastating kiss, the warm sun and Champagne. She was all feeling and need, and she wanted more, more of everything – the rough scrape of his jaw, his musky scent and playful tongue, the seductive taste of him.

A longing so intense it was painful suffused her. Her whole body was striving for something, Luke's passionate kisses pushing her closer and closer until finally it dawned on her that one of them would have to keep their wits about them, and it wasn't going to be her fiancé.

Reluctantly she pulled away.

Luke closed his eyes a moment as if to collect himself. Opening them, he smiled ruefully at her and tucked a lock of hair behind her ear.

"If you knew how much I wanted you, you'd never come near me." Standing up he held his hand out for her and helped her to feet. "It's high time I got you home."

Silently, utterly aware of one another other, they packed up the basket and headed home.

Rose was busy packing her clothes the day before they were to be married, laying each dress and undergarment neatly into the new trunk Edward and Vivian had given her as a wedding gift. Tucked deep into one of the corners and wrapped in a linen handkerchief was Nathan Byrne's soiled glove. Everything in her recoiled at the thought of bringing the glove, and all its attendant secrecy, into her new home. But her grief over her father and her love for Luke were both part of her now.

There was no dispelling the melancholy that attended thoughts of her wedding, and it went beyond her father's murder to encompass all the difficulties that came after it. Now , in addition to everything else, she worried over her aunt. Not surprisingly, Olivia's reply to her last letter was all Rose had feared. Her aunt was shocked and worried Rose was making a mistake, one she'd come to regret. And how could Rose blame her? The situation was so strange and fraught with complications, she could hardly expect Aunt Olivia to accept it with equanimity.

Edward had offered to host the small ceremony at his house, for which Rose was grateful. It would be a great comfort to take such a big step in a safe and familiar place. She and Luke would stay to celebrate with some food and drink, after which they'd leave for the house on Walnut Street.

Rose didn't know whether she wanted to rush through the events of the day or make them last as long as possible. Her wedding night loomed at the other side of the celebration, and each minute that passed increased her anxiety. What if she didn't know what to do? She was well aware Luke desired her. It might even be the only reason he wanted to marry her. What if she disappointed him?

Sally came into the room to see how Rose was getting on.

"Sally," Rose began, embarrassed before even saying a word, "may I ask you something about tomorrow night, after Luke and I go home together?"

Sally looked momentarily surprised but quickly recovered. "Yes, what about it?"

"Well, what exactly...what I wondered was...will he want to share my bed? All night? And how often do you suppose he'll want to? And will I like it, and what if I don't?"

"I suppose you've kissed already?" Sally asked.

Rose nodded, her face flushing at this understatement.

"And you liked it well enough?"

Again Rose nodded, unable to speak.

"Well then, likely you'll like the rest as well. Your Mr. Fletcher is quite taken with you. I daresay you could wrap him around your little finger, if you haven't already. Beyond that, it's hard to say. Men are a mystery, even for those of us who've lived with one. Now then, have you anything in need of pressing?"

It seemed that was all she was going to get out of Sally. But if what she said was true, then Rose had little to worry about. After all, Luke's kisses were heavenly, and he was nothing if not desirous of her pleasure. A tendril of heat unfurled in her belly at this thought, but her musings were interrupted by the sound of the door pull.

Sally hurried downstairs to answer the door, only to return seconds later.

"Rose, Mrs. Charlotte Fletcher is here to see you, and she isn't the most pleasant creature we've had call on us."

"Good Lord, whatever can she be doing here?"

Rose stood up, smoothing out her dress as she tried to imagine what possible reason Charlotte could have for calling on her. She checked her reflection in the oval mirror on the wall. Satisfied that she looked calm and unruffled, and that Charlotte had been kept waiting a sufficient amount of time, she headed down to the parlor.

Charlotte was standing in the middle of the room, her hands clasped in front of her, a moué of displeasure on her face. She turned as Rose entered the room and regarded her coldly.

"I will make this brief," she said, looking disdainfully at Rose and then at the room. "Clearly you've managed to capture Luke's attentions. Men often have no sense, even when it's obvious to everyone they're being taken for a fool. However, while I have no sway over him, I do have some say in how you'll be received in this town. I'll make certain every last Cabot, Adams, Gardner and Winthrop knows exactly what you are."

"If you came here merely to insult me, Charlotte, then consider your errand complete and take your leave," Rose said, pleased by the outrage that flared in Charlotte's eyes at the use of her given name. "If you have more to say, do come to the point."

Charlotte's nostrils flared and her eyes narrowed.

"No doubt you're quite pleased to have caught Luke. Perhaps that's what you hoped for all along. I would put nothing past you. But I will not sit idly by while you make fools of us. Make no mistake, if you go through with this marriage I will find out whatever it is you don't want Luke to know, and I will send you packing for good. All of that unpleasantness can be avoided, however, if you're smart." Here she paused dramatically before continuing.

"I am willing to offer you the sum of five thousand dollars if you agree to leave Boston. No one can know of our arrangement. You will leave town, without explanation, and Luke will never hear from you again. If you don't accept my offer, rest assured I'll do everything in my power to keep you from gaining anything from this marriage. You can save your outraged protestations, I want only an answer to my offer. You won't receive a better one."

Rose listened to this speech, more furious and disgusted with every word. She was also shaken, for though Charlotte was mistaken about her motivations, she was all too accurate about her secrets. But she would not let this woman see weakness or doubt.

Her voice was filled with cold fury when she spoke.

"You come to me in my friend's home and simultaneously insult, threaten and bribe me. Clearly you are the one capable of anything. But I'll not waste my time explaining myself to you. Your offer, your presence here, was a gross miscalculation on your part. You can see yourself out."

With this, Rose swept out of the room, so incensed she could hardly see straight. Once out of the room she flew up the stairs and she paced the parlor floor, shaking with rage.

Her first instinct was to tell Luke, but after considering all the ramifications, she thought better of it. There was nothing he could do, and in any case he knew already that his stepmother was against the marriage. Furthermore, she felt terrible about the rift she'd already caused in his family. And, all that aside, Charlotte was not wholly off the mark in her suspicions.

No, she would say nothing. She had enough to worry about with Nathan, never mind his mother.

Chapter Eleven

*T*he next morning Rose slid quietly out of the bed, careful not to disturb Vivian, who muttered something unintelligible in her sleep and turned over. Pushing aside the curtain, she looked out the window at the empty street, the other houses ghostly in the pre-dawn light. Little by little the neighborhood came awake as people left their houses and headed into the rest of their lives.

Behind her Vivian was also waking. Sitting up in bed she smiled widely at Rose.

"Good morning, Mrs. Fletcher," she chirped excitedly, hopping out of bed. "Time to get you ready for Mr. Fletcher."

There was a knock at the door and Rose opened it to find Sally holding a tray. "Oh, Sally, this is heavenly," she sighed, breathing in the glorious scent of cocoa, biscuits and jam. She couldn't remember anyone bringing breakfast right to her when she wasn't even ill.

"Pshaw. If today isn't special, then I don't know what day is. But I daresay you're likely to get anything you want brought to you at your new residence. You'll be a woman of leisure, don't forget."

"Yes, I suppose I will be," Rose replied, unsure how she felt about it.

"Eat up, girls, and then we'll get our bride ready."

Soon Vivian and Sally bustled around her, helping her dress in the delicate lace undergarments Madam Beauchamp had made for her. On her legs were sheer silk stockings held up by lacey garters. The white silk slid over her skin like a kiss and was so fragile she doubted she could wear them again.

Before Madame Beauchamp, it had never occurred to her that women would wear such beautiful, expensive undergarments. Why bother, when no one saw them? But perhaps Luke would see them. She had little idea of what to expect on her wedding night, but somehow she doubted her new husband would patiently turn around or leave the room while she disrobed.

"Stand up, child," Sally said, breaking into her reverie. "Let's get you into this dress." Obediently Rose stood and let the dress slide over her chemise, corset and petticoats and settle about her with a soft rustle.

Though the dressmaker had suggested a wedding dress in white, Rose was too practical to agree to such a thing. Instead she'd decided on something she could wear again – a lovely sage green silk so light it seemed to hover over her skin. Delicate flowers embroidered in pink and brown thread ran along the hem and neckline.

Rose grew quiet as the women fussed around her, smoothing the material and discussing what ribbon to use in her hair. She couldn't help wishing her parents could have been with her. Her father should have been the one to speak to Luke, her mother to give her advice and calm her fears.

And yet, she would never have even met Luke if her father were still alive. Though perhaps, if they'd remained in Boston, all of them together, she would one day have met him, and they'd have married in that other life as well.

Rose gave a quick shake of her head. No more what-ifs today. Tomorrow was soon enough for those.

Expertly Sally dressed her hair, threading a green ribbon through the braided knot at the nape of her neck. The front of her hair was braided as well and pinned behind her ears. Rose slipped on satin slippers dyed to match the dress and then they all stood silently for a moment.

Rose looked at herself in the long oval mirror and could hardly believe what she saw. The dress was so beautifully made and of such a soft color, it seemed to cast its own glow. Her garnet ring shone even in the mellow light. Was this what a bride looked like?

"Oh, Rose," Vivian breathed. "You're so beautiful, you hardly seem real. I think Mr. Fletcher will be quite speechless when he sees you."

Rose hugged Vivian. "Thank you for being such a good friend. I know it hasn't always been easy for you."

Now both girls were crying and hugging.

"Enough," said Sally, looking a bit teary herself. "We can't have Rose looking red and bleary from crying. But if you have to cry, at least have a handkerchief on hand," she said, handing both Vivian and Rose a delicate square of linen.

The door chimed and the three women looked at each other. Sally gave Rose a quick once-over.

"Mr. Fletcher won't know what hit him." And with that she headed downstairs to welcome Luke and his father.

Rose and Vivian stood holding hands in awed silence, listening to the voices downstairs. In another moment the chime sounded again and Rose stood perfectly still as the minister entered and was greeted. Before she knew it Edward was at the door to fetch her. Rose felt as if she might break down in quite dramatic tears when he took her hands and kissed her cheek.

"Your mother and father would be so proud of you, Rose, as am I. I'll be here for you, if ever you need me."

Rose kissed Edward on the cheek, unable to speak, then quickly blotted her eyes. She breathed deeply in and out, and then nodded her head.

"I'm ready."

The day took on a dreamlike quality as Rose listened to the minister explain the duties of matrimony. She was surprised by how vulnerable she felt, even with so few people present, as she looked Luke in the eye and repeated her vows.

Nothing could have prepared her for the sheer enormity of what they were doing. But she meant every word. Before the minister had a chance to say anything about a kiss, Luke cupped a hand behind her head, bent down and pressed his lips to hers. It was the most chaste kiss they'd ever shared, and yet it shook her to the core.

Luke kept her hand in his as they accepted the well wishes of the small party, and then they all moved into the dining room for the celebratory dinner Sally had prepared. Jonas Fletcher sat to Rose's left, and though she felt awkward at first, he immediately put her at ease. Rose liked him very much and wished she weren't causing so much discord in his household. She wouldn't have blamed him if he'd acted less welcoming toward her, but she detected no resentment on his part.

For dessert Sally brought out a lemon cake frosted in buttercream that had everyone taking second helpings while listening to a story Mr. Fletcher told about the first train he'd ever ridden. Rose listened to it all with only half an ear, for she was terrified of what would happen when she left the safety of the March home.

Without realizing it she ate and drank far more slowly than everyone else, anxious to prolong the festivities for as along as possible. She'd barely touched her cake or sipped her tea when she looked around the table and realized that everyone else had cleaned every crumb from their plates quite some time ago.

Edward smiled at her, as if he understood, while Mr. Fletcher and Vivian requested yet more tea, as if to aid her delaying tactics. Luke smiled at her and said perhaps he would have more tea as well, adding that it was quite delicious, and where did Edward get such flavorful leaves? At this Rose came to her senses and realized she could not keep them there all day, drinking tea until they could barely remain at the table.

"I think I'll forego more tea, though like everything else, it was wonderful," she said, and nearly laughed at the relieved look on everyone's faces. There was a rush of good wishes and several gifts thrust into their arms and then Luke led her from the March's and into the golden October light filtering through the oaks and maples.

⁓

Luke couldn't quite believe that the woman sitting next to him was now his wife. Every so often she glanced at him with a tentative, uncertain smile and then averted her gaze, unable to maintain eye contact.

He couldn't take his eyes off her, the line of her throat and curve of her cheek, her lush eyelashes that masked and revealed her beautiful gray eyes. He'd spent the last four months wanting nothing but her, and now he was going to have her. Today, tonight, and every night hereafter.

Jeremy dashed out of the house for the horses as soon as they drew up in front of the house, as if he'd been standing at the window waiting.

"Welcome home, Mrs. Fletcher," he said breathlessly, touching his cap before leaning in to take the gifts.

Rose's eyes were wide in her face and she looked a bit pale, but she smiled at Jeremy as Luke took her arm and led her up the brick steps. She looked so beautiful and yet so unsure as they stood at the threshold of their new life together. Though he knew he ought to be thinking about all the ways his life was about to change, all he seemed able to think about was getting her into his bed. Immediately. Somehow he needed to get her straight upstairs to the bedroom without delay.

Just as Mrs. Williamson opened the door for them he realized the perfect solution. Sweeping Rose up in his arms he headed for the stairs, delighting in the feel of the curves he would soon uncover. Her eyes widened in surprise but she threw her arms around his neck and tucked her head into his chest.

He strode with her into the bedroom before setting her down on her feet. Much as he would have liked to toss her onto the bed and ravage her, that would have to wait for another time. Today required gentleness, patience. God willing he would have enough of both to keep from scaring her.

The question was, would she understand what he wanted, or would he have to explain himself? Just how innocent was she?

Rose looked at the bed and then back at him, her hands clasped tightly as if to control her agitation. He was just about to kiss her when she spoke.

"Luke," she began tentatively, "is there perhaps a book I might read that would explain...that would detail the wedding night and what is expected of each party?"

Luke's mind went utterly blank. He opened his mouth to reply only to realize he had no idea what to say.

A deep flush had worked its way up her neck and over her cheekbones, and she was wringing her hands in agitation. All at once he realized she must be utterly terrified.

A surge of tenderness and the desire to protect her, even from himself, moved through him. Though he was already desperately aroused, he didn't want her fearing what he was so anticipating. Taking her hands in his he tried to quell her fears.

"All you need do is let me give you pleasure. If there's something you don't like, tell me and I'll stop."

He could see she was relieved by this, but still she looked unconvinced.

"Do you like how it feels when I kiss you?" he asked, leaning down to press a soft kiss to her lips.

"Of course," she answered, and he was gratified to hear the breathlessness in her voice.

He reached up and caressed the delicate line of her jaw, traced the column of her throat. "And you like how I touch you?"

She nodded her head, her beautiful eyes going smoky and heavy-lidded.

"We'll kiss and touch each other more, and I feel certain you'll enjoy it." He hesitated to continue, but clearly she wanted to know what to expect. It would be unfair not to tell her. "There is a part of making love that may be uncomfortable for you the first time. I'll do everything I can to give you pleasure, but a woman's first time often hurts."

"Yes, I had heard that," she replied, her eyes wide and serious. "For how long will it hurt?"

Now this was getting awkward.

"I suppose it's different for every woman. But I swear to you, I'll stop whenever you want me to." Lord help him if she asked him to make good on his promise.

"Very well," she said, squaring her shoulders in determination, as if she were a soldier going off to battle. "Let us begin."

_⟿_

Rose stood ready, determined to do her best. She was an intelligent person, capable of learning things quickly. Surely she could do this.

Luke stepped toward her until he was nearly pressed against her. Gone was the tender sincerity of a moment ago. Now he looked at her with fierce hunger.

She felt as if he held her in a trance, so impossible was it for her to move. She waited breathlessly as he bent his head toward her, his lips brushing over hers as if to gentle her. As soon as she felt his mouth on hers she wanted more. Mindlessly she pressed against him, finally free to ask for everything she'd been wanting.

On a groan he pulled her closer, the hard length of him pressed to her curves as he rained kisses over her face and down her throat. The rough skin of his jaw abraded her into shivers of new awareness, every point of contact igniting her already scorched nerves. His teeth nipped her bottom lip before his tongue slipped inside, stroking her into pliancy before retreating.

Rose grasped his arms, afraid she'd melt into the floor. She could feel the tensed power of his muscles and ached to feel more of him. Tentatively she lifted her hand to his face, stroking his jaw before moving to his mouth, where her thumb ran over the curve of his lower lip. So full and soft, so devastating.

She felt him go still and looked up from her study of him to find his eyes blazing down at her. Then his hands were in her hair, pulling the pins out one by one until her hair cascaded down her back. Another kiss as his hands dove into her hair, tugging on the long tresses until her head fell back, offering him her throat.

Wordlessly he turned her around so that he was behind her. She felt her dress loosen as he released button after button, his fingers tracing the curve of her spine as it was revealed. Then he was in front of her again, his hands sliding the silky material down her arms, slowly grazing it over her hips until it pooled at her feet.

When she raised her eyes to his he was watching her with such intensity that for all her fear she could not look away. He said her name, as if in wonder, and bent towards her again, his kiss voracious, his mouth giving her no quarter. She didn't want any. Her hands moved up his arms and she felt him tremble, felt how his whole body was coiled, ready to spring but holding back for her.

"Rose, my God, what you do to me."

His searing gaze moved over her. Swiftly he undid the ties of her petticoats and they too fell. Then, deliberately, his breath coming faster now, he unlaced her corset until she stood only in her thin chemise.

A flush stained his cheekbones and a muscle moved in his clenched jaw, and all at once she saw how he had been reining in his desire, how even their most passionate kisses had been but a fraction of what he held back.

His eyes never leaving hers, he pulled the chemise over her head until she stood in the circle of her gown, naked but for her stockings. Cool air brushed over her skin, and she shivered at her sudden vulnerability. Not since she was a little girl had anyone seen her unclothed.

For the space of several heartbeats she couldn't look at him, yet she could feel Luke in every pore, in every part of her. When she could bear it no longer she raised her gaze to his, breathless with her own desire.

Luke's mouth took hers again as his hand closed over her breast. His thumb ran over the sensitive nipple as heat charged through her veins and her knees went weak. She heard herself moan, heard her own breath gasping and didn't care.

Without a word Luke picked her up and carried her to the bed. Laying her down, he came to her side. His breathing had quickened and his hands shook ever so slightly as he untied the ribbons of her garters and slid her stockings down each leg, his fingers grazing the untouched skin of her thighs until they fell open of their own volition, his mouth following the retreating line of silk in a trail that set fire to every nerve ending.

By the time he slid the second stocking off she was beyond herself, her eyes at half-mast, her breathing labored. She didn't know what he was doing to her, she only knew she needed more.

Luke's weight left the bed and he began to shed his clothes.

"Let me," she said. Beyond shyness, she wanted only to touch her new husband, to make him as wild for her as she was for him.

Luke's chest rose and fell beneath her hands as she released the buttons of his shirt, pushing it off his shoulders to reveal his muscled chest and the powerful arms that held her so easily. Her hands fumbled at his trousers, and he groaned, closing his eyes as if in pain. Now she understood how close to pain this kind of pleasure was, and she didn't let anything deter her.

With his help she slid his trousers, shoes and socks off until he was as naked as she. Then she sat back on her heels and stared at him, swallowing hard at his size. How could he possibly fit inside her? Reaching out she touched and stroked him until he pulsed with life in her hand. Groaning as if he'd reached the limit of his endurance, he pushed her back on the bed.

Relentlessly now he kissed her, his tongue sliding into her mouth, teaching her a new rhythm. Then his mouth was on her breasts, sucking and licking the tender peaks. On and on the torment went, first one breast and then the other, his mouth moving up to kiss her again and again. Rose's hands raced over his skin. She felt the sheen of perspiration on his back and reached up to taste the salt of his neck.

His hand moved lower, over the slight swell of her belly, the soft hair. Her breath stopped as she felt his hand cover the part of her that ached so desperately. Her hips rose at the sweetness of his touch, the bolt of pure pleasure so intense a cry escaped her.

He was lying beside her now, murmuring praise and endearments as his finger stroked her. Need built and coiled through her until her head tossed on the pillow and she called out his name, frightened by the intensity of her feelings. She didn't know if she could go on and yet she couldn't bring herself to stop him. Desperately she sought something from him.

"Luke, please – "

Her nails dug into his arm as the pleasure crested and broke. Arching into his hand she rose to meet each wave until gradually they receded.

She opened her eyes to his beautiful face above her, his eyes blazing.

"I have to have you now, darling. Stay open for me a little longer," he coaxed, his voice tight with need.

Rose nodded, too awed to deny him anything, wanting whatever he wanted.

He kissed her long and deep as slowly he entered her. But he was so big, she felt herself stretch around him, and the stretching turn to burning pain. Panicking a little, she moved restlessly, her fingers clenched on his arms.

"Easy, darling. Easy," he soothed. His voice shook, and all at once Rose understood what he was feeling, the pleasure she could give him. Her panic subsided and she relaxed, her body welcoming him.

Once again he stroked her, renewing her pleasure as she grew accustomed to him. Soon she was responding fully, rising to him, accepting more of him with every thrust. Soon she wanted him deeper, filling her, and her hands instinctively moved to his buttocks, urging him on.

"Sweet lord," he groaned, burying his face in her neck, his hands fisted in her hair as his powerful body moved over and inside her. With one last thrust he called out her name as he shook with his release.

Rose lay cradled in Luke's embrace listening to his heartbeat return to normal. Everything had taken on a sensual dimension, and her skin felt even the simple act of lying in bed in a new way, as is she'd never felt sheets slide over her skin. She finally knew what she'd been yearning for all those nights she lay awake thinking of him.

She stretched lazily against him and gave a small laugh.

He smoothed the hair from her forehead and looked down at her. "What's so funny?"

"This is what you've been wanting to do since you met me?" she asked.

"Since the moment I laid eyes on you."

"I'm glad I didn't know how wonderful it would be. It was difficult enough to be around you as it was.

"I quite agree," he said, giving her a quick kiss on her nose.

"I can't imagine everyone feels this, or no one would leave the house."

Luke laughed and rolled her over until he was on top of her again.

"Well, my sweet wife, I don't intend to. Not for a long time."

Though they didn't have time for a honeymoon trip, Luke didn't go back to work until the following Monday. They had five days together with nothing to do but make love, eat, take long drives and explore Boston together. But though they ventured out of bed, it almost seemed as if they never stopped making love, for every moment with him was intimate and fraught with sensuality. Never in all her imaginings, either before their engagement or after, had she thought it would be like this.

Mrs. Williamson kindly put together baskets for their drives and sent trays to their room. And when they did descend for a meal, the housekeeper appeared to take no notice of their flushed appearance and addled demeanor, though Rose detected a discrete smile or two from her. Rose would have been embarrassed, were she not so woozy from lovemaking.

Yet in the midst of this profound pleasure her grief still reared its head, and with it came guilt that she could experience such happiness. Tucked away in her trunk, the soiled glove was a reminder of what she must face. But it was too soon. Perhaps in a few months she'd feel more confident in the possibility of Luke forgiving her betrayal, but their marriage was too new and fragile to burden it now. And if she were honest, she couldn't bear the thought of spoiling the happiness unfolding between them. Silently she asked her father for more time, hoping he understood.

⟿

Luke stood looking at Rose as she lay sleeping, her hair spilling over the pillow in brilliant waves, the light from the fire gilding the silky skin of a shoulder and arm, the long leg that slipped out from under the covers.

They'd had five blissful days together, but now he must leave her and go back to the office. How he would think about anything but his new wife was beyond him. He'd washed and dressed while she slumbered but found himself sitting back down just to look at her, putting off the inevitable.

Her skin, flushed from their recent lovemaking, invited more caresses, but he stilled his hand in order to let her sleep. He'd been stealing enough hours meant for sleeping.

He couldn't get enough of her, could hardly keep his hands off her even when they were both fully dressed and around the staff or out on the street. And it wasn't just the pleasure of taking her to bed that held him. Her husky voice, the slow smile that started as if unsure of itself and then lit up the room, her sense of humor – all these things made him loathe to leave her side.

Still, as much as he was discovering her, she was slow to reveal herself, and he felt that part of her was still kept from him. There was a nervousness or retreat in her manner, a shadow that came and went. They were still too new to each other for him to question her, but he often wondered what his new bride was thinking.

She stirred, her lids slowly opening to reveal those mercurial eyes. She smiled shyly and pulled the covers over her.

"What are you doing over there?" she asked.

"Trying to tear myself away from you so that I can return to work."

Rose's smile faded and she sat up, modestly holding the blankets in place. Her hair spilled over her shoulders and down her back, and in an instant he was hard. Again.

"Must you go?" she asked, her lower lip forming a delicious pout.

Bending over he nipped her lip and then drew it into his mouth before kissing her long and lingeringly. Finally he pulled away. Much as he wanted to ravish her, it would have to wait.

"I must," he sighed. "A great deal has been happening this past week, and I need to be there to ensure things don't get any worse."

"Has something gone wrong?"

Luke took Rose's hand in his, for it was impossible to be near her and not touch her. "The board still thinks there's a chance to save the original route. They insist that we make another offer to Mrs. Harris, which is absurd. But they don't listen to reason."

Luke stopped and looked at Rose with concern. All the blood had drained from her face and her hand clutched his.

"Will you do it then?" she asked.

"Make Mrs. Harris another offer? Absolutely not. We have our new route set and we're to start blasting this week."

Her hand unclenched and some of the tension left her.

"What's the matter? Why are you so upset?" he asked, unsettled by the strength of her reaction.

"I suppose I just feel sorry for that poor woman. She's already given her answer several times over. I hate to think that the railroad would continue to bully her."

"I don't like to think we've been bullying her, but I quite agree we ought to move on. You needn't worry on that score."

She gave him a small smile. "I'm sorry to overreact. You'd best go or you'll be late."

Luke hesitated, still feeling as if there was something more to her distress. But perhaps he was the one overreacting now.

"Very well. If you're sure you're all right," he said, leaning over to kiss her once more. "I'll see you at dinner."

Gathering his jacket he left the room, turning around at the last moment to see Rose lying back against the pillows, staring at the ceiling.

CHAPTER TWELVE

*O*nce Luke went back to work Rose spent her days decorating the house, visiting with Vivian, and reading every book in Luke's library. For the first time in her life she was mistress of her own home, and not since she was fifteen had she had any leisure time.

She had no chores and no particular place to be most days, a not altogether comfortable feeling after so many years of usefulness. She therefore created her own daily structure of walks to the market, reading in front of the fire in her sitting room, visits with Vivian, menu planning with Mrs. Williamson and, of course, her midday meal with Luke.

She still couldn't get enough of her new husband, and many were the times they made love rather than partake of the meal laid in the dining room. Fortunately, Mrs. Williamson was an amiable woman and without being asked always packed a basket of food for Luke to take back.

Boston was favored with a glorious October and Rose took full advantage of the clear bright days by reacquainting herself with the town. Ever since moving to the farm she'd feared her world would close in on her, getting smaller and smaller until it was so small nothing new would ever squeeze through. Now every day brought something new, not just in the places she saw but in the things she felt.

In the first few weeks of their marriage they went to a play or recital once or twice a week, but then a troubling thing began to happen. Though they continued to steer clear of any gatherings Charlotte attended, soon even that wasn't enough to guarantee they were treated civilly. Just as Luke had predicted, the very people who had greeted them so warmly now said a stiff hello to Luke, if they said anything at all, and hardly acknowledged Rose.

"You remember my wife," Luke said the first time it happened, his ferocious glare causing Mrs. Barrett to pale and her husband to stammer. But it happened again and again, until all the pleasure went out of the occasions.

Charlotte and Jonas had moved back to their dwelling in town, and clearly Charlotte was making good on her threats. Fortunately, she and Luke received invitations from people in the less elite echelons of society — well-to-do merchants and politicians, the occasional intellectual, as well as old acquaintances from Luke's earlier days in Boston. But even they employed servants, and while friendlier to her, they still regarded her as either a curiosity or a threat. As much as Rose tried to enjoy herself, she was ever on guard, worried she'd say the wrong thing.

She despaired of making any new friends until one evening late in October, when she was pleasantly surprised to see Eliza Lynch.

"Mrs. Fletcher, how lovely to see you."

Rose smiled with pleasure at Mrs. Lynch's greeting. The two had met during an intermission at the playhouse in September and Rose had been taken with her bright laugh and engaging personality. A pretty blond woman perhaps ten years older than herself, Mrs. Lynch had seemed like she might one day be more than an acquaintance. Tonight's supper was being given by Matthew Bishop, an old classmate of Luke's, and Rose hadn't expected to see anyone she knew.

"I didn't expect to see you," Rose said, taking a sip of punch.

"I know Mrs. Bishop through our charity work. I hadn't realized you'd be here either, but I'm so glad you are. I've been wanting to get better acquainted with you for weeks now."

"I thought the very same thing," Rose said, smiling with delight.

"I hope Mr. Fletcher is easier to coax out of the house than Mr. Lynch. Whenever it rains Mr. Lynch needs to be dragged kicking and screaming out the door."

"Mr. Fletcher was happy enough to come, though we stay in most nights."

"It's good to see him so happy," Mrs. Lynch said, causing Rose to blush. "He was so distraught after Catherine's loss. I've never seen a man more in love, so it was no surprise he had to leave town. A thing like that haunts a person for life."

Rose looked down at the glass in her hands, unable to speak. The woman's words seemed designed to cut her to the heart, and yet they were said with the warmth and compassion of a friend.

"Oh my dear, how thoughtless of me," Mrs. Lynch cried, her hand flying to her bosom. "What a thing to say to a new bride. You mustn't listen to me."

It was rather too late for that, but Rose managed to smile and let Mrs. Lynch lead her to a group of gossiping matrons. Luke looked at her from across the room, his gaze taking her in from the tip of her gray satin slippers to the top of her head. A private smile spread across his face and his gaze turned heated. She smiled back, heartened just looking at him, but he must have sensed her low spirits, for he frowned and excused himself from the two men with whom he'd been conversing.

"Is everything all right, sweetheart?" he asked, his breath warm on her cheek. His big capable hand gripped her elbow, and even that simple touch flooded her with awareness.

She wouldn't mention Eliza Lynch's unsettling comment, especially not here. The last thing she wanted was to remind him of the worst period of his life.

"I'm perfectly well. I was surprised by something Mrs. Lynch said, but it's of no consequence."

"What do you say we make our goodbyes and I take you home and ravish you?"

"We just got here! We can't leave yet."

"Very well," he said with an exaggerated sigh. "But I implore you not to make me stay above an hour."

"You have a bargain," she said, smiling at him. But she couldn't help thinking about Mrs. Lynch's comments. Her father had never gotten over the death of his wife. What if Luke never did either? What if everything she did fell short of his first wife?

Several days later Rose was sitting in front of her dressing table freshening up for supper when Luke returned home, entering their bedchamber with an expression so grim it set her heart racing.

"What's wrong? Has something happened?" she asked, gripped by the notion that he'd found out about her.

Luke bent down and kissed her, instantly calming the worst of her fears.

"Nothing for you to worry about," he said, taking up the necklace she held and clasping it around her neck. "It's only that I have to leave you for a time. We're planning a number of railroad lines over the next several years and I've been asked to survey a route to the north. I leave day after tomorrow."

"How long will you be gone?"

"I'm not entirely certain, but I imagine it will be two to three weeks. The last thing I want is to leave you, but I'm afraid there's no way around it. Every surveyor we've got is being sent out."

"If you must go, then you must," she said, turning around to smile brightly at him.

"You'll be all right, won't you? If there's anything you need, I'll take care of it before I go."

"I'll be perfectly fine. What could I possibly need?" she said, laughing off his worry.

"No doubt you'll hardly notice I'm gone. You'll be too busy visiting with Vivian, perhaps even Mrs. Lynch."

"No doubt," she said, matching his teasing grin with one of her own.

Two days later she found it more difficult to feign nonchalance. Her chest tightened as she watched him pack his things, and she kissed him goodbye through a haze of tears. As soon as he was gone she returned to her sitting room, the days until his return stretching out before her. She tried to read, to write a letter to Olivia, but couldn't for the life of her seem to focus.

Giving up, she went instead to the March house, where Vivian's sunny disposition was sure to lift her spirits.

"Oh Rose, I was just about to send you a note," Vivian said at the sight of her. "We've had a letter from Aunt Harriet. She's doing poorly and has no relations near, so I'm to go to Sudbury first thing tomorrow."

Rose's mouth opened but no sound came out. All she could think about was how alone she was going to be. Gathering her wits at last, she asked about Vivian's travel plans and got further details of her aunt's illness, but stayed only a few minutes more and then left Vivian to her preparations.

She took a roundabout way home, none too anxious to return to the quiet house, and when she arrived she stared about her, not sure what to do with herself.

"Is anything the matter, Mrs. Fletcher?" Mrs. Williamson asked, jolting Rose out of her troubled thoughts.

"I suppose I'm just out of sorts with Mr. Fletcher away, and now Vivian is leaving tomorrow as well."

"That is a pity."

"Shall I help you in the kitchen?" Rose asked, desperate for the company and something useful to do.

"Heavens, no. Everything is perfectly under control. Dinner will be ready in under an hour."

Not wanting to appear desperate, Rose retreated upstairs where she read for the rest of the day, stopping only for meals. But where once she would have luxuriated in all the time to herself, now it felt more like a burden.

Several more days passed this way, and then a note was delivered to the house inviting her and Luke to an evening of music at the home of Mr. and Mrs. Lacey. Mr. Lacey was a dry goods merchant with whom Luke was friendly, and Rose had found his wife pleasant, though they had spoken little the one time they'd met.

After much deliberation, Rose sent a note accepting on her own behalf. It would be good for her to be less dependent on Luke and Vivian for all her entertainment. Besides, she had always loved musical evenings.

Buoyed by this boldness, she decided to take matters into her own hands and sent a note inviting Eliza Lynch for tea.

Mrs. Lynch had not yet replied when the evening of the recital arrived. Rose sat nervously at her dressing table while Martha deftly pinned her hair. After standing before her wardrobe for close to an hour, she'd finally chosen an elegant but understated long-sleeved gown of brown silk embroidered with yellow flowers. If she recalled correctly, Madame Beauchamp had specifically told her it would suit this very sort of occasion.

Jeremy escorted her to the house and then went round to the rear entrance to join the other servants. Rose's heart beat with a combination of anxiety and anticipation as she entered the house, and it didn't escape her that she was nearly as nervous approaching the Lacey household for a social engagement as she'd been when first arriving at Cider Hill.

Making her way to the ballroom, she smiled and said hello to several people she recognized. All of them were cool to her and none stopped to talk. A feeling of dread over-took her, but still she tried to convince herself it was all in her head.

Then she saw Mrs. Lacey. The hostess was speaking to an older couple, her expression animated as she laughed at some-thing one of them said. When they moved away her gaze lit on Rose and her expression changed to one of outright displeasure. It took her only a moment to school her features, but in that time Rose saw the truth. She wasn't welcome there, not without her husband. Perhaps not even with him.

Mortified by the realization even as she stood facing Mrs. Lacey, she forced herself through all the usual pleas-antries. She thanked the woman for the invitation and told her she looked forward to a wonderful evening, all the while calculating how soon she could leave without look-ing foolish.

She endured an agonizing hour during which she stood alone, sipping punch and trying to look as if she were enjoying herself. No one approached her. After what seemed like ages a quartet began to play and everyone took their seats. Rose kept her eyes on the musicians and tried to appreciate the music, but it was no use. At the first break in the program she slipped out and asked one of the maids to fetch Jeremy.

"Did you have a good time, Mrs. Fletcher?" Jeremy asked as they walked home. "I could hear the music from the servants' hall. It sounded real pretty."

"Yes, it was. Very pretty," she said, and then words failed her.

The thought that she'd been attending soirees where she wasn't welcome made her feel physically ill, and the idea of having to tell Luke what had happened that night filled her with hot shame. Of course they'd both known this could happen, but actually being a pariah was far different from thinking about it in the abstract, in the warm aftermath of a passionate kiss.

Defeated, Rose returned home and went directly to her bedchamber. There she stood looking at her reflection in the mirror, a woman who even in the finest clothes would forever be known as a servant. She had an entire wardrobe of gowns meant for occasions like tonight, all of them a waste of money and effort.

Feeling numb, she stepped out of her dress and undergarments, leaving behind a crumpled pile of silk on the floor. What did it matter if her dress was wrinkled when she would likely never wear it again?. She pulled on the simplest cotton nightgown she owned and climbed into the big empty bed, wishing with all her heart that Luke was there to comfort her.

Rose stayed in bed uncharacteristically late the next morning. What reason did she have to rise? There was nothing for her to do, no one to see. When she went downstairs mid-morning, it was to find that Eliza Lynch had finally sent her reply. She thanked Rose for the invitation but wrote that she had another engagement on the very same day. The fact that she didn't suggest an alternate day or extend an invitation herself could not be ignored.

Had she misjudged Mrs. Lynch's attitude toward her as well?

Rose left the house only for her solitary walks after that, or to take the phaeton out in order to exercise the horses. She spoke to no one outside of Jeremy, Martha and Mrs. Williamson. The housekeeper, perhaps taking pity on her, finally relented and allowed Rose to help her in the kitchen.

Now that her world had shrunk to that of the house, she turned her attention to the rooms she had yet to decorate. The drawing room was particularly in need of help, as it had been used almost as a storage area, with several crates stacked one on top of the other. Bending over she tried to lift the top crate, only to discover it was far too heavy for her.

She stood with her hands on her hips, staring down at them in annoyance. Jeremy was at school, else she'd have asked him to help her. Perhaps she'd simply move them a little bit at a time.

Sifting through the crates to decide where all the items ought to go, she found herself staring at two sheaves of letters tied together with string. Without meaning to she read the first lines of the topmost letter.

My dearest Catherine,

Every day I wake up, amazed anew that we are to be married. If only it were tomorrow, as I do not know how I'll survive two more months without holding you in my arms.

Her breath came fast and light and her pulse thundered in her ears.

One bundle contained messages from Luke to Catherine, the other from Catherine to Luke. Standing up, she put everything back where it was, wishing she'd never laid eyes on it.

But she had, and now she had to live with the very words Luke had sent to his betrothed, and know that it was but a fraction of what the letters contained. She'd purposefully not allowed herself to dwell on thoughts of his first wife, but now she was forced to consider what he'd felt for her all those years ago.

Mrs. Lynch' words came back to her, and all at once she felt ill. The day Luke came upon her at the pond he'd told her he didn't have more to offer her than life as his mistress. What if what he'd meant was that he'd never stopped loving Catherine?

Rose spent the rest of the day in her sitting room, staring out the window. Her whole life seemed balanced on the edge of a knife. She'd risked so much, had staked everything on her love for him, and on the hope that he would one day love her enough to forgive her betrayal. But one needed the kind of love that outlived death to forgive someone of that. A man didn't feel that but once in his lifetime.

A letter from Luke arrived the next day to let her know he'd be returning in a week's time. She did little in the intervening days but help in the kitchen and take her solitary walks and drives. The crates stayed where they were, and her efforts at decorating came to a halt. Mrs. Williamson urged her to eat more, saying that Rose had lost weight and Mr. Fletcher would think she wasn't doing her job.

Luke returned home shortly after nightfall a week later, entering through the kitchen with a rush of chill air. Startled, Rose looked up from the pie she was making and stared at him.

"Did you miss me?" Luke asked, dropping his saddlebags in order to pick her up and swing her round in a circle, nearly upending her pie.

Mrs. Williamson let out a relieved sigh when nothing fell and turned back to the goose she was basting.

"You know I did," Rose said, her heart singing with joy at the ardent way he was looking at her. Once again her hopes surged. "You'd better have missed me, too."

"You have no idea," he whispered in her ear, the sound causing an instant blush to sweep up her neck. He turned to the housekeeper. "Might I drag my wife away from her duties for a short time?"

"I can spare her. Supper will be ready in an hour, Mr. Fletcher, if that suits you."

Luke's hand grasped hers and tugged her through the kitchen and up the stairs until they were in their bedchamber.

He closed the door and stood with his back to it, eyeing her like a sultry predator. Rose stood uncertainly by the bed, her heat racing with excitement. She wanted his hands on her, stroking her until all her doubts and fears evaporated.

Luke came to her, wrapping his arms around her as his mouth took hers, lips sliding over hers with increasing hunger. Then his tongue slipped between her lips and they moaned in unison.

Luke's hand covered her breast, only to find the stiff fabric of her corset.

"These blasted clothes. It'll take me a good ten minutes just to get you naked."

"Please, hurry," she said, already breathless and impatient.

His eyes went dark and a flush stole over his cheekbones. Picking her up, he laid her on the bed. Once again he kissed her until her breath was ragged, hitching in and out. She tried to widen her legs for him but her heavy skirts hampered all movement.

"Don't worry, I'll take care of you," he whispered, moving down her body until he was by her feet.

Cool air swept up her stockinged legs as he pushed her skirts up to her hips and settled between her thighs. His hand stroked up her leg and he smiled at her, as if he had a secret he was about to tell. Then he ducked his head.

"What—"

But she said nothing more. Her breath caught at the feel of his fingers spreading her open, his tongue licking over her like a flame. Her hips lifted off the bed, greedy for him. Soon she was writhing, beyond the boundaries of her own body. There was just Luke and his heavenly mouth, the hands that held her hips as his tongue slid over her, oh so slowly, until the ache built to a need so desperate she thought she might die of it. Her fingers were rigid in his hair when he slid his tongue inside her, his own moans joining hers when at last she broke apart beneath him.

When she opened her eyes he was above her, his arms braced on either side of her head as he filled her in one smooth thrust. Holding on to him she savored the feel of him all around her, claiming her for his own. His breathing came fast and hard, his muscles working beneath his linen shirt. With one final thrust he called out her name and collapsed on top of her.

Long moments passed before either could speak.

"Three weeks was an eternity without holding you in my arms at night."

The hand that had been softly caressing Luke's hair froze at his drowsy declaration, so like what he'd written in his letter to Catherine: I don't know how I'll survive two more months without holding you in my arms.

A wave of despair crashed over her, deadening her to the joy and blissful satisfaction he'd brought her. Luke rose up on his elbow, puzzled by her silence.

"Rose? Is something wrong?"

How she wished she could confess and receive his reassurances. But it was no use. He didn't love her, not yet, else he'd have said so by now. And she had no right to read his most private correspondence and then make demands of him.

She gave him a shaky smile and blinked away the tears that threatened. "Nothing's wrong. I'm just overwhelmed. And I missed you."

He smiled, kissing her once more before swinging out of bed. "I daresay our hour's nearly up," he said, rearranging his trousers and tucking in his shirt. "We don't want Mrs. Williamson's hard work to end up a cold, toughened goose."

Rose climbed slowly out of bed and straightened her clothing. Walking over to the looking-glass on the wall, she saw that her face was flushed, her hair in disarray.

One by one she took the pins from her hair until it fell loose around her shoulders and down her back. Gathering it over her shoulder she began brushing it out, her eyes meeting Luke's in the glass. He stood near the bed, frozen in the act of buttoning his collar, his eyes following her every move.

He came up behind her until he was pressed against her back, his arms wrapping around her. "You take my breath away," he murmured, kissing her neck in the spot that sent shivers along her spine.

The way he looked at her, she could almost believe he might love her. But what if it was only desire, and never anything more? Desire was potent, she knew that well enough, but she wanted more. So much more.

"What will happen when I grow old and wrinkled?" she asked, looking at him through the glass. "I won't take your breath away then."

Luke looked up and frowned at her, as if unsure what she wanted from him. "I should hope you age like the rest of us," he said, pulling away from her. "I don't know if I can take an entire lifetime lusting after you as I do. It might very well kill me."

Rose looked away from him and began plaiting her hair until it hung in one long braid over her shoulder. They had just been as close as two people could be, and yet now she felt as if there were miles between them.

She turned and gave him a brief, forced smile. Luke looked at her warily, as if sensing that something were not quite right. But he said nothing. Silently, without touching, they descended the staircase for supper.

A week of chill rain and dark skies kept Rose indoors and only added to her growing despair. All over the house, swatches of material lay draped over furniture, waiting for her to decide on the décor of each room, but she couldn't make herself care what color the walls were papered. She could barely rouse herself to care about what they ate each night. After all, Mrs. Williamson was perfectly capable of feeding them.

The activities with which she was expected to fill her days all seemed so frivolous, just a way of keeping a bored woman busy to no one else's benefit. She was sitting at the dining room table, listlessly looking at possible recipes for their Thanksgiving meal, when Mrs. Williamson gave her a letter from Lydia.

It was the first letter she'd received from her friend, though she'd written weeks before. No doubt Lydia had been hurt that Rose hadn't told her the truth about her and Luke. Lydia's naturally cheerful disposition and genuine affection seemed to have overcome her hard feelings, however, as the letter was lively and filled with the latest news from Cider Hill.

The letter painted a vivid portrait of the estate in the midst of brewing their famous cider, not to mention the effect it had on the staff, who were all being given a decent share of the beverage. Everyone seemed to be in high spirits. With Mrs. Fletcher and Mr. Byrne no longer around, things were much more relaxed and the pace of life had slowed considerably.

Though things had improved for everyone, Rose couldn't help feeling badly about how abruptly the reading and writing lessons had ended. Dottie in particular had only just begun to read, and she needed considerable help to get through even a paragraph.

In the midst of her remorse it occurred to her that there might be a way to continue them. After all, she had more than enough time on her hands, and a carriage and horses for her own use. Full of renewed purpose and excitement, she sat down and wrote to her friend.

Within the week it had been arranged. Matthew Brewster, one of the farm laborers she'd been teaching, offered his home for the use of lessons. Two evenings a week, weather permitting, Rose would drive the phaeton to his home near Cider Hill and anyone who wanted could come learn to read and write.

Rose threw herself into her teaching, spending part of each day working out lessons for the varying abilities of the students. It was a task she found deeply satisfying, particularly as she now had access to an extensive library. Best of all, she was now able to visit with Lydia and Dottie for short periods of time afterwards.

"Everyone talks about you as if you were living a fairly tale," Lydia said one day as Rose drove her back to Cider Hill. "As soon as I get back tonight they'll be asking me all sorts of questions about your new life. Abigail will be quite desperate to know what were you wearing."

"I suppose it does seem like a fairy tale, when you look at it from a distance," Rose said, not realizing until the words were out how she sounded.

Lydia gave her a sharp look. "Only from a distance?"

Rose laughed, hating the forced sound of it. "I'm not complaining. I only meant to suggest that life isn't perfect, nor should we expect it to be or we'll only be disappointed. Fairy tales are for children, not married women."

Lydia frowned at her, a concerned look on her face, and Rose feared her friend would ask questions she wasn't prepared to answer.

"It's close enough to a fairy tale when you're working for Mrs. Fletcher," Lydia observed instead, sounding a good deal like Dottie.

"Yes, I suppose it is," said Rose, and they left it at that.

⟿

"I hope I'm not keeping you from anything," Jonas said, settling into a chair in Luke's study.

It was a raw Saturday afternoon in late November, not the sort of day people tended to call on one another. But then his father wasn't just anybody.

"Not at all. Rose is at Miss March's and I was just catching up on some correspondence. What brings you here?"

His father grimaced. "I could use some easy company, that's the long and short of it. Maybe a drink as well," he said, raising his eyebrows and looking pointedly at Luke.

"Of course. I'll join you," Luke said, happy as always to drink with his father. He poured them each a generous glass of whiskey and then sat down opposite Jonas. There was no mistaking his father looked weary and troubled.

"I take it Charlotte is not yet reconciled to my marriage?"

"That's correct, but you needn't apologize again for causing me trouble. The truth is that I'm dealing with the fallout from marrying Charlotte, not just the repercussions of your marriage. Suffice it to say she and I are equally disappointed in each other. But I'll not go into all of that. I'd much rather enjoy the afternoon."

"I did have something I wanted to discuss with you," Luke said. "I'm afraid you won't be pleased by it though."

"Oh?"

Luke stood and walked to the window, looking out at the cobbled street, the houses on all sides. He turned back to his father.

"I confess I'm more restless than I anticipated when I told you I'd be staying in Boston. Working in the office so much of the time has got me itching to be outside, away from all the people and noise. I can't live in town if I'm to keep my sanity."

"Do memories of Catherine play any part in your desire to get away?" his father asked, ever calm as he watched Luke begin to pace about the room.

"I have many regrets when it comes to Catherine, but this is something else."

"You always did prefer Cider Hill," his father said with a chuckle. "There were days your mother and I barely laid eyes on you. You were gone from sunup until sundown, running wild through the forests and fields." He smiled to himself, as if reliving fond memories.

"Maybe that's all I need. A house in the country, far enough away that I can breathe but close enough to map for the railroad."

"If that's what you want, I won't try to convince you otherwise. It was enough that you came here at all when I needed you. I never expected you to stay here permanently, though you know well enough I was hoping you would."

"When I married Rose, I fully intended to stay in Boston. I suppose I was so delirious at finally having her that I forgot myself. But some things don't change."

"We are who we are," Jonas replied with a sigh. "No use fighting it."

Luke couldn't help wondering if he was thinking of Charlotte as he spoke. Surely his father would never have imagined her behaving as she had. Thank God Rose would never disappoint him in such a way. It just wasn't in her. Even so, he didn't know his new wife as well as he'd once thought. Something had changed and the intimacy of the first weeks of their marriage was eroding, but he didn't know why. Too often he caught her studying him with a sad, haunted look that squeezed his heart.

It was as if she were waiting for him to do or say something, but for the life of him he didn't know what. He did everything he knew to make her happy, and yet she grew ever more quiet and withdrawn. Whenever he asked her what was wrong, she denied that anything was amiss.

Perhaps it was the reality of being snubbed by so many people, or the sudden change in her circumstances. But he couldn't help feeling as if it were his fault. Lately he'd begun to experience the same dull dread he'd felt when he realized he couldn't make Catherine happy.

It was the first time he'd admitted this to himself, and he quickly suppressed the thought. Taking a healthy gulp of whiskey, he looked back out the window.

"It's getting late in the year for any kind of move, so we'll be here until spring at least."

"Well, that's something," said Jonas, sounding resigned.

"Perhaps I ought to build something myself," Luke mused aloud, the idea taking on weight as soon as he said it. Rose could tell him exactly the kind of house she wanted, and he'd give it to her. Maybe then she'd be happy. Boston was proving to be disappointment to her, and moving closer to her aunt would surely improve her spirits.

He was bound to make another trip to the Berkshires before winter. When he did, he'd find the perfect place for them to call home.

⟲

Rose returned home chilled to the bone from the short walk from Vivian's house.

"May I take your coat, Mrs. Fletcher?" Martha asked, appearing from the parlor door.

"Yes, thank you, Martha," she said, handing the girl her hat and gloves as well. "Is Mr. Fletcher home?"

"He's with his father in the study, ma'am."

Jonas didn't often call, as he and Luke saw each other so often during the week. It was always good to see him, but Rose still felt the weight of all that was unspoken and unknown between them.

She followed the delicious aroma of baking bread to the kitchen, where she found the housekeeper up to her elbows in flour.

"Will Mr. Fletcher's father be dining with us this evening, Mrs. Williamson?"

"I don't rightly know. They haven't come out of the study since Mr. Fletcher arrived, and I didn't want to intrude."

"It's getting late. Perhaps I'd better go check."

Heading back out of the kitchen she stopped in front of the study. The door was slightly ajar, and she was about to knock when Jonas spoke.

"If that's what you want, I won't try to convince you otherwise. It was enough that you came here at all when I needed you. I never expected you to stay here permanently, though you know well enough I was hoping you would."

"When I married Rose, I fully intended to remain in Boston. I suppose I was so delirious at finally having her that I forgot myself. But some things don't change."

Rose backed away from the door and ran up the stairs to her sitting room. Once inside she paced madly about, her thoughts whirling.

Everything she'd feared was true. He still loved his first wife, enough that he couldn't bear to stay in Boston. It was time to accept it and do what had to be done. Going to her trunk, she knelt before it and took out the glove she'd buried under layers of silk and linen, holding it in her hand as she hardened her resolve.

CHAPTER THIRTEEN

*T*wo days later Rose entered Luke's study. It was cool and dim inside, the curtains not yet opened to the day. Luke worked for the most part from the offices in town, so there would be little in the way of railroad business. What she was looking for was of a more personal nature, however, and more likely to be here than anywhere.

It took her only a few minutes to find the letters. Tucked into a leather box on the highest shelf of his bookcase was his correspondence with his family. Kneeling on the floor she opened it to find letters from his sisters, father and even his mother. She pulled out letters from Jonas dated from February and began to read.

6 February, 1841
Dear Luke,

I hope this finds you well and surviving the winter in relative comfort. Did the necessary supplies reach the fort as expected? I confess that I myself am too old and used to my comforts to tolerate the harsh conditions of life in the Territories. Of course, you are used to living rough. I expect it is the people you find most troublesome.

Lately I find myself feeling the same way. Many of the troubles of planning a new route lie more with the people involved than the track itself. Which brings me to my latest news.

While there was never any hope of replacing you, did I even wish it, I have out of duty and necessity asked Nathan to bear some of the burden of the Western line. While he has not the skills, knowledge or discipline you have, he does seem willing to learn. In fact he seems all too eager to prove himself, even where doing so is not warranted.

Charlotte has high hopes for him which I am afraid have to date been thwarted, whether by bad luck or poor choices I could not say. However, I have now given him responsibility for handling the landowners in Lenox, and I have hopes that over time and with my guidance he will prove to be an asset to the company.

But enough on that score. I have heard from your sister Annabelle. They are all quite well and hoping to visit Boston within the next year. I do miss them and have not yet seen the youngest. I look forward to the day we will be able to get to Woodstock by rail, and many other places besides. There is no stopping this kind of progress. It has all the force and momentum of a train at full speed. These are exciting times, and would be all the more so were you to return.

Forgive me for once again inserting my own selfish hope. If you cannot come here I may just drag these old bones to you, wherever you may be. I daresay I am not as indispensable around here as I think I am.

As ever,
Your father

3 March, 1841

Dear Luke,

How I miss your rational mind. I could use you around here, and of course a man can always use his son near him. How did my children all end up so far away? I suppose I prevail upon you that much more because I cannot ask the girls' husbands to return them to me. But what of you? I wonder whether you feel the need for a home. A man can go a long time without one, but it exacts a price.

Over the years I have managed, I think, not to write you letters coercing you too baldly. I suppose I have been less restrained of late due to recent difficulties. The railroad encounters obstacles at every turn, and my efforts to teach Nathan about the business and give him meaningful employment seem to be for naught, or so it appears these last weeks. I recently sent him to Lenox to make another, more generous offer, and by his account Mrs. Harris is close to selling, for which I am grateful. Yet his manner of late has been most erratic. He is querulous, sullen and undependable. His behavior gets worse even as he prevails upon me to give him more responsibility. Were he not my wife's son I would dismiss him. My hope is that this is a phase that will pass, for he was at one time, if not a brilliant businessman, at least an eager one.

I see I have covered a fair bit of paper airing my grievances. This is what happens when one writes in the midst of frustration. No doubt things will be much improved by the time this reaches you.

As ever,

Your father

Rose sat for long minutes, absorbing the import of the letters. Nathan had ridden out to the farm in February and yet neither she nor her aunt knew of such a visit. This was the confirmation she needed that he'd had been to the farm. Between the letter and the glove there could be no doubt. It was also clear Mr. Fletcher knew nothing of her father's murder.

Why had Nathan done it? Was he so desperate to prove himself that he would try to weaken their family just to get the land? Or had he become so angry that he shot her father in the heat of the moment?

Now that she had all the pieces, or at least all those she could get on her own, she needed to tell Luke. But it was only morning and he had told her he wouldn't be home at midday. She would have to wait until evening. Shaking and sick to her stomach, she replaced the letters and turned to leave the study.

Something caught her eye just before she opened the door. A leather portfolio lay on the corner of his desk, several pieces of paper protruding from it. Picking it up, she untied the string binding it and opened it up.

There were half a dozen sketches, all of them of her. Some were of her reading, others sewing, and one portrayed her asleep, the twisted sheets revealing a bare arm and leg, a few inches of her breast. She was smiling in her sleep, as if pleasure had followed her there.

All of them were rendered in careful, even loving detail. But whatever he felt for her, it wasn't enough. If it had been, he wouldn't be running away from memories of Catherine.

Upstairs in her chair by the window, she sat with her head in her hands. She'd hoped that when this moment came their marriage would be strong enough to sustain the blow, but they were more distant now than when she'd been a maid in his father's house.

She'd been sitting in the chair, staring out the window for what could have been hours, when she heard Luke come in the door. With a feeling of unreality she listened to him mount the steps until he stood in the doorway, his masculine beauty a knife in her heart. She would have loved him all her days if he'd let her.

"There you are," he said, coming toward her. "I hoped I'd find you."

Roes struggled to keep her composure. "I didn't expect you before evening."

"I'm afraid I must leave for Stockbridge this afternoon," he said, walking over to the wardrobe where he began filling a valise with clothes.

"But why so suddenly?"

"I received a letter this morning from Whistler, asking me to come immediately. They seem to have run into yet another snag."

Rose could say nothing for several seconds.

"I see," she finally replied. "When do you expect to return?"

"I imagine it will be at least three weeks. You'll be all right, won't you? I know things were difficult the last time I left, but Vivian will be here to keep you company."

Three weeks. Should she risk telling him the truth now? Then again, could she stand to wait weeks more before telling him? That thought was even worse than the first.

"Don't look so down, darling," he said, leaving off from his packing to come over to her.

Taking her hands he urged her to stand, his arms coming around her in a warm embrace. Slow and deliberate, his kiss tore down her meager defenses. Her body responded instantly, as if there were no tomorrow, no imminent betrayal. She let him lead her to the bed where he pressed kisses along her jaw, down her throat, along the neckline of her dress. Restlessly he made quick work of her clothes, revealing her little by little as he removed each layer.

Her fears subsumed in desire, she gave in to his caresses, opening to him and demanding more in return. Fueled by her urgency, Luke pressed her back into the softness of the blankets, holding her hands above her head as he devoured her. His mouth on her throat, her breasts, he kissed her until she knew nothing but him. Twisting and turning she writhed beneath him, every nerve ending painfully alive.

Releasing her hands he moved lower, pressing kisses down to her naval and then further still to the center of her need. She opened for him, her hands twining in his hair, her hips rising to his clever tongue.

Higher and higher he took her, holding her hips as she bucked and tightened around him. She called out for him, needing him inside her. Rising up, his eyes intent on her and his breathing labored, he entered her. She held on to his powerful body, delirious with the feel of him as he filled her. When release broke over her she shook and held him tight while tears streamed down her cheeks. On a hoarse cry he emptied himself inside her, shaking as he lay on top of her in the aftermath.

It was a few minutes before either of them moved. Luke lifted his head from where it lay buried in her neck and looked at her.

"What's this?" he asked, running a thumb over a tear. "Did I hurt you?" he asked worriedly.

"No, of course not. You mustn't pay me any mind."

Though he was only inches away, a sense of loneliness swept through her. Getting out of bed she pulled on her wrapper before turning to him. "There's something I must tell you before you go."

Luke sat up and swung his legs over the bed.

"You're not with child, are you?" he asked, his expression somewhere between panic and pleasure, and it was all she could do not to weep then and there. Wordlessly she shook her head.

"Perhaps you could tell me in a letter," he said, rearranging the clothes that had been thrown into disarray. "I'm sorry darling, but I'm afraid I'm running late as it is. It'll be nightfall before I make it to Worcester."

Coming to her he cupped her face in his hands and kissed her. "I'll miss you," he said, and then he was through the doorway and out of sight, though the feel of his lips lingered long after he rode away.

The next week passed in a blur, with Rose going through the motions of her life without feeling any of it. At night she slept ill, tormented by dreams in which she lost Luke a hundred different ways. Not even waking from these brought relief, for she was stuck in a purgatory of her own making, not yet condemned but not able to live either.

She left the house only to teach her classes and visit Vivian, but her friend persuaded her to come out with her and Edward one evening to meet with a group of people raising funds to build a public library. Rose had been excited to hear of it the previous week, as it sounded like just the sort of project she'd enjoy, and one unlikely to include anyone from Charlotte's circle of influence.

"It will do you good to get out among the kind of people who'll be present tonight," Vivian cajoled. "Think how uplifting it will be to take part in such a worthy project, and one so dear to your own heart."

Rose finally acquiesced, her interest great enough that it overcame her initial reluctance. When Edward and Vivian came to her door that evening she was ready, and the three of them headed out into the December chill, their breath misting before them.

"Where is the meeting to be held?" Rose asked.

"George Ticknor has offered his home as the meeting place," Edward answered. "He's been trying to raise interest in the library, as well as money, for some time. Ticknor was an old classmate of mine at Harvard, and now he's a professor there. I wasn't the least bit surprised to hear he's heading the initiative. He's always been a most liberal thinker."

Rose felt a moment of alarm at this. Her father, Peter, had been a Harvard student as well, and quite a brilliant one, according to his friends. He'd been close with a number of Harvard professors up until Rose and he left Boston, and had corresponded with them until his death. But even supposing someone recognized her tonight, she couldn't imagine how any harm could come of it.

They arrived at an enormous white house, complete with white pillars and stone veranda. A number of people were streaming toward the door, and carriages lined the street. Vivian and Rose looked at one another in surprise. They'd expected a sedate gathering, but one would have thought Ticknor was hosting a ball tonight.

A servant stationed just inside the door took their coats while another directed them to the ballroom. Rose found herself wishing she'd dressed with more care, for many of the guests were in full evening attire.

A tall, gray-haired man with great bushy sideburns and a ruddy nose greeted Edward the moment they walked into the ballroom.

"Edward, so glad you could make it. Miss March, it's wonderful to see you. How do you do," he said, bowing to Rose while Edward made the introductions. "Quite a turnout, is it not?"

"I should say so," said Edward. "How did you manage it?"

"Everyone's come to see Vattemare. No one can resist an eccentric Frenchman. Word seems to have spread about his talents, and I haven't bothered to squelch the notion that he'll be performing. Let them think what they want if it brings them here. Maybe some of them will empty their pockets for once."

"What sort of talent?" Vivian asked.

"Vattemare's a ventriloquist. Have you ever heard the like? Of course, that's just his hobby. His main interest is in efforts of this sort. He has a most creative and enterprising mind."

Rose and Vivian looked at each other, incredulous.

"So good of you all to make it," Ticknor continued. "Do find yourself someplace to sit. I shall hopefully speak to you later," he said, rushing away as he was summoned to the front of the room.

Edward led them toward the rows of chairs that had been set up to face the front of the room. It was as they were winding their way through the crowd that Rose caught sight of the woman in a plum-colored evening gown, her dark hair precisely coiffed, her head turned in profile.

Charlotte Fletcher. And she was deep in conversation with Eliza Lynch.

Rose clutched Vivian's arm, unable to believe what she was witnessing. The two women were leaning toward one another in intimate conversation when Mrs. Lynch let loose with the very same laugh that had so charmed Rose.

"What is it?" Vivian whispered in alarm.

But before Rose could reply, Mrs. Lynch's gaze landed on her. An expression of surprise crossed her countenance, followed quickly by cool amusement.

"Mrs. Fletcher," she said, one eyebrow raised in arch amusement. "How unexpected."

Rose stood where she was, unable to move or breathe for a moment. Then fury roared through, and with it a steadying determination not to let either woman get the best of her. Smiling, she walked over to them.

"Mrs. Lynch, Charlotte. How surprising to see you here. I thought only to meet people who concerned themselves with the greater good."

Charlotte's mouth tightened and her eyes narrowed, but Mrs. Lynch looked delighted by the confrontation.

"One should never underestimate others, Mrs. Fletcher. I'm sure you'll agree that leads to much misery."

"Indeed," Rose said, looking directly at Mrs. Lynch. "I seem to be forever underestimating the depths to which others will sink. How fortunate for you that you already know."

Nauseated, her composure eroding, she turned to go only to be brought up short by someone standing in her way. She stared in surprise and disgust at the sight of Nathan.

Nathan laughed. "Goodness me. It appears my sister-in-law is not at all pleased to see me. How very hurtful when I've missed you so."

It was all Rose could do not to accuse Nathan of killing her father then and there. Fortunately, Mr. Ticknor chose that moment to begin speaking, and everyone hushed at once and began taking their seats.

Turning away, Rose hurried to the empty chair beside Edward and Vivian, her breath light and fast. Up front, several rows beyond where she sat, George Ticknor made his case for the first-ever free public lending library. Rose heard almost nothing that was said. Her mind was taken up in remembering Eliza Lynch's seemingly innocent comments about Luke and Catherine. The cold-hearted calculation of it went beyond anything she could have anticipated.

Ticknor finished his speech and then introduced Vattemare. The applause as the Frenchmen took his place in front was so thunderous, it succeeded in jolting Rose out of her trance. But though even a day ago she would have hung on every word he said about the importance of sharing knowledge, now she wanted only to go home so she could think in peace.

After what seemed hours, the attendees were encouraged to partake of the refreshments laid out in the back of the room. Rose was desperate to leave, but she couldn't very well drag Edward and Vivian away when they were so enjoying themselves.

"Wasn't that splendid?" Vivian asked, her eyes shining with excitement. "I cannot wait to contribute to such a worthy endeavor."

Unable to match Vivian's delight, Rose murmured her agreement and hoped her friend wouldn't notice anything amiss. She didn't want to discuss what had happened until they were away from the house.

"Rose Stratton, is that you?"

Rose turned at the sound of her name, an instinctive smile forming as she recognized her father's old friend.

"Mr. Winthrop. It's good to see you."

"I'd know you anywhere, though it's been, what, six years? My sincere condolences on the loss of your father. Mrs. Harris wrote me of it only last month, but she didn't mention that you'd left Lenox for Boston."

Someone behind Rose made a choked sound. Turning around, she saw that Nathan stood only a few feet behind her. It was clear he'd overheard, for the blood had drained from his face and he stared at her as if seeing a ghost.

She'd been found out.

"Please excuse me, Mr. Winthrop," she said, with as much calm as she could muster. "I'm afraid my friends were just about to leave." Terrified of what she might see if she looked back, she hastened over to where Vivian stood beside her father. "I must go at once. Please tell your father I'm ill. I'll explain later."

She was trembling all over and her skin had gone clammy. It was all she could do not to bolt from the house, but it would be folly to leave by herself. Who knew what Nathan would do if he found her alone?

Finally, after waiting an agonizing amount of time for Edward to extricate himself from a conversation and retrieve their coats, the three of them left the house. Every moment Rose felt sure Nathan or Charlotte would come chasing after her, demanding answers, but when she dared look back there was no sign of them.

By the time Rose made it back to Walnut Street, she was fully panicked. She stood in front of the door and embraced Vivian while Edward stood just a few steps away lighting his pipe.

"Stay with us tonight, Rose," Vivian urged, alarmed at what Rose had told her on the walk back.

"I can't. Nathan knows who I am, I'm sure of it. It's not safe to stay here, and anyway I have to find Luke and tell him everything before someone else does."

"But Rose—"

"I'm sorry. I must go now if I'm to leave in the morning. Promise me you'll be careful. Nathan may wonder what you know as well."

Guilt settled over her at the stricken look on Vivian's face, but she remained resolved.

Once she had made her decision she wasted no time. Going immediately to Mrs. Williamson, she explained her plan to leave early the next morning. Though the housekeeper looked surprised, she made no objection. Rather she insisted Jeremy go with Rose, as it would be much safer than staying at inns by herself.

Upstairs Rose set about packing only the most necessary items. The lighter they traveled, the better time they would make. They would reach the farm by the evening of the fifth day if the weather held. She'd overnight there and then set out for Luke the next morning.

Once she had packed she sat down and wrote apologetically to Lydia and Matthew Brewster for the short notice of the break in their lessons, promising to write again on her return to Boston. She wouldn't let herself contemplate what would happen if Luke didn't forgive her.

She had decided they would ride rather than take the phaeton, as the roads through the Berkshires wouldn't permit a carriage. Five arduous days was far too long to ride sidesaddle, so she decided to forgo convention and use one of Luke's saddles.

Jeremy tacked up the horses in the dawn chill, thrilled to be going on an adventure, as he'd never been more than ten miles outside of Boston. Even Rose's subdued mood couldn't quell his excitement. Mrs. Williamson saw them off with food enough for a week, looking rather forlorn as she said goodbye to her son. She bade him look after Rose and mind himself, and Rose promised she would write as soon as they arrived.

Rose was anxious to be make good time and urged the horses into a canter whenever possible, but they couldn't keep up such a pace for long. Luckily the weather, though raw and overcast, held the whole way.

The land, originally covered entirely by trees, had been cleared in huge swathes for the many farms that now covered the hills and valleys. Even so the landscape was heavily forested, the bare braches etched against the pale sky. Rose found the barren landscape beautiful and a balm to her melancholy spirits, the cold air and the smell of woodsmoke from nearby houses fueling her desire to reach the farm.

They rode from sun-up until sundown, pausing only for an hour at midday to take their meal. The inns they stayed at each night were unexceptional, providing mediocre but edible sustenance and a passably clean room for the night.

The last day was spent winding their way through the foothills of the Berkshires on narrow, rutted roads, the forest close around them. This combined with the elevation had them shivering while their horses labored up the grade. Rose was exhausted, dirty and so anxious to see her aunt she had to force herself to let the horses pick their careful way along the trail.

In late afternoon they reached the top of a hill and she saw the farm spread out before them. There was the cornfield, harvested and turned for the spring planting. She could see where the squash, pumpkins, and beets still grew. A man she didn't recognize – he must be one of the recent hires – came out of the barn and headed for the house.

"Is that it, miss?" asked Jeremy, his eyes never leaving the view below.

"Yes, that's it. And never was I so happy to see it. They'll probably put you to work, you know. No one stays on a farm without working."

"Oh, I don't mind. I'll help with whatever's needed, just like I do for you and Mr. Fletcher."

Rose's stomach clenched at mention of Luke, but she said nothing. Turning her horse, she led the way down.

Aunt Olivia came to the door as they rode into the yard, staring at Rose as if she couldn't believe her eyes. Then she smiled and stepped outside, her arms wide open. Rose fell into her aunt's embrace and held on for dear life.

"What's happened?" Olivia asked, pulling back to look at her.

Rose glanced over at Jeremy, who stood holding the reins of both horses, staring wide-eyed at Rose. It was only then that Rose realized she was crying. Her confession would have to wait until they had some privacy.

Olivia quickly took the situation in hand, directing Jeremy toward the barn to care for the horses before coming inside the house for a meal. As soon as he was out of earshot, Rose looked at her aunt.

"The very worst thing has happened. Or one of the very worst things. There are so many of them now it's hard to say which is more horrible."

"Come inside where it's warm and you can tell me everything over tea," her aunt said, as sensible as ever.

Gratefully Rose followed her into the house, her tears renewing as she laid eyes on the place she'd called home for so many years. Here she had no secrets, she was only herself, with all her hopes and flaws.

Ten minutes later her aunt set a cup of steaming tea in front of her, exactly as she'd done so many other times when Rose was feeling low. Then she sat down across from Rose at the kitchen table and listened without interrupting as Rose recounted the events of the previous night.

"Heavens. What happens now?" Aunt Olivia asked.

"Tomorrow morning I'll ride out and find Luke so I can tell him the truth. After that, I hardly know."

"The crew is working in Stockbridge, not fifteen miles away, from what I hear. Some of them are being put up by families in town. It shouldn't be too hard to track him down. Mind that a storm is coming tonight, be it rain or snow."

"If travel is possible, then I'll be going regardless. I can hardly stand to be in my own skin anymore." She paused, looking down at her hands. "I'm sorry this isn't a proper visit. I've wanted to see you for such a long time, but somehow..." She stopped, guilt overwhelming her as she tried and failed to explain the last few months.

Aunt Olivia took Rose's hands in hers and looked directly into her eyes. "It's been too long since I've seen you. Let's not waste our time on regrets. You know how I felt about you going to Boston, but I understand why you had to." She sighed and shook her head. "You're brave and loyal, and not many could do what you've done. But I can't help worrying that you married Luke Fletcher to avenge your father. He would never have wanted you to throw your life away on his account."

"It's not like that at all. I love him, which may be even worse, because he doesn't love me back."

"Oh, honey. If he doesn't he's a fool."

Olivia, Jeremy, Rose and several farm hands sat down to supper, the farmhands wanting to know all about Boston while Jeremy wanted to know all there was to know about the wilds of the Berkshires. Rose had trouble holding up her end of the conversation. She was too busy imagining what the next day would bring. Would Luke forgive her? Would she forgive him if the circumstances were reversed? Perhaps it wasn't a fair question. After all, was not a person more likely to forgive someone they loved?

After supper she did the chores while her aunt took several dishes of food and headed over to the home of an ill neighbor. Jeremy headed out to the barn to see to the animals and the house quieted around her.

Chapter Fourteen

$\mathcal{L}$uke was tired – tired of riding, of sleeping rough, and most of all of being away from Rose. This time out, traveling hadn't given him his usual sense of freedom. Instead he'd thought about little but her since he left Boston two weeks ago.

He couldn't wait to get back home and tell her about the fifty acres of land for sale in Great Barrington. If she liked the sound of it, he'd purchase the land immediately and build on it come spring. He was fairly certain she'd be excited, as it would mean being closer to her aunt, though come to think of it, she'd never said exactly where her aunt lived. In any case, it would suit both their purposes. They could even keep the house in Boston and live there for several months out of the year.

But his surprise would have to wait at least five more days, and from the looks of it he would not make great progress today. The sky had darkened in the last hour and now looked as if it would open up any minute.

He was miles from the nearest inn and didn't relish the idea of getting caught in a freezing rain. Looking around, he realized he was no more than three miles from the Harris farm. Perhaps Mrs. Harris would consent to letting

him bunk down in her barn for the night. She'd been cordial enough with him. Hopefully that would extend to
providing him shelter.

The farm came into view a mile ahead, an orderly
array of buildings and a patchwork of fields, some shorn
of their harvest, others bearing the fruits of a fall planting.
His horse picked its way down the steep path to the main
house where he dismounted. As there was no one about,
he walked up to the front door and knocked. He heard the
sounds of feet approaching and took off his hat, ready to
flash his most agreeable smile for Mrs. Harris.

Except when the door opened it was not Mrs. Harris
but Rose.

Dumbfounded, he stared at her, unable to conceive
of why his wife was here when she should be back home
in Boston. Rose looked even more shocked than he felt.
She had gone deathly pale and one hand fluttered to her
throat. She was wearing one of the plainer dresses Madam
Beauchamp had made, a rich brown wool with a high collar. A red checked apron was tied around her waist and her
glorious hair was plaited and pinned in a coil at the nape
of her neck.

A feeling of dread fell over him, the dull knowledge
that what he was about to learn would change everything.

Wordlessly she opened the door and came out, her
movements stiff. She looked at him directly and took a
deep breath, as if stealing herself for what she was about to
say. Finally she spoke, her words halting and unsure.

"I didn't mean for it to happen this way. Please believe
that. I wanted to tell you so many times, but I was afraid."

"What the devil is going on here?"

"I've lived here since I was fifteen years of age. My father and I moved here to live with my aunt and uncle after my mother died."

Luke could do nothing but stare at her as comprehension slowly dawned. Still he said nothing, his body rigid with tension.

"This past February my father died. I told you about that." She took a deep breath. "What I didn't tell you was that he was murdered. I found him in the wood back there," she said, pointing behind the house. "He was shot in the chest and I couldn't save him. But before he died he said the name 'Fletcher.' I didn't understand what that meant until I learned of the letters from your father offering for this land. At the time he was killed he was expecting a visit from someone with the railroad."

"What does this have to do with you and me?"

"It has everything to do with us. Don't you see? I had no choice. The sheriff wouldn't listen to us, wouldn't even talk to anyone from the railroad company. I felt so helpless, and I couldn't bear that whomever killed my father should get away with it. So I found a way to work in your father's house. I wanted to find out who was responsible. And I did."

Luke heard nothing beyond the fact that everything had been a lie.

"You were spying on us." he said, his voice flat and emotionless, as if coming from someone else.

"I had to do something. If your father bled to death in your arms, then you'd understand why I did what I did.

He was taken from us and no one would help me learn the truth. I know I should have told you sooner, but I was afraid to. And when I tried to tell you before you went away, you wouldn't listen."

"So all this time you've suspected me, my family?"

"No, it wasn't like that. I realized soon after I met you that it couldn't have been you."

He stopped for a moment as a realization hit him like a fist to the gut.

"When I kissed you in my father's study, you weren't cleaning at all, were you? There I was, falling all over you like a fool, and you'd been searching through my father's things."

Her eyes fluttered closed and she nodded her head. The feeling of betrayal was so swift and sharp he nearly doubled over. Turning away he headed for his horse.

"Luke, wait!" she called, but he didn't stop.

He reached his horse before she caught up to him. "Please let me explain. It's not like you think. I care about you. I love you."

The pain of hearing those words now, when she had just exposed her deceit, seared through him. They were a lying woman's desperate attempt to keep him from seeing the truth. She was crying now, the tears streaming down her face making her somehow more beautiful and more treacherous. If he hadn't known better he would have thought she actually felt something. But now he knew what a good actress she was. His mind raced, looking back over the months he'd known her, reconfiguring it with the knowledge he now had.

"Luke, I was right. I suspected it was Nathan and it was. I'll explain everything if you'll just listen. Please."

Luke swung onto his horse and took up the reins. Her hand reached out to touch his. That touch, those elegant, sensitive hands.

"I'll have your things sent here as soon as I can arrange it."

Her hand dropped to her side and she looked at him helplessly, heartbreak in every line of her face. Except everything she did and said, every expression was a mask, a false front. The woman he knew had disintegrated before his very eyes.

Wheeling Arturo around, he urged him into a gallop and rode as if his life depended on it, easing up only when he reached the steep ascent to the trail. He told himself not to look back, that she was as good as dead to him, but even now he was as drawn to her as he always had been.

Looking down from his perch atop the hill, he saw her sink to the ground as her skirts pooled around her, her hands clasped in her lap. She looked straight ahead without moving even as the first cold drops of rain fell. He watched for a few minutes, expecting her to rise as the storm began in earnest, but she remained utterly still, as if not even a breath passed through her. He turned back around and urged his horse on, but the image haunted him for miles.

⸏

Despair immobilized her. There seemed no point in moving, though some part of her registered that she was wet and cold. She didn't know how long she sat there on the hard ground, the chill soaking through her skirts, but finally she roused herself to move, fearing that Aunt Olivia would return and find her there. Slowly, as if she'd aged many years since Luke's departure, she got to her feet and wandered away from the house, seeking the solitude of the lower fields.

Dazedly she headed past the house and barns, across the gardens to the wood that bordered the fields. When she first arrived at the farm she'd often come this way to mourn her mother in private. She felt as if she were mourning Luke now, for if he meant what he said, she would likely never see him again.

An overwhelming sense of loss descended on her at the thought of never falling asleep in his arms. Never again knowing his touch on her skin, seeing his smile or his beloved face. She felt as if she might break apart, as if every step she took were the last she would ever take.

Without realizing where she was going, she found herself in the place where she'd held her father as he died in her arms. She fell to her knees, seeing her father's face as the life passed out of it, and then Luke's face, his expression hard and unforgiving, before he rode away. When the tears came it was with such force that they shook her, her sobs tearing through her as if they would never stop.

Which was why she didn't hear Nathan until it was too late.

"Hello, Rose."

Rose looked up, horrified to see Nathan standing over her, his face haggard, his clothes and hair dirty and disheveled.

Unsteadily she got to her feet. Her heart, which had seemed a moment ago all but dead, began to race.

"That was quite a trick you played on us. Only my mother suspected you were so conniving. The amusing part is that my charming stepbrother isn't so lucky after all. You aren't quite the prize we both thought you were."

"Why are you here?"

"I should think that would be obvious. I know who you are now, and after witnessing your little tiff with Luke, it's clear you know what I've done. I could hardly just let you go without first having a little chat about it."

"Tell me why you did it," she demanded, her fists clenched at her sides. "Why kill him?"

"You can't imagine how much pressure I felt when Jonas asked me to meet with the widow. All I wanted was to prove that I could do as well as the exalted son I heard so much about. I made the miserable journey here just as he asked, but before I reached the house I ran into Peter Stratton."

Rose felt lightheaded as he spoke. She knew what came next, knew she couldn't change what happened, and yet she wanted with everything in her to hear a different ending. Nathan looked up as a sob tore from her throat, but his gaze was abstracted and indifferent to her suffering. He continued on.

"Before I even had the chance to introduce myself, he told me he was sorry I'd wasted my time coming all that way out. Nothing I said made a difference. He cared nothing for the money we'd lose, the plans we'd made. I picked up the rifle that was leaning against a tree and threatened him, thinking to scare him into selling, but even that didn't work. A moment later he was lying on the ground, bleeding before my very eyes. I don't even remember pulling the trigger."

He looked at her then. "If he'd only agreed as he should have, none of it would have happened."

"You killed my father on his own land and you dare say it was his fault? I see no remorse in you, no regret. How do you live with yourself?"

"Oh, I felt both remorse and regret at first. But I soon realized what useless emotions they are. They change nothing. And oddly enough, after a time I found what I'd done almost liberating. I had already done the worst by taking a man's life. What I did after that hardly mattered."

A bolt of fear pierced through her horror and fury. He was looking at her with speculation, and it struck her that he was in more command of himself than she'd ever seen him.

"You may as well go now and leave me in peace," she said. "The sheriff paid me no mind before, and Luke doesn't believe me. You have no reason to fear me."

"Oh, but I do. Your precious husband may still put two and two together, and then Jonas will become involved. No, it's far too risky to go back to Boston. Besides, this is the perfect opportunity for us."

"If you think I'd have anything to do with you —"

"You've lied and deceived everyone around you for months. You even swore before God to love another under false pretenses. I'd say we're perfect for each other."

Bile rose in her throat at Nathan's portrayal of her. She backed away from him, her mind whirling as she tried to work out a way to escape him.

"Come now, Rose," he said, closing the gap between them and grabbing her wrist. "You know I can't simply let you go."

A chill coursed along her spine at this.

"You're hurting me," she said, trying to pull away from him. His grip tightened.

"I won't hurt you if you do as I ask. Come with me," he said, directing her towards his horse.

"Yes, of course. But I must tell my aunt or she'll wonder where I am," she said, hoping to get free of him. "If you'll wait here, I'll just be a moment."

"No, that won't do at all. I'm afraid I can't let you go and risk losing you again, not after all I've been through. You can send your aunt a note when you're settled."

Rose looked at Nathan's burning blue gaze and saw there was no reasoning, no way out.

Without looking back, she ran toward the house, hoping her aunt was not yet returned. Her wet skirts clung to her legs, hampering her, and her corset restricted her breathing. She ran until she felt as if she would faint, her heart pounding in her ears, her breathing so labored she could hear nothing else.

She didn't get far. Nathan caught up with her in seconds, jerking her back by her hair and spinning her around until she faced his maddened eyes. She tried to wrench free, but he only twisted her hair tighter until she cried out. Desperately she fought, twisting and lashing out.

She heard a furious yell from the woods and then Jeremy came out of the trees and launched himself at Nathan, knocking him off his feet and sending Rose tumbling to the ground. Looking up, she saw with surprise that Jeremy had gotten the upper hand and was punching Nathan with all he was worth. Rose moved to help but Nathan, recovered from the surprise attack, threw Jeremy off and regained his footing. He kicked the boy hard in the side and Jeremy curled himself into a fetal position, wheezing for breath.

Sickened, Rose flew at Nathan, and the next thing she knew was a blinding pain across the right side of her face. Dimly she realized he'd hit her, hard enough that she would have fallen over had he not grabbed her. When she looked up he was pointing a gun at her.

Would this be her fate, to die by his hand? For surely a man who had killed once might do so again, perhaps more easily the second time.

Numbly she did as he insisted and climbed onto his horse until she sat astride, her sodden skirts clinging to her chilled skin. She thought she might scream when he climbed up behind her and, reaching around her, took hold of the reins. She looked over at Jeremy, terrified he was too hurt to get up, but he stirred and rose shakily to his feet with a groan. He took a few steps after them and fell to his knees, rising again with a cry as Nathan urged the horse into a gallop and out of sight.

CHAPTER FIFTEEN

Luke rode hard at first, pushing Arturo to full speed along the trails, as if he could outrun his thoughts. But gradually he realized how risky and foolish it was to make his horse run full out on such wet and dangerous footing, and at the start of a long journey as well.

And his thoughts could not be outrun. They raced from one memory to the next. Rose in bed, her flaming hair cascading over her shoulders and onto his chest, the feel of her as he moved inside her. Her silken depths, her sighs and moans. Rose opening the books he'd given her, full of yearning and anxiety. Rose beaming with pride as her students performed Shakespeare. Then he pictured her rifling through his papers and the feeling of betrayal was so intense he could hardly see.

Had all of it been an act, every word and deed calculated to help solve her father's murder? Had she married him only to skulk about, looking for evidence against his family?

But no, that wasn't right. Not really. He'd pursued her from the beginning, even against her wishes. Her character had been consistently sweet and generous, though there were times when she'd seemed remote or uneasy.

Her father had died in her arms. Would not he have gone to the ends of the earth under the same circumstances? But what made her think his family had anything to do with it? Was she so desperate at the loss of her father that she would cast about for villains in the homes of strangers? No one in his family was capable of such a thing. The idea was absurd.

And then he recalled what she'd said about Nathan and his blood ran cold.

Nathan's behavior surrounding the farm had always been odd, and he'd declined precipitously since February, the time of her father's death. His father's letter's had said as much, and the dates corresponded.

Rose was telling the truth. Nathan had killed her father and she'd been too scared to tell him. But why? Hadn't he shown her how he cared, earned her trust? He had no love for Nathan, so why had she not confided in him, either before or after their marriage?

Had she really been trying to tell him the day he left?

The image of her sitting so still in the circle of her skirts, heedless of the rain, came back to him. Wheeling his horse around he headed back toward the farm. Back to Rose.

He'd gone just a quarter of a mile when he saw some-one coming toward him on horseback.

"Mr. Fletcher, Mr. Fletcher!" The rider was coming at breakneck speed, slowing down only when he was nearly upon him. Fear shot through Luke as he saw that it was Jeremy, bruised and bloody and covered in mud. He was pale and shaking, barely able to sit his horse.

"What's happened?"

"It's Mrs. Fletcher, sir. Mr. Byrne's taken her away. I ran at him, I did try to stop him, but he kicked me something awful and then I couldn't do nothing, even when he hit her."

A fear so desperate and dark swept over Luke, he nearly missed what the boy said next. But he made himself focus, knowing he had to stay clear-headed if he was to help Rose.

"I got up just as they was heading into the trees on the north side of the lower field. I'm so sorry, sir. I couldn't help her."

The boy was crying now, tears streaking his grimed cheeks.

"When?"

"An hour ago, no more. I started out after you right away, and it took that long to catch you."

Luke was worried about the boy, but more worried about what Nathan might do to Rose.

"Are you well enough to show me where you last saw them?"

Jeremy nodded, his eyes big in his face at the responsibility.

"There's a good lad. Lead on."

⸺

Rain came down in a drizzle punctuated by stronger bursts. Rose was soaked through and chilled to the bone, but what was worse was being in such close proximity to Nathan, who kept one arm around her waist so that she was pulled against him. Her skin crawled at the unwanted contact, but she focused instead on her surroundings so she would know where she was at all times. She knew this land better than Nathan and would use that to her advantage at the first opportunity.

They had been riding for thirty minutes, perhaps a little longer. But instead of heading through one of the nearby towns, or at least past the farm of someone she knew, Nathan kept to the lesser used trails, those used more for hunting than travel. At times he veered off the trail completely and occasionally seemed to lose his way.

Eventually they came in sight of an abandoned house. The forest, as if waiting for the chance, had swiftly retaken the land and rutted road, and now one had to be nearly on top of it to know it was there. It was dingy and peeling, the windows all broken. The sagging roof had large gaps in the shingling and looked as if one more snowfall would cave it in entirely.

Nathan dismounted and pulled her down beside him. Taking her arm he forced her into step with him, pushing her through the front door.

It was a small house – a kitchen, parlor and two tiny bedchambers, all of it on one floor. Rose had been in it once or twice when the family was still here. They stood now in the main room and she saw that the stove had been torn out and the wet floor was strewn with glass, leaves and branches. A smattering of raindrops fell through the gaps in the roof.

She forced herself to think, to shut her mind to all the horrible possibilities that lay before her and instead concentrate on how to get away. The Henry homestead lay about four miles north. If she could just get into the woods without Nathan seeing her, she had a chance. He was faster on horseback, but if he never saw her it wouldn't matter. The trees provided less cover this time of year, but still grew close together, with a good deal of evergreens in between the deciduous trees.

"I didn't want it to be this way, Rose," Nathan said, breaking into her thoughts. "If only you didn't make things so difficult. But I know if I give you time you'll understand how it has to be. We're connected now, you and I. Your father's death has brought us closer than ever. In time you'll come to see it."

"What is it you plan to do? Keep me here until I fall in love with you?"

"This is no place for us to stay. In the morning we'll move on. But you needn't concern yourself with those matters. You'll soon see how reasonable, how constant I am. Luke would never be as indulgent as I'm prepared to be."

Rose said nothing. What did one say to a madman? She would simply cooperate until she could get away.

Nathan smiled apologetically. "I'm sorry I can't offer you anything better tonight, but I'll risk a small fire in order for us to dry off."

Rose looked down and saw that her clothes clung to her skin and her hair, entirely loosed from its pins during her struggle with Nathan, fell in wet strands to her waist. Nathan had faired even worse than she, as Jeremy's attack had sent him rolling around the muddy ground.

Gathering broken branches from the floor, Nathan lit the kindling from a box of matches he pulled from his jacket.

A few tiny flames flickered to life and he added bigger pieces until it gave off a steady heat. Shivering uncontrollably, Rose moved closer and knelt down to hold out her hands.

Despite the extremity of the circumstances, she found herself instantly comforted by the warmth. Gradually the desperate tension left her. In her depleted state she fell into a near trance as she watched the orange and blue flames. She was not aware of Nathan near her until she felt him stroking her hair.

"So beautiful, like silk," he said dreamily.

Rose leapt to her feet and backed away from him, too disgusted to pretend otherwise.

"Is this how I'm to be repaid for my kindness?" he asked, a dangerous new look in his eye.

"I'm not ready. I need more time."

"Perhaps I'm not as patient as I thought," he said, eyes narrowed as he considered her.

"Given that you're a lunatic and you murdered my father, no amount of time will be enough."

Nathan's equanimity vanished. His face paled before turning deep red.

"I see. Then I'm afraid you leave me with no choice."

Rose backed away from him, measuring the distance to the door and wondering if she could make it. But she got only a few feet before he hauled her back against him and spun her around.

"I'll always love you, Rose," he said, his hands encircling her throat.

Grabbing at his wrists she struggled to loosen his grip. Desperately she kicked and twisted, succeeding only in sending the two of them to the rotten floorboards. He was on top of her, his weight holding her helpless as her vision grayed. Her strength gave out and her mind narrowed to a small pinpoint of light. Her hand fell limply to the floor and she felt a sharp sting as something cut her.

A shard of glass.

Nathan was but a shadow above her, his hands relentlessly crushing her neck, but she drove the glass into his side with as much force as she could at such an awkward angle. Nathan screamed and reared backwards, falling to the floor. Gasping for breath, she rolled over and scrambled to her feet, dizzy and nauseated as she ran out the door toward his horse.

Her left foot was in the stirrup, her hands pulling herself up when she heard him behind her. Then his hands were on her waist dragging her off. The horse shied and reared, knocking both of them to the ground. Once again Nathan was on top of her, only now she was too weak to fight him.

I'm sorry, Pa, she thought, a terrible sorrow opening up in her as she felt her strength give out. *I'm sorry, Luke.*

A bellow of rage sounded, as if from far away, and then her throat was released. Wheezing for breath she rolled over, her chest heaving with the effort. Gradually her vision cleared and she saw Luke, his face contorted with rage as he stood over Nathan, pummeling him mercilessly. Nathan was curled into a ball and begging him to stop, but his pleas had no effect. Luke said not a word but continued to hit him until Nathan went limp. For a moment Rose wondered, without caring, whether Nathan was dead, but the rise and fall of his chest indicated he was only unconscious.

Then Luke was kneeling beside her, gently helping her to sit up, crooning soft words of comfort. His touch, which she had thought never to feel again, instantly warmed her, and when he drew her into his arms, she luxuriated in his strong embrace. His big hand stroked her hair as he pressed kisses over her cheeks.

"It's all right, you're safe now. I won't let anyone hurt you ever again."

His feather-light fingers stroked the bruises on her cheek and neck, as if he might erase them. Noticing the cut in her right hand, he stood up to retrieve a clean hand-kerchief from his saddlebag, his hands trembling as he bound the wound.

"Rose, I'm so sorry..." he began, his voice hoarse with feeling.

Rose tried to tell him it was okay, but so sore was her throat, she could not get out any words. Instead she smiled and kissed him, telling him with her body what she couldn't say aloud.

"I had better get you someplace warm," he said. "Wait here and let me deal with Nathan."

Getting up, Luke hauled him onto his shoulder and then slung Nathan over his own horse, tying him down with rope from his saddlebag. Nathan roused as Luke was tightening the knots, and Luke calmly punched him, knocking him unconscious again.

Coming back over to Rose, Luke removed his coat and pulled it around her shoulders. She tried to stand, but she was so weak her legs couldn't support her. Picking her up, Luke looked down at her with an expression of such tenderness and gravity, it was as if no harsh words had passed between them.

Effortlessly he lifted her onto his horse and then swung up behind her, and she was pleasantly reminded of the night they rode together through the streets of Boston. He'd rescued her from Nathan then, too. This time at least she knew it would be the last time Nathan would threaten her. The nightmare was finally ending.

But did Luke's attentions mean he'd forgiven her? Would he want her back in his home, in his life? Too weary and fragile to ask, she was content for the moment to bask in his presence.

Luke led Nathan's horse behind them as they made their way back to the farm. Aunt Olivia flew out the door as they rode into the yard, crying at the sight of Rose. It was with relief that Rose saw Jeremy standing in the yard, bandages covering his face and arms, but otherwise well. Several local men, hearing of her disappearance from Olivia and the farmhands, had come to the house, and they removed Nathan to a stall where they proposed to guard him until the sheriff came.

Exhausted by the effort it took to stay on the horse, Rose swayed as soon as she was on her feet. Luke carried her into the house with Aunt Olivia following anxiously behind. Gently Luke laid Rose on her bed.

She tried to thank him but he wouldn't hear of it.

"Hush now. If you only knew what it does to me to see you like this, you would not thank me for doing so little.

If I hadn't arrived when I did..." he stopped, and Rose watched with wonder as he struggled to compose himself, tears in his eyes. His voice was rough with emotion when he finally went on. "Can you ever forgive me?"

Rose stared at him in shock. "Forgive you? But it was I who drove you to it by deceiving you. I could never blame you for how you felt."

"I ask forgiveness for what my family has done to yours. That's something I can never repair or make up to you, though I would do anything to undo what's been done."

Rose clasped his strong hand in hers as she gathered her thoughts.

"When I first came to Cider Hill, I was so angry, so full of hatred and the need to avenge my father's murder," she admitted, her voice quiet. "But hatred is too simple for what I found at your father's house. I found love there, and kindness. No one but Nathan is to blame for what happened, least of all you."

He leaned over and kissed her, and all her aches and pains seemed to fade away.

"As I forgive you and you forgive me, I suppose we ought to forgive ourselves as well," she said.

"Yes, my wise and lovely wife, I suppose it does," he said, pressing a kiss to her forehead. Then he glanced out the window. "It looks as if the sheriff has arrived. I'll go speak to him. If he needs to see you, he can do so tomorrow when you're rested. I won't be long."

Speaking to the sheriff didn't take long, especially as Nathan, unhinged by the turn of events, raged at everyone who came near him and all but confessed to killing Rose's father. The sheriff listened grimly to Luke's account and agreed he would come by and speak to Rose the next day. He had enough evidence already to take Nathan to Becket where they would deal with him.

Luke watched as Nathan, riding astride between two armed men on horses, was led away. He didn't care to think what effect this would have on his father and Charlotte, but there was nothing to be done about it. He just hoped they would understand why Rose acted as she had. Surely Nathan's guilt would convince at least his father that she'd done nothing wrong. But whatever happened, nothing would come between him and Rose again. He'd see to that.

With Nathan safely gone, Luke headed back to Rose, anxious to be near her and assure himself of her wellbeing. But even knowing she was safe didn't entirely vanquish the knot in his stomach. Never would he forget the all-encompassing fear as he tracked them into the woods, or the sight of Rose fighting for her life against his own stepbrother.

When he arrived at her room her aunt had just brought up a tub. Rose looked bone tired as she sat on the bed, her face pale, her bruises standing out in sharp relief. She looked as if she might fall asleep where she sat, but she was covered in dried mud and cuts that needed tending.

He made several trips to the well and stood awkwardly in the kitchen with Rose's aunt as she heated several large pots over the stove. He could see that she was taking his measure, but she didn't seem to resent his presence. All in all, he thought she was taking the situation much better than could be expected.

"I can't tell you how sorry I am for what my family has put you through, Mrs. Harris. If I'd had any idea..." Luke stopped, the destruction his family had wrought on them overwhelming him. He cleared his throat.

Mrs. Harris looked at him and smiled wearily. "You're forgiven, Mr. Fletcher. From what Rose tells me, your stepbrother acted entirely on his own. What I want more than anything is to put this behind us so she can start to heal. I'm counting on you not to cause her more hurt. You've got a rare woman in Rose. I only hope you know that."

"I do know it, and you have my word I'll not hurt her."

She looked at him appraisingly before nodding her head. "Go on up then and take care of your wife."

Rose had fallen asleep on top of the counterpane, but she woke as he was pouring the last pot of steaming water into the tub.

"That's going to be heavenly," Rose said, smiling shyly at him.

She looked so frail, though she'd proven she had a will of iron and wasn't nearly as fragile as she looked. But strong or not, she'd endured more hurt the past few months than anyone should have borne.

Walking over to her he sat on the bed, reaching for the buttons down the back of her dress. One by one he released them until the material fell open. Standing up, Rose pushed the sleeves off and let the dress drop to the floor. He untied the laces of her corset and felt her breath release on a relieved sigh.

It was so like all the other times he'd undressed her, and yet so unlike them, for though his desire for her was undiminished, his primary feeling was of tenderness. He was bemused by the rush of feeling he felt in putting aside his own needs for hers. Or rather, her needs had become his own.

He held her hand as she stepped out of her chemise and petticoats and into the tub, blushing like an innocent at his attentions. Though they had been intensely intimate during their brief marriage, somehow this felt even more so. Perhaps it was because it was not about making love but about caring for her.

She sank with a moan of contentment into the hot water, her head falling back to expose fully the ugly bruises Nathan had left, the sight of them like a punch in his gut. The bruise on her cheekbone was turning purple and she had other myriad scratches and bruises over the rest of her. He could have killed Nathan with each newly revealed injury.

Luckily Rose was past noticing his reactions. Her eyes were closed and she looked too tired to even pick up the soap. He took it upon himself, though he worried his calloused hands would be too rough for such skin. She deserved better, silk and soft sheets, nothing harsh or threatening ever again.

She gave a low hum of approval and sank deeper into the water as his hands slid over her. The candle he'd set on the chest of drawers flickered on the walls and burnished the length of her hair. He washed that as well, the rush of warm water and his massaging hands coaxing a soft moan from her. At last he sat next to the tub, glad just to be near her as she soaked.

How was it that he'd never bathed his lovely wife? He'd been remiss, but he would make up for it, that was certain. She would never wash her own hair again if he had any say in the matter. He hadn't even begun to love her properly, or to live the kind of life they could have.

When the water had cooled he helped her into her night-gown and applied salve to her cuts. Together they sat before the fire, and when her hair was dry he brushed it for her, yet another pleasure he'd never known. Feeling brave, he even went so far as to braid it, though his efforts were clumsy.

Rose laughed softly at him.

"This was my first time. I'll improve."

"I don't doubt it," she said, her voice husky, eyes heavy with fatigue.

"You can hardly keep your eyes open. Let's get you to bed," he said, helping her to her feet.

"Only if you come with me."

"I thought you'd never ask," he said, gratitude flooding him at being able to hold her all night.

⁓

Rose lay back against the pillows and watched with pleasure as Luke began to undress.

It was as if she'd woken to a new life. Her burden had been lifted, one she'd carried for so long that she'd forgotten what it felt to be without it.

"It will be wonderful to get back to Boston," she said, watching him. "I can be myself without worrying that I'm going to lose you. I won't let all the silly things bother me like they used to. I was so worried about how I compared to Catherine, but it doesn't matter anymore. You don't have to feel for me what you did for her. I understand that now."

Luke stopped in the act of unbuttoning his shirt.

"Rose..." he began, and then stopped, shaking his head as if unsure how to go on. "Are you saying you think I loved Catherine more than you?"

Rose nodded mutely and watched in surprise as Luke pulled the chair closer to the bed and sat down, dragging his fingers through his hair.

"I'm such a fool, and I don't deserve you," he said. "If I'd known you thought that...I should have told you about my marriage to her long ago, I see that now." He stopped and looked down at his hands, then up at her, his expression pained. "Our marriage was not a happy one. When she died I blamed myself – for taking her from England, for not being what she wanted. Even for the baby that killed her. Looking back I see we were simply ill-suited to one another."

Rose stared at him, unable to believe her ears. "All this time I thought I wasn't measuring up," she said, dazed by his revelation. "Only, I did overhear you tell your father you wanted to leave Boston."

"And you thought it was like the first time I left?"

Rose nodded her head, embarrassed to be airing her most private worries.

"Wanting to leave Boston has nothing to do with Catherine. I just feel too penned in there. I'm not cut out for city living, or being cooped up inside all day." He paused a moment. "I hoped being someplace more hospitable, and closer to your aunt, would be better for you as well. But I should have shared my thoughts instead of waiting to surprise you."

"Surprise me with what?"

"I found a beautiful piece of land in Great Barrington. I thought we might live there, in a house I'll build for you. We can keep the house in Boston, as well, and stay there as often as we like."

Rose couldn't help it. Tears of relief and joy overwhelmed her and slid down her cheeks.

Luke tilted her chin up until she was looking into his eyes.

"I love you, Rose, more than I've loved anyone or anything. I was afraid to admit it, and for that I'm sorry."

"I've loved you for so long," she said, trembling in his arms as emotion overwhelmed her.

Tenderly he cupped her face in his hands, his thumbs wiping away the tears. Pulling back the covers, he climbed into bed beside her, the warmth of his body flowing into hers. Holding her close he whispered to her all the things they would do together, all the places he'd take her, the ways he would indulge her every desire.

Rose lay in his arms, basking in the feel of him. He was really and truly hers. Only minutes ago she had thought she was as happy as she could be. Now she saw there was no limit to it.

About the Author

*I*sabel Morin started reading romances when she was thirteen years old and hasn't stopped since. Now she writes them, too. She lives in New England with her husband, the inspiration for many of her heroes, and a frisky Bengal cat.

Also by Isabel Morin: *Tempt Me* and *Set Loose*, available as ebooks.

Email Isabel at: authorisabel.morin@gmail.com or visit her at www.isabelmorin.com.